POST

POSTAGE ONLY
FOR COMMUN...

POST CARD.

THE ADDRESS ONLY TO BE

CARD

Brixton Beach

Also by Roma Tearne

Mosquito
Bone China

Brixton Beach

ROMA TEARNE

Harper
Press

HarperPress
An imprint of HarperCollinsPublishers
77–85 Fulham Palace Road
Hammersmith, London W6 8JB
www.harpercollins.co.uk

Visit our authors' blog: www.fifthestate.co.uk
Love This Book? www.bookarmy.com

First published by HarperPress in 2009

Dedication on page 273: an unsourced passage (originally in German)
that Wilhelm Hesse pasted in Eva Hesse's first Tagebuch;
EH 1, inside back cover, 1939. Courtesy of the Estate of Eva Hesse
Lines from *White Flock*, 1917, by Anna Akhmatova on page 374 © Anna Akhmatova

1

A catalogue record for this book is available from the British Library

This is a work of fiction. Names, characters, places
and incidents are either the product of the
author's imagination or are used fictitiously.

ISBN 978-0-00-730154-6

Typeset in Minion with New Baskerville display by
Newgen Imaging System (P) Ltd, Chennai, India

Printed and bound in Great Britain by Clays Ltd, St Ives plc

Mixed Sources
Product group from well-managed
forests and other controlled sources
www.fsc.org   Cert no. SW-COC-1806
© 1996 Forest Stewardship Council

FSC is a non-profit international organisation established to promote the
responsible management of the world's forests. Products carrying the FSC
label are independently certified to assure consumers that they come
from forests that are managed to meet the social, economic and
ecological needs of present or future generations.

Find out more about HarperCollins and the environment at
www.harpercollins.co.uk/green

In memory of N M C whose story,
discarded for forty years, is told at last.

And for Barrie,
Oliver, Alistair and Mollie.

All of life is a foreign country

Jack Kerouac,
letter (24 June 1949)

Bel Canto

THERE ARE POLICE EVERYWHERE. From a distance it is the first thing he sees. Even before he hears the noise of sirens, the screams. Even before the BBC team appears. Acid-green jackets move grimly about, directing the traffic, securing blue-and-white tape, herding people away. That's what he sees. A red, double-decker bus stands parked at an odd angle, black smoke pouring out of its windows. There is glass everywhere. His feet crunch on it and he notices shards glinting dangerously in the light. His first thought is, Someone might cut themselves; his second is, There must have been a fire.

'Move along, please, clear the path,' the policeman shouts, roughly.

He pushes several people back with the palms of his hands. Then he speaks into his radio. There is a smell of sweat and rubber. And explosives.

'We need another ambulance over at checkpoint four,' the policeman says. 'Quickly. They're bringing more out. Have all the hospitals been alerted?'

'We need the reinforcements, now!'

'Yes. They're on their way.'

'What happened?' Simon asks, urgently. 'Was it a fire?'

His voice is hoarse; his throat has tightened up. There is an even tighter constriction across his chest. He has been running. All the way over Lambeth Bridge, along Horseferry Road, up Park Lane towards

Edgware Road. He wanted to go in the opposite direction, towards the Oval and the house named Brixton Beach. For a moment he had wavered, wanting to call at the house, knock on its blue-fronted door, but then he had carried on running. There are no taxis to be had. The traffic is gridlocked. It will be gridlocked for hours. He should be at work, he should be at his post, standing by waiting for the admissions, triaging the flood of casualties, but he has fled, unthinkingly. Never in the whole of his professional career has he behaved in this irresponsible way. Panic chokes his voice; fear grips his limbs as he scans the faces in front of him.

'Clear the path, please.'

The noise of yet another ambulance siren deafens him. He isn't used to hearing the sirens from the outside. He is used to the calm of the operating theatre, the controlled energy of work. Scalpels placed where they are always placed, nurses ready to second-guess his moves. He is not used to chaos.

'Oh my God! Oh God! Look! Look!' a woman screams.

Her voice goes on and on screaming, making sounds but no sense. It is only then Simon glances up and sees the bus. Its top has been completely blown off. Roof, seats, windows, people. Half a bus really, standing motionless save for the thin wisps of smoke sailing lazily out, upwards like a kite; into a sky of startling blue. A man in rags with blackened face and arms walks past holding on to a young boy. Tears furrow his face leaving rivulets of white flesh. Two new ambulances edge their way slowly forwards, sirens blasting, driving the onlookers aside, clearing a path, deafening in intensity, removing all possibility of speech. Three policewomen stand forming a barrier with their arms stretched out, faces braced for what they are about to receive. In a moment the ambulances are swallowed up in the crowd. Simon can smell burning. As the sirens grow fainter he begins to hear other, human sounds and he struggles to move forward.

'Jesus! What is it? What's happened?'

'Does anybody know?'

'Don't touch them … for God's sake!'

'Oh my God!'

'Mummy!'

4

A child's voice with its upwardly rising intonations, distinct and pure above the cacophony of cries, drifts towards him. The blood pounds in his head, blurring his eyes, making him nauseous. He was hot from running, now he is shivering. A motion of a different kind grips his whole body.

'Let me through,' he says. 'I'm a doctor.'

Inside the blasted double-decker bus, as his eyes focus, he sees that trapped bodies are burning. Some of them are simply torsos without heads.

'I'm a doctor,' he shouts. 'Let me through.'

'I'm sorry, sir, can I see your ID, please?'

The ambulancemen are moving a stretcher and two blood-covered individuals are helped inside. Simon reaches for his doctor's pass then realises he has left the meeting without his jacket. He has nothing. No ID, no mobile phone, no wallet. If she were trying to reach him she would not be able to. He has rushed out, knowing ... knowing what? That he couldn't wait? That he needs to see for himself?

'Could you move back, please,' the policeman says.

His voice is edged with panic, bewildered and with a threat underlying the calmness in it. The glint of metal on his belt is the firearm he is prepared to use in case of necessity. Sweat pours down his face as he answers his radio. He is young, mid-twenties, and what has just happened is overwhelming him. It will mark him forever.

'We don't know what's going on, sir. We've only been told there's been a series of explosions. In the underground. Yes, sir.'

But the bus?

'Al-Qaeda?' asks another voice, uncertain, shaky, on the verge of hysteria. A woman's voice. 'Oh my God no! Not *here*, not in Britain?'

'Don't know, madam. Not at this stage. Sorry.'

Simon feels weak. He *has* to get to the entrance of the tube station; he *has* to find out what's actually happened. He needs a mobile phone desperately. Then he remembers, of course, all his phone numbers are in his own phone. He can't remember any of them. So he pushes his way across the crowds that are gathering and crosses the road, weaving through the stationary traffic. Another policeman stops him.

'Sorry, sir, could you step aside, please. This area has been closed off to the public.'

'I'm a doctor,' he says again, his voice barely above a whisper.

'Can I see your ID, then, sir?'

But of course he hasn't any. Helplessly he is shepherded across the road, along with a few other onlookers. The sun is exceptionally strong. There isn't even a small breeze. It is a morning of tropical intensity, a day for spending on the beach, perhaps. There are more sounds as another fleet of ambulances rushes past. The sirens have hardly stopped since Simon arrived.

'Must be sending them out from several hospitals, I reckon,' the man beside him remarks.

'It means a lot of people are involved,' adds a woman nearby. 'My mobile isn't working.'

'Nor mine.'

'The network is blocked,' someone else informs them. 'Or they've been reserved for the emergency services.'

Voices cut across each other, conversations interlock. A woman with a pushchair is crying helplessly.

'My daughter was going on a school trip today but she had a tummy bug so she stayed at home.'

'Really?'

'Yes. They would have come to Leicester Square and gone across to the National Gallery.'

'Some poor parents must be going mad.'

There is another wave of wailing ambulances, louder than before, nearer. How many more are needed? One stops on the wrong side of the now deserted road, flagged down by two police officers who have parked their car diagonally across the kerb. Sniffer dogs prowl at their feet. Simon runs towards the paramedics stepping out of one of the vehicles.

'John,' he cries, before the policemen can stop him. 'John!'

The sniffer dog bares his teeth. Overhead a plane flies slowly through the sky. It is so low that everyone looks up, startled. The moment is frozen, trapped within a bubble of terror. Held steadily.

The plane, it has a blue and yellow tail, glides smoothly above the trees and disappears between two tall buildings.

'Dr Swann,' the paramedic says in surprise, and the policeman hesitates.

'I was in the area,' Simon says quickly and with deathly calm. 'Can I help?'

'They're on standby, sir. At Tommy's. And at Charing Cross. It's okay,' John tells the policeman, who discreetly lowers his gun. 'He's one of ours, off duty.'

And he nods, grimly, as though he has already braced himself for the sight they are expecting.

'I think it's a big one, sir, judging by the fuss. Everyone's on the highest alert. Top priority. Must be bad.'

He shakes his head. He has just been called away from a pile-up on the slip road to the motorway. How many miracles are they supposed to perform in a day?

'Let me come with you, John,' Simon pleads as they move off together towards the tube station.

At the entrance to the underground a shudder runs through him. It travels from his feet upwards towards his head. The scene before him is of biblical proportions. A man, or is it a woman, head swathed in a makeshift bandage cut from a shirt, is being helped across to the emergency post recently set up on the grass verge. For a moment the figure hovers, stumbles, its veiled face catching the light. A photographer clicks his camera. This image of a bandaged face will become iconic, one of the images of the year, the decade, even. Someone somewhere loves the face under these bandages. Simon moves towards the emergency post. A waiter has brought chairs for the walking wounded; the lucky ones. There are others not so lucky.

Firemen are bringing out stretcher after stretcher of wounded, mutilated bodies. Cries fill his ears. A charred body, indistinguishable in every way except for a bracelet on a blackened arm, lies motionless. A man, lying face up, stares at nothing, unaware his guts are exposed to the summer breeze. A woman, legs gone from the knees downward, sliced clean, unconscious but still breathing, waits to be whisked off in an ambulance. Two paramedics are already triaging the arrivals. Some to ambulances, some to be treated first for minor injuries, others, with a sheet over them, to be identified later. A cameraman is recording the scene silently. Picasso's *Guernica*, thinks Simon, before he can stop himself. And something else, too, he thinks. He sees a room, lit from above, as though with searchlights, and a cupboard that opens out to reveal the hull of a boat. He hears voices. *Searching for Lost Time.* A figure lies before him, long dark hair, caked with blood, eyes closed. He has seen so much blood in his life. Blood and its seepage has been the thing he deals with best. But this blood, this flesh is different. He cannot bear it. All around the drenching terrible smell of burning flesh and soot fill the bright blue sky. Scorched limbs, voices pleading with him, voices giving out instructions.

'Help me, help me!'

'This one's lost a deal of blood …'

'This one for Tommy's …'

He is working on autopilot, going through the routines, but all the time he's looking, looking. Every face, every limb, searching for what he dreads finding, but looking anyway. His heart is crying, he should not have come; he should have stayed in the hospital. Waited. But he is here now and he will not leave until he knows. One way or another. Perhaps, he thinks, the thought forming into words, springing into life, perhaps she's in the tunnel. Suddenly all his strength deserts him and he feels the ground heave up towards him.

'I'm sorry,' he mumbles, but no one hears him.

Perhaps if he goes back she'll ring. Perhaps she is still at Brixton Beach. Safe, trying to get hold of him. Wildly he looks around, not knowing what to do, and in this fraction of a second a woman dies in front of him. The colours of death, he thinks. Why is he thinking this now?

'Who has done this terrible thing?' a voice cries. 'Who could want to hurt us this much?'

'The people of London …' the BBC journalist says into the microphone. He has been the first of the media presenters to arrive on the scene, the first to file copy; sensitive, sharp, precise.

'Bastards! What have they done?'

The cry of rage reaching his ears is an ancient one, repeated from time immemorial. Arms rise heavenwards as though in prayer. Humanity's unanswered question asked on this ghost of a morning in July. Helplessly, Simon turns towards the speaker, a man old enough to have seen the sands of Dunkirk, a man old enough to have witnessed the Battle of Britain. For on this beautiful day, even as Big Ben strikes the hour and swallows fill the summer skies, a lesser God descends. Fraught with terrible intent. Here, in the very heart of London.

Paradiso

1

ONLY THE YOUNG CAN FEEL THIS WAY. Unaware of time's passage, only they can be so trusting. It is their good fortune to live without question, storing up memories for that later day when middle age allows them to re-visit the past. Time of course will change things; time will mould and distort, lie and trick them with all its inconsistencies. But in the brief interlude, suspended between dreaming and waking, before the low door of childhood swings shut behind them forever, the young, with luck, can experience complete happiness.

On the night before Alice Fonseka's ninth birthday her father Stanley brought home two bright red apples. Stanley worked at a factory that imported all the foreign fruit for the rich Cinnamon Gardens Singhalese who could afford to live like the English.

'Apples are a luxury,' Stanley told her. 'But because it's your ninth birthday, you must experience the taste of luxury!'

He smiled without joy, being preoccupied with things other than his daughter's birthday. Tomorrow, Alice's mother Sita planned to take Alice up the coast after school to stay with her grandparents for the weekend. The baby Sita was expecting was due in a month and Alice's trip to her parents was partly to give Sita a chance to rest.

'But you can only stay for two nights,' she warned Alice, peeling the apple and cutting it into segments.

The flesh was pale and spongy. Alice ate it reluctantly.

'Why?' she demanded. 'Why can't I stay longer?'

'Two nights,' her mother said firmly. 'Finish your apple now and get ready for bed. You've got school in the morning.'

Alice scowled. She was not the slightest bit sleepy.

'I want to stay for a week.'

Visiting her grandparents was the best part of any birthday.

'Will Grandpa Bee meet us at the station?'

'Yes, he will. Now be good and get ready for bed. It will make your birthday come sooner.'

'Oh! I can't wait to see him,' Alice cried, slipping off her chair and running around the satinwood dining table excitedly.

Sita ate the left-over piece of apple. As a small child, Sita had nicknamed her father Bee. She no longer remembered her reasons for this, but the name had stuck and now everyone called him Bee, even his wife Kamala.

The next day when Sita collected Alice after school she brought the remaining apple with her, packed carefully between her daughter's overnight clothes in her blue plastic visiting bag.

'You can share it with Grandpa Bee, if you like,' she said when she met her.

Alice nodded, her eyes shining. She had been too excited to sleep last night, but although she was tired happiness rose in her like the spray from the sea. It was midday. The church clock was striking the hour. Children swarmed out of the school gates dressed in the starched, immaculate white uniforms of St Clare's College; the girls had neatly plaited, coconut-oiled hair, the boys wore gleaming shoes. Only her daughter, it seemed to Sita's critical eye, looked as though she had been rolling in the scrub again.

'*Anay*, Alice, how did you become so filthy? Have you been sitting in the dirt again? And just look at your hair!'

The child's hair, carefully plaited that morning, had come undone. There were bits of twig stuck in it and her uniform was streaked with paint.

'You've been climbing the tree again, haven't you?' Sita asked in exasperation. Her daughter's knees were covered in cuts. Alice hopped from one foot to the other, ignoring her mother.

'I'll never be eight again!' she shouted at some of the children rushing past, waving at them.

She was carrying a paper bag with presents from her classmates.

'Can we go now, Mama?' she cried, dancing about and rubbing her already filthy shoes deeper into the red earth.

Sita sighed. The year was 1973 and with every birthday her daughter seemed to become more of a tomboy.

Mrs Perris the teacher came out to talk to them. She stood in the boiling heat just outside the gate, in the road where the beggars were gathered, close to the women selling spiced ambarella and mango *sambals*, close to the palmist chalking up sherbet-pink marks on the ground. Mrs Perris hardly noticed the noise and the confusion that cartwheeled around her. She was glad to get out of school for a moment, she told Sita. But Alice saw her teacher look nervously over her shoulder as though she expected someone, the headmaster perhaps, to come out and tick her off. Several mothers collecting their children looked curiously in their direction. It was unusual for a member of staff to talk to a parent in this informal way outside the classroom. The tight security since the bomb had gone off made it difficult to be as free and easy as in the old days.

'Alice ought to be very tired,' Mrs Perris said, wagging her finger. 'I have to tell you she hasn't stopped talking today. I couldn't get a single piece of work that was worth anything from her. In fact, I moved her away from Jennifer to sit by herself, didn't I, Alice? Lucky it's a special day, huh, or I might have had to cane you!'

But the teacher was only teasing and Alice grinned, knowing this. She had the feeling Mrs Perris hadn't come out to talk about her.

'Nobody got much sleep last night,' Sita said, absent-mindedly pulling her daughter away from the hole she was digging so energetically with her foot.

Alice gave an exaggerated sigh. Her mother's hair, she thought indignantly, was no better than her own. Strands of it had escaped from its pleat and stuck to her sweaty face. Opening her mouth to comment, she caught Sita's eye and fell silent, sensing instantly and with perfect understanding that her mother was in one of her tricky moods. Sita was tired.

Her tiredness was a constant uneasy presence, a weight as heavy as the humid monsoon-imminent air around them. It was clear to Alice that it was simply the fault of the wretched baby her mother was soon to have. Alice did not want this baby, she had been hating it from the very moment her mother told her the news. What was even worse was that she was absolutely certain no one else wanted it either. Not long ago Alice had overheard a conversation between Aunt May and her grandmother.

'There couldn't be a worse time to bring a child into the world,' Aunt May had said.

Alice, who was expert at eavesdropping, had been taken aback. She had not realised the grown-ups disliked the thought of it too. So why didn't they just get rid of it?

'They cry all night,' her best friend Jennifer had warned her. 'You won't be able to sleep for months and months!'

Jennifer had burst out laughing at the look of horror on Alice's face.

'Well, I'll get rid of it, then,' Alice had said.

She had spoken offhandedly, hiding her unease.

'If it won't behave, no one will want it,' she added with more bravado than she felt.

The other children in the class had asked her what she intended to do.

'Kill it, of course,' she had said without hesitation, making the boys guffaw loudly.

The conversation however had made her a little guilty and she was glad when it was dropped. Then it turned out that Jennifer's mother was expecting a baby too. Alice scratched her leg, thinking about what she had said, brushing away a mosquito. It had surprised her that both mothers were having babies at the same time.

'Must be because they're friends,' she had said.

'Oh, don't be stupid,' Jennifer had scoffed. 'Everyone knows men give them babies.'

Jennifer was the class encyclopaedia.

'How?' demanded Alice. But Jennifer, having reached the extent of her knowledge, pulled a face, refusing to say another word.

After that Alice had been silent, sharing her dark thoughts with no one, not even her grandfather. She simply hoped the baby would die.

'I know,' Mrs Perris was saying in a low voice, moving her head from side to side. 'Ayio! I heard it on the news. Rioting in Wellewatha, for the second time in a month. This is turning into a witch-hunt against the Tamils. I thought of you last night, child. Is your husband okay?'

She glanced towards Alice, who pretended to examine the scab forming on her knee.

'Yes, yes,' Sita said, lowering her voice.

'Thank God he came home before it started, you know.'

There was a pause and both women fell silent. Then Sita looked around nervously.

'Did I tell you our passports have arrived?'

'Really! That's good news, isn't it?' the teacher said encouragingly.

Sita nodded.

'At least now we know for certain we can leave.'

Mrs Perris placed her hand on Sita's arm and squeezed it. Alice looked curiously at them both, not understanding but struck by the look on their faces.

Earlier in the year Mrs Perris had been widowed. The change in her had been shocking. Her husband had been killed in the riots in Jaffna. Everyone agreed he had been in the wrong place at the wrong time. Alice had wanted to find out what the wrong place was, but again no one would tell her. She tried asking her father but Stanley told her to go away and stop bothering him, and Sita told her not to talk so much.

'They're all bastards,' she heard her father tell her mother.

He was in one of his bad moods at the time. Alice was aware that her father knew all the bastards in Colombo. Even Grandpa Bee was impressed by this fact.

'Well, Stanley certainly knows a bastard when he sees one,' she had overheard Bee say.

At the time, Alice had been standing behind the door listening intently, wondering if she too would be able to recognise a bastard if she ever saw one. Bee had been speaking quite softly, under his breath, but even from behind the door Alice had detected a curious note of triumph in his voice. Bee had been unaware that Alice was nearby.

It was only her grandmother, being more knowing, who had shushed him sharply.

'Be quiet,' she had scolded. 'The child might be listening.'

At that, Alice, pretending to be a stork standing on one leg, balancing on the ball of a foot, nearly toppled over. It was true she was always eavesdropping. Listening was something that had become second nature to her; straining her eardrums until they nearly burst, standing with her mouth open behind half-closed doors, worrying a piece of information as though she was a dog with a fallen coconut, coaxing it to split open and reveal its secret. Even Jennifer had congratulated her on her skill.

'You do have a nose for scandal,' she had observed.

Alice hadn't known what a scandal was, but she did know that the world was full of unresolved, interesting stories that everyone conspired to keep from her.

After the bastards had killed her husband, Mrs Perris had eventually returned to school. The children waited curiously to see how she would behave. Thirty pairs of eyes swivelled silently towards the teacher as she walked into the classroom. She wore a white sari, the Kandyian way. It was meant to make her look more Singhalese, but all it did was make her unfamiliar. Every time anyone spoke to her she looked as though she might burst into tears. Very soon the whole class, which collectively was more cunning than people realised, saw that Mrs Perris was completely changed. Once she had been a woman who loved teaching. Now she appeared not to notice when the children misbehaved. The class, working together, seized the opportunity. Led in part by Jennifer, they became unruly. The noise brought out the teachers from the other classrooms, stampeding like a herd of elephants. Everyone wanted to see what was going on in Mrs Perris's once perfectly behaved class. Some of the teachers tried to stop the noise. Some of them looked at the widow with pitying eyes, as if they were thinking, 'Well, she's done for!' It was as if a gong were sounding in Mrs Perris's head, stultifying her. *I'm finished*, it banged.

'She looks terrible,' Jennifer declared with conviction, 'especially around the eyes.'

Alice disagreed. Jennifer was her best friend, but often Alice felt the role was unsustainable. Being friendly with Jennifer was like taking a ride on the back of a tiger. You held on or got eaten alive.

'My mother said Mrs Perris's husband turned blue when they killed him,' Jennifer told the class with relish. 'As though someone had coloured him with dye!'

In spite of herself Alice was agog, her eyes turning into saucers of amazement. But she liked Mrs Perris and did not want her hurt by gossip, so she decided to challenge Jennifer.

'How does your mother know?' she demanded.

Jennifer scowled, unused to being contradicted.

'She went to look at him, silly,' she said, her face so close that her sugary hot breath from the toffee she was secretly eating poured threateningly over Alice.

'Like this!' And she pinched Alice's arm, hoping to make it blue. 'He was in his coffin, you know, men,' she added, making her voice rise and fall. 'And his lips were swollen, just as if a mosquito had bitten him.'

She narrowed her eyes and stared intently. Was Alice by any chance squeamish? Alice hesitated.

'I don't believe you. Dead people are supposed to look peaceful,' she said finally.

Jennifer snorted.

'You're scared,' she had observed shrewdly, and then in a final insult, 'baby!'

After that she had refused to say any more on the subject. And Alice, whose passionate thirst for knowledge palpitated vainly in her chest, was not prepared to beg for any further information. There was a peculiar sad stillness in Mrs Perris's face that made her appear frail and strangely beautiful. It both puzzled and fascinated Alice. Once or twice she had tried talking to her father, but Stanley just yawned and poured himself another whisky.

'Those bastards get away with everything,' was all he said in his predictable way. 'Sita, can you get me some ice?'

Alice had watched as her mother left the clothes she was sewing for the baby and went to fetch the ice.

'Time for bed, Alice,' she had said, noticing her hovering about.

Still Alice continued to be preoccupied by Mrs Perris. On her last visit to her grandparent's house she brought the subject up with Bee.

'Mrs Perris looks transparent,' she told Bee.

Transparent was a word that interested her.

'It's as if you can see right through her.'

Bee listened gravely. He waited until she finished speaking and then he nodded.

'It's called an afterglow,' he said re-lighting his pipe. 'Like a star as it falls; full of light. Like a blessing. Why don't you try to draw her?'

So Alice had drawn her, and Mrs Perris had asked if she could keep the drawing. Alice wrote her name in wobbly paintbrush writing and gave it to her without a word. Privately she told her grandfather it had not been a good drawing.

'I didn't want to draw her as if she was crying,' she said, 'because she *never* cries.'

Bee had chewed on the end of his pipe.

'Absence is a presence,' was his only comment, but she sensed he understood. There was nothing her grandfather did not understand, thought Alice, her heart overflowing with love for him.

'Enjoy the rest of your birthday, Alice,' her teacher was saying, now.

'I'm taking her to my parents tonight,' Sita murmured. 'To be on the safe side, you know.'

Mrs Perris nodded. Then she planted a spontaneous kiss on Alice's head.

'We'll see you on Monday, no?'

'God willing,' Alice's mother answered.

It was a short walk to the station, weaving their way amongst street-sellers, beggars and the roadside shrines that were tucked between the corners of buildings and covered with crude drawings of Gods and demons. All around were small, open-fronted shops stacked high with plastic containers, stalls selling bunches of dirty-green plantains and rambutans, ambarella and piles of mangoes fingered by huge spiders. There were spice shops and sari shops filled with iridescent colours. Sita walked quickly, head bowed, looking neither to left nor right, holding her breath. Occasionally she turned to Alice, urging her to hurry because she did not want to miss the train.

'Have you brought my water bottle?' Alice asked as they boarded the train.

Even though the compartment was empty her mother looked around nervously.

'Speak in Singhalese,' she said softly.

Alice ignored her, taking her bottle. The water was warm and tasted of hot plastic. When she had finished drinking she turned towards the window and watched the view of the city as it moved slowly past. The train gathered speed. Very soon they had left Colombo with its dirt and overcrowded buildings, and an empty beach stretched for miles before them. Two white gulls with enormous wing spans sailed lazily by. Alice narrowed her eyes to slits against the glare and watched them dive bomb the waves. She swung her legs vigorously, wanting to put them on the seat opposite but knowing she would be scolded if she did. Her thoughts spun like candyfloss in a fairground tub. She had a thousand exciting questions, a million wants swimming in her head.

The day had reached its hottest but a cool sea breeze streamed in though the open windows as the train swung and hooted its way along the coast. The air quivered with expectancy and even as she watched, the view took on a mysterious, luminescent quality that made it almost too painful to behold. In spite of the familiarity that years of travelling this route had given her, she was aware in a dreamlike and fleeting way of some deep and unspoken love for all she saw. It was a sight she had been used to seeing all her life. It was her birthday today and she was coming home to her grandparents. That was enough to make her want to shout with unbridled happiness. In a sudden desire for her mother's approval she remained still, staring out at the sea while the tight drum of blue sky wrapped its feverish brilliance all around, closely mirroring her ecstatic happiness. The train clattered on, past trees that gave off a faint elusive perfume filling the compartment with sweet fragrance. Alice, breathing deeply, her eyes fixed at some spot in the distant blueness, was hardly conscious of where she was. Reality and dreams mingled with the motion of the train as the sweep of water expanded endlessly like a dazzling blue desert beside her.

The train slowed down, nudging them backwards and forwards, almost, but never quite stopping. Then it speeded up again and they passed through several small villages screened by coconut palms. Scraps of washing flapped on a makeshift line and a slender dark-boned woman pulled water from a well around which a group of semi-naked children played. They passed a level crossing where two Morris Minors waited patiently for the barrier to rise. On and on they went, with glimpses of a lagoon, men chopping wood, other people's lives distanced and therefore enchanting. Alice glanced at her mother, who was fanning herself slowly, staring straight ahead. She looked enormous. I hate the baby, thought Alice again and with a surge of rage. She had forgotten about it for a moment, but it was still here, the one blemish on the day. Her mother wanted a boy.

'Boys are best,' Jennifer had said, quoting her older sister. 'In this country everyone wants sons.'

The train began to curve around the bay hooting a warning to all the children who played on the line. And here we are, thought Alice with another surge of delight, forgetting about babies, for the very best moment of the day was approaching. There in the distance, still only a speck, was the station and the hill where later she would fly her kite. And somewhere amongst the little clutch of white buildings facing the sea was her grandparents' house. Sunlight touched the rooftops. They were drawing closer. Below her the sea broke through the trees, coming into view once more, startlingly close and full of noise. With a shiver of excitement Alice turned to her mother, but Sita had closed her eyes and was breathing heavily, her mouth slightly open, faint beads of perspiration on her brow. The train was slowing down again; the carriage was almost empty. Alice looked worriedly at her mother, wanting to wake her.

'Will Aunty May be there too?' she asked carefully, in perfect Singhalese.

Bee Fonseka stood in the shadows waiting for the train. Beside him were potted ferns and two ornamental rubber plants that grew out of a hole in the ground. The afternoon was bathed in an intense luminescent light. It fell in low, late slants but because of the breeze gave no hint of its strength. Bee waited, watching, as the turquoise blue Sea Serpent emerged through the thick bank of coconut and plantain trees. He was wearing a pair of trousers that matched his whitening hair. Several people, recognising him, raised their hats and he bowed in acknowledgement but made no move to speak to any of them. There had been no rain for months and the air smelled of salty batter, frying fish and *suduru*, white cumin seed. He had left the house almost half an hour ago. The train had been delayed and Kamala, he knew, would be getting anxious. He had left her fussing over the food, putting the finishing touches to the birthday cake, while the servant woman brought in piles of bread and juggery. Enough to feed an army, Bee had observed wryly. The servant had placed a tall jug of freshly squeezed lime juice on the teapoy and draped a heavily beaded cover over it. Then she had gone to pound the spices in preparation for Alice's favourite evening meal of rice and curry cooked in plantain leaves. How anyone would be able to eat anything after the mountain of cakes and biscuits and patties, Bee had no idea. Normally he would have walked to the station to meet them but because of Sita's condition he had taken the car. Then, as he had been about to leave, Kamala had caught sight of his hands, black from the etching inks he had been using.

'For goodness' sake, clean that ink off before you go to the station!' she had grumbled.

Bee grunted, ignoring her, wishing he had left sooner.

'How can you go to meet them with hands like that?'

'I don't have to clean my hands for Alice,' he said vaguely. 'She's an artist too, she'll understand.'

'Well, think about your daughter at least,' Kamala said, but he had gone. The car door slammed and the next moment he was driving out through the front gate and towards the station.

Now he waited impatiently thinking of the child and the present he had for her, wondering if she would like it. He knew that Sita, although tired, would insist on getting back home to Stanley. At the thought of his son-in-law, Bee's jaw tightened.

Fourteen years ago his eldest daughter had married in secrecy. Bee had not even known of Stanley's existence until then. Sita had travelled to Colombo one morning, pretending she was visiting a school friend, returning a week later a married woman. At first Bee had been too furious to speak. He had no prejudices against the Tamils. Indeed, the few Tamil families that lived near him were courteous and intelligent. They were large, close-knit families who worked hard and mostly did very well at the local school. Still, it was impossible to deny the change that was sweeping across the country. Life would not be easy for Sita. Rumours of violence in the north, in Jaffna and the eastern part of the island were rife. If they were correct, then it would only be a matter of time before prejudice spread down south. None of them, least of all Sita, would be able to predict how things might go. Worried and deeply hurt that she had not trusted him enough to tell him about Stanley, Bee had withdrawn into silence.

When they had finally met, he had found the relationship genuinely puzzling. What was the attraction? he asked Kamala. Kamala had no idea either. Night after night they lay awake discussing their eldest daughter, getting no closer to the truth, for Stanley was a strange, uncommunicative man. Nothing the family could do, not even May's winsome ways, had succeeded in drawing him out or dispersed the coldness that was, they felt, part of his character. Sita, the daughter who had been the closest to Bee as a child, now seemed uncomfortable in her father's presence.

On their first visit to the Sea House the couple had stayed only for the evening. Sita had hardly spoken. It had been an awkward distressing event and the little information they did glean was unsatisfactory. Stanley worked in an office in Colombo. He was a stenographer, he told Bee, working at a firm that imported fruit from abroad.

'Why do we need fruit from the British?' Bee had asked, forgetting to hold his tongue. 'Haven't we enough wonderful fruit of our own?'

His wife and daughters had frowned disapprovingly. But Stanley hadn't seemed to mind.

'Apples,' he had said. 'The British living here miss having things from their homeland. So we get apples for them. After all, we should encourage them to stay. It's better for the country, safer for the Tamils, anyway.'

Bee made no comment. He took out his pipe and tapped it against his chair. Then he lit it.

'I want to go to England one day,' Stanley had confided a little later on.

He was eating the cake his new mother-in-law had baked hastily. There had been no time to make an auspicious dish for the bride and groom; this was all she could offer. The servant woman standing in the doorway, waiting for a glimpse of the eldest daughter, shook her head sadly. This was not the way in which a Singhalese bride returned home. It was a bad omen. The bride and groom should have been given many gifts. Jewellery, for instance, a garland of flowers, a blessing at the temple. The bride should have entered her old home wearing a red sari, to be met by her sister and fed milk rice. And before all of this, right at the very beginning, the servant woman believed, before the wedding date had even been set, the couple's horoscope should have been drawn up. But none of these things had been done. It was very, very bad. As far as the servant woman could see, shame had descended like a cloud of sea-blown sand on this family. Sita had brought it to the house, trailing her karma carelessly behind her, fully aware but indifferent to the ways in which things worked in this small costal town. The servant felt it was a wanton disgrace.

'I want us to go to the UK,' Stanley had said, taking Sita's hand in his.

Watching him, Kamala had become afraid. She thought he sounded a boastful man.

'After we have children, of course,' Stanley continued. 'This bloody place is no good for children to grow up in. Everything is denied to us Tamils. Education, good jobs, decent housing – everything. The bastard Singhalese are trying to strangle us.'

His voice had risen and he had clenched his fists.

'Stanley!' Sita had murmured, shaking her head.

Bee had seen with a certain savage amusement that at least his daughter had not quite forgotten her manners.

'Does your family know you've got married?' he had asked his new son-in-law finally, ignoring his wife's look of unease.

What did Kamala think? That he too was going to behave badly?

'Yes, yes. I've just told my mother. We'll be visiting her after we leave here,' Stanley said dismissively, lighting a cigarette without offering Bee one.

He would not be more forthcoming. No one had known what to say next. May went over to her father and sat on the floor beside him.

'Well, let's have some tea, huh?' Bee had suggested, returning his wife's look defiantly. 'What are we waiting for?'

And that had been all that had happened at that visit. They had simply taken tea and made small talk. At one point Sita had gone to the bedroom she shared with her sister and collected a few of her belongings. She had shown them her wedding ring. Heavy filigree Tamil gold, not what the Fonsekas cared for, she knew, but they had admired it anyway. The newly weds would be living in Stanley's old bachelor pad, an annexe in Havelock Road, she informed them. The family listened politely.

'We'll stay there for a while,' Sita had said. 'Once I get a job and we can afford something better, we'll move.'

It was no good any of them visiting, she told her mother.

'The place is too small to swing a cat,' she said.

The Fonsekas stared at her, not understanding the strange phrase. Why would they want to swing the cat? And it was then, for the first time, that Stanley had laughed. Ah! thought Bee, understanding at last, startled by the sudden animation in the man's face; yes, he could see what the attraction was.

That had been fourteen years ago. Fourteen years that had given Ceylon time to change for the worse. Time enough for corruption to rise unchecked and burn like a forest fire. Riots, demonstrations, the bitterness accumulated from a century of foreign rule, all these things combined to unhinge the nation. While the British, Bee observed bitterly, had de-camped, the Ceylonese had no concept as to where on earth they were going.

Bee gave up talking about his eldest daughter and buried himself in his work. Eventually the servant woman persuaded Kamala to have Sita's horoscope drawn up. The sea of superstition still remained. Bee watched, refraining from comment. What was done was done. Slowly, aware of his own weaknesses, he tried to be fair to Stanley, refusing to tolerate any comments on their differences in his home. It was the British who were the enemy, not his son-in-law's. The plight of the Tamil people since independence was what needed to be addressed, not petty family differences. But for the first time Bee understood how complex a business this was. Determined, in spite of his son-in-law's covert challenges, he tried to patch the rift. If he was disappointed, he did not show it.

'It's just his nature,' he would say to Kamala whenever she became upset. 'Human nature is the same the world over.'

But the easy affection he had once shared with Sita vanished. He did not expect it to return. Now all was correct and careful. Slowly his work had begun to sell and he became a prominent figure in the tiny artistic community that existed on the island. Once or twice a painting had sold to collectors in Malaysia. So, with one daughter married, and another growing up, he buried his disappointment and painted instead. Two years passed in this way. Sita visited, sometimes with Stanley, but more often than not alone. Her new husband was always busy. He still wanted desperately to go to the UK.

'When we have saved up a little,' Sita told her parents without a tremor of regret in her voice, 'then we'll leave.'

Bee understood. What else can the man do? Even while Kamala wept, he accepted the inevitable.

'She chose a difficult path,' Bee said, 'and in spite of everything I can't help admiring her.'

He spoke as he believed, never knowing how his words would return to haunt him.

Then five years and three months into their marriage, in the cool of the rainy season Sita announced she was pregnant. Bee responded to the news with astonished silence. Kamala, thinking he was angry, eyed him warily. But Bee was not angry. Far from it. On the same evening in the deepening twilight, he went on his usual walk across the beach to watch the ships taking up their position on the horizon and to marvel at the way in which this simple piece of information had altered his perception of the entire world, forever. A child, *his* grandchild! A blessing that, after so many years, brought such hope. I am glimpsing eternity, he thought, speechless with amazement. Out there in the void, between the fore and aft of his own life, was an extraordinary vision of the stars. He was delirious with happiness. Standing on the beach, gazing out towards the sea with nothing beyond him except Antarctica, he had fallen in love with this notion of immortality. Here was a life to be, not of his own time yet joined to him by time's common flow. They would be bathers in the same sea, he and this child; time had brought the generations together. This was how he felt, even before he set eyes on her, the little scrap they were to call Alice. As far as Bee was concerned it was love at first sight, paradise regained. Alice, returning from the hospital in her mother's arms, ready to be shown the sea for the very first time, could anything top that? In that instant he had seen her great dark eyes roaming curiously towards the ocean and he knew that forever after the shore and the sea would be bound up with Alice, his first grandchild.

Things changed rapidly after that. *He* changed. All that had been falling apart began to reassemble. Kamala watched him indulgently, secretly breathing a sigh of relief. May laughed, teasing him. The neighbours became accustomed to his long discourses on the child and the nature of childhood. Her intelligence was soon legendary and had quickly become an established fact in this part of the coast. Bee didn't care. They could laugh at him as much as they wished, but his painting now began to be influenced by the child's interests. He stopped the sweeping watercolours of the ocean and began to paint in miniature: small sea plants that grew in cracks, minute white seashells buried on the edges of rocks, fragments of marine life washed up in the monsoon storms, fish scales, raindrops on the edges of a coconut frond. All the things in fact that he had begun to show his new grand-daughter. The dealer in Colombo came to visit and liked what he saw. Life in miniature, he called it, and urged Bee to paint more. There was, it appeared, a market for this closely observed minutiae. Bee allowed the dealer to take a few paintings. But mainly he was reluctant to sell this new work, for it felt too private to be seen by others. He re-decorated the room facing the ocean, for before long, Alice was old enough to be left with them. And finally he saw, to his greatest joy, the child *wanted* to be near him as much as *he* wanted to see her.

'Grandpa!' she cried, as soon as she caught sight of him, waking from a sleep, carried in her mother's arms, delighting in the sight of him.

Stanley wanted her to speak only English, of course, but somehow both Singhalese and Tamil slipped into her vocabulary. Bee made no comment, the gleam in his eye saying it all. The child could do no wrong. Kamala produced small, dainty cakes whenever a visit was eminent and May, grown tall and very lovely now, embroidered white frocks for her niece.

Time passed slowly as the sea and the old whitewashed house absorbed these moments thirstily. Memories moved lightly against the sun-warmed walls. It was a long golden moment stretching over almost a decade. Sita gave up her job as a teacher and began to write a small column for the woman's page of the *Colombo Daily News*. An uneasy existence between Singhalese and Tamils existed lulling them into a false security. She wrote her articles under a pen-name and Alice, without anything being discussed, was taught to use her mother's Singhalese maiden name. By the time she was ready to go to school she thought of herself as Alice Fonseka.

Then one night, when Alice was five, Stanley was beaten up on his way back from work and his money stolen. When he arrived home he was bleeding from a wound on his head and his clothes were torn. Luckily Alice had been staying with her grandparents. Sita called for their usual doctor, but he refused to come out, telling her to take her husband to the hospital instead. The police too were indifferent. There was a travelling circus in that part of town, the policeman said, shrugging. Best to keep away from Galle Face for a bit. It would be impossible to find the culprit.

'And besides,' the policeman had said smiling broadly at Sita, taking in the fact that her husband's name was Tamil, 'these things happen to everyone. Not just the Tamils. You mustn't be so sensitive.'

Sita stared back at him, speechless. The men had hurled racist insults at her husband in Singhalese. How could the policeman think this was not a racist attack?

'Why doesn't your husband think of going back to Jaffna?' the officer had suggested.

He sounded reasonable and was, he told her, trying to be helpful. Sita couldn't believe her ears.

'I'm doing this because I like the look of you,' the policeman said, swaggering a little, holding his paunch with both his hands. 'I'm doing this as a favour, d'you understand?'

When he smiled she had seen the prawn-pink undersides of his heavy lips and shuddered.

'My husband is *not* from Jaffna,' she had shouted, 'not even his relatives came from Jaffna.'

The policeman had stared at her suggestively, warningly. Afterwards she felt violated.

'He asked me what a nice Singhalese girl like me was doing married to a Tamil,' Sita had told her parents when she came to collect Alice.

Bee, listening grimly, wanted to go to the chief constable in Mount Lavinia, but neither Sita nor Kamala would let him make a fuss.

'Everything's fine here, Father,' Sita had said, shaking her head, calming down a little. 'Don't make trouble. It's safe for Alice here and for May, too. Leave it.'

So against his better judgement he had consoled himself with the fact that it was just one incident. One corrupt policeman in a disturbed country was not as bad as all that.

The Sea Serpent emerged through the trees, lumbering towards the station and breaking into Bee's thoughts. He smiled as with a grinding of metal the train came to a halt. A moment later Alice leapt out at him followed tiredly by Sita.

'Hello, birthday girl!' he cried, kissing the top of her head and taking his daughter's bag.

'I can't stay very long,' Sita warned. 'I've got to catch another train back this evening.'

'Have you brought the car? Is Aunty May with you? And is Esther coming? And Janake?' asked Alice.

'Steady on,' Bee said, talking with his pipe in his mouth in the way she loved. 'Now you're such a great age you must try to act a little bored. It's more grown up that way.'

'But I *have* been bored!' cried Alice, her eyes like the polish of water on wet stones.

'She talks too much in class,' Sita said, irritated. 'It was so bad today, her teacher made her sit by herself. No, Alice, it isn't funny,' she added in warning.

Alice grinned, wrinkling her nose. Later on, when she had her grandfather all to herself, she would tell him what her day had really been like.

'Why go back tonight?' Bee asked, helping his daughter into the waiting car.

Alice could not wait. She sucked in the air like a lollypop and shot straight into the back wishing her mother would simply leave quickly. The back seat of the car had the familiar smell of warm leather and love. There were other smells too, of sea, sand and grease and long, younger days sitting on tedious journeys in the heat. It held the memory of sticky Lanka lime and hot winds blowing and can-I-eat-the-patties-yet whines. The sea was out of sight for the moment, screened by a tangle of bougainvillea, but still its presence remained powerful. Sea sounds were everywhere, tossing about and fragmented by the breeze.

'So,' Bee said wryly, glancing over his shoulder, for she had been silent for at least a minute, 'how's the birthday girl? Asleep?'

He pretended to look stern and Alice squealed with pleasure. She felt as though she was sucking on a sherbet dib-dab, or running with a kite. Excitement made her want to shout and wriggle her toes all at the same time but her mother was talking and so, impatiently, she tied a string to her pleasure and reined it sharply in. The sound of her mother's sombre voice always deflated her a little. Bee glanced at her in the mirror. Then he coaxed the old Morris Minor slowly up the hill. Tantalising glimpses of the beach followed them.

'Esther and her mother want to see you,' Bee said.

His daughter had leaned back and closed her eyes.

'That's nice,' she said, shutting out the view.

A man with a white loincloth looped over his legs was drawing a catamaran across the sand. Alice blinked; unknown to her, the image fixed itself in her mind forever. Two sun-blackened boys were collecting coconuts in a sack. In the high bright daze they appeared silhouetted like matchstick men. The car climbed up Station Road with a sound like an old cough tearing at its throat. It passed the small *kade* where Bee bought his tobacco. Bougainvillea choked the stone walls all along the way. Magenta and white; too bright to look at without squinting. A golden-fronted leaf-bird flashed past, heading for a canopy of hibiscus bushes, leaving a searing after-burn of colour, and all around the seagulls' cries made invisible circles in the air. It was almost four o'clock. Nine years had scuttled away like a crab.

'I wish today would slow down,' she said, as the car clutched the hairpin bend, turning higher and higher until suddenly, sprawling in front of them and with no warning, the Sea House appeared.

The light had changed the colour of the house. Everything was clearer and more beautiful than Alice remembered. Someone had sharpened the picture of it, making the verandah and the old planter's chairs and the garden appear brighter too. In a moment Kamala appeared and Alice was enveloped in a juggery-scented hug. On the table was a selection of *rasa kavili*, Singhalese sweetmeats. She did a quick count in her head. *Alu-Eluvang* and *hakura appa*, juggery, hoppers and jelly. No, nothing had been forgotten. All her favourites were there: the *boroa*, the small delicious Portuguese biscuits she loved, and the jug of freshly squeezed lime juice. In the middle, in pride of place, was a magnificent love cake with nine candles waiting to be lit. Her grandmother had not stopped smiling. Beside her, tied with a pink ribbon, was a lime-green bicycle.

'Well,' Bee asked, 'so, what d'you think about the colour?'

'A bicycle!' Alice said, astonished further by this day of surprises.

And she rushed full tilt towards it.

Then she stopped.

'But I can't ride,' she wailed.

'Ah! Yes, that's a problem,' agreed Bee seriously. 'Well, someone's got to teach you then. Now, I wonder who that might be!'

'I'm not hungry, Amma,' Sita was saying even before she sunk awkwardly down on one of the old planter's chairs. 'All I want is a cup of tea.'

Alice scowled. Why was her mother spoiling everything? Or rather, she corrected herself, why was the *baby* spoiling her birthday?

'Sita,' Kamala said, 'you look exhausted. How can you go on like this? Think of the baby. Why didn't you let your father collect Alice? And why don't you stay the night now you're here? Stanley can manage for a night, can't he?'

But Sita was shaking her head in a way Alice recognised. Stubbornness was the thing she had given Alice in bucketloads, and stubbornness was written all over her own face now.

'No, Amma, you know I don't like him being alone. And after last night and the riots in our area, I must go back. You didn't see what we saw; you don't know what these people are really like. There were neighbours in the crowd who *knew* us, people we thought were our friends, the same as us. Singhalese, like me!'

Her voice was beginning to rise; Kamala put out her hand as though warding off her daughter's fear.

'How can I *ever* trust anyone?'

They surveyed the tea table in silence. Alice washed her hands in the bowl of water that the servant held out to her. Then she dried them on the soft cotton hand towel and started on the sandwiches. She was tense with waiting for her mother to go home. Guiltily she anticipated the evening with her mother gone and the moment when she had her grandparents all to herself. And then, forgetting about everything, she realised she was enormously hungry.

'Ayio!' Kamala said, pouring out the tea.

Two tea leaves floated on a brown sea in the cups.

'It isn't the riots,' Bee told her, handing over his cup. 'We shouldn't place too much emphasis on them.'

His eyes had closed into narrow slits in the way Alice loved. It made him look like the picture of an owl in one of her books. Bee's voice was noncommittal. It changed the atmosphere, taking the tension away from Sita's face.

'Human nature has no surprises. All the riots do is make it more obvious.'

'Well, we all know it's the fault of the British,' Sita murmured. 'It's their mess.' But she spoke sleepily, without conviction.

This was too much for her father.

'Don't talk to me about the British,' he said, sitting up instantly, eyes flashing open, alert, as though sniffing out any stray British.

'Now, Sita, don't start him off,' Kamala warned, but Bee waved his arm irritably.

'They'll pay for all this, all right. One day they'll be called to account, just wait.'

Alice yawned. The conversation was going its usual way and she was losing interest.

'Enough, enough, Benji,' Kamala warned. 'Nothing is going to change the past.'

She glanced sharply at her granddaughter's face, reading it accurately.

'And please don't forget it's Alice's day today.'

'Just one more thing,' Sita said.

She hesitated, holding out her cup for more tea.

'Stanley got the passports this morning.'

The silence was electric.

'For all of you?' Kamala asked bleakly.

'Yes, of course!'

Alice saw her grandmother's hand shake and the cup she was holding rattle on its saucer. The next moment the glass door opened and Alice's aunt May walked in, followed by Esther and Esther's mother Dias, in a flurry of birthday visitors, a rustle of birthday presents.

'Happy birthday, Alice,' Esther cried, giving her a kiss.

Alice looked at her with interest. Esther was chewing on something.

'Many happy returns, darling,' Aunty May said, handing her niece a small parcel. 'It's all the books you put on your list.'

'My God! You're a regular bookworm, child,' Aunt Dias laughed, pinching her cheeks with her hand as though she was squeezing rubber out of a rubber plant. 'She looks just like you, Sita!'

And she too handed Alice a small parcel.

'Where's Janake?' Alice asked, seeing he was not with them, trying not to be disappointed.

'He's gone to his aunt's,' Kamala told her. 'He'll be back tomorrow.'

'Oh!' Alice said. She *was* disappointed.

'Their passports have arrived, did you hear?' Bee told the visitors grimly while Alice opened her presents. His voice was muffled as if he was somewhere far away.

'Ayio!' Kamala said again.

'Oh, thank you, Aunty May,' Alice said. 'I *wanted* the new Secret Seven book! And the *Wind in the Willows*.'

'Good! But don't read it too fast!'

'And look at these paints!'

Kamala was beginning to look as though she might cry.

'Now,' May said briskly, 'I need some tea.'

'Why did Janake have to go to his aunt's?'

The servant handed round white china plates edged with gold. Aunty May gave everyone another change-the-subject kiss, but couldn't resist one comment of her own.

'Those bastards in the government have done this,' she said under her breath.

Alice finished her piece of cake and reached for another.

'There are bastards everywhere,' she said matter-of-factly, making Esther giggle and May hoot with laughter.

'Hear, hear!' she said, clapping her hands.

Even Sita smiled a thin, watered-down smile. Bee's shoulders shook.

'Our birthday girl's thought for the day!' he chuckled.

His eyes were the colour of cloudy glass. The tension eased imperceptibly. Perhaps now they could get on with the business of enjoying her birthday, thought Alice. She was longing to try her bicycle. Sita leaned back in her chair, shutting her eyes, and once again without warning the moment became fixed in Alice's mind, with the sea glimpsed through the doorway and her aunt May's sari the colour of ripe mangoes.

'Why don't you children sit out on the verandah,' May suggested.

'I'm not a child,' Esther frowned.

She went in to see the cook, to get a small handful of hot rice.

'Aren't you going to eat anything?' Alice asked curiously when she returned and sat down on the step.

Esther rolled the rice up into a small ball and popped it into her mouth. Then she chewed it in silence. She was wearing her polka-dot dress and a pair of pretend sunglasses. Her hair was tied in a ponytail and she wore a brooch in the shape of a heart with Elvis's face on it. Alice stared at her.

'Why don't you swallow the rice?' she asked curiously after a while.

Boredom flitted across Esther's face like a passing cloud.

'Because it's meant to be gum, silly. You don't swallow gum!'

'Why don't you get some real gum, then?' Alice challenged.

Esther gave her a withering look. Then she picked up her hoola-hoop from the ground and began to swing it on her hips.

'Elvis the pelvis,' Alice said.

Everyone knew Esther was Elvis-mad and that the whole of her house was a shrine to him. Alice continued to gaze at her.

'Why don't you get some proper gum?' she asked again.

'They don't sell gum at the kade,' Esther said at last. 'And it's too expensive at the hotel shop.'

'Come on, children,' May called out from the dining room. 'Time to cut your cake, Alice.'

They sang 'Happy Birthday' and Alice blew out all nine candles in one go so she knew her wish would come true.

'How much longer before the wedding, Aunty May?' Esther asked.

If there was one thing Esther envied Alice for, it was having an aunt like May. Her own family consisted of just her mother and herself, for her father had died when she had been born. Esther had known the Fonsekas all her life and May with her large dark eyes had all the glamour of the film star Esther wanted to become when she grew up. May smiled and handed out the cake plates.

'Three weeks and four days after the new baby arrives,' she said, winking at her niece. 'You'll be the big sister then!' she added, laughing at the expression on Alice's face. 'Don't worry, darling, you'll always be the eldest. The baby won't count! Look at me, once a baby always a baby!'

May was ten years younger than Sita, less remote and easier to talk to. She worked as an English teacher in the boy's school at the top of Mount Lavinia Hill. She was the only woman who taught there. Everyone joked that she had got the job because of her looks and that the masters were all a little in love with her. Even after the scandal of her sister's elopement, no one had turned against May. She was too beautiful for that. Then a few years ago May had met Namil. He was from a well-respected Singhalese family and had been to the university in Peradeniya where he'd qualified as an engineer. Very soon Namil had fallen in love with her.

'He'll never be short of a good job,' Alice's mother had said wistfully when she heard.

Namil was very tall. Together, he and May made a striking pair. Esther was constantly admiring them.

'You're so lucky,' she told Alice, 'having an aunt like May. It'll be such a stylish wedding.'

'Aunty May is lucky that Namil is a Singhalese,' Alice agreed. 'Not like my dada.'

Startled, Esther raised her eyebrows.

'Don't go passing on such information to everyone, men,' she said loftily. 'Not in this day and age, or you'll get into trouble.'

'Alice!' May called. 'Don't neglect your guests. They're dying for more cake! Come and serve them.'

'I'd better make a move,' Sita announced without moving.

'Why on earth can't you stay the night?' Dias asked.

Being both neighbour and family friend, she felt she could say those things others could not without giving offence.

'It's no use, Dias. I've already asked her,' Kamala said.

There was an awkward pause. Sita shook her head without speaking and the conversation moved on in sharp staccato sentences overlaying each other. Every word seemed as heavy as the heat outside.

'Are you going to the fair tonight, Alice?' Esther asked.

'Yes, yes,' May called out, laughing at them. 'It was meant to be a surprise, Esther! Namil and I are going to take you tonight, Alice.

It's your birthday treat. Your *second* birthday treat in one day, you lucky girl!'

May came over to where they sat on the cool verandah beside the pots of ferns.

'Are you going to live in England, then?' Esther asked suddenly.

'No, of course not!'

'Oh! Why have you got a passport then?'

Alice didn't know. Her father's older brother lived in England. He had gone long before Alice was born.

'I think he sent it,' she said dubiously. 'As a present.'

'You don't give people passports as presents,' Esther scoffed.

'It's always good to have a passport,' May told them lightly.

'Why?' asked Alice, but May had turned and was taking Sita's bag out to the car. There was a scraping back of chairs and the grown-ups came out on to the verandah. They no longer looked happy.

'I think,' Esther said softly, 'you'll find you *are* going.'

She spoke under her breath and Alice, glancing up at her mother, did not hear. Although she did notice that Sita had a funny, closed expression. It was the look that usually followed an argument. Her grandfather was frowning and staring at the ground.

'Come, then,' Bee said finally. 'I'll take you.'

He sounded cross.

'Will Stanley be waiting for you at the station?' Dias asked.

'Oh yes,' Sita replied. She spoke easily but Alice knew, from the way she spoke, that she was lying.

'Can I learn to ride my bicycle now?' she asked, kissing Sita good-bye.

'Don't wear your grandparents out,' was all her mother said.

'You must get out of your school uniform first,' her grandmother added.

'We must go too, child. Just look at the time,' Dias announced, yawning. 'Come on, Esther. If you're going out tonight you must help me in the house first.'

'I'll be back soon,' Bee called.

He turned to Alice and now he was smiling again.

'So be ready,' he warned. 'We'll go to the beach and I'll teach you to ride your bike!'

Outside, the sea beckoned invitingly. It hissed and rolled restlessly, catching the last of the radiant light. Ahead of them, three white ships had positioned themselves against the horizon, and as the last train to Colombo hooted its way towards the station a small kite rose and fell languidly in the breeze.

Later, when he returned, Bee and Alice set off on foot, down to the sea.

'Like in *The Water Babies*,' said Alice, who had just finished reading the book.

'Don't be long,' Kamala warned. 'And hold her hand when you cross the line.'

'Yes, yes,' Bee waved impatiently.

But then at the level crossing he stopped and took her hand, waiting and listening for the sound of any stray trains.

'Just to keep your grandmother happy,' he told her. 'So you've finished *The Water Babies*, huh? You read that quickly.'

Alice skipped beside him.

'Aunty May has given me all the books I asked for,' she said.

'Good!' he nodded. 'You must read as much as you can. English is a beautiful language,' he said thoughtfully. 'It's a language of grace and culture. We have been very foolish to confuse such a language with our government's anti-British attitude.'

Alice yawned. This was the moment she had been waiting for. Going down to the sea with Bee. At last, she thought, wondering what they might find today. He was always finding her things on the beach to add to her collection of objects. Mostly it was glass that he found, but sometimes it was other things: driftwood and rusty bits of tin that made Kamala scream with horror.

The barrier was up. An old woman carrying two chickens crossed the lines. She beckoned them to cross with her.

'*Eney, eney,*' she called, showing betel-red teeth. Two boys on one bicycle rode across.

And then, at long last they reached the sands where several bigger boys shouted hello as they passed. Bee heaved Alice up on to the bike and began pushing.

'Right,' he said with a grin, 'let's go!'

They wobbled off.

'Pedal, pedal,' he shouted above the roar of the waves. 'Keep going, faster! *Faster!*'

On and on they went, Bee breathlessly behind her. A train roaring past. There was spray against her face. She could hear Bee's encouragement, as, head down, she pedalled furiously. The sand was completely unmarked and very white. A half-buried shell flashed by. The wind ran through her hair, wet and heavy with water.

'Am I doing it?' she asked, but there was no reply.

Turning, she looked behind her and wobbled.

'Watch out!' Bee called too late as she went crashing into the water.

He was laughing now.

'You stopped,' he cried, going to help her. 'I told you not to stop pedalling!'

He was still laughing as he pulled her up and righted the bicycle.

'That's enough for today,' he said.

Her dress was soaking and her knee hurt.

'Your grandmother will kill me!'

'Oh, please, please,' Alice pleaded, her eyes like saucers. 'I don't want to stop yet. I have to learn now!'

Bee hesitated. He was done for with Kamala, he knew.

'Come *on*,' Alice insisted, tugging his hand.

Bee laughed.

'Oh, all right, all right, just one last time, then,' he agreed. 'It's true. You *have* nearly got it. But this time, don't look behind you, for God's sake!'

Some of the boys had gathered round to watch. They knew Bee from his daily visits to the beach to buy fresh fish and talk to some of the fishermen. They were used to seeing Alice, too, had watched her learn to swim and now they wanted to see her learn to ride her bicycle. One of the boys whistled encouragingly and wheeled his own bike in the air, showing off. Alice ignored him, wishing Janake hadn't gone away. She wasn't going to admit defeat, not in front of these grinning idiots.

'Ready? Let's go!'

Once again the sound of the sea was close to her ear, mixed up with Bee's footsteps thudding softly in the sand behind her, telling her to pedal faster. And then it was only the sound of the sea, insistent and haunting, that filled her head. She could go on this way forever, she thought, raising her head. Startled, she saw her grandfather was no longer behind her as the horizon righted itself in her sightline. So that finding she was riding the bicycle entirely by herself she laughed so loud and so much that she wobbled and fell off again.

It is evening. Alice can see the sea through the horses as they fly round and round. Gilded hooves, flying sea-spray that disappears to be replaced by the sky. Then they're back, flying high, dipping low, back and forth. She sees Bee's face as he chews on his pipe. He is waving at her. Music belts out; its beat riding the sea from side to side, swinging the fairground lights, the pink-and-green paper lanterns strung around the stalls. Round and round. There's Esther eating candyfloss wearing her polka-dot dress. Even her ponytail swings as she waves at Alice before strolling off. Aunt May holds on to Alice tightly and laughs. Uncle Namil stands on the grass verge watching solemnly. He is still wearing his Colombo office clothes and doesn't seem part of the fair at all. Maybe, thinks Alice, that's why Aunty May is laughing so much. Alice throws her head back, feeling the wind running through her hair, the dress her aunt made, cool and lovely against her legs. Above her the stars blink in the vast tropical sky. I will never forget this, she thinks, shouting into the air that rushes by. She wants it to never end. Three kites fly lazily, flicking home-made tails, while the sound of the barrel organ is loud in her ears and the smells of roasting gram and fried fish and burnt sugar seemed to gather together and explode around her like Catherine wheels.

In another part of the island, in Colombo 10, a woman screams. It is an old familiar scream, primeval and ancient, travelling down the corridors of centuries. In this darkening hour, in the brief southern twilight, the woman screams again, this time more urgently. A child wants to be born. Nothing can stop the need, the desire to exist. Nothing, not the Colombo express rushing past, nor the poya moon gliding tissue-paper-thin across the fine tropical sky can stop it. The child is coming before its time; its clothes, lovingly embroidered, are piled inside a shoe-box in the woman's house. The clothes are small enough to make this possible. Blue; most of the fine lawn clothes are as blue as the sky, for the woman is hoping for a son. She has already decided on a name. For months now she has been saying the name to herself in a whisper.

'Ravi,' she says, 'Ravi.'

She speaks softly for fear of the evil eye. But now she is in pain, three weeks too early, and here in the government hospital. It is late. Too late to inform her mother. Or her sister. Her husband has been sent home, told to return in the morning. This is women's business, the nurse tells him.

'Don't worry,' the nurse says. 'Three weeks is only a little early. And Doctor will be here shortly.'

So the husband goes, the sounds of his wife's whimpers resounding uneasily in his ears.

The carousel has stopped. Alice and May stagger down the steps with shaky feet, fresh sea air cool in their faces. They are still laughing. The puppet master has begun his show. Beside him is a huge neon-coloured inflatable man who sways in the sea breeze. The monkey screams in terror. Namil buys them all an ice cream, but Alice can hardly eat it she is so excited. She can't decide what to look at first. The world is a spinning, rocking, top of sparkling lights. Someone has climbed the tallest coconut tree and strung the coloured bulbs amongst the branches. The carousel starts up again. Alice watches as the lights swing across her face. Her grandfather, yawning, has gone home, leaving her with her aunt. May stands close to Namil and watches the carousel begin again slowly at first and then gathering speed. She smiles a secret smile, thinking about her wedding. Not long now, she thinks. There will be lights threaded across the trees in the garden for the wedding party, just like these at the fair. They will serve iced coffee, May tells her niece. And wedding cake.

'It will be the height of sophistication,' May says, laughing.

Esther, strolling by, hears of it and stops, impressed. Esther has won a baby doll at the coconut shy. As she's too old for dolls, she gives it to Alice, but Alice isn't really interested.

'Give it to the new baby, when it's born,' Esther suggests.

'What if it's a boy?' Alice asks.

Esther shrugs; she is already bored with the conversation. There is a boy called Anton in the crowd. He is here with his school friends. They are from the boys' school and Esther thinks he likes her. She would like to borrow Alice to go with her to the lady card-reader's tent.

'Don't be long,' Aunty May warns. 'We'll wait here.'

The lady card-reader's tent is occupied. Esther takes some money out of her purse. Then she sees the boy called Anton.

'Here,' she says, thrusting the money into Alice's hand. 'You go in, instead. I'll stay here. I want to talk to someone. Go on, I'll wait here for you.'

Alice doesn't want to go. She can't comprehend something as vast as the future, but Esther and the fairground atmosphere are too insistent.

'Go on,' Esther urges impatiently. 'You can ask her anything. Ask if you are going to have a brother or sister.'

The customer inside the tent has come out now and there is no excuse. Esther pushes her inside the tent, nodding encouragingly.

'I'll wait here,' she promises.

The tent is dark with a small glow from a red-shaded lamp. The lady card-reader sitting at the table points to the chair beside her.

'How old are you?' she asks in Singhalese.

Alice tells her. It is her birthday today, she says and the woman moves her head as though she wants her to stop talking now. Then she begins to lay the cards out on the table. They aren't the same cards that Alice has seen the servant boy playing with. These cards have pictures. The lady card reader uncovers three sevens.

'Not so good,' she observes. 'Can you swim?'

Alice can swim, although her grandmother doesn't like her to go into the water here because of the strong currents. And all because once a servant had remarked she could drown if she weren't careful. The servant had seen how Alice's hair grew at the back of her head in a whirlpool. Ever since then her grandmother had been frightened of the sea. Nothing her grandfather could say or do could take away this fear. But yes, Alice tells the lady card reader, she can swim. The woman stares at her for a moment. Then she nods, satisfied.

'I see lots of water,' she says. 'Cold water, grey faraway skies. And you have a good memory. Don't forget anything. One day you will find happiness, so don't give up.'

She looks at Alice and hesitates. Then she holds out her hand for the money. When Alice gives it to her, she stands up.

'You are very talented,' she says. 'So do the best you can. It won't be easy.' And then she holds open the curtain.

'What on earth were you doing in there?' Esther greets her crossly. 'You've been ages. Your aunty's going to be worried.'

'Did you see Anton?'

Esther nods.

'Well, are you going to have a brother or a sister?'

'I forgot to ask,' Alice tells her.

'Idiot!' Esther bursts out laughing at her.

In the bright heart of the fair the carousel is still turning and blasting loud music as the two girls walk back, carrying their thoughts with them.

The doctor is drunk. His breath smells as he squints at the notes the nurse gives him.

'What?' he asks in high-pitched Singhalese. 'You called me in just for this Tamil woman?'

'She isn't Tamil, sir,' the nurse tells him. 'Just the husband.'

'Exactly!' the doctor says, trying not to belch but without success. 'That's my point. Why should we help breed more Tamils? As if this country hasn't enough already!'

Outside, the trees rustle in the slight breeze. Tonight is quiet, no drums, no police sirens, no sudden violence. A perfect night on which to be born.

'All right,' the doctor says, bored. 'Take me to her.'

The woman lies groaning in a pool of sweat. Moonlight falls on the ripeness of her belly. Catching sight of the doctor, she begs him for something to relieve the pain. She speaks in perfect, old-fashioned Singhalese. The nurse bends and wipes her face and offers her a sip of water.

'Give her some quinine,' the doctor tells the nurse.

Then he examines the woman. Because he is drunk, because he has driven here in haste, leaving his dinner guests still at the table, he has forgotten his glasses. Roughly he inserts two fingers into her dilating uterus and the woman screams. The doctor tells her sharply to be quiet, and stepping back half loses his balance. The nurse glances at him, alarmed.

'Sir?' she asks tentatively.

The doctor does not know that this nurse is still a student. She should not be here alone, but the midwife has been called out on an emergency. The student nurse thinks *this* is an emergency too, but she doesn't know what she could say. She is frightened. The doctor prods the woman, ignoring her screams, then, having satisfied himself that all is well, leans over the bed.

'Do you understand English?' he asks slowly.

It is important he does not slur his speech.

'Yes,' the woman says faintly, in Singhalese. 'I do.'

'Good. Then you will understand when I tell you these pains are perfectly normal. They are just called Braxton Hicks contractions. The baby will turn soon and then you'll go into labour. It may take a few hours; you just have to be patient. Nothing to worry about. It's a perfectly normal process. You Tamil women have been doing this for centuries!'

And he laughs, washing his hands.

'The nurse will take care of you,' he says, gesturing to the nurse to give the woman the quinine. 'This will calm you down. I'll be back later.'

The woman, feeling another contraction coming towards her in a wave, tries to ride it and begins to cry out again. The nurse holds her head and she drinks the quinine, the bitterness hardly registering on her. The doe-eyed nurse wipes her face again and follows the doctor out.

'Don't bother calling me. I'll be back in a couple of hours. She'll be fine till then,' he says.

'But, sir, I think it's a breach,' the nurse says tentatively.

She isn't sure, of course, and doesn't want to look foolish in front of this famous consultant.

'Nonsense,' the doctor tells her. 'Do you think I don't know a breach when I see one!'

Again he laughs in a high-pitched manner, peering at this pretty girl's anxious face.

'What's a nice girl like you doing here?' he asks.

He has a sudden urge to run his hand across her back and further down. He begins to imagine the places his hand might reach.

'You should be in my nursing home,' he says, a little unsteadily.

The nurse, her dark eyes made darker by tiredness, smiles a little.

'We must see what we can do,' promises the doctor, thinking how good it would be to have such a lovely face at his private clinic.

And then he goes out into the car park and towards his Mercedes, parked sleekly beside the stephanotis bush, back to his lighted house and his dinner guests.

'Just one more ride,' Alice pleads.

She feels as though they have only just got here. The puppet master is beginning another show and the Kathakali Man of Dance can be heard beating his drum. Alice does not want to miss anything. May and Namil hold hands in the darkness, swaying in time to the music as though they were one person and not two. Namil has brought May some bangles that glitter and jangle as she moves. Alice notices her aunt has some jasmine in her hair and her eyes are shining. She thinks May looks even more beautiful than usual. Namil is looking at her solemnly.

'All right,' May says, smiling at them both.

She can hardly keep still; the music makes her want to dance.

'One more, then we go, no?'

This time Alice goes on the merry-go-round on her own. Slowly her eyes adjust to the faint line of sea and sky as she rides, swaying to the music. Is this what flying is like? Alice wants to move through the night forever, swooping down from the tops of the trees, scooping up the dark water below the cliffs. She can no longer see the faces standing below; all is a blur of rhythm and bright light. Everything reduced to sensation.

The woman screams. She is pleading. The baby inside her struggles, it turns and turns again. In the darkness she sees her stomach heave and rise up in another wave. It turns into a shape too grotesque to be normal. The woman is petrified, she doesn't recognise her own body. It has become something separate from her, dragging her along into an unknown place. She screams, not wanting to go.

'Please, please,' she cries.

Even as she watches, her stomach lurches in a landslide movement to one side of the bed. The nurse who has been holding her is terrified.

'Wait, I'll get someone,' she says. 'Wait, hold on.'

The young, sweet nurse is crying too in great gasping sobs of panic.

But the woman is past listening. Her cries have changed. They pierce the air, becoming something other than despair, sounding inhuman. They are the cries of an unseen child. The child she once used to be, the child inside her, maybe. In the darkness outside, jasmine flowers open, bursting their pouches of scent. Large spiders move haltingly amongst the leaves of the creepers that grow against the whitewashed wall. This is the tropics; insects and reptilian life flourish. A drum is beating in the distance, its regular beat out of step with the cries of the woman in the hospital bed. The spiders and the snakes move relentlessly through the long grass, deaf to the fact that she is pleading for her life now.

They walk back down the hill carrying their prizes. The moon paints a long silver strip across the ground. The road has been recently tarred and the smell of hot bitumen mixes with the smell of the sea. Alice breathes it in deeply. The fair is following them home in magical bursts of heady lights and smells and cries, and the faint jaunty sound of music. She dances ahead of her aunt, waving her thin arms in the air. The moon picks up her shadow and throws it on to the empty road, turning her into a child on stilts.

'Is this child not tired yet!' sighs May, pretending despair. She is swinging Namil's hand as she walks. She too takes little dancing steps.

'I'm not a bit,' Alice sings out in time to the music. 'I'm never going to be tired because I'm nine today!'

They all laugh. They are still laughing as they reach the house. Bee, who has been working in his studio, comes out to greet the revellers. Kamala is shaking her head and trying to look stern.

'Come, come, Putha, it's very late,' she tells Alice. 'You must have a wash and go to bed,' she says, giving the little girl a hug.

'Amma, she still has bags of energy,' May cries in mock complaint. 'Namil and I have been trying to wear her out with no success!' she adds, kicking off her sandals and throwing herself down on one of the many planter's chairs that dot the verandah.

'Well, I'm taking her to the beach early tomorrow morning, so she'd better get some sleep or she won't be able to wake,' Bee tells her slyly.

'Yes, yes, yes,' Alice says, knowing when she is beaten.

Everyone laughs and she follows the servant in, the faint music from the hill still luring her like the tune of the pied piper.

In the last hour, the darkest moment of the night, just before dawn breaks, a doctor hurries into the room. He is a different, younger doctor. He too is a Singhalese; a family man, a father. Capable of hiding his feelings under a mask of professionalism. The woman on the bed has bled so much she is only semi-conscious, and the doctor knows he has not got much time. The baby, the girl child, he knows, is already dead. Later he will fill out the death certificate. *Still birth*, he will write. And although no one will be watching, his hand will have the faintest tremor; his jaw will tighten imperceptibly with anger. That will be all.

Later, in disgust, he will apply to leave his wretched country, unable to stomach what he has always known. For he, more than anyone, knows that life is cheap in this Third World paradise. It comes and goes like waves on its many beaches. But all of this will happen later. On this long, solitary night the doctor will do his job and deliver another dead child. He will see the baby's soft downy hair as it comes away on his hands, when he lifts the body out of this woman. The woman, herself semi-conscious now, far beyond tears, has one last request.

'Let me see her. Please, let me see her,' she begs.

But the doctor, his face softened by pity, his heart filled with pain, shakes his head. The woman sees the compassion in his face in the growing light of the new day.

'What the eye doesn't see, the heart doesn't grieve over,' the doctor says.

It is his only mistake that night.

2

DAWN WAS STILL AN HOUR AWAY. The caravan of delights had packed up its brightly coloured lanterns. Dulith the puppet man, long fingers drumming against the side of his truck, headed for the coast road. He was followed by a trailer carrying the carousel horses and another with the stilt-man at the wheel, trailing tinsel through the window. The clowns slept, chuckling softly, traces of make-up still on their grimy faces; and the helter-skelter men, having concertinaed the helter-skelter down to almost nothing, moved their trailer with hardly a sound. Leaving in silence was what they always aimed to do, waking no one, refusing to disturb the children and their dreams. The monkey lay sleeping beside the lion tamer, exhausted and dour, and the lady card reader, having taken his wig off, urinated on to the road from his moving caravan. It was all part of the fun of the fair. It was all part of life for the fire-eater and the shadow dancer and the inflatable man. Another town, another crowd, another group of noisy punters eating freshly spun candyfloss. All in a day's work; here today, gone tomorrow, with no time for regrets. The sea rose and fell as they hit the coast road, heading north. They would be back in a year; same time, same place, right here on the hill where the short, rough grass would have grown over the chalk numbers that had marked the positions of the rides.

Alice stirred. A telephone was ringing in her dream. It rang and rang again insistently, pushing against the carousel that played out its tune in her head. The feet running across the coconut-polished floors sounded like a thousand galloping horses. It was still dark, the sun had not risen; the mosquito net around her cot was undisturbed. Opening her eyes, Alice saw the sky on the point of being punctured by light. Her dream fled the room, leaving behind a puzzling echo. She frowned, trying to recall the music that played on the merry-go-round, but it evaded her. Nothing moved. Even the sap, bluish-white as mother's milk, had stopped dripping from the rubber trees in the plantation nearby. But *something* had disturbed Alice. The edges of a peculiar awareness nudged her gently, like an old shell murmuring, insisting she awoke. She sat up, fully awake, alert now. She was hot and the flower-scented garden was calling out to her, so in a swift movement she threw off the mosquito net, stood on the low window sill beside her bed and launched herself on to the gravel below. It was the water pump dripping outside the gate that had woken her, she decided. Someone had forgotten to turn it off. Further along the garden a long beam of light extended across the ground. With one blow it cleft the garden into two. She saw with surprise that her grandfather was up and working in his studio. Alice hesitated, wondering whether to disturb him. Overhead, the beginnings of dawn poked a hole in the sky. Faint rose-pink light flooded out, spreading across the horizon, seeping into the sea. The air was filled with a selection of newly unwrapped scents from the jacaranda tree. Alice crossed the gravel in her bare feet and stood on the empty coconut oil drum near the window of the studio. Her grandfather had his back turned to her. He was bent over his etching press, but the studio looked tidy, not at all as it usually did. Black scrim hung neatly on their nails, stiff with dry ink; his cleaned rollers were stacked on shelves above his head and none of his copper plates were in sight. Alice craned her head. What was her grandfather doing at this hour? Something about the angle of his body bothered her and she hesitated for a moment longer, not knowing whether she should disturb him. Bird-arias exploded into the morning. She heard a soft, puzzling sound and then she froze in terror as Bee sunk slowly to his knees. The next instance she toppled over and crashed down into the gravel.

The noise brought him to his feet. He stood in the doorway, a thin man in a white sarong that matched his hair. His face looked strange, as though it was a jigsaw puzzle that had been put together in the wrong way. Confused, she stared at him and it was another moment before she saw with cold, creeping horror that he was crying.

'Your mother has lost the baby,' he told her simply, spreading his hands out in front of him.

Seagulls carried his words in circles above her head, their keening cries tangling with the breaking waves so that forever afterwards Alice would be unable to separate any of these sounds from what had been said. Forever afterwards she would connect the lost baby with the birds and the vast drum of the sky pouring out light as though from an open wound.

Time stood still for her as the events fixed themselves on her mind. Gradually, as the sun gained strength, a thin line marked the horizon, separating the sea from the sky. The waves became transparent as lace while the sky continued to lighten. The waves arched their backs, crashing, concussed against the beach. People passed by, silhouetted against the sun. Far away in some other reality a train hooted its way across the coast. It was the Colombo express, travelling up from Dondra, the very tip of the island.

'Come, Alice,' Bee said, when he could speak again. 'The worst is over for her.'

But he looked terrible, making no move towards the house either. Where had they been when Sita had needed them most?

'Let's go for a walk on the beach,' he said finally, taking her hand.

A baby girl, he told her, haltingly. Her sister. Not the brother called Ravi as her mother had hoped.

'She didn't live to see the day.'

He was exhausted. A delicate eggshell sheen spread across the water even as they watched. Fishing boats were bringing in the night's catch, trailing long nets full of silvery cargo through the shallows. An arrow-head of gulls streamed behind, heralding the day with their shattering cries. The fishermen, splashing through the water, dragged the boats on to the beach; then they unloaded the catch and threw it carelessly into the flat woven baskets that would be taken to the fish market later. Dead fish and sea-rot smells drifted on the breeze, swooped on by hosts of fluttering gulls. A sense of unreality hung in the air.

'The doctor was responsible,' Bee said. He seemed to be talking to himself. 'A Tamil child's life is worth nothing.'

'I hate Singhalese people,' Alice told him.

Her voice sounded unfamiliar, uncertain. She was bombarded by emotion, tossed in a cross-current of confusion, feeling she ought to cry. No tears would come. Instead, small evil thoughts danced in her head and swam behind her eyelids. Had the baby been blue like Mrs Perris's dead husband? Did it cry? And hanging over all her questions, terrifying her, was the memory of the wish she had made. She glanced at Bee. He had stopped walking and Alice now felt a cold wind clutch at her heart.

'I want you to understand,' Bee was saying quietly, looking directly at her, searching her face. 'People will think you're only a child and they will hide things from you. Later they will tell you it was for your own good. But you won't stay a child forever. And I don't want you to misunderstand.'

Some of the shock in his voice was replaced with anger.

'You must know the difference between hating one person and hating a whole race. Don't make that mistake. The doctor was a man, a pariah man. Not even a dog can be that bad. Chance made him Singhalese, remember that, Alice. He would have been bad anyway.'

They walked on silently. I have a dead sister, thought Alice, trying out the words in her mind. She shivered inwardly. Already she felt different.

'Such a little life,' Bee murmured.

They were walking along the same road that Alice had danced on just hours before. Now it had become a remote and distant place and everything had changed in a night. The day lay crushed before her. With a flash of insight she realised she was struggling with events beyond her control. She had become a girl with a dead sister. Nothing was certain any longer. They reached the beach. She could hear the sounds of children's voices carried by the breeze towards her and she saw a few boys pulling a boat out of the water. They were the boys who lived in the little cluster of huts close to the railway line, children of fishermen. Squinting against the sun, Alice watched them silently. Sadness tugged at her, bringing with it a threat of tears. But the tears still would not come and the unmistakable feeling of aloneness made her feel she was no longer part of the beach or these children. Perhaps, she had never really belonged here, she thought in dismay. The sea breeze was making it difficult to breathe and there was a queasy, empty feeling in the pit of her stomach. She wished her old friend Janake would return. The dead sister hung as heavy as a Tamil thora chain around her neck. Other children had had dead relatives, but they had not willed them to be dead. Frowning suddenly, she wanted nothing more of it.

'Alice,' her grandfather was saying, 'your father wants to take you to England. Did you know?'

Alice stared at him. Understanding knocked against her like a ball in a socket. She heard the words, curiously familiar and yet not believable.

'You don't get a passport unless you're going to travel,' she said slowly, remembering Esther.

'Yes.' Bee nodded, the tone of his voice confusing her. 'That's true, darling.'

He hesitated.

'In England,' he said, 'you will be quite safe.'

She was silent, digesting this.

'We cannot keep you safe here any longer,' he continued. 'You must go; the young have no future here. It is best, for a while, at least.'

He stopped walking and stared out to sea. She could not read the expression on his face. All she knew was that in the wide-open aspect of the beach he looked frail and very dear to her. I *am* safe here with you, she wanted to cry, but the words seemed to lodge in her throat and the sea breeze whipped her breath away and lost them.

When they got back, after her father had phoned, Alice heard the facts, such as they were. By the time they filtered down to her they had become simpler, softer. A tale murmured in the shocked voice of her aunt May.

'In England,' May told her, 'childbirth is safe. But in this country it depends on who you are and who your doctor is. Your dada is not a rich man. He could not pay for the private hospital.'

May had been crying on and off ever since she had heard the news; her eyes were bloodshot and swollen. After school had finished she was going to Colombo to visit her sister. And sometime after that, Kamala told her granddaughter, there would be a very small funeral.

'Can I come?' Alice asked cautiously.

She was too afraid to voice what she was beginning to suspect; that she had willed this to happen.

'No, you must stay here. Grandpa Bee is going to bring your mama back here to recover. She won't be going to the funeral either. She's too weak. You can stay and look after her.'

Alice said nothing. What would she say to her mother when she next saw her? Would her mother have bloodshot eyes, too? Guiltily she wondered how much Sita would guess of her part in the baby's death.

'Is she thin now?' she asked in a small voice.

And only then did she remember her friend Jennifer.

'Jennifer's mother is having a baby too,' she told Kamala in dismay. 'She said they were going to have a boy. A Hindu astrologer told her mother that finally, after five girls, she would have a son.'

It was too late. Jennifer would tell everyone that Alice had wanted the baby to die and then everyone in the class would say she had made a curse. Perhaps, thought Alice in panic, she would be sent to the police.

'Do I have to go to school on Monday?' she asked, wanting to cry. 'Can't I stay here a bit longer?'

'Yes, darling,' her grandmother said, looking at her in a funny way.

Perhaps she too had guessed the terrible secret, thought Alice, really frightened now.

'You'll stay until after the funeral. Then you must go back to school. And if Jennifer asks you, simply say the baby died. There's no shame in that, Alice. It wasn't your poor mother's fault.'

Stanley rang again.

'You'll have to be kind to your mother,' he told Alice, as if even he had discovered her secret. Reluctantly she agreed, aware of Bee's watchful eyes on her. Afterwards, without a word, Bee got the car out to drive May to the hospital. He would go with Stanley to the undertakers to organise the funeral. Kamala gave May a food parcel of rice and bitter gourd with chillies. The cook had baked it with fenugreek in the clay oven, knowing it was Sita's favourite dish.

'She'll be hungry,' Kamala whispered, 'even though she won't realise it.'

Kamala too sounded close to tears. She gave May a flask of coriander tea.

'To dry the milk.'

Alice glanced at her.

'She may have a fever.'

Kamala was speaking hurriedly, avoiding looking at May. Alice watched them from the corner of her eye, both fascinated and repelled by the whispering voices. Everyone was avoiding looking at each other, as if they feared something awful would show in their faces.

After they had gone the house fell silent. There was still no sign of Janake, as Alice wandered around aimlessly.

'Why don't you see if Esther is around?' Kamala asked.

But Esther was nowhere in sight either and Kamala, busy getting the room ready for Sita, had no time to talk.

Alice looked around for something to do. On her grandmother's instructions, she reluctantly decided to do a drawing for Sita. The thought of her mother's return was beginning to curdle uneasily within her. She drew a picture of the view from Mount Lavinia Hill with its bougainvillea-covered houses, its coconut grove and its glimpse of the sea. After some deliberation she decided not to draw the ships that were so constantly present on the horizon. The ships that she had taken for granted all her life had, since this morning, taken on a new and more sinister meaning. So instead she drew the three rocks beside the hotel where she had often swum. She hoped it would bring back happy memories for her mother too.

The servant had taken a mattress out on to the verandah and was dusting it. Then she began to sweep Sita's old room. Sita would sleep alone so she might rest properly. The servant took all the furniture outside and began to clean it.

'Move away, Alice, baby,' the servant said. 'You'll get covered in dust. Why don't you lie down for a bit?'

Alice went into her room. She didn't want to be called baby. She stared at the mosquito net hastily thrown aside earlier that morning. She had known this room all her life. It was as familiar as her own hand. The deer's head that her great-grandfather had brought back as a trophy from England stared down at her. A bowler hat worn by one of her ancestors hung over its face, covering its sad, dead eyes. Alice shivered. The hat had been put there by Kamala years before when a much younger Alice had been frightened by its eyes. No one had ever bothered to remove it, and the deer now stared eternally into the dark interior of the hat. Sitting on the end of her bed, Alice glanced around the room. There was a faint smell of camphor and polish and washed cotton. The lump of clear green glass that she had found on the beach during her last visit stood on the window sill, exactly where she had left it. Everything was as before; only she, Alice Fonseka, had changed. Her guilt hung on an invisible hook in the thickening midday heat. Once, when she had been very small, a servant told her a story about a child who had done something bad. Afterwards, the servant told Alice, every time the child moved, every time she walked or sat down or played in the garden, the devil would walk behind her, dragging his chains. Recalling the story, Alice wondered if she too would be hearing chains soon? She listened, but nothing happened. Through the dazzling bright sea light far down below the cliff came the sound of a passing train. Its echo went on and on.

She stared blankly at the sea. There was no way of explaining her unhappiness to herself. On the beach another group of children jumped in and out of the waves. From this distance they looked like small birds darting about, waving their arms in the air, free. Janake was still nowhere in sight. She watched the boys for a moment longer, hearing their faint laughter. Until this moment childhood had held no threat for her. But as she stood watching the scene below, for the second time that day, the idea that things had in some irreversible way altered began to take shape in her mind. The sun reappeared with renewed force from behind a cloud. She longed to be down on the white sand, laughing at nothing and getting soaked. She longed to see Janake and have him tease her. Standing beside the open window, recalling her grandfather from earlier in the morning, she emulated what he had done moments before he had seen her. Raising her arms up, letting her body descend slowly to the ground, curiously, she tried to imagine how he must have felt. Such was her absorption that she did not hear the gate bang shut or the footsteps on the gravel. Esther's face looking up at the window startled her.

'What are you doing, Alice?'

'Nothing,' she said crossly, frowning, standing up. 'What are you doing here?'

'We heard the news,' Esther said. She sounded shocked, unsure of herself. 'Amma sent me to ask if you would like to come over to our house.'

Alice was puzzled. Esther sounded unusually friendly.

'What's done is done,' Alice told her, unconsciously echoing her grandfather's words.

Esther stared back at her. In the bright paintbox-coloured daylight her dress looked strangely tawdry, the traces of lipstick on her lips, drab.

All afternoon Bee sat helplessly beside his eldest daughter while she slept a drug-induced sleep. Then the doctor who had delivered the baby came in. Together they had watched Sita. Her womb had ripped, her uterus would need stitching, and when she finally began to remember she would have to bear a different kind of pain.

'I'm sorry,' the doctor had said.

Bee noticed how dark his eyes were, just like pools of rainwater.

'She'll recover,' the doctor had told him, 'physically, anyway. There will be no more children, but she'll recover. The stitches will heal, the scars will be hidden, outwardly everything will be in order. I've made sure of that.'

He shook his head. Then he told Bee he had decided to leave the island. He was no longer able to stay silent about all those things he was witnessing, he said.

'I became a doctor so I could alleviate suffering, not add to it. But this place –' he had lifted his hands in a gesture of incomprehension – 'is turning me into a coward. I fear for my wife, my family. I am no longer able to do my duty as I should.'

Bee listened without comment.

'I'm going to Australia,' the doctor had continued.

Outside the room the noise of the ward drifted towards them. Bedpans clattering, newborn babies mewling, laughter, even.

'Yes,' Bee agreed finally, expressionlessly. 'My daughter will be leaving too. They want a better life for my granddaughter.'

That had been all they had said. The doctor placed his hand lightly on Bee's shoulder. Then he nodded briefly and left. His face had been full of a grave pity. It had almost been the undoing of Bee.

At dinner that night Esther and Dias came round again and the talk turned on the events of the day. They were all in shock. Looking around at his family, Bee said very little. He still felt numb from this terrible day. Darkness was encroaching. The servant came in silently and switched on the light. Instantly two large orange-spotted moths flitted in and began to circle around the bulb. Alice and Esther finished eating and went quietly on to the verandah, seeming to be swallowed up by the dark garden. They too were quiet. Bee waited until he was certain they were out of earshot.

'First let them bury their dead,' he said, turning back into the room.

I am accepting the inevitable, he thought in silent pain.

'We must let them go in peace to the UK,' he told Kamala.

'Something more should be done,' May said, angrily. 'Someone should be told, for God's sake! He should be struck off, Amma. How can we stand by like this and do nothing?'

May was crying again, but this time she was angry as well.

Later, when the visitors had left and Kamala had coaxed her, Alice went without fuss to bed. But she could not sleep. A full moon shone in through her window and once or twice she sat up and looked out at the sea. She could hear the grown-ups out on the verandah now and she could smell tobacco from Bee's pipe. The low hum of their voices blended with the drone of the insects.

'How *can* you?' Aunt May was asking.

'We can't afford the lawyer,' Kamala said in a low, sad voice. She sounded as though she too was crying.

Then Alice heard her grandfather tap his pipe against his chair. Until now he had been mostly silent.

'It isn't a question of money,' he said hesitantly, and Alice strained her ears to catch his words. 'Even if we found the money for the lawyers, and even if the nurse could be called on to testify, who would believe this was done simply because she has a Tamil name? Would anyone believe us? We would be taking on the government doctors. I can't think of a single lawyer in this country who would want to do that.'

The sound of his voice, quiet and incomprehensible, comforted Alice, so that closing her eyes, finally, she drifted into a dreamless sleep.

The funeral took place early on the following Thursday. May stayed with her sister in the hospital. Only Stanley and Bee were present. They paid the gravedigger and Stanley carried the tiny white coffin himself. The scent of orange blossom marked the moment, fixing it in Bee's mind. Murderers, he thought, as the first fistful of soil hit wood. Then, when all that remained was a fresh mound of earth, they turned without a word and headed for Colombo. The sun was beginning its climb in the sky. The city was wide awake and filled already with the bustle of rickshaws and horns and the sounds of a thousand indifferent lives. Bee glanced at his son-in-law. He had never been close to Stanley; this was, he saw, their closest moment. Driving home along the coast road, in an afternoon of unbroken heat, his mind brimming with images of his daughter's exhausted face, Bee felt the light, unbearable and savage, scythe across him. Then with its sour, stale smell of seaweed and other rotting vegetation, the day disintegrated slowly before his eyes.

While the funeral was taking place in Colombo, Kamala gave alms to the Buddhist monks. Dias had come to help, bringing her cook with her to the Fonsekas' house. The priests were praying for the life that had passed briefly by, blowing out like a candle. All morning they had sat cross-legged, head bowed, their tonal chants filling the house as they blessed the white cotton thread. Their voices rose and fell, sometimes flatly, sometimes softly, always with a deep vibration. They were dressed in traditional saffron robes, so starkly bright that even the familiar sitting room with its ebony and satinwood furniture, its old sepia photographs and plants, took on a dreary air by comparison. The heat in the room, in spite of the doors and windows having been thrown wide open, was oppressive and unusually cloying. Janake, back from his aunt's house, was present with his mother.

'Let's go outside,' Esther whispered. 'How much longer is this *pirith* chanting going to last?'

No one could eat until the monks had been fed. It was bad form and disrespectful to do so, but the savoury smells drifting out into the garden were tantalising.

'I'm starving!' Esther said flatly, and she sneaked off, leaving Janake and Alice on the verandah.

'Where's she going?' frowned Janake. 'She can't eat yet.'

'She's gone to steal some rice to make chewing gum with,' Alice told him.

'What?' Janake laughed. 'She's off her head!'

Alice said nothing and Janake looked at her sharply. He was four years older than her and had known her all her life. Yesterday when he had returned from Peradeniya his mother had told him about Sita. His mother had also told him that Alice was probably going to England because of what had happened. Janake had been shocked.

'But, Amma, Alice *loves* it here,' he had cried. 'And it would break Mr Fonseka's heart if she went.'

Janake had been present on the first day Alice had been shown the sea as a tiny baby. He had been with her when she took her first faltering footsteps across the sands. It had been Janake who had held her hand, watched over by an anxious Bee. As she grew, it was always

Janake who played with her whenever she visited her grandparents. A few weeks ago he had gone with Bee to buy a bicycle for her. The idea of Alice going to England, of her never being here, was incomprehensible to him. He glanced at her. His mother had told him not to mention the subject to Alice in case she didn't know, so he couldn't question her. Alice was staring straight ahead with an unusually serious look on her face. Janake scuffed the ground with his feet and then he picked up a stick and began whittling it.

'Esther's a fool,' he said angrily. He felt both helpless and full of an unaccountable rage.

Esther returned with a handful of hot rice. She squeezed it into two balls, offering one to Janake.

'Here, have some home-made chewing gum,' she grinned.

'No thank you,' Janake said, scowling. 'That isn't real chewing gum,' he scoffed.

'Fine!' Esther cried, tossing her ponytail and offering it to Alice instead.

Alice became aware of a certain shift in the order of things between the three of them.

'You're supposed to keep moving it in your mouth like gum,' Esther laughed, not unkindly. 'And don't swallow it!'

'But it isn't real gum, and I'm hungry.'

'Why do you want to be so American?' Janake asked curiously.

He was watching them with narrowed eyes and Alice had the distinct feeling he wanted to pick a fight with Esther.

'You should stop trying to be like other people and just be Ceylonese. We are a great country!'

'This is a boring place,' Esther said shortly. 'And in any case, I'm not one of you Singhalese types, men. I'm a Burgher, remember. See?'

She held out her arm, which was several shades lighter than Janake's.

'Huh!' Janake snorted. 'Alice is fairer than you. Put your arm out, Alice.'

'That's because she's half-caste, idiot. Her father is a Tamil.'

'So? So are you! Idiot yourself.'

Esther shrugged, losing interest. She stared out to sea. Later on, when she got home Anton, the boy from the fair, was coming to call.

She chewed her mouthful of rice more slowly. Anton had a distant Tamil relative and this made Dias nervous.

'Just look what happened to Sita,' Dias had warned. 'I don't want that to be your fate. We're Burghers. Who knows when it will be our turn to be kicked? We should be careful.'

But Esther didn't care. She would be fifteen soon. She hated this country. She hated the way things were changing, and she did not want to study in Singhalese.

'But soft, a light shines from the east,' she murmured.

'What?' asked Alice.

Janake began to laugh. Esther was silent. She was thinking of Anton, wishing he had kissed her at the fair. In reality he had grinned and offered her some real American gum. America, that was where Esther wanted to go. Not England.

'"Gallop apace, you fiery horses,"' she said loudly, forgetting where she was.

Until the new law had stopped them learning in English, they had been studying *Romeo and Juliet* in school. No one would ever translate it into Singhalese.

'What are you saying?' Janake asked.

'Nothing you'd understand.'

And she turned to Alice instead, for Janake was annoying her.

'I was just thinking, you know, men, your sister will have been buried by now.'

Alice too was thinking. She wanted to write a letter to Jennifer. *My dear Jennifer*, she wanted to say. *My sister died yesterday. I will be coming back to school soon.* Calling the baby 'sister' made a difference to how she felt about it. How odd it all was. A mottled brown, dusty rattlesnake writhed in the dust. Alice imagined her mother in her hospital bed, writhing as if she too was shedding a skin. It occurred to her that, had her sister lived, there might have come a time when the two of them would have sat on the verandah just as she was doing with Esther. Alice would have been the eldest. It was the hottest moment of the day. Her grandfather had still not returned from the funeral. How long did it take to bury someone? Inside the house, the sounds of pirith had stopped and the food was being brought in. Esther moved restlessly.

'Dust to dust,' she intoned. 'But life must go on, and I'm ravenous!'

'Alice,' someone called.

'They want to tie the thread on you. Go, quickly,' Janake said. 'Go, Alice. Tomorrow you can show me how you can ride your bicycle on the beach.'

Esther gave her a small shove.

'The sooner that's done, the sooner we can eat, child!'

The monks were having their food at last. Strangely, now that they had stopped chanting, Alice could hear the melodious echoes everywhere. She could hear it within the hum of the cicadas, rising and falling, and the imperceptible rustle of the leaves on the murunga tree, and in the waves that spread like ice cream on the beach. She wondered what her school friend was doing now. *My dear Jennifer, my sister was buried today and now I'm going to have the pirith string tied around my wrist to help her into the next life.* The leaves on the mango tree were covered in fine sea dust. A thin black cat limped in from next door's garden; she stretched out on the parched flowerbed and licked her wounds. Two thoughts like brightly coloured rubber balls juggled in Alice's head. One concerned her mother and the other her sister. There wasn't a single cloud floating in the sky. Eternity was up there, but she was starving. She went hurriedly in to have the thread tied to her wrist.

After they had finished eating, the monks washed their hands in the jasmine-scented finger bowls. They wiped them on the white cotton towels, blessed the house again, bowed and left. Everyone bowed back with their hands together. *Aybowon.* The house seemed to sigh. It remained a house in mourning, but at least it had been blessed.

'Nothing more will happen here,' the servant told Alice confidently. Everyone helped themselves to food in a quiet, subdued manner. Murunga curry with coconut milk, *kiri-bath*, milk rice, or plain boiled rice cooked in plantain leaves, whichever you preferred. There was jak-fruit curry, and dhal and coconut *sambal.* Dias gave Alice such a big hug that she squeezed the food all the way up to her throat and Alice thought she might vomit. Then Dias kissed her hard and she lost the two Indian rubber balls of thought she had been juggling. They dropped on the floor and rolled away to be retrieved at some later date. For the moment, Alice concentrated on getting away from Esther's amma. Janake had disappeared again.

'Your mummy will be coming home soon, child,' Dias said, her lipstick-kissed-away-lips looking sad.

I'm fine, Alice wanted to shout, with the defiance for which she was renowned. She wanted everyone to look somewhere else because, more than anything, she wanted to forget about her mother and the baby. She did not want to be reminded about them. She wished her aunt May would come home; she wished her grandmother wasn't so busy supervising the food. She wanted Janake to come back from whatever he had been sent to do. But most of all she wished her grandfather would return. *Dear Jennifer, it wasn't really a proper baby, but everyone is making such a fuss.* She rubbed the letter out of her thoughts.

The afternoon dragged on. There was still no sign of Bee or May.

'You know, the child is grieving too,' Dias whispered to an aunt. 'They must keep an eye on her, cha, make sure she doesn't get withdrawn or anything.'

Alice could hear her from across the room. Her grandfather had always said her hearing was very good.

'Where's Janake gone?' she asked.

Esther shrugged.

'I'm going home,' she yawned.

She had had enough drama for the moment and she wanted to curl her hair before Anton came.

'Cheerio,' she cried, waving good-bye.

Alice heard her whistling 'True Love Ways' as she left. Dias heard it too and hurried after her daughter, annoyed with her behaviour in this place of mourning. It was a signal that the afternoon had ended. Kamala told Alice that it was time for her to get out of her alms-giving clothes, have a wash and then a nap. So by the time Bee drove his car in through the gate, the house was quiet. The servant boy closed the gate after him and stood waiting.

'Shall I wash it, sir?' he asked.

Bee nodded and gave him the keys. Then he went up the steps into the house. One of the monks' black umbrellas rested against the door. Kamala and the cook had cleared the food away. There was a covered dish and a place set for Bee at the table.

'Do you want something to eat?'

He nodded and went to wash his hands. When he came back she was standing by his chair.

'How was she?'

He sat down.

'As you would expect,' he said shortly. 'She wanted to go to the funeral. The doctor managed to persuade her she was not strong enough.'

He ate a mouthful of food in silence.

'I think the doctor was wrong,' Kamala said slowly. 'They should have let her see the body.'

Bee grunted. He had no desire to eat, but he let her serve him.

'Did Janake come?' he asked instead.

Kamala nodded.

'Did he leave a note for me?'

'Yes. It's in your studio.'

'Good!'

They were silent. Kamala waited until he finished what he was eating. Then she served him another ladleful of rice.

'Did you tell her?' she asked softly. 'Her second child looked like her first?'

Bee shook his head.

'I don't suppose that husband of hers had much to say?'

'He was crying most of the time,' Bee told her. 'He wants her to write something for the papers. He wants the world to know about the murder of his child.'

Kamala opened her mouth to say something, but, changing her mind, closed it. There was no point in talking about Stanley.

'She *should* have seen the child,' she insisted instead.

'Where's Alice?' Bee asked, pushing aside his plate.

The taste of the food made him feel sick.

'Sleeping. Dias thought she was unusually quiet. She thought we should talk to her because she noticed she was eavesdropping all the time.'

'So what?' Bee asked sharply. 'What's wrong with that? It's perfectly normal for a child of her age. Why doesn't Dias mind her own business?'

He took out his pipe and began to fill it with tobacco.

'Alice will be fine,' he said irritably. 'And tell Dias that Sita will be coming back with May in a few days' time. They'll be fine, too. That woman should look after her own daughter instead of interfering with other people's affairs.'

Kamala sighed and Bee pushed his chair back and stood up. He would be in his studio, should anyone want him.

'Tell Alice to come and find me when she wakes,' was all he said.

Kamala watched his receding back. A small rush of cooler air made her shiver. There was something he was not telling her, but she knew Bee was stubborn and would speak only in his own time.

They had been together for thirty years. When they had first married, she had been a girl of only eighteen. Bee had been the new teacher in the boys' school. Kamala's father had decided Bee was a suitable match for his daughter. Both sides approved and Kamala was introduced to him. They had both been young; the British had still been in power. After they were married, every time Bee had seen the British flag flying he would swear. At first Kamala had been amazed by his fury, but later on it had delighted her. Until that moment she had no real idea of his true character. Politics had never crossed her mind. In this backwater she had not met anyone as forthright as Bee. Her father and brothers were very conservative, diplomatic, quiet. Bee was different and Kamala liked his hot-headedness, his passion. Later, as she got to know him better, she felt the weight of this passion turn itself towards her with astonishing force. She fell in love. They had been married for three months when she fell both pregnant and in love almost simultaneously. Not for her this English notion of romantic love before marriage. Kamala's love had come slowly like a small stream, appearing first as a trickle, then gathering pace until it grew into the great river that it was today, flowing steadily down to a larger sea. For this reason Kamala had puzzled over Sita and she had found Stanley an even greater mystery. Her daughter had hardly known the man. Given their different backgrounds, how could Sita be sure she loved him? But when Kamala had tried to discuss these things with Bee he had refused to be drawn. Not for the first time in their marriage she came up against his stubbornness. From this she had known how deep his hurt had gone, and because of this she had kept her own counsel. It had not been easy. Then Alice had arrived. The child had switched on the light they so desperately needed. Although, Kamala reflected sadly, she had also brought them a whole different set of anxieties.

Preparing to go to bed at last, Kamala thought back to the day Alice had been born. How happy they had been on *that* day. Moonlight fell across the garden sending great shadows from the lone coconut tree on to the gravel.

'I'll just have another look at her,' Bee said, coming in, glancing at her, 'check she's asleep.'

Kamala nodded and waited. She was praying silently to the Buddha for peace to return to the house. Incense drifted through the open window. The night was cooler as they lay, side by side, in their old antique bed in a room steeped in bluish moonlight and scented as always by the sea. This was the bed where first Sita and then May had been born. Life and death, thought Kamala sadly, here in this house.

'We might need to prepare for another visitor,' Bee said quietly.

'When?'

'Not sure. After the demonstration, is my guess.'

Outside a solitary owl hooted and the moon moved slowly across the sea.

'So at least you can still help someone,' she murmured.

She felt infinitely old. Turning, she faced Bee, moving closer to him as she had done every night, without fail, all these years. He smelled faintly of tobacco and of linseed oil; he had been smoking too much in the last few days. It wasn't only this news she was waiting for. She was certain there was something else. A train rushed past.

'What is it?' she asked at last, fearfully, in Singhalese.

Bee said nothing. He lay motionless for so long that she wondered if he had heard her. She hesitated, a cold fear in her mouth, willing him to speak. Finally he moved restlessly, his face unreadable.

'Stanley leaves in a month,' he said. 'He's got a passage to England. He decided to leave first and get a job, then send for them. I've told him that I will pay their fare. That way they won't be parted from him. It will be better that way. Alice needs both her parents and the family must not be split up. They'll be gone in four months at the most.'

Outside, the sea moved softly. The beach was empty, the water a churning mass of silvery black. Nothing could distinguish it from the dark unending emptiness of sky.

3

WHEN THE MOMENT SHE HAD DREADED finally arrived and she saw her mother walking slowly up the garden in her faded orange sari, Alice felt her legs grow unaccountably heavy and turn to stone. Kamala coaxed her out on to the verandah and reluctantly down the steps, a bunch of gladioli thrust out in front of her face. Long after she had forgotten her mother's lop-sided expression of trying not to cry, Alice remembered the deep, burnt orange of the flowers and the shimmering sea-light. She gave Sita an awkward hug and the scent of the flowers passed violently between them. Dazzling sea colours of a certain unbelievable blueness flew into the house while the sound of the cicadas rose and fell in feverish cadence, reminding Alice of the Buddhist monks. It was Kamala who took charge of the situation, enfolding her daughter in a loving embrace, recalling the day Sita had walked in with the newborn Alice. No one else was capable of much. Within minutes Sita was installed in a chair and a cup of weak coriander tea was in her hand.

'I'll put your mama's flowers in a vase in her room,' Kamala told the child, smiling encouragingly, aware of some indecision. 'She can see them when she has her rest.'

Alice nodded. She was a murderer. In the awkward silence that followed, Sita stared straight ahead at the sea. Two catamarans with dark patched sails stood motionless in the distance. Alice stole a surreptitious look in the direction of her mother. Sita had wanted a boy named Ravi but, because it had been a girl, they would have called her Rachel after the child in the film, *Hand in Hand*. Alice swallowed.

'Did it hurt?' she asked eventually.

Without warning her mother began to cry, a thin long howl followed by great choking sobs. Her sari was coming undone. Alice stared at her in dismay, wishing she hadn't spoken.

'Mama,' she said uncertainly, looking around for her grandmother, wishing Janake would come over as he had promised. Sita looked frightening and unfamiliar. Her body was its old shape with her stomach almost flat again. She began to speak in a high, strange voice that wobbled on the edge of hysteria. Panic-stricken, Alice called her grandmother.

'I thought my legs were being pulled apart,' Sita was saying through a storm of tears. 'And then my stomach collapsed. They didn't let me see her, they didn't want me to!'

She wrung her hands and her face twisted with the effort of trying to speak while she cried.

'We have to leave this place, Alice. We must go far away from these murderers. We must go to England. Your dada is leaving first, but we must follow.'

Alice stood rooted to the spot. Her mother looked like one of the puppets she had seen at the fair. Her grandparents, coming in just then, moved swiftly.

'Come, come, Sita, don't upset yourself and Alice with talk like that. Let's take you into the bedroom.'

'Give your mother a kiss, Alice,' Bee said calmly, 'and then she must rest. After that I want you to come with me; there's something I have for you. I've been waiting for the right moment.'

They stepped out into the hot afternoon, and turned towards his studio, a small shadow walking close to a larger one. Her bicycle was leaning against the mango tree exactly where they had left it. Seeing it, Bee stopped and sighed.

'Child …' he said.

And then he shook his head.

'Can I ride my bicycle?' Alice asked, stalling for time uneasily.

Her grandfather was beginning to sound frightening too. Whatever it was he was about to say, she did not want to hear. Bee nodded absent-mindedly. She wanted him to be angry with the government or her father. She wanted him to look fierce, but all Bee did was continue to stare at the sea. She sensed that shockwaves were going through him. At last he took a deep breath.

'Alice,' he said, and to her relief he sounded stern. 'There are certain things you need to know.'

She froze. He knew! She had wished the baby dead and he was going to hand her in to the police. Bee was looking at her. The heaviness that she had been carrying around for days shifted and the sun on her neck was as warm and comforting as a hand. Mango scents from the tree pressed against her. It was such an ordinary day. On the dry parched ground a yellow-spotted gecko moved haltingly, back and forth. Alice watched it until it disappeared under the debris of fallen leaves and then her grandfather's voice was suddenly very clear and steady in the pause.

'It is not the end of the world, you know,' he was saying lightly, as though he was talking to himself. 'And it isn't for almost four months.'

'What?' she asked, startled.

'Huh?' he said gruffly. 'What d'you think? That you won't come back, huh?'

When she looked up, he appeared to be laughing, with all but his eyes.

'It won't be forever. When this trouble stops, you'll come back, you know that! Just you wait and see. I shall be right here, waiting for you. Now come, Putha, I want to show you what I've been saving for you.'

'Are we going to England?'

Bee nodded. His lips were pressed firmly together. They crossed to the back of the house where he had spent his life battling with the wind and the monsoons to create his garden. Most of the plants he grew were in containers he had stolen from the kitchen, much to the annoyance of the cook, who was always complaining to Kamala. Bee never took any notice. Going over to the old cupboard that lived outside his studio beside the murunga tree, he searched inside and handed Alice a small box with drawers attached. When she opened it each compartment held all the seeds he had collected from his garden.

'See, child, there's a whole garden here, waiting. I've been saving all of them for you. See, here's a forest sleeping in your hand!'

It was obvious he had been preparing for this for some time, that in fact he had always guessed they would leave one day.

'So you can take my garden with you wherever you go,' he told her firmly. 'And you must grow the plants just as I've shown you. Hmm?'

She nodded, silenced. The shadows lying in wait on the edge of her bright looking-glass world jostled with each other, inching a little closer. Certainty was seeping into her like sea water from a hole dug on the beach. Alice stared dumbly. A confusion of thoughts swam in her head. The view of the sea, the yellow-spotted gecko now darting across a branch of the murunga tree, and her grandfather, all the well-loved sights of the slowly baking afternoon became as insubstantial as a mirage. Again her heart flexed with sadness and a faint sense of pre-monition brushed against her. The rush of the sea was faint as though from a shell held to her ear. Blinking, she observed her grandfather in the mottled shade of the tree.

'And there's something else I want to tell you,' he was saying, ignor-ing the look on her face, frowning at her. 'Having certain thoughts about things won't make them happen. We all have those sorts of thoughts. Sometimes we have to *think* them in order to see what we feel, d'you understand?'

Alice nodded as the vomity thoughts moved up her throat. And then subsided back into her stomach. She felt like the blocked gully at the back of the garden. Sometimes the servant poked it with a stick and the dirty water went away. But a blocked gully, the servant had said, was always a blocked gully. You never knew when it might overflow. Her grandfather was looking at her closely, so she carefully put her don't-care face on. Bee wasn't easily fooled. She needed to be careful.

'We all have thoughts, Alice,' he repeated softly. 'Understand?'

Again she nodded. Luckily her grandfather had turned and was looking far out to sea again.

'She should have been allowed to see the baby,' he murmured. 'What you don't see stays in your mind longer. It haunts you. D'you understand?'

Alice waited. It occurred to her that this was another way in which she was changing. Because I'm nine, she decided, I don't get impatient any more. I've learned to wait. She knew that her dark secret about the baby was inside the gully. Out of sight for the moment, at least.

'This will always be here,' Bee said, pointing to the view and the garden. 'Waiting for you to return.'

He spoke fiercely.

'You know that I will never, never leave you.'

Then his face cleared.

'I'll take you for the cycle ride later, after I do a bit of work,' he said in a different voice. 'And you can look for Janake.'

But later things got worse. Three weeks was not long in the cycle of recovery. Sita was in a terrible state. Her breasts still leaked milk and she had been warned that the tear in her uterus would take months to heal. Walking was painful because of the stitches and despite constant sedation she slept only fitfully. In the end they moved her bed into her sister's bedroom so May could talk to her whenever she woke. What frightened Alice the most was that her mother could stay silent for only so long before she began her story again. The family doctor came to call. He had been a friend of the Fonsekas for as long as they could remember. He had delivered both Sita and May. Now he came to examine Sita, to check her wound was healing and to change the dressing. He came just when the four o'clock flowers were closing. Alice tried filling her head with the sound of the sea in order to blot out her mother's cries. After the doctor had left, Bee called Alice and she wheeled her bicycle over the level crossing towards the beach. They walked without speaking, pausing only at the kade for Bee to buy some tobacco. When she had been younger, Alice used to love to stand at the level crossing watching the express as it roared towards Colombo. Tonight they were late and the train had already gone and the beach when they reached it was empty, scribbled all over with small sand worms. Two enormous gulls walked sedately in front of them, managing to keep a fraction of an inch away from the waterline.

'I'm going to sit on this rock,' Bee told her, 'and draw the view and smoke my pipe. Why don't you see if Janake is around by the huts?'

He had not told Alice, but he had begun to draw her. The drawings were to be his talisman against the coming departure. The sun had not set and the light had a curious candescence. It hung over the sea uncannily as Alice rode in a wobbling line towards the huts. Janake, when he wasn't out with the fishermen, helped his stepfather to collect coconuts. Today, to her delight, he was still on the beach chopping firewood. She stood watching him for a moment. He was as much a part of this place as she was, so constantly present in her life that she had hardly noticed him until now. The savoury smell of cooking drifted from one of the fishermen's huts making her mouth water. Janake, stripped to the waist, raised his arm high in the air before bringing it down on to the log. The way the axe struck the wood looked easy, but Janake was sweating. There was a slowly growing pile of wood nearby. Turning, he saw Alice and addressed her in Singhalese.

'Where've you been? I've been waiting for you.'

'Why does the tree smell of perfume?' she asked.

'It's a special tree,' Janake said. 'It can cure many things.'

He smiled a flash of very white teeth. Then he told Alice the townsmen had finally given his mother permission to chop down the tree. They had needed the permission because of the tree's medicinal properties. Early this morning the tree men had come and taken the tree down and now his mother wanted him to saw these parts up. Some for firewood and a piece to make a table.

'I've been doing this all day,' he said. 'And waiting for you. How is your amma?'

Alice picked up a small chip and smelled it.

'That's a medicinal smell,' Janake told her. 'The herbal doctors will pound it up and make it into a poultice.'

'Shall I take some for my mother?'

'If you like. Ask the cook to grind it for her. Is she bad?'

Alice nodded. She was reluctant to tell Janake how bad her mother was, or that she didn't want to look at her face. He was a boy who would stop a bus on the road if there were a tortoise crossing. How could she tell him she had caused a death? She frowned. Janake was absorbed in stacking the wood into piles.

'Can we go to the sand dunes?' she asked.

'Okay,' Janake said without looking up. 'Wait a minute till I finish this. We can walk to the next bay. You might find things for your collection.'

He was right. They found some old driftwood with paint on it and a piece of blue fishing net.

'It must have come from one of the catamarans,' Janake said, examining it.

The wood revealed two colours, one underneath the other. Aquamarine over-painted by cobalt blue. It was scratched and peeling, still damp from the water. The evening stopping train passed slowly by. It was half empty. Glancing up, Alice saw a woman with bright red lipstick eating a samosa. When the train slowed down at the level crossing a man in a white shirt leaned out of an open window and watched them. He smiled and waved at Janake. Alice had a feeling she had seen him before. Then she remembered that he had come to her grandparent's house during the riots one Singhalese New Year. He had slept in her grandfather's studio for a few days. He had looked very frightened at the time and then he had gone away. The train began to move off and the man waved at them both.

'That's my uncle Kunal,' Janake said as the train gathered speed. 'D'you remember him? I was visiting him the week you had your birthday.'

'Does he live with your aunt then?'

'She's not my real aunt,' Janake said and then he gave a shout. Half buried in the sand was a beautiful piece of wood. He began pulling it out.

'Oh, can I have it, please, Janake,' Alice cried excitedly.

'I'm getting it for you, wait! Don't pull it, you'll break it.'

'Oh! Look!'

'What are you going to make with it?' Janake asked curiously.

Alice shook her head. She couldn't say, but she wanted to take it home anyway.

That night, when the household were finally in bed and Sita turned restlessly in her dreams, Bee told Kamala about Alice's afternoon of foraging.

'My studio is full of her finds,' he said with admiration. 'She's going to be a maker of things when she is older.'

It was only to Kamala, and under cover of darkness, that he dropped his guard.

'It's as if …' he paused, 'the only way she can make sense of what she's leaving behind is through these random finds. They are her way of finding direction.'

Kamala was silent. What could the child possibly store up? How could she make any sense of what she was losing when she had hardly begun to understand what this place was about?

'She knows,' Bee told her stubbornly. 'She's no fool, she has her instincts. She knows what matters. And in any case, it won't be knowledge needed by her for years.'

On their return from the beach Alice, asking him for some glue, had started to make a small construction. Bee had hidden his amazement.

'Has it sunk in, then?' Kamala asked. 'That she will be going.'

How could it have sunk in when even she could not comprehend any of it?

'What's all the fuss about? She'll be back, you'll see. In no time at all,' Bee said roughly.

Oh yes, thought Kamala, then why are you so upset? The crescent moon appeared from behind a cloud. The same moon that would shine in England. We will have the moon as connection, Bee told himself, firmly.

'Dias thinks we should get her to talk about Sita and the baby,' Kamala told him hesitatingly.

'Why can't that woman keep her mouth shut?' Bee asked irritably. He moved restlessly. 'I don't want her trying her hand at British psychology on this family.'

In spite of her sadness, Kamala wanted to laugh. Bee had no idea how he sounded.

'When she feels the need to, Alice will talk,' he declared. 'At the moment all she needs is for us to stay as we've always been. There'll be time enough for change in her life.'

The clock in the hall struck the hour. Outside beyond the trees the sea barely moved. Someone had ironed out the waves. In the distance they could hear the faint wail of police sirens. Tonight the sounds were coming from the direction of the town. This is how it begins, thought Bee, his mood changing swiftly. We are the witnesses of the start but who knows what it will lead to. Yesterday a drunken Singhalese doctor was careless with a Tamil life. Tomorrow will be different again. And what will happen when the Tamils retaliate? What then? In the darkness, Kamala reached for his hand.

'Children work these things out through their play,' she agreed, knowing it was her reassurance that he really wanted.

'She won't be a child for so very long. The journey ...' he stopped. When it came down to it, a life without her was unthinkable.

'She'll be fine,' Kamala said, not believing it, frightened too. 'And anyway, before all of that there's the wedding.'

They lay side by side, turning over their thoughts, discussing May and her forthcoming wedding which would now have to be post-poned, at least until Sita could cope better. May, the easy child, always happy, always laughing thought Kamala. She still laughed. She had been born blessed, with the knack of making her life easy. And now she had picked a loving man. Since the stillbirth, knowing how upset May was, Namil had taken to visiting her every single evening.

'When is Stanley coming?' Kamala asked softly, knowing she was on dangerous ground.

Although Stanley had rung most nights to speak first to his daughter and then his wife, he had not left Colombo since the funeral.

'I don't care if I never see the man again,' Bee said. 'I'm sick of the way he thinks he's a white *sootha*.'

He knew he was being unfair, but Bee no longer cared. Stanley did not interest him.

'I suppose he's busy at the moment,' Kamala said placatingly. 'Sita says he has to work overtime at his office in order not to take a cut in his last pay cheque.'

Two moths danced in and out of the window, lighting up the moonlit sky. The smoke from the mosquito coil rose upwards in thin white tendrils.

'What if he doesn't send for them?' Kamala asked, voicing the question in both their minds. 'What if paying their passage makes no difference? What if he just forgets them?'

Someone was shining a searchlight on the bay and all sorts of colours appeared out of the night.

'If he doesn't send for them, it's simple. They'll stay here,' Bee said. 'But I don't think it'll come to that.'

Two days later Stanley came to see them, travelling up the coast by train. It was a Saturday. He brought some chocolate and something called bath cubes sent by his brother for the niece he had never met. Sita sat out on the verandah to talk to him. Even from a distance they looked like awkward strangers meeting for the first time. Not like husband and wife, thought May. Alice, eating her chocolates, watched them. Her mother looked all wrong.

'You know I'm going to England in April,' Stanley told his daughter. 'To get a house ready for you.'

Alice yawned. She was still waiting for Janake to arrive as he had promised.

'You must look after Mummy for me, huh?'

He was going, he said, to send for them both as planned, in three months.

'You can come on the boat together,' he said with an enthusiasm she hadn't noticed in him before. 'And there will be a new English school and new English friends. You are a lucky girl!'

Alice frowned. She didn't want new friends. She wanted to play with Janake and to see Jennifer. A lot of things had happened since she last saw Jennifer. The thought made her frown deepen and she opened her mouth to argue. Seeing this, her mother smiled nervously. Two deep dimples, from her life before the baby, appeared on Sita's face.

They stayed there long after her smile had gone, as though wanting to remind everyone of what Sita had once been like. Ah! thought Kamala triumphantly, you see, she *will* be happy again. It's time she needs, you fool, thought May angrily, looking at Stanley. Why can't you touch her, you cold bloody fish!

'Don't frown, Alice,' Sita said. 'We have to get out of this place. The way your father has been treated, what happened to me, all these things mean we can't stay here any longer.'

The dimples seemed at odds with Sita's words. A large garden spider ran across the verandah floor making her shiver. There were so many things Sita hated about this place. Things that now would never go away but would only get bigger. Alice was thinking of the baby in her own way. Dead or alive, she saw the baby would have always been a problem. From her mother's surprising determination and her father's suppressed anger she could see that leaving had become a reality and there was no room for negotiation. But she understood too, with uncanny insight, the baby would come with them. The servant boy in the house opposite was tuning his transistor radio. The music reminded Alice of the fairground ride on that now distant birthday. A wave of rage, unexpected and frightening filled her chest. She didn't want to cry in front of anyone, but where *was* her grandfather?

'You'll miss my wedding, Stanley,' May was saying without sounding the slightest bit sorry.

'Yes, he will,' her sister agreed.

'There have been more riots,' Stanley said.

He appeared to be challenging them all in some way. He was glad his father-in-law wasn't present. It was impossible to speak freely in front of him. Pig, thought May. She too was glad her father was absent. Tamil pig! Her father would have read her thoughts and reprimanded her.

'They killed my child, men,' Stanley shouted, losing control without much effort.

Watching impassively Alice saw his face had grown darker. Her mother looked like a coconut frond beaten by the rain.

'Singhalese bastards!' Stanley shouted, Bee's absence giving him courage. 'A wedding is hardly a priority, men. We need to get out before any more damage is done to my family.'

The music on the servant boy's transistor had changed. Alice knew it was the song called 'True Love Ways'. Esther would be wearing her taffeta dress and dancing in time to the music.

'The overseas Tamils are fed up,' Stanley said. 'I'm telling you, they're becoming a force. One of these days this damn government will be whipped.'

'What are they planning?' May asked, fear leaping like a fish in her throat. 'What about us? What about the thousands of Singhalese who are innocent, who have no problem with the Tamils?'

But Stanley wasn't interested.

'They're *your* people, men,' he said. 'Speak to the butchers who killed my child. When the time comes, there will be no pity left in us, hah!'

'Stanley,' Bee said calmly, 'you're speaking like a fool.'

He had come in unnoticed. 'A butcher is a butcher. Don't forget the doctor who saved your wife.'

But Stanley, either from the strain of keeping his mouth shut for too long, or the confidence brought on by his imminent escape, couldn't stop.

'No disrespect, men, but it's your people who are asking for a civil war. If that's the case, they'll get one, just wait a little. Remember that all's fair in war.'

Sita began to weep silently. Bee took out his pipe and tapped it against the side of the wall. Alice saw his jaw tightening. Then with a visible effort and no change in his voice he spoke.

'I understand how you feel,' he said. 'I know you have to go. The situation is getting intolerable. Of course you must go. But it need only be for a while. There are many, many Singhalese who think as you do. These people will not allow this to develop into a civil war.'

He took out his tobacco pouch and began packing the pipe. He didn't look at Sita, he did not even look in her direction, but his whole body strained at the sound of her weeping. The transistor music was still playing insanely and the sea had a beautiful silvery line on the horizon. The cook was scraping coconut, and next door the servant boy was sweeping the verandah. A crow cawed harshly in two-part harmony. The sound went on and on turning in the dazzling air. The day had been transformed into a bowl of blinding light. Of the sort that had dazzled their English conquerors, thought Bee, as he stood in the doorway, quietly. It had made the English mad, he had once told Alice.

He had only been half joking at the time and Alice had laughed at the thought of the *soothas* going mad. But it was true, they had come here to conquer and instead the light snared them.

'Don't they have light like us in England?' Alice had asked at the time.

'Oh, heavens no! The English went back home blinded, and of course they wrote about our light. The nineteenth century is full of it,' he had said, grinning. 'The tropics became a strange, magical place in their imagination after that. They went away different!'

Kamala had laughed. 'Stop it!' she had said.

But Bee had continued looking solemnly at Alice, the devil in his eyes.

'It's true!' he had said. 'They were drugged by too much sensation. Their books are full of it, as you will read when you get older. English gentlemen seduced by the narcotics of jungle love!'

And now she was going there, he thought. He felt ill. She had asked him what it would be like.

'Will it be different in England?' was what she had asked. The question had rendered him helpless.

'I believe it will be,' he had said eventually. 'Probably in ways you would not expect. Not better, not worse, you understand. Different. Anyway, you'll see, soon enough.'

'Do I have to go?'

That was what she had asked next. But how was he meant to answer that?

'Listen, Putha,' he had told her, trying very hard to be fair, to keep himself out of the story, '*this* is your first home, you were born here. That's a powerful thing, don't ever forget it. But it may not be your last, you understand. And that's all right, too. It will be beautiful in

England even though the difference will surprise you. You'll just have to search for it.'

Standing in the doorway he recalled that conversation. Wondering if he should have told her what he really believed; that this place with all its tropical beauty was where she should remain. And also that he believed it would make no difference. For although she would leave Ceylon, Ceylon would never leave her. Listening to the rush and crush of waves now he wondered how long it would take for them to see the consequences of such a violent uprooting. And he thought of this small beautiful place, once the centre of his world. Without her it would be the centre of nothing. Stanley's voice buzzed in his ear like a large bluebottle. With a great effort Bee dragged himself back to the present.

'Then go for a time,' he said out loud, without looking directly at Stanley, making his voice as neutral as possible. 'This situation will not last forever and the change will be good for you all after what has happened,' he said, thinking too that Alice needed her parents' attention.

'But come back before she changes too much,' he added brusquely, 'give her an education and then come home.'

And he went outside, as though the matter was settled, to mix some colours for a new print he was making, calling to Alice to come and help him.

Soon after that Sita and Alice went back to Colombo to prepare for Stanley's departure. Back to the rickshaw-clogged streets lined with ramshackle buildings. A new harsh mood was in the air. As if a whole secret way of life had died while they had been away and the city was now preoccupied with different things. Sita walked slowly. She was still bleeding internally. At the crowded outpatients she queued with other mothers, nursing their babies. The air was filled with a tinnitus of flies as she sat, one more saried woman in a colourful line of reds and yellows against a lime-green wall. Smallpox inoculation had come to Ceylon for the first time. All around them infants screamed. Sita watched dully. She could not understand how a broken heart could still palpitate with such pain. Alice sat quietly beside her, swinging her legs. After her injection they were going to see Jennifer's mother and the new baby. Then tomorrow she would go back to school. The thought of facing her class teacher Mrs Perris made her nervous. Before she had left, her grandmother had told her again not to worry about telling her friends that the baby had died.

'Many people lose babies in this country,' Kamala had said consolingly. 'You mustn't worry.'

'Why should she worry what people think?' Bee had demanded, overhearing the conversation. 'Alice has better things to think about. She understands these things happen, don't you, Putha?'

Alice had nodded and then begun to giggle because her grandfather was tucking in a small parcel at the foot of her bed.

'What is it? Can I see?' she said, struggling to get it.

It was a book she had been wanting. Another Enid Blyton.

Waiting in the clinic, watching the other children being given their vaccinations, Alice half closed her eyes, thinking of the Sea House. Her mother stared ahead not speaking. When it was her turn, the nurse told her she was having a tetanus injection as well.

'Put your arm out,' the nurse said. 'You mustn't forget to collect your smallpox certificate,' she reminded Sita. 'You won't be allowed into England without it.'

Sita nodded.

'You are a lucky girl, going there!' the nurse continued, smiling encouragingly.

'I don't want to go,' Alice told her.

She spoke softly and the nurse didn't seem to hear. The needle branded a small circle of pinpricks on her arm. Alice clenched her fist, saying nothing.

'There might be a small reaction,' the nurse told her mother, after which they went out into the burning sun. Suddenly Alice didn't want to go to Jennifer's house or see Jennifer's mother or the baby boy she had just had. The sun boiling down on her hatless head made her feel sick.

'Why do we have to go now?' she whined.

'They're expecting us,' Sita said shortly. 'It will be rude if we don't go.'

She was carrying a parcel of some of the exquisite dresses made for her own baby.

Jennifer lived in Colombo 7, where the gardens were lush and green and freshly watered. They took the bus, leaving the broken beauty and the chaos of the city. Even the bus appeared subtly different to Alice; emptier, cleaner. Not many people had reason to go to Colombo 7.

'Look, all the signs have changed,' Alice told her mother in English.

'That happened weeks ago,' her mother said.

Sita clutched her parcel close to her chest. Alice swallowed. She didn't want her mother to give away the baby dress, but she could see from the expression on Sita's face it would do no good to bring the subject up. In the last few days, her mother had stopped her terrible crying and Alice was afraid if she mentioned their baby it would all start again.

'My arm hurts,' she said instead, hoping to give her mother something else to think about.

Sita ignored her.

'Don't scratch it,' was all she said.

At Ratnapura Road they got off. The streets had widened out and were tree lined and shady. Jennifer's house was in a cul-de-sac. A manservant opened the gate. Orange blossom and shoe-flowers cascaded over the wall. A water sprinkler was watering the grass and underneath the murunga tree stood a large shiny pram. Some dogs tied up and out of sight began to bark hysterically. Instantly they heard the alarming high-pitched cry of the baby. Sita pulled Alice along sharply, nodding at the servant woman who led them into a large cool room with tiled floors and air conditioning. Things happened in quick and disjointed fashion after that. Jennifer arrived and hugged Alice but couldn't stop staring at Sita. Alice watched her mother try to give Jennifer's mother the present, but because she was holding her baby Sita had to put the parcel on the table. Sita looked small and a little frail. It made Alice suddenly very angry. The baby cry was like a siren, urgent and impossible to ignore. Jennifer's mother laughed delightedly and began to feed him.

'Take Alice to play,' she told her daughter.

'Is it true, you are going to England?' Jennifer asked as soon as they were out of earshot of the grown-ups.

There was a Russian doll on the window ledge. Alice picked it up and began to take it apart, each doll getting smaller and smaller until the last one was so minute that she fumbled and dropped it.

'Leave it,' Jennifer said sharply. 'Don't break my things. When are you going to the UK?'

'In a few months' time. My dada is going to send for us.'

The baby's thin cry went on and on in Alice's head.

'Does it cry all the time?'

'Quite a lot,' Jennifer said importantly. 'Baby boys are like that, you know.'

She hesitated.

'Yours was a girl, wasn't it?' she asked.

Alice looked at her. She had never noticed how very black Jennifer was. Her lips were so large that their pink insides showed even when she wasn't smiling. She looks very Singhalese, thought Alice.

'Your mother married a Tamil, that was the problem,' Jennifer said, knowingly.

The baby's cry was less intrusive, now. Outside the window a crow hawked harshly and they could hear the sound of saucepans being scraped. Singhalese voices rose and fell in the hot, lovely air. Without warning, Alice felt she too might start to cry. She wanted to go home. The air conditioning was too cold and her arm was hurting.

'My head hurts,' she told Jennifer. 'I think I'm reacting to the smallpox, you know. I had to have it because of going to England.'

After their hurried departure into the sunlight her arm hurt less. And much later on, in the evening, she listened to her mother recounting the visit.

'She wanted me to leave,' Sita was telling Stanley.

From behind the door where she listened, Alice heard her mother's terrible pleading tone. She was certain Sita's face was pleading too. It made Alice grind her teeth.

'You shouldn't have gone,' Stanley said, sounding bored.

'I didn't want her to think I was jealous. We went to all the hospital appointments together, I had to visit at least once.'

'Well,' Alice's father said, 'we'll be out of this hell soon enough. Thank God!'

The next day at school Jennifer avoided Alice. She had made friends with a new girl who had joined their class while Alice had been away. The new girl was called Vishvani and she too lived in Colombo 7. The chauffeur drove Jennifer to school with her.

'There's no point in my being your friend,' Jennifer told Alice. 'You're going overseas soon.'

She paused imperceptibly then added: 'Oh, and by the way, we threw away your mother's dead-baby clothes. My brother has plenty of things to wear. We don't need your bad luck clothes.'

4

LONG BEFORE HER SISTER'S WEDDING DAY, Sita's heart had become hard as a rambutan stone; shrunken and dark and unbreakable. It happened so stealthily that very few people noticed. A week after the visit to Jennifer's house, Sita started wrapping her preoccupations between the folds of the baby clothes so painstakingly embroidered in her other life. Those long monsoon afternoons, when she used to dream of the unborn son who would change the world, had vanished. Knowing there was no longer any point in resurrecting her hopes, she packed her soft-cotton sorrows carefully inside the large empty trunk that seemed to have invaded her mind. Then, quietly, she climbed into it and shut the lid. As the first terrible shocks subsided to tremors, she saw what she needed to do in order to survive, so without fuss she simply disappeared. No one appeared to notice. No one remarked on her absence; most people thought the concertinaed, crumpled person walking around, going about her daily business, was the same old Sita, mother of Alice who asked too many questions, returning after a little personal misfortune. Headstrong wife of that Tamil man Stanley whom she had married in haste and who could not even afford to pay for a private confinement.

'What can you expect?' asked a distant relative, paying Sita a visit in order to find out how things were progressing with this wayward woman. 'God is punishing you for marrying a Tamil.'

'Never mind,' added a cousin who had had four miscarriages and couldn't understand what all the fuss was about. 'Try again, child. These Tamil fellows can breed, I tell you!'

And the cousin laughed suggestively.

'You mustn't make such a fuss,' a neighbour told Sita. 'It's over now, forget it. You're still alive, that's the main thing.'

Sita made no reply. Stanley was leaving in less than three weeks. Her world was slowly disintegrating and speech came only spasmodically to her. Defending herself was an impossibility. Bee visited several times in the week after their return to Colombo. There had been another outburst of rioting and he was worried about the family. Sita had no idea that her father, also silent, was fully aware of her disappearing act. She had not realised that she was no longer functioning properly, nor that her womb had turned into a steel utensil, too cold and harsh a place to be inhabited ever again. Her tears, like her milk, had dried up, and outwardly her wounds were healing. A thick angry scar was forming across her abdomen, just in case she might be tempted to forget what had happened. She felt as though she were growing horns inside herself. At nights while Stanley lay beside her and Alice slept across the hall in her own room, Sita would lie awake feeling a devil had placed sharp objects inside her belly. It worried her that this devil might burst out and kill someone. In the mornings when Stanley awoke she said nothing to him about her tormented night. He looked and acted fresh as an English daisy.

Kamala, listening to Bee's account of her daughter's state of mind every time he returned from these visits, became increasingly anxious. Instead of growing closer to her husband, it appeared that Sita was moving away from him. Kamala's greatest fear now was that Stanley might disappear altogether and that Sita with her indifference was encouraging him to abandon them and vanish to that story-book place called England.

'No, Amma, he won't,' May disagreed, interrupting Kamala's thoughts, certain he would not. 'How can he, when her passage is booked anyway?'

Kamala did not answer, but her worry became so great that May took a day off work and visited her sister to see for herself. But when she got there Sita didn't want to talk to her, either.

'What do you understand?' she asked May rudely. 'All you can think about is your wedding.'

In spite of knowing what her sister was going through, May was hurt. Her hurt seeped out like morning light sneaking through a shutter. No matter how tightly she tried keeping it out, there was always a sliver present. May's wedding was the only interesting thing that had happened to her in her whole life, and now Sita was belittling it and making her feel guilty as well. Namil, listening to her grumbles, shook his head, disagreeing.

'Karma cannot be changed,' he said gently. 'Hers is bad, so we must take pity and not be angry.'

Bee tried to refrain from joining in the discussion. He was waiting with angry passion for Stanley to leave. After that he would help Sita pack the annexe up in Havelock Road and then he would move their few remaining possessions to the Sea House. When it was time for them to leave for the UK, Sita and Alice would travel to the harbour from the coast. That was Bee's plan.

'The man is just spoiling for a fight, so best if he leaves,' was all he said when pressed. 'If he doesn't send for them, will it be such a tragedy?' he asked Kamala privately.

During Stanley's last week, on the pretext of taking some etchings to his dealer, Bee decided to visit Colombo again. He wanted to check up on Sita and Alice. Sita was making some last-minute alterations to a pair of trousers for Stanley to wear on the ship. She barely glanced at her father when he walked in. Alice was still at school.

'I've come to take some of your things back in the car,' Bee said easily.

Sita pointed to a large trunk and two small packing cases.

'What about the books?' Bee asked, surprised. Sita had always been surrounded by books. But Sita shook her head. She would not be needing books where she was going.

'I won't be reading any more,' she told her father with finality.

Whatever life they might or might not have in England, it did not involve books; of that she was certain. What was she planning? Bee wondered. To switch her mind off permanently in England? He stayed all day, partly because he could not leave without seeing Alice, and partly because he wanted to force Sita to eat something. He didn't want to add to Kamala's worries, but he was aware that Sita had almost stopped eating. Reluctantly, she cooked a little lunch and they ate in semi-silence. It was Stanley's last day at work; he would not be back until much later.

'They'll get him drunk,' Sita said, unable to stop a small, bitter smile hovering across her mouth.

Bee refused to be drawn. A vein pulsated on his cheek. The annexe had an air of impermanence and disarray. Stanley's unpacked things were strewn everywhere. Bee noticed a pair of new leather shoes.

'Oh, he brought them from Gamages,' Sita said, following his eyes. 'Well,' she added, slightly defensive, 'he needs good shoes for the trip, I suppose.'

Feeling the weight of his fury bear down on him, Bee closed his eyes. It would do no good to criticise Stanley. At two thirty, they drove to St Clare's College to pick up Alice. Bee stopped the car outside the school gate.

It was like this, coming out of her last lesson, stepping into the blistering sun that Alice caught sight of them. Her heart leapt; she had not expected to see her grandfather today. Pushed forward on a huge crest of emotion she rushed towards them. She had had the most terrible day.

'Grandpa!' she screamed, running towards the car. And then, before she could reach it, she burst into tears.

In the two weeks since she had been back at school, Alice had struggled to recover the position she had lost within her class. Jennifer had stopped talking to her and Alice was sure it was because the baby had died. Perhaps it was because Jennifer blamed her for killing it? Everything, thought Alice, had gone wrong, and it was her fault. There was no one else she wanted to be friends with. The Tamil girls in the class looked at her curiously. She was supposed to be a Tamil, but she didn't look much like one; nor could she speak proper Tamil. Even the food in her tiffin box was different from theirs. What was the point in being friendly with her when she was probably a spy for that

Singhalese mother of hers? The Tamil girls had been warned to be very careful when they went to school, not to talk to dangerous people. Alice was not to be trusted and they did not want her near them. Lunchtimes had got progressively worse. This lunchtime had been the worst ever. She had gone to school that morning taking the picture postcard of Piccadilly Circus her uncle had sent her, hoping that Jennifer might be interested. But Jennifer, giggling in a corner of the playground with her new friend from Cinnamon Gardens, would not look at Alice.

'Don't then!' Alice had shouted, stung.

And in a last desperate effort at indifference, she had cried out:

'I don't care, anyway, I'm going to England. I'll have lots of friends there, wait and see.'

There was more to come. The last lesson of the day was always Singhalese. When Mrs Maradana the Singhalese teacher collected up the homework at the beginning of the lesson, Alice realised with dismay that she had not brought hers to school. Mrs Maradana stared at her.

'Come here, Alice,' she had said, her voice very soft. 'Did you think you didn't have to do your work because you are going to England? Hah?'

Alice shook her head. The class quivered with silent anticipation. Everyone guessed what was coming. Mrs Maradana was known as a Tamil hater.

'Well?'

Alice said nothing. There was an agonising pause while the teacher opened her drawer.

'Hold out your hand, child,' she had said coldly.

The class craned their necks, all together, like atrophying plants. The air vibrated as once, twice and then, once more the cane stung her hand. Someone sniggered. The humiliation was far worse than the pain.

'Sit down and get on with your work,' Mrs Maradana said, putting the cane away.

Alice, her mouth tightly shut, swallowing hard, had walked a chin-wobbling journey back to her seat. Twenty pairs of eyes followed her as she opened her desk. The rest of the hour had passed in a blur.

When, after an eternity, the bell rang signifying the end of school, the class rose and stood to attention, placing their hands together as though in prayer.

'*Aybowon*, children,' Mrs Maradana said.

Jennifer raised her hand.

'Yes, what is it, Jennifer?'

Jennifer's parents supported the school very generously.

'I'm so sorry you lost your father, Mrs Maradana,' Jennifer said softly. 'I hope he reaches Nirvana.'

Mrs Maradana's eyes widened dangerously. Once more the class held their breath, but this time the teacher smiled thinly.

'Thank you, Jennifer,' she said, adding, 'give my regards to your parents. I hope that baby brother of yours is letting them sleep finally!'

Outside, the air shimmered translucently and the sky was a relentless gemstone blue. Children spilled out of the school building like a swarm of mosquitoes. It was out of this swarm that Alice emerged and spotted her grandfather's car. She caught a glimpse of her mother in her old green sari, exactly the colour of an over-ripe mango. Sita hadn't worn it for a long time, not since before the baby. In that instant the surprise of her mother looking her old self, her grand-father's unexpected presence, and her smarting hands struggled within her and was no longer containable. Her tears, once begun, were unstoppable; hurling herself into the back of the car, she howled.

'What on earth's the matter with you?' Sita asked, knocked off balance.

'What's wrong, Putha?' Bee cried, switching off the engine and turning round to face her in alarm. 'What's happened, Alice?'

'Alice,' her mother was saying, 'don't cry for no reason. Tell me what's wrong.'

Alice let out a thin, lonely wail. She had not known she possessed such a terrible sound within her. Just hearing it frightened her.

'I don't want to go to school any more,' she cried.

That night, when she was in bed, and her grandfather had gone back, Alice went over the events of her day. In the end it had turned out to be the nicest day since her birthday. Bee had wanted to go in and have a word with Mrs Maradana, but Sita would not let him. Bee had been very, very angry.

'There's no question of her going back to that place,' he kept saying, over and over again. 'She must stay with you until you come home.'

For once Sita had not disagreed.

'No more bloody Singhala,' she had said.

Alice was surprised to see her mother so angry. Her hand had stopped hurting and now that Bee was here she was beginning to enjoy herself. But Sita was working herself up into a rage.

'You see why we have to leave, Thatha? You see what a waste of time it is, trying to make a life in this place?'

Sita's face was alive with rage.

'No Singhala,' she repeated, grimly. 'No Tamil either. Only English. The language of the Just.'

Alice glanced at her grandfather. He too was watching the sudden animation in Sita's face.

'Come, Putha,' he said neutrally. 'Let's forget about school. I'm going to take you to the Galle Face Hotel for an ice-cream to celebrate our decision!'

And that was when the day had suddenly got a whole lot better. No one mentioned the subject after that.

But later that night when Alice had gone to bed everything got bad again. She heard her parents arguing with each other and held her breath. At first their voices were only a murmur. Then something thudded against the wall and her mother started screaming. Instantly her father's voice got louder. Alice lay rigid in bed feeling her hand throb. This was how it always started. Closing her eyes, she tried to blot out the noise by imagining her room in the Sea House with its long wispy curtains. Whenever she was there the last sounds she heard as she drifted into sleep were of the sea mixed with the whirling of Kamala's sewing machine. All there was here was her mother's voice, distorted by rage, her words engulfed by great dry sobs. An object was hurled across the room. Alice strained her ears. Her mother was throwing empty coconut shells at her father. The shells fell with a thud, one after another. Where had she found so many shells to throw at him?

'You're crazy,' Stanley was saying, over and over again.

He was no longer calm.

'Crazy bloody Singhalese cow!'

Alice could hear him laughing an unhappy, pinched, laugh. The sounds issued from his mouth like a series of shots being fired from a gun. Her father sounded as though he would never stop. There was an out-of-control feeling within the noise. Alice covered her ears. The laughter changed.

'Losing the baby has made you mad,' Stanley screamed. 'Crazy bloody woman!'

More coconut shells flew across the room. Alice heard one crack against the wall as though it was a head. There was the sound of water pouring out.

'Now look what you've done!' Stanley said.

In the silence that followed, his voice sounded uncertain and frightened. Alice could hear her mother. She was still crying but now the sound had changed. Her mother was crying in the way she had cried on the day she returned from the hospital; softly and without hope. Alice stared into the darkness, her mind a hide-and-seek of evasion. It was a moonless night; her hand ached. The day and all its many facets began to blur sleepily in her head. Since her birthday everything had become complicated. Before she had turned nine, life had been full of nice things, she decided dreamily. Now everything was a series of never-ending confusing events. Jennifer had come out into the playground to watch her this afternoon, satisfied that at last she was crying, giving her the proof needed that the caning had hurt. But it wouldn't happen again, thought Alice, feeling her eyelids grow heavy. She would not cry like that ever again. In the darkness, lying on her back, she pushed her chin out stubbornly, trying to hide the fact that inside herself she felt defeated. Her friendship with Jennifer was over. In her heart of hearts she had known it would not last. I am not like her, thought Alice sleepily. Outside in the starry night there was the usual wail of police sirens and *byla* music. The sounds pulsed, like her hands. A drum was beating slowly beyond the trees and beyond that, in the distance, she heard the faint hoot of the Colombo night train leaving for Dondra. Closing her eyes she thought of her grandfather, who would hear it too as it passed Mount Lavinia in an hour. The thought filled her with contentment.

The next morning, Stanley's last complete day on the island began with the usual bright unending sunshine. In twenty-four hours he would be on the ship sailing towards the Suez Canal, heading for England. At last his dream was coming true. He had looked at the small route map that came with his ticket so often that it had torn along its folds. The ship he would be travelling on was coming from Melbourne. It would make its way via Aden into the Mediterranean. Even the name signified romance for him. Greece would follow, he thought sighing with pleasure. Ever since his boyhood days he had had a secret desire to visit Greece. There was a slight possibility that he might be able to leave the ship when it docked. He wanted to see the Parthenon, hear the Greeks speak in their language, experience the cradle of civilisation for himself. He kept all such plans to himself, knowing Sita would only fuss about his safety or the added expense of disembarking and joining a tour. The only thing that seemed to interest her was that he got a job in England.

'The sooner we can get Alice out of here, the better,' she kept telling him.

Of course he would do his duty, Alice needed to get to a safe place, but Sita did not seem to recognise he would not have another chance for a holiday.

Stanley stared at the molten light flickering on the ceiling. He moved his legs lazily across the bed. Tomorrow at this time he would be heading for the harbour. He smiled. Then he remembered they had had another fight last night. What had this one been about? Perhaps it was because he had been late home? Had he been drunk? He couldn't remember. It's my money, anyway, thought Stanley, and he swung his legs on to the floor. Coconut shells littered the ground. What the devil are they doing here? he wondered. He was just opening his mouth to call Sita when what had happened came back to him. Crazy woman, he thought, shaking his head. Mad as a hatter! He gave a short, barking, laugh and followed the sound of the sewing machine into the sitting room. What the hell was she sewing now? His trunk was packed and ready. Sita looked up at the sound of his footsteps. Her eyes had dark rings around them and Stanley looked quickly away.

'You need to weigh it,' she said, pointing at the trunk. 'You'll have to find a pair of scales from someone.'

Stanley nodded, relieved she wasn't shouting. Yawning, he started buttoning his shirt up.

'Where's Alice?'

'She's playing with the cat next door.'

Stanley snorted but refrained from comment.

'Do you want some tea?

He nodded, glancing at her as she left the room. Sita's face was closed; she looked as though she might have been crying again. He sighed heavily. What the hell, he thought. It wasn't that he hadn't any sympathy for her. He had. He felt the injustice of what had happened, if not the physical loss of the baby, as much as any husband in his position could. Sita came in with a tray. She had a plate with an egg hopper on it and some juggery. There were two teacups, a pot of tea and a jug of boiled milk. She had made hoppers for him, knowing it was his last day. Unexpectedly he was overcome by a feeling of pity for her. She was still a good-looking woman, he decided, glancing at her sideways. Although the doctor had said there should be nothing intimate for a few months, he wondered if she would refuse him, on this, his last day. Who knows what might happen to me, he thought, a chill of self-pity passing over him. I might be the one to die next. But at that instant he heard the child's voice through the doorway, talking to next-door's cat. Sex would not be possible with her around.

'I'll get some scales from Aruguna,' he said, picking up the cup of tea she held out to him. 'I've got to go over there anyway, to say good-bye.'

After Stanley had gone to get the scales, Sita closed up the house. She had two errands. One was to pick up a sari for her sister, and the other was to go to the spice mill for her mother to have some chillies ground into powder. She called to Alice to put her shoes on and they went out. Sita felt desolation walk beside her. The reasons were so many she could not decide which pained her most. There was the ghost of the baby, lying in her arms. Sometimes she felt this was the greatest ache, but then she would decide the child and all she had suffered was a thing apart. So what was it, she wondered dully, for it wasn't the thought of Stanley's departure that bothered her. Last night when he had thrown his indifference at her, taunting her, turning all she had suffered into useless mockery, she had realised that his leaving mattered less and less. She did not care about the new life he kept talking about because she had no life left in her to start. The real problem she felt was that she no longer had the will to go on. This morning she had noticed a rope at the back of the kitchen yard. She had no idea where it had come from, but it was dark and heavily coiled. She imagined it hanging neatly from the rafters, turned into a knot, a noose, a gallows.

'Why do people say "a bolt of silk", Mama?' Alice asked, tugging at her hand, breaking into her thoughts. 'Why do thunder and silk come in bolts?'

Sita didn't reply and Alice's chatter continued. Why, why, why? thought Sita bitterly. The ordinariness of every single day was more than she could stand.

First, they headed for Pettar and the sari shop. The sun was beginning to dry the mud as they dodged the garbage spilling out on to the roadside. Sita held her sari above her ankles with one hand and Alice with the other. Overhead the trees were alive with whistling bulbuls; bright yellow sunbirds. Alice stared upwards as she walked. Always after it rained she noticed the colours glowed more vividly and the air became scented with the smell of temple flowers.

'*Anay*, look where you're walking, Alice, please,' her mother said, tugging at her hand. 'There's filth everywhere.'

The shops were opening their shutters again. Men in sarongs squatted on the ground, their bodies curved in long bent question marks; street sellers and beggars rubbed shoulders as the tiffin boys ran back to their kitchens with empty curry tins.

They turned towards the railway station, going deeper into Pettar where the silk merchants had their emporiums. May's going-away sari was ready to be collected. Guilt filled Sita's head, it stopped up her ears and filled her nose with its sweet sad scent. In spite of the disgrace Sita had brought to her family, May was getting married. No thanks to me, thought Sita, with a bitter smile. I'm being punished, she decided, this is my fate. All around the tropics teemed with life and colour; with the frantic hurry of rickshaw men's feet, the grating sound of gears on antiquated London buses and the intermittent cries of the streets, while never far off, like a steady heartbeat, was the soft sound of the ocean. Sita heard none of it. A slow refrain played in her head: I should have died, I should have died, I should have died. Taking my shame with me. Removed myself from this place.

At Lukesman's sari shop she handed the assistant her receipt. Bee had insisted he pay for her sari as well as the bride's trousseau.

'I've not bought you any clothes in a long while,' he had said gruffly, his face inscrutable.

No one had commented, but they all knew that he was thinking of the wedding he had never been able to give her. Sita had not wanted to accept until Kamala, for the one and only time, had rebuked her privately.

'Do it,' she had said. 'Don't hurt your father.'

Any more than you have already, was what she meant, Sita decided.

'Would you like to see them first?' the assistant asked, opening the brown-paper wrapping.

'Oh yes, yes,' Alice said, peering over the counter.

The shop was dark and lined with shelves all the way up to the ceiling. It rustled with new cloth and tissue paper; it glowed gently with lavish silk colours. May's going-away sari was crimson and magenta embroidered with small gold birds. Six and a half yards of the finest Kashmir silk. With half a yard to be cut off for the jacket.

'Yes?' asked the assistant, watching their faces.

The silk draped itself and spilled across the counter, catching the light as if it had an amorphous life all of its own.

'A bolt of silk,' Alice said experimentally, and the shop assistant nodded.

'How beautiful,' a voice said in English close to them. 'Hello, Sita, hello, Alice.'

Sita turned. It was Jennifer's mother.

She was trapped, by a trick of fate, in this place of dead silk worms. Pramless, lifeless and incomplete. Oh God! thought Sita, wanting to flee. Jennifer's mother was smiling at them. Behind her was Jennifer and dimly, just entering the shop, was the servant woman carrying the baby.

'Someone getting married?' Jennifer's mother asked in a friendly voice.

She was smiling uncertainly now. In the background the servant woman jiggled the baby, who made gurgling noises whilst chewing his fist. The servant woman came towards them. When the baby saw his mother he stared for a moment, fixedly. Taking his fist out of his mouth, he broke into a huge toothless grin.

'You weren't at school,' Jennifer whispered. 'Why not?'

She too sounded uncertain.

'I'm not coming back,' Alice told her, triumph turning like a boiled sweet on her tongue.

'But you'll get behind with your studies.'

'The work done in this country doesn't amount to much,' Alice said scornfully, repeating something she had heard her father say.

She hesitated, wanting to say something that had the word 'bastard' in it, but her mother was within earshot and with a flash of perception she saw her mother too was struggling. Jennifer continued to stare at her. She looked taken aback. Some regret for this lost friendship hovered on her face. She hesitated.

'Did it hurt? The cane? Is that why you're not coming back?'

Alice shook her head. She glanced at her mother and felt her own anger flapping like a kite in the breeze.

'No, of course not!' she said. 'I'm not coming back because it's a waste of time if I can't study in English.'

The sight of Jennifer, lost for words, wanting at last to be friends was more than she could bear.

'I have no interest in this backward country, you know,' she said, gaining confidence, speaking loudly. 'I'm going to make new friends in England.'

And she turned her back on Jennifer, slipping her hand into her mother's cold one, ignoring the small space of loneliness that lodged inside her.

They hurried out. Neither of them said anything more about the encounter. In the mill, they joined the queue. Great mounds of spice spewed out of the machine into gunny bags. Saffron, cumin and coriander. The fine particles of chilli in the air made their eyes water and their throats sore. Sita covered her mouth with her sari train and told Alice to put her handkerchief over her nose. The air was full of red dust. An old woman sneezed without covering her mouth and Sita drew Alice aside, angrily. Small things made her angry, very quickly, Alice observed.

'There are thirty thousand germs suspended in the air,' she whispered.

Alice tried to imagine thirty thousand germs somersaulting in the spice mounds, grinning and deadly. The old woman sucked her breath in and Sita frowned. The queue was moving very slowly and all she could see was the rope, lying quietly coiled beside the broom, out in the kitchen yard.

Stanley had lied to Sita. It was a small lie that she would never think to check up on, but he wasn't going to see their friend Aruguna. He was on his way to visit Neville, his Tamil friend. Neville worked at the Colombo News Agency. Stanley headed towards Main Street and the bus stop, but as he approached the number 14 bus drove swiftly past, laden to bursting point with passengers. Stanley cursed under his breath. He knew there wouldn't be another bus for half an hour, at least. Deciding to wait, he glanced at his watch. It was by now a quarter to eleven and already the day was hot. By early afternoon he would be walking in a pool of sweat. He hated this wretched climate. He leant against a piece of guttering and watched a crow foraging for food in a drain, his mind a contented blank. When he heard the soft thud, followed a moment later by the sound of breaking glass, he hardly registered it. There was a short, stunned silence and then screams. The back end of the number 14 bus lurched towards the pavement and was ripped apart. Smoke belched out. Stanley froze. He had missed the bomb by a whisker. There were people running in all directions. Stanley hesitated, not wanting to go too close just in case there was a second bomb. Almost immediately it seemed the screams were overlaid by the sounds of ambulance sirens. The police arrived and began cordoning off the area with tape, moving people on and shouting to the paramedics carting off the bodies. The army, appearing swiftly, began directing operations at gunpoint. Onlookers began to move hastily away. No one wanted to get tangled up with the army. Stanley stood in a shocked haze of sweat and horror, watching. But for a stroke of luck he would have been a victim.

He quivered with fright and superstitious thoughts, never far off, made him shudder. Only this morning he had watched as a silver fish had dropped down from the rafters, narrowly missing his face. Stanley swallowed. Marvelling at his good luck, he wished he were safely on the boat to England. The army were aggressively herding people in all directions, looking for a scapegoat. Stanley didn't want to be noticed. Forcing himself to slow down and behave normally, he began to walk in the direction of home. But then it occurred to him there was nothing to go home for, just yet. Sita would be at the spice mill and after that she had some other shopping to do.

Last night's unhappiness, his wife's insatiable obsession in recounting their recent tragedy and the guilt she always induced, exhausted him. It sapped his energy and was slowly driving him mad. When she wasn't crying about what had happened, she was crying about leaving the island. But then again she didn't want to stay here either. It was a nightmare and the only certain thing was that, somehow, it all boiled down to being *his* fault. What was he meant to do? he wondered, unhappily. He half suspected she wished she had not married him. Often he wished it too. The wish lay between them, replacing the sex they no longer indulged in. Sita, with her small beautiful face, her delicate frame, her lovely friendly smile, had ensnared him in some distant lifetime and only now did he understand that the things he had once found so attractive were becoming a noose around his neck. Reluctant to spend his few hours in Colombo with her, bone-tired of her neediness and her constant desire for more than he could offer, he hesitated. They were as different as Eskimos and Greeks, he thought gloomily, dodging the potholes and avoiding the cow dung on the road.

He crossed Pettar, looking nervously around him. The streets here were subdued, people were standing in shop doorways talking softly amongst themselves, fearful. Only further along, near the fort, was life untroubled by the bomb. An old man, a palmist, sat cross-legged on the ground, doing readings. Who could have predicted, mused Stanley following his own line of thought, that the relatively harmless act of falling in love could have had such a disastrous effect on my life. He groaned inwardly, thinking of the added complication of the child. Everyone had warned him of the foolishness of marrying a Singhalese. Courting disaster, Neville had said. Well, he had ignored their advice and now he too was part of the huge melting pot of suspicion and mixed race mess. While slowly, in the face of the Fonseka clan, his excellent sense of self-preservation was being eroded. Well done, Stan, he told himself. Time you left. He began to whistle tunelessly.

By now, it was nearly eleven thirty. Luck had been on his side for once today and he was suddenly badly in need of a whisky. Turning away from the main road, he headed for the docks. Neville was alone in his office.

'Ah!' he said, waving Stanley in. 'Here's the intrepid traveller! Come in, men, come in. All packed and ready?'

He laughed boisterously.

'What's the matter? You look as though you've seen a ghost!'

'There's been a bomb.'

Neville nodded. 'Of course, of course.'

'You heard about it?' Stanley asked, taken aback. 'So soon?'

It always amazed Stanley that his friend knew everything that went on in the city without moving away from his desk.

'I've a bit of an emergency on at the moment, you know,' was Neville's usual excuse, when asked to join in on any social events. But as far as Stanley could see, these emergencies emerged out of nothing and went away equally quickly. Neville's business appeared to be conducted exclusively on the telephone, of which there were three in his office. Every news story came to him in this way. And yet he always had his finger on the pulse, knowing the latest scandal long before anyone else did. He was a useful man to know. When Stanley, for instance, had first applied for his passport it had been Neville who had helped him with the application, making sure it was processed quickly and then, later on, it had been Neville who had told him where to get the cheapest ticket for the crossing.

'Buy from the Greeks, men,' he had said. 'Trust me, they are the cheapest.'

Stanley had trusted him and the passage was booked in a single phone call. It was only after it was fixed that Stanley had remembered Bee wanted Sita's ticket bought too.

'Really? Hah, these Singhalese buggers have plenty of money, don't they?'

And Neville had fixed two more tickets for late July with no other comment, although Stanley had a strong feeling he disapproved.

On the night Sita had gone into hospital, Stanley had visited him quite late. Neville had welcomed him in the usual easy manner and, taking a bottle of whisky out of his safe, had plied Stanley with drink. In the early hours of the following morning it had been Neville who had been first to ring him with the news that Sita had lost the baby. In the panic that followed it had not occurred to Stanley to ask how his friend had known.

Stanley often thought how refreshing it was being in the company of one's own people. You knew where you were with them.

This morning Neville was in his usual avuncular mood.

'You look like you need a drink,' he said shrewdly, taking a new bottle of whisky out of a drawer and a jug of ice from the fridge. The ceiling fan gently moved the papers on his desk. Stanley pushed some books off a chair and sat down. It was well past the middle of the day.

'I can't believe I'll be on the high seas tomorrow, away from this bloody country,' he sighed. 'Thank God!'

He had only eaten half the hopper at breakfast and the whisky on an empty stomach was making him feel light-headed. When the telephone rang a few minutes later, Neville answered it in Singhalese.

Stanley sat gazing idly out of the window, not really listening, clinking the ice in his glass as he watched the rickshaw men hurrying on bare feet, spitting betel as they ran. Beyond him the sea moved restlessly in the confines of the harbour, glistening in the sunlight. Soon, thought Stanley, with a feeling of exquisite pleasure, I won't have to look at this any more. Colombo was so overrated, he thought, and he wondered what it would be like meeting up with his brother after nearly fourteen years. Stanley, the younger of the two, had stayed close to his mother's side after she had been widowed. The last to leave, never to return, he thought with happy finality. He would break his mother's heart, he knew, but it couldn't be helped. In any case, according to his mother it had been Sita who had taken him away.

This morning's bomb was the second explosion in two weeks. No doubt someone would claim responsibility for it later. Some poor sod from the resistance movement, an uneducated Tamil, would pay the price. Neville finished his conversation and swivelled around on his chair.

'Another drink?' he asked, switching smoothly to Tamil.

Stanley shook his head, envious of such fluency. It suddenly occurred to him that Sita might have heard about the explosion and be worried.

'I ought to go, men,' he said uneasily. 'She'll create merry hell otherwise. I just wanted to say good-bye and thank you for everything.'

'But you've only just got here!' Neville said in surprise. 'Was there something in particular I could do for you?'

Stanley hesitated. He wasn't sure if he could ask again.

'I was wondering if I could ring my brother?'

'Of course, of course, men, why didn't you say? Here, go ahead.'

So Stanley dialled the number and waited. Rajah worked in an office somewhere in London. Having persuaded Stanley to leave the island, he had promised to find him a job. It would not be easy, he had warned, for with Sita and the child to support money would be tight but, Rajah had paused tactfully, there was only one child! A blessing in disguise in some ways. When he had first heard these words, Stanley had felt an enormous lightening of his heart.

'A bomb went off on the bus this morning,' he said now, as soon as he heard Rajah's voice. 'I just missed it.'

'Well, it's time you left,' the voice answered faintly, after a pause during which Stanley fancied he could hear the sea. 'How's Ma?'

Stanley noticed his brother now spoke with a slight accent. He sounded like a lot of the UK returned people, not quite a white man, not quite belonging at home.

'I haven't seen her since after the funeral. Have you news about a job yet?'

'Relax, relax; wait till you get here. Go and visit Ma, give her my love.'

They chatted for a moment longer. When he had finished, Stanley handed the phone back to Neville.

'He's doing very well, you know,' he said, a touch of envy in his voice.

Neville finished his drink.

'Well, you will too, soon,' he said casually. 'The Tamil diaspora are very successful, men. They are also an important part of our fight against all the injustices we are enduring here. You mustn't forget that either!'

'Of course not,' Stanley said automatically, draining his glass.

He should go home, he thought again.

'Thanks for everything, Neville,' he said.

They shook hands. As he took his hat off the table, he noticed a book on Marxist theory and a pile of sealed letters with Canadian postmarks.

'See you,' Neville said. 'I'll try to come to the harbour tomorrow.'

As Stanley closed the door, he saw Neville was already reaching for the telephone.

Sita and Alice had just finished at the spice mill when the bomb went off. There had hardly been a sound, just a muffled thud. Had it not been for her constant worry over Stanley's safety, the sense of violence brought on by the bomb would have been a welcome relief for Sita. At least a bomb had a certain energy to it. The possibility of danger released some of the tension locked inside her.

'Let's go home,' she said, paying for the b
to check Dada's all right. He'll probably ring.

She hurried out of the mill, dragging Alice
the sunlight was unnaturally bright, forcing thei.
eyes against the glare. Looking up, Alice saw the
filter of fine red dust. A man on a bed of stones beg.
for things he would never get. Alice stared at his open, t
mouth.

'Where did the bomb go off, Mama?' Alice asked.

There was nothing to be seen, no broken glass, no policemen, nothing. The ambulancemen would gather the scrapings of human life,
moving it out of sight quickly and with practised hands. And out of
sight would mean out of mind, thought Sita bitterly. For wasn't it true:
what the eye didn't see did not matter. The phrase was a refrain that
never left her. The less she said it, the more she heard it.

'Come on,' she cried, pulling Alice sharply by the hand. 'We'll walk,
it's safer.'

As they walked they heard the sounds of sirens and ambulances
sweeping past, washing over them with an excess of sounds. Sita's heart
was pounding. Pushed and bumped against her mother, Alice dropped
her bag of chilli in a hole filled with rainwater. The powder fanned out
like coral in an explosion of colour. The city air smelled of a thousand
different things: orange blossom hidden in a secret garden, and
drains, and the blistering smell of freshly ground turmeric. There
was something else, too, something sweet and metallic, like the smell
of the fireworks on New Year's night. They rushed back as quickly as
they could.

It was where Stanley, returning home, his breath smelling of whisky,
found them. The first spots of rain were leap-frogging on the dusty
ground. The monsoon was breaking with a vengeance.

'Couldn't you at least ring?'

'I'm sorry,' Stanley lied. 'I had to go for questioning at the police
station.'

'And they gave you whisky there, did they? While taking down your
statement?' Sita asked.

yes glinted dangerously. Alice watched yet another argument break like the rains. Unlike the monsoons, her parents' rows never showed any sign of stopping.

That evening, their last together for some time, the meal was eaten in silence. Each of them was deep in their own thoughts. The wind had died down and the rain was abating, leaving faint streaks of washed-out colour against the sky. The dusty sun-faded garden looked as though it had been touched with a coat of paint. Large fruit-bats took up positions on the telegraph line and sparrows that had made nests under the eaves of the house squabbled noisily, but the air of unhappiness inside the house recycled itself over and over again. Stanley glanced nervously at his wife, helping himself to a little more *seeni sambal.*

'Is there any more mulligatawny left?' he asked timidly.

It occurred to him that he would never overcome his inbuilt fear of Sita. Her quick tongue paralysed him, making him feel a fool, leaving him no space to hide. Tonight, she seemed to have finished her litany of woes. The irony of this latest row did not escape him. Sita thought he had been to the Skyline Hotel to waste money on whisky. He could not tell her it was Neville who had been his supplier. Stanley sighed heavily. Was there anyone this wife of his liked? Without warning, the lights went out.

'Good!' Alice said, pleased. 'Can I light the candles?'

Her parents didn't seem to hear. Her mother was already lighting the oil lamp and her father was scraping the last morsel of rice on to his plate. The sound of it was somehow very sad to Alice's ears. Perhaps her mother thought so too, for she asked him in a conciliatory voice:

'There's some fish left, would you like some?'

Alice watched her father curiously.

'What are you staring at?' he asked suddenly. 'It's rude to stare, especially when someone is eating.'

'Why?' asked Alice.

But as always, no one answered her. Her father pushed the last of the food into his mouth.

'Alice,' her mother said quietly, 'don't be rude. Haven't you finished eating yet?'

'Are we going to the Sea House tomorrow?' Alice asked. 'You said we'd go tomorrow.'

'Stop pestering,' Stanley told her sharply. 'Your mother and I have a lot to discuss before I go.'

'Are you going to have another fight?' Alice asked.

'Alice!' Sita and Stanley said together.

She didn't care. She knew they would fight anyway. If not now, then later, before they went to sleep. Why were they pretending they would not? All she wanted was to go to the Sea House. Alice looked at her parents. Her mother's face was still pretty, but her eyes were unhappy. Her father's face, glistening with sweat, had a different look altogether. She felt he was excited about something and she suspected he wanted to hide this from her mother.

Lowering his voice, Stanley began to talk to Sita. He found dealing with his daughter a tricky business. It wasn't that he felt no affection for her. He was mildly fond of Alice, but he told himself that, with him gone, the child would need to stand on her own two feet, learn to fend for herself. Survive.

'Tomorrow,' Sita was saying, placatingly, 'after Dada has gone, we can go to the Sea House.'

Alice could hear that her mother did not sound excited at all.

And then, in no time at all, it was the day of Stanley's departure, at last. A bleary-eyed, tearless Sita watched the dawn rise. So he was going, leaving her alone with not one small gesture of love. Her life with him had begun with the dawn, she thought sadly, remembering the milk train that had brought her to him, hugging the coastline, thrusting onwards with the promise of a new beginning. On that day the sea had been flat and full of possibilities; now it was this same sea that was taking him away to his new life. He was trying to hide it, but she knew all about his delirious excitement. It only served to increase her own sense of isolation.

The black-hooded golden oriole woke Alice. It had rained hard in the night, but now the sky had almost cleared and the crows were drying out their feathers in the sun. When she went in search of her mother, she found a stream of red ants coming in from the wet, marching steadily through the kitchen. She shuddered, forcing herself not to scream, knowing it would get on her mother's nerves. The roof in the hall had been leaking again. Sita had adjusted the plastic sheeting over the small hole in the night and placed a bucket under it. Alice could hear her mother moving in the kitchen. There was an unfamiliar smell of *kiri-bath*, milk rice. Her mother was making the auspicious dish for her father's departure. The smell reminded Alice of the Sea House. Her grandfather would be here soon, she thought happily.

She found Sita crouching beside the low stone sink in the dark kitchen, washing saucepans. The old gas stove stood against one wall and there was a series of clay pots lining a shelf. Sita had her back to the door. Alice stood silently watching her. There was something beaten about the way her mother bent over the low sink, washing the pans so quietly. Even her sari, the red and yellow silk, a present from Alice's father, worn long ago only for special occasions, had lost its lustre. It was old now; Alice could see a tear in it that had not been there before. They were too poor to afford a servant. Staring at the sari, it occurred to Alice that her mother spent too much time in this damp dark kitchen. Her heart flexed wordlessly, she wished she could make her mother happy. Turning to place a lid on the pot of rice that was cooking, Sita gave a start at the sight of her.

'I didn't see you,' she said sharply. 'What are you doing? Go and have a wash. Grandpa will be here soon.'

Fully focused on her mother's face, Alice saw the sunken cheeks and the dark smudges under her eyes. Sita was painfully thin. Caught unawares by a new emotion, Alice opened her mouth to speak but her mother had already turned her back.

'Where's Dada?' Alice asked instead.

'He's gone to the kade to buy some shaving cream,' Sita said shortly, sounding tense. There was the sound of a car turning outside and Alice ran to the front door.

'Ah!' Bee said. 'Well, look who's here, then.'

He alone sounded happy. Alice grinned.

'What have you brought for me?' she demanded.

'So, I have to bring something each time, do I?' he asked, raising one eyebrow. 'We're going to have to be strict with you once you come to live with us in Mount Lavinia,' he said seriously. 'Or you'll get spoiled. Spare the rod ...'

'And spoil the child,' finished Alice, laughing happily.

'Absolutely!' Stanley remarked, coming up swiftly behind them with his shopping. 'Nearly ready,' he added, nodding at Bee.

'Good!' Bee said, noncommittal.

They drank tea and toyed with the *kiri-bath*. The air was tense with unspoken thoughts. Only Alice, overjoyed at the sight of Bee, stopped caring. Finally Bee stood up and began loading the luggage into the boot of the car. Stanley looked around at the annexe where so much of his life had been wasted. Suddenly, desperately, he wanted to be gone, freed of the chains that held him. Good, thought Bee, looking at the ground. Just go. Get the hell out of here, then. Oh God, I shall have to face his mother, Sita was thinking. And his aunts. I shall have to endure it all.

'Who wants to come with me on the launch?' Stanley asked with false jollity as the car was speeding towards the harbour.

'Me!' Alice said instantly.

'Right then!'

Once again Alice detected the curious note of suppressed excitement she had heard earlier in Stanley's voice. Bee must have heard it too, because he looked sharply in the mirror, accidentally catching Alice's eye. She had a feeling her grandfather was trying not to laugh. Instantly, happiness rose in her. The sky was clear and very blue.

'I don't think I will,' Sita said quietly. She knew she would not be able to face it. 'I'll say good-bye on the jetty.'

No one said any more for the rest of the journey.

The harbour was a strange mixture of tension and emptiness. Passengers were decamped everywhere. Luggage labels spelt out the names of exotic places.

'Sitma Line. P&O Liners, Port Said, Aden, Gibraltar, Genoa ...' Alice read out aloud, wishing she knew where these places were, glad she wasn't going there.

Sita shivered. She thought the place was terrible. Women in saris carrying their whole life in a bundle, children eating gram for the last time, old grandmothers, pressing a last bottle of *seeni sambal* on a relative they would never see again. Alice stood open-mouthed and riveted, absorbing the noise and confusion. Never had she seen such a place as this. They had entered an alien world. At last Stanley handed in his ticket and his luggage was whisked away. Instantly, he appeared apart from them, holding nothing except a small plastic briefcase with his few travel documents. He had slung his sweater around his shoulders, but now found this made him unbearably hot.

'Here, hold this for me, Putha,' he said to Alice, who stood quietly absorbing the activity.

Bee turned away and lit his pipe and she slipped her hand in his when he had thrown away the match. Looking down at her excited face, Bee winked.

'Should you buy something to eat?' Sita asked Stanley.

No one answered her. She felt superfluous to the buzz all around her.

'I think I'll get something to eat when we embark,' Stanley said, at last. 'Oh, look!'

Ahead of him, in a line of faded cotton saris, were five dark Tamil women. It was Stanley's mother and her sisters. As she came nearer they could see his mother was crying. She took her son's face in both her hands and kissed him. Then she nodded in the direction of Sita. It's all your fault, the nod seemed to say.

'You don't know how lucky you are,' she told her daughter-in-law. 'You at least will see him again.'

Sita could think of nothing to say.

And then, in the smallest space of time, with no warning, Stanley, still smoking his last cigarette, was gone. Like a condemned man, thought Sita dully. Thank God, at last, thought Bee and Stanley simultaneously and with enormous relief. The tannoy announced the arrival of the motor launches to take passengers and relatives to the ship that sat a little way out in deeper waters.

'Okay, I'm off then,' Stanley told them awkwardly, kissing each one; his mother, Sita, his aunts. Then he shook hands with Bee.

'Look after yourself,' Bee said, adding quietly, 'and don't forget the family.'

Stanley swallowed, wanting to say something, not averse to marking the moment, but not knowing how best to do so. Picking up his brief-case, he glanced at Sita and gave her a last quick hug. Pity touched down fleetingly on his heart; then took off again. He took hold of Alice's hand.

'She's coming with me,' he said, grinning, 'as a stowaway!'

'No,' Alice replied, her voice panicky. 'I'm only coming to see your cabin.'

'Go with her, Thatha,' Sita murmured with soft, keening desperation so that, seeing her face, Bee nodded quickly and followed them out on to the launch.

The ocean liner, white as snow with two black funnels, lay at anchor surrounded by a flock of large seagulls. The sea was calm in spite of the night's storm, reflecting the sun's rays through a clear lens. Alice caught a glimpse of coastline from an angle she had never seen before, wide sandy coves and fringes of coconut trees looking strange from the water. The land seemed small and the fishing huts and harbour buildings shabby from her low-slung position on the motor launch. They climbed the long, swaying gangway. People seemed to be hanging from every part of the ship, through portholes and on the decks, watching as they climbed. Once on board, everything grew in size. The ship was bigger than it had appeared from land.

'Come on, quickly, quickly,' Stanley called. 'If you want to see my cabin, you mustn't dawdle.'

But even as they hurried to find it, using the map Stanley had been given, getting lost amongst the faceless corridors, struggling with the heavy doors, climbing lower and deeper into the boat, the great boom-ing sound of the horn was heard and a voice advised all guests to leave. The sound of the ship's engine had changed and there was a slow creaking of wood. Suddenly Alice had had enough. It was hot and the sickly smell of diesel everywhere made her feel slightly sick.

'I want to get off,' she said, pulling at her grandfather's hand. 'Now!'

'Yes,' Stanley agreed.

He too had had enough of this protracted farewell and his father-in-law's obvious disapproval.

'It's just a cabin, after all.'

He turned to Alice.

'Give your Daddy a kiss. Be a good girl,' he said meaninglessly.

Alice was hardly listening. Fear was rising in her.

'You'll have exams as soon as you get to your new school in London,' he said. 'So do some reading every day, and look at the history book I gave you.'

'Yes,' Alice agreed.

The corridors had become crowded with relatives making their way to the exit as the horn sounded again, more urgently.

'Let's go, Putha,' Bee said. 'Hold my hand.' And he led the way down the ladder, past the waving, noisy crowds, down to the waiting hands on the motorboat returning home. But by the time she had found a seat and looked up again at the great ship, it was impossible for Alice to distinguish her father from all the other smiling faces.

5

FOUR RED CACTUS FLOWERS BLOOMED on the window ledge in the annexe in Havelock Road. For months Sita had wanted them to flower.

'There's no point taking them with us,' she told Alice.

Alice picked one anyway; then she went outside. The ginger cat from next door came up and rubbed itself against her legs.

'I'll be coming back, Roger,' she told the cat.

Picking him up, she buried her face in his fur listening to the thunderous purrs, but the cat leapt fastidiously from her arms into the jungle of next-door's garden and disappeared. Alice narrowed her eyes until they were slits, trying to turn them into cat's eyes. Roger would be here tomorrow and the day after that, while *she* would be far away at the Sea House. She didn't like the annexe; it was coated in rain-damp sorrow, dead feelings and useless hope. Nothing had come to much here. Not her mother's baby or the landlord to mend the hole in the roof. And now they were leaving. The morning tightened like a rubber band around her throat. The lime tree under which she had played for as long as she could remember, squeezing out lime juice into her toy teapot, stood impassively. The sky was becoming overcast again and rain threatened. Sita emerged carrying the suitcase and, almost instantly, as if they had been hiding behind the jasmine fence, one or two of the neighbours, all Singhalese, came out to say good-bye. They kissed first Sita and then Alice. Mrs Pereira gave Alice a round of juggery wrapped in a palm leaf. It had been tied with twine. And Mrs Mehdi gave Sita a packet of tea from the estate where her relatives worked.

'We're not going to England yet,' Alice said. No one took any notice of her.

'Well, don't forget about us,' Mrs Pereira said, her head rocking from side to side. '*Anay!* Remember you're still a Singhalese, child!'

The women stood on the pavement under the plantain tree, holding up their umbrellas, waving until the rickshaw turned the corner and Havelock Road was no more.

'Thank God that's over!' Sita said in English, sitting back in the comforting darkness. 'Two-faced bitches! Here, give me that juggery. We'll give it to a beggar. I don't want to eat anything that comes from that filthy house.'

Alice snuggled into the mysterious space within the rickshaw. Their seat smelled of incense and other hot rainy-day smells. The downpour began again in earnest, beating a tattoo on the canvas roof as the rickshaw man ran barefooted across the puddles. Through the slits in the flaps, they saw glimpses of roadside life speeding by. Piles of pink and yellow flowers wrapped in shiny tin-foil shrines flashed past in a dream while mango skins and cow-dung swam in the dirty water that over-flowed the sides of the roads. Sita remained silent all the way to the railway station. May's homecoming sari was neatly wrapped in her suitcase, along with the silk for the jacket Kamala would make when they reached the Sea House.

The sea had been disturbed by a storm last night and now there were giant waves, high and foamy. Once on the train, Alice began counting aloud until Sita told her to stop.

'Dada is on this sea, Alice,' she said. 'I hope he isn't being seasick.'

Silenced, Alice belatedly remembered her father. It was strange to think of him on this very same sea. She felt neither sad nor glad, but she knew she had to be very careful with her mother this morning. Yesterday, returning from the jetty, Sita had not been able to stop crying. Bee had tried to persuade them to come back to the Sea House with him that night, but Sita had been adamant; they would spend one last night in the annexe and leave in the morning by train. In the end, Bee, understanding that Sita needed a night alone, had piled all their belongings into the car and driven reluctantly away. When Alice had woken in the night wanting a drink she had found the house unusually quiet. Already her parents' quarrels were a thing of the past. She wondered if her mother was lonely without them.

The train was slowing down. A man on a bicycle sped along the road that ran between the railway line and the beach. Alice could see his face rigid with concentration as he raced the train. His face seemed familiar. They were approaching the level crossing. The barrier was coming down. Alice leaned out of the window and saw a white van speeding behind the bicycle. It hadn't been there a moment ago.

'Don't put your head out,' Sita said automatically.

Sita was staring straight ahead. The last time I did this journey I still had the baby, she thought, dully.

The strip of beach that ran along beside the track was completely deserted. The rain had stopped and left behind a curious, ethereal light. It hung over the horizon with mute softness. As the train clanked and creaked to a standstill, in the silence that followed, the roar of the waves was suddenly very loud and close by. Crisp sea-smells filled the carriage and they heard voices, faintly at first but then becoming more insistent. The train lurched slightly and went no further. Alice, ignoring her mother, craned her neck out of the window. Other people had begun to look out too. There were voices were coming from some point beyond their sightline. An argument was taking place. The ticket collector appeared on the track, gesticulating furiously. Then with a sharp squeak of the brakes the train began to move backwards before it stopped again. Everyone in the carriage groaned and looked at their watches. What was the delay?

'I have an appointment in an hour,' the man opposite them said to no one in particular. He spoke in Singhalese. He wore a smart tropical suit and kept brushing imaginary dust off it. 'Now I'll be late.'

An elderly Tamil woman shuffled into the compartment and sat down. She produced a dirty plantain leaf tied up in a parcel which she proceeded to undo. The parcel was full of rice and the old woman began eating with her fingers, licking them clean after each mouthful. Alice stared at her with interest. The woman cleared her throat of phlegm and belched so loudly that Alice giggled, but Sita turned away in distaste and nudged her to do likewise. Then a few people began complaining loudly about the delay. The man opposite stood up impatiently and climbed down from the train. Alice saw him walking on the gravel towards the ticket collector. The guard joined them and very soon there was a whole group clustered together out on the track.

'What on earth is going on?' asked one of the passengers impatiently.

The old woman finished her rice and tucked her plantain leaf between the sides of the seats. Some uneaten rice fell to the floor. She stared at it fixedly, then she licked her lips and wiped her nose on the corner of her sari. Everyone in the carriage looked away politely.

'Look, Mama,' Alice said excitedly. 'Police!'

Two police cars had driven up and stopped beside the level crossing, their lights revolving pointlessly. The group around the ticket collector and the guard had grown by now and there was a lot of excited talk.

'What the hell is happening, men?'

The suited man returned to his seat.

'Body on the line,' he said shortly, mopping his brow.

It was getting hot. The carriage gave a collective, weary sigh and resigned itself for the inevitable delay.

'What the devil, men! There's a body on the line every day. Why can't they find a more convenient place to do away with themselves? Stop inconveniencing others!'

'Some Tamil, I expect,' the man in the suit said, opening the window a little more. 'Ambulance on its way. Won't be long now before we move. The guard said they'd make up time.'

'Don't believe a word these guards say. They're all liars.'

The suited man opened his newspaper, ignoring everyone. Almost instantly they heard the sound of the ambulance siren and moments later it appeared in view.

'Sit down, Alice,' Sita said in a low voice. 'And don't stare.'

Most of the passengers had by now moved to a window facing the sea. The Tamil woman belched again and stood up.

'They kill Tamils,' she said loudly in hesitant Singhalese. Everyone ignored her; Sita moved closer to Alice.

'Have you packed your history book?' she asked.

Alice nodded.

'What's happening?' she whispered back in English.

Sita frowned warningly. The suited man was watching them slyly over the top of his newspaper. At last the train appeared to be disengaging itself. It moved backwards a fraction. Then it began to edge slowly, inch by inch, along the line. Alice saw the ambulancemen at either end of a stretcher. A white sheet was draped over it. The train was moving more smoothly now. It passed the giant cacti that grew all along this stretch of coast. It passed a few coconut trees, bent towards the ground. The passengers crowding around the window moved away and suddenly they had a complete view of the sea and the road; clear of the rain, very empty, with the sand, wide and smooth. And as the train gathered speed, moving swiftly onwards, she caught sight of a soldier, his gun cocked and ready, standing beside the mangled wheels of a bicycle. He looked very young, no more than a boy. An army jeep had pulled up beside the police car as the policeman in his white uniform raised his arm and waved them on. The train rattled along and at the same instant Alice saw, with a thrill, in the soft, beautiful light beyond them, the gentle curve of the line that was taking them to the white houses rising steeply above Mount Lavinia Bay.

Bee was waiting at the station. Because it was Saturday the ticket office was closed and the station was quiet. Such had been the force of the rain that it had swept on to the platform, flooding it completely. The seats in the waiting room, the cinema posters on the platform wall and the plant pots with their mother-in-law's tongues swam in water. A particularly large squall had even knocked against the overhead light and broken the bulb. The station sweeper was clearing it up. The station master, who had been on the telephone moments earlier, came out when he saw Bee.

'There's been a delay further up the line,' he told those waiting on the platform. 'I've been talking to the guard. They'll be about ten minutes late.'

'What happened, Gihan?' Bee asked, going towards him.

He took his pipe out of his pocket and lit it with some difficulty.

'Not sure,' Gihan said loudly, shrugging.

Then, because it was Bee, he dropped his defensive air and lowered his voice.

'I believe the army got on the train at Weltham Point. Who knows why!'

He raised his hands and let them fall to show his helplessness in the matter.

'Did you hear about the incident yesterday at Morotowa?'

Bee shook his head and looked at the station master sharply. I don't listen to gossip, his look said. He had known Gihan Ranasingha since they had both been boys. In those days Gihan had been the only child in the school on a scholarship and while the other boys in the school had tended to look down on him, Bee had made a point of becoming his friend. Years later, after they had grown up and Bee had returned to Mount Lavinia with his new bride to take up the post of headmaster, they had met again. By then Gihan Ranasingha was married with four children of his own.

'How are you?' Gihan asked now. He was looking at his feet and spoke casually. 'Haven't seen you for a while. How's Kamala? I heard the wedding was cancelled.'

'Not cancelled,' Bee said shortly. 'We've just put it back a bit, to give Sita a chance to recover.'

Gihan nodded.

'Yes, yes, of course. I understand. It must be an auspicious time, of course.'

'No,' Bee frowned. 'I told you, we've simply postponed it until Sita is stronger. A matter of a few weeks.'

'Of course, of course,' Gihan said soothingly, smiling at his old friend.

The whole town knew about May's wedding and that it was being delayed. Once again, because of Sita.

Bee continued puffing on his pipe in silence. He did not return the smile. For some time a certain coolness had existed between the two of them. It was not obvious to anyone else. They still spoke whenever they met, Gihan still asked after Kamala and May. Outwardly, nothing had changed since they had been boys playing cricket together against the English. But Gihan never mentioned Sita, and Bee had lost the easy trustful air he once had. These days he never accepted, as he once would have, the invitations to share a glass of arrack while waiting for a train that was delayed.

Gihan looked thoughtful.

'How long is the little one with you? She won't be leaving for some time, I hope?'

He had only a vague idea of Alice's age.

'No.'

'Oh good, good,' Gihan nodded, not really listening, rubbing his hands together.

All this rain had made him feel cold. Who would want to go to the UK? he thought, shuddering.

'Bring them over if she gets bored,' he said, unable to stop himself. 'Indira would like to see the child.'

Indira was his wife.

'Come for lunch, men,' he hesitated. 'With your daughter, too, if she likes.'

He couldn't bring himself to say Sita's name, but he couldn't stop his affection for Bee, either.

'Indira was saying only the other day she hadn't seen anything of you for ages, huh.'

Bee was too tall for Gihan to reach his shoulder, so he patted his arm instead. Bee smiled faintly. They both knew he would not take the offer up, but it didn't stop Gihan from issuing invitations as easily as tickets or Bee from appearing to accept. Neither of them, thought Bee sadly, were able to put a halt to this futile ritual.

When Sita had eloped and the news first spread across the community, Gihan had not been able to keep quiet.

'How could this have happened to the poor man!' he had fumed the day he heard. And after that he had made the mistake of telling Bee what he thought.

'What a disgrace!' he had said before he could stop himself. 'Such a terrible thing to do. And she's the eldest too!'

At the time, Gihan had advised Bee to disinherit the girl.

'She's made her bed, men,' he had shouted, his heart going out to Bee, thinking it would be better if the community knew what his friend's feelings really were. 'Better all round,' he had advised. 'You should make a stand. For your own sake, men. And for Kamala and the other girl.'

Bee had stared at him disbelievingly.

'You have the younger one to think of,' Gihan had said, oblivious to the signs. 'She'll never find a husband otherwise.'

Subsequently, having learnt the cost of his tactlessness, Gihan kept silent, but by then the damage had been done. With time, Bee appeared to weather the storm. But he changed, became more withdrawn, less visible, and, after that first moment, although he always listened politely, he took no notice of anything Gihan said. Very soon the whole town saw Bee walking openly on the beach with the girl and her Tamil husband. Gihan had shaken his head at the foolishness of it, but then the child had been born. For a while it seemed everyone would forget Sita's disgrace. Things might have recovered had Sita not lost the second child.

'*Anay*, she's bad news,' Indira told Gihan, fuelling her husband's dislike. 'You shouldn't see her face first thing in the morning. It will only bring bad luck!'

Gihan didn't know what to believe.

'You know what people are saying, don't you?' Indira insisted. 'That Tamil grandmother must have put a spell on the baby. She didn't want another Singhalese bastard, I suppose.'

It wasn't as far-fetched as all that. Everyone knew the Tamils were unnatural, crazy people, Indira told her husband, shaking her head knowingly. Gihan, listening with a slight feeling of revulsion, agreed, but then he had seen Bee in the distance walking on the beach, and the look of him, the loneliness that exuded from him, the slowness of his pace, as opposed to his usual brisk step, had filled Gihan's heart with pity. How much could the poor man bear? So Gihan had gone out on

to the track and shouted to Bee, but the wind had whipped away his
voice and the waves had drowned his words. After that, every time he
saw Bee waiting for the four o'clock Colombo express and the arrival
of his granddaughter, Gihan made a point of talking to him.

Standing on the platform, waiting for the delayed train, Bee inclined
his head by way of thanks for yet another useless invitation.

'We'll have to see what the women are planning,' he said lightly.

'Of course, of course. A wedding is women's business, after all!'
Gihan said, wagging his head understandingly.

A cream butterfly flew out through the open window of one of the
compartments as though it had been waiting to alight from the train. It
sailed between the wrought-iron fretwork in the roof and out through
the barrier. Five Singhalese solders stepped out of the guard's carriage
and walked briskly towards Gihan Ranasingha. They were followed by
a small flock of people. Bee saw Sita walking slowly along the platform
and hurried towards her. Her suitcase was feather light but she carried
it as though it were a lead weight. Alice leapt out from behind her and
the afternoon shifted focus, becoming brighter and full of purpose. The
sun came out simultaneously as they went towards the car. Gihan had
disappeared into his office with the soldiers and closed the door.

'What's going on?' Bee asked, inclining his head towards the train as
it slid out of the station. 'Gihan's just been giving me the party line.'

They told him about the accident and the mangled remains of the
bicycle.

'That was no accident,' Bee said quietly, shepherding them out to the
car. 'But I'm glad you're here, at last.'

The air was fresh off the sea as the car wound its way up the hill
towards the house. Bougainvillea flashed past them again, hibiscus
flowers lined walls and arches as Sita leaned back in her seat and half
closed her eyes. There was an unusual brilliance today that she remembered from her youth. A feeling of sorrow cut the light as though it
were butter. She had forgotten how peaceful it was here, how much
she loved the place and how soon she would be leaving it behind.
Alice's voice, talking non-stop to her grandfather, came to Sita from a

long, bright distance. She heard the waves as they rolled and fell. This
stretch of the journey was so much a part of her that she had no need
to fully open her eyes. She knew every inch of the road by heart and had
lost count of all the times her father had picked her up from the station.
Coming back from boarding school in Colombo for the holidays,
returning from a visit to her friend Girlie's house in Cinnamon
Gardens. Successful Girlie, making the proverbial good marriage to a
member of the newly formed cabinet, and at whose society wedding
Sita had stood as bridesmaid, smiling for the photographer. Looking,
by all accounts, prettier than the bride. Yes! thought Sita, life held many
possibilities once. The car was slowing down. Alice had fallen silent
and, opening her eyes, Sita saw Bee bending over her with grave
tenderness. She had not seen such a look on him for a long time. How
grey he is, she thought fleetingly, her heart reaching out to touch a
long-forgotten emotion. Smiling very slightly, she got out of the car.

'Sorry, I must have dozed off,' she murmured.

'They've just announced a curfew on the radio,' Kamala greeted
them. 'There's been an incident at Morotowa.'

'We saw it,' Sita nodded.

Her mother too, now she was so near to leaving her forever, came
into a clearer focus. She was tired, more tired than she could say, but
how good it was to come home.

'What sort of incident?'

'Must be the man on the bicycle,' Alice told them calmly. 'I saw him
racing the train. He looked scared.'

They turned to look at her.

'You *saw* the man?' Sita said. 'Why didn't you say?'

'I didn't know they were going to kill him, did I?' Alice said, glad to
be noticed. 'I thought he would escape. He was a Tamil.'

No one spoke.

'How d'you know?' demanded Sita sharply.

'Ssh! Ssh! Don't shout at the child,' Kamala said.

'Because he looked Tamil,' Alice told them matter-of-factly.

What was the matter with her mother? Had she forgotten the Tamils
were hated?

'So much for innocence,' Bee remarked.

'*Anay!*' Kamala cried.

The child had been robbed of her childhood. Every day that passed brought yet another reason for her being taken away.

'Let's have some tea,' Bee said. 'Now they are here at last!'

He surveyed the room with satisfaction. No one spoke. A known quantity of days stretched before them.

In her room, Alice unpacked her book of drawings and brought them out to Bee.

'Look, here's Mrs Maradana,' she said, finding the page, grinning at him.

Bee burst out laughing. Alice had drawn a picture of her Singhalese teacher using the new Biro pen Bee had bought for her. Biro pens were all the rage at the moment. She had, with a few vigorous, confident lines, captured something of the spirit of the woman. Staring at it, Bee thought, This is good; this must be developed. It is a talent that will hold her in good stead. I shall not see the end of it, he thought, but at least I see what she has brought into this life. Maybe I have even contributed to it.

'This is very, very, good, Alice,' he said aloud. 'Keep drawing, look as hard as you can at everything.'

Memories were all he could give her. No matter how far she travelled, no matter if she never returned, still her memories would last forever. He tapped his pipe and re-lit it, half listening to her voice chattering on. He was not a man who frequented the temple, but Buddhism remained part of his life. Whatever good thing a man did, he believed, would return to bless him. Or haunt him; depending on the way he lived. Yes, he thought, Stanley would send for them soon enough but just for a brief moment, on the first of these last remaining evenings, as he watched the setting sun, listening to the child's happy talk Bee was comforted.

A routine of sorts slowly established itself. For Alice, mornings meant the beach. Bee took her for a swim or a bike ride. Sometimes, when he was not out with the fishing boats, Janake came for her, and occasionally even Esther visited. In the afternoons, after her nap, she was allowed to visit Bee in his studio when he let her loose on his paints. They worked together in companionable silence. As it was term time, May was still working. The wedding was now to take place in June and in the evenings the talk was mainly about the preparations for it. Namil was often present and, were it not for the fact that Sita's mental state was no better and that they were counting the days, things might have been pleasant enough. Sita's lethargy was a constant reminder of the borrowed time they lived on. Having detached herself from everyone, she spent long hours in her room, often having her meals brought to her. All attempts to draw her out proved useless. Nearly two weeks passed in this way.

On one such night when the house slept and the moon appeared a milky blue in the phosphorescent sky, Kamala sat sewing alone. The darkness had drawn its sea-misty wings over the beach and the waves exploded in clouds of spray. Regardless of everything the house turned over and sunk deeper into sleep. Bee was still working in his studio. Kamala put away her sewing. She folded the jacket she had sewn for Sita and rubbed one hand over the other. The blue sapphire in the ring Bee had given her years ago shone in the pinprick of light. Both her children were briefly under the same roof again. Watching the moon disappearing from view, aware these nights were numbered, she felt the impending loss hover a hair's breadth away. All of this, she thought, surveying the silent room, appears to last forever but will vanish in a moment. She imagined her daughters, her *girls*, running in and out of the open house, laughing, teasing each other, fighting too, as if they were a pair of boys. Clearly she saw it, as though it had been yesterday. Living for so long in this way they had mistaken 'so long' for 'forever'. Ah! but time has flown while they grew, thought Kamala, feeling the year turn over, dry as a leaf. Bee was depressed and would not admit it. Twisting the rings on her finger, Kamala's thoughts went round in circles. From the day it had broken open, her love for him had never faltered. On the night that he had returned from the port he had sat smoking his pipe on the verandah. May had been out walking with Namil. The house had been silent. Packing away her sewing, Kamala

126

had come to stand beside Bee. She had stood without speaking for so long that in the end she thought he didn't realise she was there. But in the end he held out his hand without turning round and made her sit beside him, his eyes moving towards her like a star in the darkness.

'I was thinking today, they have taken after you,' he said softly. 'You are very beautiful.'

In all these years the tenderness had never left his voice. Kamala looked down at her hands, smiling in the darkness, remembering his words. The house slept as though it were an animal, as though it were well fed and at peace, tucked away on its perch above the bay, surrounded by rustling coconut trees. Moonlight shredded the water into small fragments. The rain had died down and the air was full of the sharp smell of seaweed, while the sea, moving on its seabed, sighed too, peaceful like the house. It was a sea she loved, almost on the equator, a width away from India, furthest of all from Antarctica. Somewhere out beyond the reef, currents swirled darkly and fish as black as night swam, but here within the bay all remained safe. A thousand years of coral splendour protected their bay, keeping it safe for bathers and fishermen alike. But into this quietness Kamala heard the faint sound of drumming further inland. It was coming from the town. The only discordant note, it had gone on and on since the curfew and was now part of the background noises of the night, slipping in with the whirl of insects and the slap of water. The servant woman, who knew of these things, had told Kamala there was a sick man in one of the villages. The drummers were hoping to drum the devil out of his body. They wanted to drum it out of town, but they had been working all night and still nothing had happened. That was how hard it was to remove the devil once he had taken hold, the servant woman said. Maybe by dawn the sick man would be cured. Maybe not. Either way there would be an offering left for the gods by morning. Kamala went to bed. It would be hours before Bee finished work in the studio.

A thin light shone under the door that led into Bee's studio. It flickered faintly. Every now and then a shadow passed over the crack as if someone inside the room was walking around. It was what Alice noticed first when she awoke and went outside. On these occasional night forays, her grandfather's studio was the first place she thought of. Tonight something had woken her; she moved swiftly, her small bare feet silent on the cool gravel, wanting to find Bee and tell him about it. Voices drifted towards her, then stopped. Straining, she listened. A bullfrog croaked and dark shapes fluttered past her face, making her duck and lose her balance. She fell against a flowerpot and froze. It was like the last time, she thought, in sudden panic, not knowing whether to run back to the house. The voices had stopped. Nothing moved. Then the door opened and she saw a pair of familiar feet, the edges of a white sarong.

'Well, well. Now that's a surprise, I must say,' her grandfather said, his voice an odd mixture of sharp anxiety and relief.

'I couldn't sleep,' Alice said, looking beyond him wonderingly into the studio.

'So it would appear,' Bee said wryly. 'How unfortunate!'

He was standing in the doorway, blocking the view. It wasn't like the last time, she decided, searching his face with relief, although she had a distinct feeling he didn't want her there.

'Alice,' he was saying, 'this won't do. D'you know what the time is? You should go back to bed. I was going to wake you up very early to go to the beach.'

'But I'm not tired,' Alice began, and then she too stopped.

Someone else stood behind her grandfather. Alice stared. The man's face was familiar.

'Hello,' the man said.

He smiled tiredly.

'I know you,' said Alice, puzzled.

Bee sighed.

'You better come in,' he said resignedly.

'I'm sorry, sir,' the man apologised.

He shrugged his shoulders.

'She's just a child. It will do no harm.'

'No,' Alice announced, shaking her head. 'That's what everyone thinks. But I'm not.'

Bee raised his eyebrows. This quiet certainty was new.

'Alice,' he began, eyeing her.

Then he made up his mind.

'Okay, come in, come in, quickly.'

He pushed her gently into the room and shut and locked the door. She was startled to see his studio so transformed. Bee had closed up his etching press and all his colours and rags had been pushed hastily to one side of the shelf. A small camp bed had been opened up against one of the walls and there was a bowl of water stained dark crimson on the floor beside it. Someone had torn a bed sheet into strips. Her grandfather had turned off the electric light and instead two candles burned on the table. Alice looked around her, astonished. The man had rolled his trousers up and there was a bandage on his leg. She could see blood seeping out through it.

'Alice,' her grandfather said again.

He was watching her.

'You say you're not a child. So I'm trusting you with my secret. You must not breathe a word of any of this, you understand?'

He had never spoken to her so seriously before. Not even when he had taught her to mix his precious pigments. Alice nodded. She pushed the hair out of her eyes; all sleep had fled from them. Bee looked grim.

'This is Kunal,' he said reluctantly. 'He's been shot in the leg by the army and he's hiding here until morning. I'm going to have to get Dr Mutumuruna to come over and look at his leg, but I can't leave until the curfew is over. It's too dangerous.'

He paused.

'Kunal is staying here for the moment. No one knows about this, Alice. *No one*. Kunal will be taken by the army and killed if they find out. Do you understand?'

Alice nodded. The seriousness of his words had rendered her speechless.

Kunal was sitting on the camp bed. He wasn't looking at them any more. His head was bent.

'He's lost a lot of blood,' Bee muttered. 'I'm going to have to get hold of the doctor as soon as it's light.'

He was talking to himself. Alice looked at him. She was concentrating so hard that her head hurt with the effort. She swallowed quickly.

'Yes,' she said clearly. 'I understand.'

Bee did not seem to hear. He opened the cupboard that held his inks and took out a bottle of whisky. Then he washed a tumbler and poured the whisky into it. Next he held the glass up to the light. It was golden like a wasp's sting.

'Kunal used to be one of my staff at the boys' school,' he said.

Alice gasped.

'Were you on a bicycle recently? Near the level crossing,' she asked.

Kunal finished the whisky in one gulp and shook his head. Alice saw his eyes were bloodshot with weeping.

'No,' he said.

He paused, struggling. When he spoke again his chin wobbled in a way Alice fully understood.

'No. That was my friend. You were probably the last one to see him alive.'

And then he began to weep.

At dawn Bee went out to get the doctor. Alice could not be persuaded to leave Kunal. She sat cross-legged and stubborn on the ground beside him.

'I'm not sleepy,' she told Bee, again with quiet certainty. 'Don't worry.'

Again Bee hesitated.

'All right,' he said finally.

If he were going, he would have to leave now.

'I won't wake your grandmother just yet. Lock the door after me. I'll be gone about twenty minutes.'

Alice nodded, silent with concentration. Kunal seemed to have dozed off, head slumped against the wall. He hadn't moved since drinking the whisky. The empty bottle stood on the floor. Alice stared at him. The edges of his trousers were frayed and she noticed his shoes were old and broken. She could see his feet peeping out. She sat very still. After what felt like a long time, Kunal opened his eyes blearily and saw her.

'You're still here,' he said faintly.

'Grandpa won't be long,' Alice whispered. 'I'm looking after you until he gets back. Don't worry. You're safe here.'

Kunal smiled vaguely.

'I know.'

He struggled to sit up and Alice went over and adjusted the cushion behind his head.

'Bee told me your father has gone to England.'

'Yes. But I don't want to go.'

Kunal nodded, agreeing.

'To leave your country is terrible, Alice,' he said. 'Your country is such a part of you. It's in your skin, your eyes, your hair, all of you. You *are* Ceylon, you know. And whenever someone from this place leaves, a little bit of it leaves with them and is lost forever. If too many people leave Ceylon, it will become another sort of place entirely.'

Alice narrowed her eyes. Kunal was shaking and she noticed there were beads of perspiration on his forehead. The bandage on his leg had become redder. She wondered what she should do.

'But some of us don't have any choices,' Kunal continued, after a pause. 'I had another friend who was about to go to the UK when they killed him. So now all that is left of my family is his son Janake and my sister. Maybe he too will go to England one day.'

'Janake?' Alice asked.

She was astonished.

'He's my friend!' she said. 'He lives in the next village with his mother. How do you know him?'

Kunal's face twitched slightly.

'His father's brother was married to my sister. One day some thugs came and killed my sister and then went looking for Janake's father.'

'Did they kill Janake's father too?' Alice asked, breathlessly.

Kunal nodded.

'Janake won't talk about his father.'

'Janake was only about six when it happened. His father was hiding his brother, my sister's husband, after my sister was killed. But then they came and found him. They took both of them, Janake's father and his brother, out on to the beach.'

'They killed them?' Alice asked.

Kunal nodded. 'I shouldn't be telling you all this. But it's the way this country has become. One of them or one of us, that's what it has come to,' he said.

'I got caned in my Singhalese lesson,' Alice said. 'That's why I'm not going back to school.'

'I know. Your grandfather told me. He was very upset. I know what happened to your mother too.'

Alice wriggled. She did not want to discuss her mother.

'When you go to the UK you will have a better chance in life. That's all any of us want in the end. A chance to breathe the air around us, to live our lives freely, without fear. There are too many dead here to haunt us.'

He appeared to have forgotten Alice, whose velvet dark eyes were fixed steadily on him.

'I'm coming back,' Alice said into the silence. 'When I'm sixteen. After I've made some friends and finished my studies, I'm coming back. I'm going to live here and look after my grandparents.'

Kunal nodded. He looked as though he might start crying again.

'You must return if you can,' he said finally. 'If everyone who leaves comes back, there might be some hope. A country needs its young if this madness is to be stopped.'

The candles were almost out and through the papered-up window they saw a little daylight seeping in.

'For people like me, there is very little hope left. It's too late, really,' Kunal whispered.

He stared at his bandaged leg.

'Alice in Wonderland,' he said at last. 'Who gave you this name? I don't know how much you understand, but your grandfather is a very fine man. He's a wonderful painter, too. And he tells me you show signs of becoming an artist. Is that right?'

She nodded, frowning. Words spun round in her head. No one believes me, she wanted to say. But I'm coming back.

Kunal had dozed off. The candles blew out, the light outside had become insistent. Alice too closed her eyes. She had no idea how long she sat like this before the door opened very quietly and her grandfather came in. The doctor was behind him. And close behind the doctor, with an expression of annoyance on her face, was a bleary-eyed Kamala.

'Hello, Putha,' the doctor said. 'Have you been looking after my patient?'

Alice smiled faintly. She was tired.

'Bed,' Kamala told her firmly, glowering at Bee.

The look said plainly, I'll talk to you later.

'I don't know what your grandfather was thinking about. Come on.' She took hold of Alice's hand, ignoring her protests.

'Could I have some warm water, please, Kamala?' the doctor asked.

Her grandfather had got another bottle of whisky out of his cupboard and was pouring some into the glass. He was looking very serious again and Alice could not catch his eye.

'Come back, Alice,' Kunal called softly. 'Come back to Wonderland one day.'

The last thing she saw was the doctor, his head bent in concentration, rolling his shirtsleeves up. And then her grandmother hurried her out into the astonishing early-morning sunlight. It was as though the night had not occurred at all, such was the blueness of the air. The sun touched her cheeks warmly and a crumpled tissue-paper moon glided across the sky. She yawned. She was hungry too, but her grandmother's face told her there was no chance of food at the moment. She knew it would have to be bed first.

After the doctor had removed the bullet from Kunal's leg, Kamala made up the small room in the annexe and had him moved there. The annexe had been newly whitewashed in readiness for the bride and groom, who were to live in it until their new house was ready. The wedding was still weeks away and the doctor thought it a good idea for Kunal to remain in the annexe for the moment. Everyone who knew the Fonsekas knew Bee had a studio in the garden. If someone wanted to search the house, the studio would be the obvious place to look first. Bee and the doctor moved Kunal in silence. He was dizzy with the loss of too much blood and protested weakly, saying he did not want to be moved. He was, he told them, ashamed to be the first occupant of the bride's new home. But there was little choice. The army might decide at any moment to patrol the beach. It was already late, the risks were enormous and the doctor needed to get back to his surgery. He would return later, he promised.

'No need to phone,' he said, giving Bee a meaningful look; and then he hurried out into the light through the footpath in the coconut grove.

Bee walked with him for some of the way. A brief storm the night before had shaken the two mango trees that stood at the bottom of the garden. Spoiled fruit lay everywhere. The green sickly scent of their skins filled the air. Battalions of ants were already feasting on the yellow flesh exposed by the fall. The doctor kicked a mango over and stepped on another, flattening it with his shoes as he hurried.

'What's the plan?' he asked.

'Jaffna?'

The doctor made a face.

'Tricky.'

They walked on in exhausted silence.

'He should be fine until tomorrow. Any problem, send for me up at the house. Don't come to the surgery. I think it's being watched.'

'Dias Harris has contacts. As soon as he is recovered enough, I'll drive him there.'

The doctor shook his head in disgust. He pressed his lips together into a thin line.

'This place is full of the worst kind of thugs, men. There's a lot of people hell-bent on destruction.'

He was silent again. A branch crackled underfoot and a small bat flew swiftly past.

'How's Sita?' he asked, after a moment. 'I noticed she came in when we were cleaning Kunal up.'

'Everything has gone inwards, Sam,' Bee mumbled. 'She won't talk, not to me, anyway. It all remains, festering. Perhaps it will get better when they go.'

He spoke without conviction, hopelessly.

'When do they leave?'

'Three months minus one week.'

The doctor glanced sharply at Bee.

'What about you? How will you deal with all that?'

'Same way as you,' Bee said grimly. 'Doing what we're doing now. Helping those poor buggers that we can.'

They walked on. The sky had become a brilliant, parrot blue. Behind them the sea threw up a gentle breeze, cooling the air. At the end of the coconut grove, Bee paused.

'See you,' the doctor said. 'I'll bring the Anti-Par Kamala wanted for the child. We can't have her getting worms just as they are leaving! I'll bring it tomorrow.'

Bee nodded and raised a hand.

Then he turned and slipped through the trees, disappearing the way he had come, hurrying soundlessly down the hill.

When he got back to the house, he went looking for Kamala.

'I'm going into town this morning,' he said. 'I won't be long. Where is everyone?'

Kamala put her finger to her lips. She was still a little cross with Bee.

'Alice is asleep and May has gone to work.'

She looked over her shoulder in the direction of Sita's room and lowered her voice.

'I think she's gone back to bed, too. Honestly,' she added, 'why didn't you tell me there was catch?'

It was the word they used whenever they hid someone. There had been no one to hide for months.

'I didn't want to worry you.'

'Hah! Why do you want to go to town, then? That worries me!'

'I want to show my face a little. I'll be back soon.'

In the town Bee found that the army had set up posts everywhere and were carrying out random identity checks. The outdoor fish and vegetable market was closed and Main Street was subdued. Bee went over to Talliman's and bought some arrack. The shopkeeper serving him raised his eyebrows. He knew Mr Fonseka as the man who only drank the best whisky.

'I haven't been to the Colombo shop for a while,' Bee explained.

The shopkeeper nodded. He knew all about Sita's baby. He thought Mr Fonseka looked worn out.

'With these curfews, it's become impossible to travel and be back in time for nightfall, sir,' he agreed.

Life was very difficult these days. The shopkeeper looked with pity at Bee. No doubt Mr Fonseka was still grieving over his daughter's miscarriage. Did he know about the shooting in the town? Bee shook his head and asked for an ounce of tobacco.

'Well, the army had a tip-off about some Tamils,' the shopkeeper told him, leaning confidently over the counter. '*Anay!* One of them was a ring-leader behind those bombings in Colombo, you know. All those poor innocent people! He was responsible for killing them. There's a rumour the army caught one of the group and shot him dead close to the railway line. But there's another dog at large. They wounded him on Wednesday, so hopefully he won't go far. It won't be long before he's caught too. They should all go back to Jaffna,' he said. 'Best for everyone, no?'

Bee paid for his arrack and his pipe tobacco.

'How long are the army staying, d'you think?' he asked.

'I don't know, sir. Probably until they find the last man. Although I think he's escaped. Surely they would have caught him by now, if he were still in the town. This is not a big place.'

Bee nodded and picked up his purchases.

'Don't worry, as soon as they've gone, the curfew will be lifted and you'll be able to go to Colombo for the whisky!' the shopkeeper laughed, his face brightening.

By the time Alice woke again the sun was high in the sky and Kunal had plotted her horoscope on a thin sheet of cake paper the servant had brought for him. When he was younger he had been renowned for his accuracy at drawing up these charts. It had been a lucrative sideline, providing extra cash in addition to his teaching. He had not drawn a horoscope for a long time. Now an inability to sleep coupled with gratitude made him want to do it for this child. Kunal had barely known either of Bee's daughters. Occasionally, in the past, when he called at the house he had come across them, going about their business, preoccupied with their own lives; but after he had left for Colombo twelve years ago, he had not seen them again. When he heard the rumours that Sita had married a Tamil man he alone had been unsurprised. Sita had always been the idealist in the family. Like her father, Kunal had thought. Even in the early days when she had been young Kunal had had the feeling that Sita's life would not be easy. She had been a beautiful girl then, but stubborn in a quiet Singhala way. People had thought her shy. Only Kunal had sensed a determination underlying everything she did. Now that she and the child were leaving, Kunal was aware of another anguish in the house. So he asked Kamala to tell him Alice's birth hour in order to plot her future, in the hope of giving them a little comfort. But when he had drawn up the horoscope he was no further forward. Alice was a gentle loving child, he told Kamala, who smiled and nodded in acknowledgement. She liked eating meat. The servant woman sneaked in to listen, nodding her approval. This horoscope should have been plotted long ago. She would grow into a beautiful woman, Kunal told them. And marry young. All this he could see. But he was puzzled by some obstruction, a blockage that presented itself with no clear explanation. Perhaps it was his calculations that were wrong, but the child would not use her strengths in the way she should. Perhaps it was the fever he was running, thought Kunal, confused, for he could not see clearly beyond this opaqueness.

'Never mind,' Kamala said quickly.

She felt guilty. Bee hated horoscopes, but, she comforted herself, if Kunal thought Alice would marry early, nothing much could go wrong. She would not be alone in a strange country.

The servant went to fetch some coriander tea. Kunal's eyes were shining too brightly for Kamala's liking. Hearing footsteps, she hastily put the horoscope into the pocket of her housecoat. But it was Alice and not Bee who came in.

'I'll look after him,' she told her grandmother. 'Mama wants to talk to you.'

'Only a few minutes,' Kamala said warningly. 'You mustn't wear him out.'

'Little missy,' the servant asked, smiling, 'come, I'll bathe you.'

'Not yet,' Alice said firmly.

She sat gingerly on the edge of Kunal's bed. She wanted to talk to him about last night, which, in the light of day, had taken on the aspect of a dream. Last night Alice had felt different. As she had waited for her grandfather to return, she had felt that what she was doing might make up for the terrible thing she had wished on the baby. No one had ever trusted her in this way before; no one had relied on her. Kunal, slumped beside the bowl of blood, had made a powerful impression on her. She wanted to ask him about his friend and about his sister and her husband, Janake's uncle. Janake was the one friend she had who was always kind to her. It had not occurred to her that he too might have had bad things in his life. It had not occurred to her because Janake was always laughing, always happy. Janake's life, now she thought about it, was charmed and quite unlike her own. She wanted to talk to Kunal and find out how it was Janake was always happy.

'I don't go there too often,' Kunal said faintly. 'I don't want to cause the boy and his mother any more trouble than they've already had to endure. You know Janake's clever; he should be at school. Since his father was killed he's been going out with the fishermen, doing odd jobs, helping his mother. It's a great shame, but the locals have spread all sorts of rumours about his father. All because my sister came from Jaffna. So stupid!'

Alice was surprised. She hadn't taken much notice of Janake's home before. He was simply her friend who always lived near the Sea House and sometimes played with her. That was all.

'Your grandfather has been very good to that family. He's the only one who takes any notice of them. He doesn't care what people think, you see, Alice. Your grandpa Bee is like that; he helps *everyone*. Now he's going to get me to Jaffna somehow.'

'What will you do in Jaffna?'

'I'll be amongst my own people,' Kunal said softly. 'After all, it is my spiritual home. And home is always where we want to be in the end. There is nothing to beat it.'

His voice tailed off. He had closed his eyes. Alice waited. Hoping he might go on, wanting to know more about Jaffna, but Kunal had dozed off. The servant woman, hovering anxiously outside the door, beckoned to her to come out. She disapproved of Kunal sleeping in the room that had been meant for the bride. It was an ill omen to put this broken man in it. But as always, no one took her advice.

Dinner that night was later than usual. They were all present, even Sita. The servant had been wrapping wedding cake all day, for Ceylon wedding cake needed to mature for at least a month before it was ready to be served. Only after that did she make her special mulligatawny for Kunal. When May returned from school Bee took her aside. She had left too early for him to tell her the full story. Did she mind that Kunal was sleeping in the annexe? May did not mind. While they were eating the doctor arrived, by the back door.

'Don't get up,' he said, when Kamala tried to clear a space for him. 'No, no, thank you, I've eaten. I'll just take a look at the patient.'

He smiled, looking around at their anxious faces.

'It's like the old days,' he said. 'Seeing you all together.'

And he went in to see Kunal.

After he dressed the wound and had given Kunal something for the fever, the doctor paused. He had a slight suspicion that an infection had set in.

'I'll know by tomorrow,' he told Bee privately. 'Give him plenty of liquids, but no more whisky.'

From the expression on the doctor's face, Kamala suspected that things were serious. The wedding was uppermost in her mind. What if Kunal were to become really ill? How could they have guests with a fugitive in the house?

'We'll worry about that when it happens,' Bee told her impatiently.

'He'll have to leave,' Kamala warned. 'He can't stay here if that happens.'

'There's plenty of time,' Bee told her calmly. 'He'll be on his way to Jaffna by then, you'll see. Stop worrying.'

Kamala was annoyed. Throughout their married life she had accepted all her husband's causes. Some of them had led to complications, some even flirted with danger. She had always supported Bee, but this time was different; this time she was putting her foot down. She was determined that May should have a decent wedding.

'I'm very sorry for him,' she told her husband firmly, 'but he *must* be gone by her wedding day.'

Bee opened his mouth to argue and then he stopped. Through the half-opened door of Kunal's room they could both hear voices. Bee raised an eyebrow enquiringly. Kamala shook her head in warning. Sita was talking to Kunal.

Sita had been in her room all day. She had slept for most of it and then Alice had woken her for dinner.

'I don't want any. Tell Granny I'll eat later.'

'Why don't you get up?' Alice had asked, and when Sita remained silent she had gone on to tell her mother that Kunal was in the annexe next door. Sita hadn't cared. She had gathered from something her mother had said when she had visited her that there was a fugitive in the house. It did not surprise Sita. Her father was always doing crazy things.

'He's sick,' Alice said, looking solemn.

Sita glanced at her daughter. The child needed her hair cutting. Her fringe had grown over her eyes again.

'Tell Granny to cut your fringe,' she said listlessly.

'Mama, will you?'

Sita ignored her daughter's forlorn tone of voice.

'Will you?'

'I'm too exhausted,' she said, ignoring the desire to cry. 'Ask Granny.'

And she turned her face to the wall, willing Alice to leave. Pushing her guilt away, she waited. She must have dozed off again because when she woke it was to the sound of voices in the annexe. Alice had left the room and the sky was now a deep dusky blue. Soon it would be dark. Suddenly she heard an unearthly scream. Sita sat bolt upright in bed. She broke out into a cold sweat. The sound triggered something terrible within her. It was in this way that she too had screamed. Only in my case, thought Sita wildly, it was in the middle of the night and I was alone. Opening the door, she listened. The house was silent. She was about to close the bedroom door when Kunal screamed again. Sita burst into tears and ran out into the garden. She felt as though her heart would explode.

Standing under the mango tree she rubbed her face, trying to make sense of her tears. For the two weeks since her return home she had felt, without caring very much, her parents' concern for her. Colombo and Stanley's departure had receded from her thoughts. All she felt was the constant bottomless pit of tiredness. Nothing else. Since she no longer had to get up each morning to take Alice to school, it was easier to stay in bed, letting the hours run on unnoticed. Each day her sojourn in the bedroom had become longer. Each day she blotted out her parents' anxious looks, staring out to sea, reflecting on the direction her life had taken. May left early every morning for school. Then in the evenings when she had finished her marking Namil usually visited and Sita was forced to listen to their voices, like small sleepy birds, emerging from the garden. Unable to bear this either, she retreated even further into her shell. Today had been no different. But now the scream had jolted her. For the first time in weeks, standing in the garden, out of sight from her parents, she heard the faint beating of her own heart. Wiping her face with the edge of her sari she cautiously made her way back into the house and headed towards the annexe. She could hear her father on the front verandah, talking to the doctor. Hardly aware of what she did, she opened the door of Kunal's room and went in.

Kunal had been silent all day, drifting in and out of consciousness. Apart from the brief conversation with Alice that morning, he had not registered anyone. Bee had visited him and sat for an hour and Kamala had brought him food and washed his face several times, but he had not noticed. The doctor, examining his wound, had woken in him a storm of pain. The doctor had tried talking to him but he had no idea what was said. When his door opened for the second time he thought he recognised Bee.

'Can I have some water?' he asked in Singhalese.

When he had finished drinking he turned towards the light from the window, his eyes disorientated by the fever.

'You have been so good to me, Headmaster,' he said in English. 'I'm afraid of being in your way. I shall leave for Jaffna in the morning.'

In spite of herself, Sita was shocked. This man was very sick. Sweat was pouring down his face and his eyes were bloodshot. She took the towel beside the bed and wiped his face. She pushed his hair back. Then she lifted him up a little and held a glass of water to his lips, noticing how they stayed pressed against the glass so that he might feel its lingering coolness. When he lay down again she saw the wetness remaining on his cracked dry lips.

'I've been talking to your granddaughter,' Kunal said. 'She is a child with an uncommon sensitivity.'

He spoke in Tamil. Only in Tamil did he have the ability to express those things dear to him. A lifetime of learning what was expected of him, English, Singhalese, could not do for him what his mother tongue did. Love, he thought, sorrow, every emotion learnt at his mother's knees could only be expressed in Tamil. It was the language of his heart. Sita felt her eyes fill with tears. She understood Tamil.

'I am Sita,' she said hoarsely. 'Do you remember me?'

An immense darkness had descended. The canopy of stars, acquiescent and soft, were beginning to puncture the sky. Somewhere out of sight the sea breathed heavily and the room filled up with its echoes. He was looking at her now, without surprise.

'Sita!' he said. 'The beautiful Sita! Of course I remember you. Today I saw you in her face,' he said quietly. 'You know, perhaps at this moment it isn't much, just a small pin-prick of light, she is so young, but wait …'

He fell silent, again. It had begun to rain, long fingers drumming on the roof, drowning the moon in the sea.

But after all, what does my suffering amount to? thought Sita. Given the thousands of Tamils who are suffering daily.

'Not any more,' she told him, her face twisting into a smile. 'Those days are over. It must have been my karma.'

The rain continued, lightly.

'You mustn't worry,' Kunal continued, still in Tamil, as though they had been talking for hours. 'All of it will grow in her, *you* will grow within her as she matures. I saw it. Today.'

He did not talk of the other things he had seen, the obstructions that would get in the way of a simple life.

'She will go far, far,' he told Sita, certain. 'Wait and see.'

'My baby ...' Sita began, but she could not go on.

Kunal had closed his eyes. When they stayed closed for a sufficient time, Sita tiptoed out.

By Saturday morning Kunal's condition was no better. Bee, Kamala and Sita, much to everyone's surprise, had taken turns sitting up with him all of Friday night. The doctor arrived, dodging the curfew to look at the leg with what seemed to be a detached air of melancholy. Kunal moaned softly, thrashing about on the bed. He wanted the bandage off. It was too tight. He was too hot; he could not get comfortable. The doctor touched the swollen leg gently. The bandage was caked with blood again. Then without warning and with unexpected force, he ripped the gauze off. Sita, standing beside Kunal, holding his hand, saw the flesh rise savagely up, refusing to be parted from the bandage, clinging for a moment before abruptly letting go of it. She saw it break open again, freshly. Then she saw blood gush out. Kunal screamed and Sita felt a wave of horror and nausea wash over her. The doctor placed the stinging antiseptic swab down on the leg and Kunal cried out. The servant woman appeared with fresh water and the doctor began to clean the wound. When he had finished, he gave Kunal a shot of painkiller. Then the doctor went outside to talk to Bee, leaving Sita to instruct the servant woman on the clearing up.

When it was done and Kunal had begun to drift back to sleep, Sita too went outside. It was very early. May and Alice were still sleeping.

'What can I do to help?' Sita asked quietly.

She was standing against the door and looked very pale. Startled, Bee and the doctor turned round. They had not seen her standing in the shadows.

'Sit with him,' the doctor said quickly, before Bee could speak. 'Stop him thrashing about. I'm afraid for the leg,' he told them in a low voice. 'I'm afraid of gangrene.'

Kamala, coming out with a pot of tea in her hand, gasped.

'Ayio! No!'

The doctor nodded grimly. He knew that the next twenty-four hours would decide things one way or the other and that it was no use contemplating the hospital.

'Wait,' he told them. 'Just a little. Don't worry, yet. I'll be back this evening. Give him some *cothemalli* if he wakes. He must drink plenty of fluids.'

'I'll make some now,' Sita said.

She tightened the belt of her housecoat and headed for the kitchen. Kamala looked after her daughter, astonished. The doctor nodded.

'Good,' he agreed heartily.

'Tell Alice when she wakes I'll take her to the beach,' Bee told Kamala abruptly. Then he escorted the doctor out of the house.

In the kitchen Sita watched the *cothemalli* tea bubble up. The light outside was achingly beautiful and the sea was flooded with it. When the tea was ready she went in to Kunal who now lay in a transparent sac of pain. Heat was radiating from him. Sita sat down, letting him sip the tea, quietly waiting until his confused delirium subsided a little. She understood everything about this hot crumpled bed of pain. Kunal's face looked grey and exhausted as he dipped in and out of consciousness. She did not know how long she sat with him. Now and again she stood up and, in the defused light coming in through the shutters, wiped his face. He was handsome. She remembered him only slightly from her younger days, even though she must have seen him quite often. It interested her to see that looking down on a person's face was different from looking at them on eye level. All his vulnerability fell open like the pages of a book when she stood over him. Had she appeared this way to the nurse on that night? she wondered. All morning, sitting with the coriander tea, waiting for Kunal to sip it, Sita went over the events of her own night of suffering with a calm detachment she had not possessed before. At some point she slipped out into the kitchen to fetch some freshly squeezed orange juice. When she returned his eyes were open and he was staring at her through a thick gauze of pain.

'You are not very old,' Kunal mumbled suddenly.

Sita held the glass of liquid to his lips.

'What happened to you can only happen to a woman who is still young. Do you know that? Your husband is young; *you* are still strong. There will be a life beyond this tragedy; perhaps even beyond this island. Don't let this hurt get in your way. They will have won if that happens.'

Sita stared at him. No one had dared to talk to her in this way. Kunal was looking up at her with eyes that burned with a fever, and yet he was smiling. Then slowly, haltingly, hardly aware of doing so, she told him how it was for her, with the love for her dead child trapped within her, inescapably. How day by day, moment by moment, she kept trying to save the child, remove it from harm's way. And how each time she failed, it became important that she try again. Because maybe, on another occasion, she might succeed. It had become an enactment, she told Kunal, like the ritual of washing her hands before eating. Something she no longer thought about or had any control over. She continued talking to Kunal in this way even though he had gone back to sleep. Speaking quickly as if she needed to get the words out before she was interrupted, before her mother or her father or even the servant woman came in, Sita found she could not stop. For she was certain now that she would never speak of these things to another living person again.

Kunal dipped in and out of consciousness for most of that day and the next. The doctor came and went. He spoke to them in whispers. Two men had been arrested in the town and then released again.

The army were doing a house-to-house search further up the hill. They would have to be ready to hide Kunal in the coconut grove. It would be a gamble, but it was better than them being caught harbouring a Tamil. Bee's jaw was tight with anger.

'Oh my God!' Kamala cried. 'What shall we do?'

'There is nothing else you can do,' the doctor said. 'Not with all your family in the house. But don't panic yet. It might not come to that.'

On Monday while Sita was sitting with Kunal once more, Bee took Alice to the village beyond the town. It was a place he often visited in order to paint. The view of the sea was unexpected and lovely here, fringed by coconut palms and with only a few picturesque fishermen's huts in sight. The doctor had told them to be as normal as they could. So he took his painting things and Alice took her bicycle.

'We'll be gone about an hour,' he told Kamala.

It was late afternoon. The sun had moved some way across the sky. There had been torrential rain earlier that had ceased as abruptly as it had started and now the air was filled with a pearly glow. They walked across the beach on the unmarked sand, both unusually silent, preoccupied with their own thoughts. Bee bent down and picked a small piece of transparent aquamarine sea glass that had caught his eye; pebble-shaped, smoothened by the sea.

'Look,' he said, giving it to Alice, 'all its edges have vanished.'

Alice held the glass up to the light and the horizon showed through it in a dark line. She put it in the pocket of her dress and they walked on. As they approached the hamlet they passed a pile of beach debris. Dead fish and rotting driftwood and old rags, piled into a mound, ready to burn. And beside it, on the sand, a breadfruit lay open; its innards like vomit on the sand. A little further on they passed a roadside shrine and then the huts came into view.

'Can I wait here with Janake?' Alice asked.

A group of children, including Janake, were playing beside the three large rocks. They were the same children she had seen on her birthday from her grandparents' garden.

'I shan't be long,' Bee said. 'I just want to talk to Janake's mother.'

The late-afternoon sun drenched the water with discs of light and the rocks appeared starkly defined against the sky. Such was the complexity and confusion of Alice's thoughts that she barely noticed the children had turned and were looking at her. She could not see, as Bee might have done, had he glanced up from his conversation, that she stood on the brink of an important discovery. That the difference between herself and the group of children playing in the water was slowly becoming clearer. Standing beside the beach debris, with its coconut husks and its rotten fruit, with the smell of sea and weeds all around, Alice watched the little group and in particular Janake as they played. Here they were again, lithely jumping in and out of the shallows, as Janake's mother listened to news of her relative. And here was Janake, looking his usual happy self. A chisel of loneliness shot through her. She watched for a moment longer, taking in a scene that was vanishing even as she looked, and was saddened without knowing quite why. Janake suddenly looked up. Detaching himself from the group with a shout of welcome, he ran towards her.

'You've come to join us? We're catching the small crabs.'

She stared. Since Jennifer had stopped being her friend no other child except Janake had wanted to know her. Esther Harris did not count. Esther was almost a grown-up. Eagerly, Alice kicked off her sandals as Janake grabbed her hand tightly. He was bigger than her, thin and wiry, and burnt by the constant exposure to the sun.

'Quickly, before the next wave.'

The children had found a group of crabs nestling in a hollowed-out bowl of sand close to the rocks. Every time a wave crashed against the rocks, the bowl got larger and the crabs tried harder to scramble up on to the beach.

'Where've you been?' Janake shouted above the roar of the sea.

'I've been busy,' Alice said, not knowing how much to tell him.

Janake grinned as though he knew all about it.

'Come on,' he said. 'Get in the water.'

The children were picking up the crabs and putting them into a bucket, but when the bucket became full Janake ordered them to throw the crabs back into the sea. He spoke in Singhalese and was clearly the group leader. After some time the other children grew bored and wandered off. Janake turned to Alice as another wave hit him. The water had soaked his hair and beads of sea-spray shone on his bare chest. He stopped in mid-laugh.

'I wish you weren't going overseas,' he shouted abruptly.

'I don't want to,' Alice shouted back. 'I hate England.'

She realised she had said something she meant. Janake was looking at her with the strangest expression on his face.

'Don't go,' he said, above the roar of the ocean.

'There's nothing here for us,' she cried, sounding like her mother.

He said no more and the waves washed and swirled around their feet.

'It's your aunt's wedding soon, isn't it?' he said finally.

'Yes.'

Janake nodded. He would be going with the fishermen to catch the fish.

'Will you come back?' he asked after a moment.

'I want to,' Alice said, realising all in a rush, with a closing up of the gap in her knowledge, that what she wanted did not always happen.

She had the strangest feeling of standing at the edge of a beach that dropped steeply a hundred fathoms. But Janake was nodding again. He produced a small penknife from his pocket and showed it to her.

'In that case,' he said, 'you must carve your name on the rocks. Over there –' he pointed, grinning at her, his good mood restored.

His teeth gleamed white. Overhead the seagulls were screaming.

'Let's walk there, it's not deep. I'll help you. Then you *will* come back. Because it's a magic trick!'

6

THEY DOCKED IN PIRAEUS AT FIVE THIRTY in the morning on the twenty-first of April. Freak, icy winds from the sea swept across Athens. Stepping ashore, Stanley caught his first glimpse of the Parthenon. To his astonishment there was snow on the mountains. Real snow, he thought, disbelievingly, like the snow in Alice's picture books. His tropical suit was rendered useless in a moment; the wind cut straight through to his flesh as though he wore nothing. He sat timidly in a café and wrote a postcard to his daughter but he had no idea how to describe any of it. The temperature had to be experienced to be believed. Should he say, it was cold like an ice cube? No, he thought, that wouldn't do, she would simply think of the *refreshing* coolness of ice cubes, though there was nothing either refreshing or comfortable about this. It made him want to rush back to the hotel.

During the two weeks of the voyage Stanley had made friends with a Swedish girl on the deck above him. What else could I do when we're all stuck together? he asked himself defensively. Of course I had to talk to her. When they arrived in Athens she had been given a room next to his in the hotel and this morning they had made a tentative arrangement to meet at some point. Stanley glanced at his watch. He felt as though Sita was watching him. The waiter brought him his coffee. It was in a cup so small that he wondered if he had been cheated, but when he looked around there were others drinking out of tiny cups.

It tasted bitter and too hot. Stanley stirred two sugar lumps in it wondering what to write.

The coffee is bitter, he wrote. *But not expensive,* he added, knowing Sita would read the postcard. He didn't want her to think he was wasting money.

One of the engines caught fire. The company have put us in a hotel, which is how I came to buy this postcard. We will probably be here for at least another week. And in the end it will probably take much longer than twenty-one days to reach England.

He paused, staring outside at the view. All around people were speaking in a language he had never heard before. It gave Stanley an extraordinary thrill, as if he was at last in the real world, to hear a language that was neither Tamil, Singhalese nor English. An ancient language, with no sinister undertones attached. The sun fell weightless and golden on the Parthenon. In spite of his precarious position, here in semi-penniless limbo, Stanley felt weightless too. All the years of struggling against prejudice, the desperate ways in which he had tried first to hide his Tamilness and later, to flaunt it defiantly, were falling away from him. Like dead skin, he thought. He stared at the Parthenon, willing it to fix itself on his mind forever. In case he never came back. It staggered him to see the remains of a civilisation that had vanished exactly in the same way as the ancient Ceylonese city of Polonnaruva. He felt he was living a dream. The ground beneath him moved as if he was still on the ship and he thought of the Swedish woman again. It had amused her to see him brace himself against the cold.

'You should buy some proper clothes,' she advised, trying not to laugh. 'Not this paper suit!'

Stanley was too embarrassed to tell her that the clothes he was wearing had cost him a whole month's salary. There were many things he was finding difficult to articulate. And perversely, there were other issues that had mysteriously begun to matter less, people who already were beginning to fade. His wife's face, for instance. Stanley frowned.

Colombo seems already a long way away, he wrote hurriedly.

He paused, trying to imagine the postman, wheeling his bicycle slowly up Mount Lavinia Hill in the burning heat, sweat glistening on his face, delivering his postcard to the Sea House, but try as he might the sense of scorching heat eluded Stanley. Instead, the face of the Swedish woman swam back into view.

In about a week we will be entering the Bay of Biscay, he wrote. *Everyone is worried because the purser says it can be stormy there. I don't want to be seasick again. Please give Mama my love and tell her I will write as soon as I get to England.*

'Will you come and see the rock later, Aunty May?' Alice asked.

They were in the garden. The doctor had been summoned and was having a private conversation with Bee and Kamala. He had been talking to them for ages. Kunal, it seemed, was much worse. Alice had been sent out into the garden to pick the mangoes that had fallen and were not bruised. May followed behind with a basket but she kept looking nervously back at the house.

'What does it say?' May asked.

She sounded distracted.

'*Alice Fonseka, Age 10, Mount Lavinia, Sri Lanka, Asia, The World, The Universe.* "The Universe" isn't very clear,' Alice said regretfully.

Even though Janake had gone over the words with his penknife the rocks had been hard to mark. They had got soaked.

'Of course, darling,' May said. 'We'll look at it tomorrow.'

The servant woman was sweeping the verandah, collecting the dead hibiscus flowers that the day's rain had reduced to a pulp. As a result of the monsoon the garden had turned virulent. The ground was teeming with insects. There were spiders and lizards, ants and beetles all rushing to feast on the water-drenched fruit and the vegetation littering the ground. A snake slithered past and disappeared in a flash into the undergrowth. No one saw it. May, holding her sari high above the wet grass, dodged the fruit bats that nose-dived, fighter pilot style, in and out of the roof. A few crows protested loudly at the encroaching darkness while the air of waiting increased to a fever pitch. Eventually Kamala called the servant woman in and at that May stopped what she was doing and went inside, carrying the basket now filled with mangoes. They gave off a scent like no other. The doctor, deep in conversation with Bee and Kamala, nodded. Then he strode into the annexe.

'Come,' Kamala told Alice, taking her hand. 'Now we must wash these mangoes.'

Kamala was looking drawn.

'I'm going to the studio,' Bee said. 'I'll be back in a moment.'

And he disappeared. A moment later the door of the annexe opened and Sita let herself out.

The room in which Kunal lay was in darkness. The doctor stood looking quietly down at him. Slow, muffled garden sounds crept in through the shutters as the doctor walked slowly over and opened them slightly. All the doctor's gestures were like that: slow and very quiet.

'Are you awake?' he asked. 'Can you hear me?'

Kunal opened his eyes. He felt very tired with the feeling that he had been struggling for a long time. The effort was suddenly too much. He tried to smile politely, but his lips were cracked and swollen and nothing happened. All he wanted to do was sleep. He had a vague sense that Sita had been reading to him. A book lay on the chair beside his bed. The doctor picked it up and sat down. Then in the same, quiet, soothing way, he began to speak. He spoke softly and Kunal struggled to understand what he was saying. One word repeated itself.

'Hospital?' Kunal asked, not understanding.

'You should be there now,' the doctor went on saying very gently and slowly. 'But if we admit you, the army will take you. You will not be seen again.'

His voice dipped in and out of focus like the headlights of a car. He too seemed to be struggling with his own words.

'You want me to leave?' Kunal said, understanding.

He had been waiting to be turned out. He knew what danger he was putting this family in. I can hide in the coconut grove, he thought, until the morning at least. He must have spoken out loud because he saw the doctor shake his head.

'No,' the doctor said slowly. In the pale honeyed light from the lamp his face looked drawn. 'This isn't what I'm talking about.'

His voice was down to a whisper. It came from a long way off with infinite kindness.

'I find it difficult to tell you,' he said.

Still Kunal did not understand.

'Probably you would have to have the leg off anyway. Possibly in brutal circumstances. The gangrene has taken hold. I will bring the surgeon from the hospital. He can be here by tomorrow. It will take us that long to get the morphine. We will make sure you don't feel anything during the operation.'

Kunal startled. Terror leapt into his mouth like a fish. It slithered and swam up his throat. It filled his lungs and his nose, stopping him from breathing. He could not understand what steps he had taken to get to this point. And then the horror of what he was faced with, the terrible truth, hit him like a wave. He thought he heard himself crying out. His breath was coming in short bursts. The doctor's face blurred and changed. His mouth was distorted, the words coming from it slowed.

'No!' Kunal screamed. 'No! No! Please, no!'

When he had finished writing his postcard, Stanley stood up and paid for the coffee.

'Coffee no good?' the waiter asked.

Stanley smiled and shook his head. Then he paid for it with some of his precious drachmas and made his way back to the hotel. He would have to get a stamp. On the way back he stopped several times. Each time he caught a glimpse of the Parthenon from a different angle. The cold had worsened to such a degree that he couldn't stop shivering. He took a wrong turning then tried to retrace his footsteps but turned into a blind alley instead. There was a barber's shop on the corner; he was sure it hadn't been there before. Someone spoke to him but he didn't understand what they were saying.

'Hotel Patria?' he asked, but then didn't understand the reply.

This is ridiculous, he thought. If I can find the Parthenon then I'll be able to find the hotel. But the Parthenon was nowhere in sight. He turned left. Perhaps he could find the docks and the seafront. The cold had numbed his hands. People were wearing gloves, he noticed. As he walked down towards what he hoped was the seafront, he noticed a small restaurant with an inviting array of meat on sticks and a curious flatbread rather like a roti. It made his mouth water. There were bottles of wine in the window. He was hungry and wondered if he could afford to stop for something to eat. But all he had was a little Greek money and a traveller's cheque. Hesitatingly he opened the door and went in. The place was empty. Stanley stood, uncertain as to what he might do next. Somewhere in the nether regions, behind a beaded curtain, a radio droned endlessly. He couldn't understand a word.

'Hey!' he called out tentatively. 'Hello!'

There was no reply. He looked at his watch. It was almost midday. He had told the Swedish girl, Marianna, that he would meet her for lunch. Making a small sound of impatience he walked out of the restaurant. But things outside were no better. To his utter amazement the sun had vanished. The sky had taken on a milky, greyish tone and the small, regular dots of wetness falling on his face were not rain but snow. As for the Parthenon, that might very well have existed in his imagination only. There was no sign of it whatsoever. Grimly, fearing he would die in this place, unable to stand the cold any longer, he went in search of a shop. In order to buy a map and find the Hotel Patria.

Sita, washing the mud-splattered mangoes, listened to the house breathe. It was late. The doctor, having talked to Kunal, having given him something to help him sleep, had left. Alice was in bed and Bee was back in his studio. Sita could hear Kamala out in the garden light-ing joss sticks at the house shrine. Both Kamala and May had been praying beside the old statue of Lord Buddha for an hour. They had prayed for Kunal and the ordeal that lay ahead, so that he might have strength to bear those misfortunes he had brought into his life. They had prayed his karma might be good in his next birth. After that, Sita suspected, they would have prayed for May's forthcoming wedding, and for her own impending journey. Sita had not joined in the prayers to the Buddha. Her prayers, she knew from past experience, would not be answered. Eventually she heard May going to bed. Their mother was still praying and Sita waited patiently, counting the mangoes and thinking. Earlier that evening, when she had first heard the word 'amputation' she told the doctor instantly that she would help as much as she could during the operation. She would help Kunal to let go of what belonged to him. The doctor was relieved. The capacity of the human heart for bravery never failed to surprise him and he accepted Sita's offer gratefully. Kamala and Bee, he told her, would be best employed fending off any unwanted visitors and keeping the child out of the way.

'You will make a perfect nurse,' he had told her, smiling sadly.

Sita finished wiping the mangoes. Half an hour later, Kamala came in and the two women began cleaning. They started with the kitchen. By tomorrow morning they would have worked their way across the house, leaving it spotless. By the time the surgeon arrived, the annexe and Kunal's room would be ready. Putting a kettle of water to boil, listening to the rhythm of the rain and her mother's instructions, for the first time in many weeks Sita felt a strange, youthful energy fill her troubled mind.

It rained all that night. Great swathes of water washed everything. Towards midnight Sita insisted Kamala went to bed.

'We've nearly finished,' she told her mother, still with a curious sense of well-being about her. 'You're exhausted. Go to bed. I'm not tired, yet. I can do this last bit by myself.'

Knowing her daughter wanted to be alone, reluctantly, Kamala went. Outside the whole world was veiled in rain. Sita worked on. It was well after midnight before the cleaning was finished. The kitchen had become an oasis of order. No one had cleaned it in this way for years. Fully awake, Sita wandered through the sleeping house breathing in the fresh smells of rain and sea air. She felt exhilarated. Walking quietly through the rooms she had the distinct feeling of a momentous change going on within her. She felt her home, with all its well loved books, its blue-and-white Portuguese plates and carved ebony elephants was imbued with an air of loveliness she had never noticed before. It was as though she were seeing the place for the very last time. And yet, she thought, at any moment, memory itself might fail her, wiping out this place she had called home. Why had she not treasured it more?

'Kunal,' she said softly to herself.

She had not said his name out loud before. He was teaching her to look, she thought.

For the first time in days she thought of Stanley. He seemed to have disappeared from her mind completely, she saw, becoming part of a betrayal she was trying to forget. The child they had lost had belonged to them both, but she had hardly spoken of what happened with Stanley. Yesterday afternoon, while she sat with Kunal in the hours before they had been told of his impending loss, Sita had felt her tongue loosen once again. To distract him she had brought out her shoebox and showed him the tiny garments that had never been worn. He had watched her silently.

'You still have Alice,' he said finally, as she closed the lid of the box.

But Sita had shaken her head. There were dead things buried within her, leaving no room for Alice, she told him. It wasn't love that was missing. Simply energy to exercise that love.

'You mustn't say that,' Kunal had said feverishly. 'Don't underestimate your daughter's power over you.'

Running her hand across the clean scrubbed kitchen table, remembering the conversation, Sita paused. Kunal did not know yet; one leg did not make up for the loss of another. Yesterday afternoon, after she had closed her box, Kunal had been inclined to talk. His eyes were bright with the raging temperature they could not bring down.

'I have a story for you,' he said suddenly.

And he told her about his own family. His parents had lived in Trincomelee once, making a living in the sea.

'I did not want to be part of the fishing community,' he said. 'I was desperate to study and get to the university. But, as you know, when the British left, all education for the Tamils stopped.'

He paused and she gave him a drink.

'Your father was wonderful to me,' Kunal told her. 'He was the new headmaster at St Aloysius. When I went to him and told him my story he gave me the job on the strength of the unfinished qualifications. That was how I came to teach the fifth standard.'

Things were going according to plan, he told Sita. He sent regular money home even though he couldn't afford to see his parents often. There had been no prejudice in the school, Bee made certain of that. But then Kunal had fallen in love with a Singhalese girl.

'Just like you.'

He smiled at Sita, his face taking on a rumpled, blurred look. Sita wondered if he should try to sleep a little. They had married against her parents' wishes, Kunal told her, and after that he had been determined to get a transfer to Trincomelee. To be close to his own parents in a place where there were other Tamils. He wanted his young wife to have some relatives who cared about her.

'She was pregnant, you see.'

Bee had been wonderful. He promised to talk to a headmaster in Trincomelee, try to get Kunal a transfer. And in the end that's what happened.

'We arrived at the school-teacher's house one January day,' Kunal said. 'We were full of hope, ready to begin our new life.'

The house was small, just two rooms and a bathroom. But the garden was glorious. It was full of frangipani and tiger-striped lilies, he remembered. A paradise with brilliant blue kingfishers darting by the water and air that was clear and smelled of lilac.

'My wife was very happy. She had been afraid she would miss the sea, coming from the south. But, you know, in Trincomelee the sea is all around.'

So they had started their married life in earnest. Every day Kunal went to the school where he taught, returning late with piles of marking. His wife grew big with their child. His parents adored her and the small community they lived in welcomed them without prejudice. All was perfect. Until, that is, his wife went into premature labour.

'I had to borrow a car to drive to the nearest hospital, almost fifty miles away.'

Even that had not worried him unduly. It was what he had expected. The drive through the jungle was not hazardous. It wasn't a particularly dangerous road, there were no big cats, no elephants. But they had reckoned without the complications of the labour. The umbilical cord had wrapped itself around the baby's neck, strangling it. And his wife had bled to death.

He finished speaking and Sita hadn't known what to say. They sat for a long time without speaking, listening to the sound of the servant scraping coconut in the yard. Then Sita stood up and wiped Kunal's brow. He had fallen asleep again, exhausted by so much talking. Sita had sat on silently holding her shoebox until Kamala came in to relieve her. Later, when she heard about the amputation, she knew what she must do for Kunal.

By the time he got back to the hotel, Stanley was soaking and the snow was beginning to settle. If he hadn't been freezing, he might have enjoyed the sensation of walking through it but, as it was, all he wanted to do was get out of his clothes. He knocked on Marianna's door but there was no answer. Possibly she had got fed up with waiting for him and had gone out. He decided to order something to eat in his room and have a bath. His brother had told him that baths were the thing in England and as the ship only had showers this was his first experience of a bath. He ordered his food and turned the tap on. Outside the window the view was changing as though by magic under the snow. Stanley stared at it, mesmerised. He could hardly believe that he could be having such an adventure. In a few short days his world had been transformed like the street outside. Sita, Alice (the postcard to her lay soggily in his coat pocket), his in-laws, even his mother, had taken on the appearance of photographs in an old family album. Why, he wondered dreamily, had he ever thought marriage and a family was the answer?

He bathed. The water was soothing and wonderfully hot, wrinkling his skin, filling him with well-being. Then he drank the beer he had ordered and ate the thing called kebab, which was delicious, not at all like the bland food they were served on the ship. He decided to write a letter to Alice as well. It occurred to him that he would need different clothes if the weather was to remain this bad. Money, thought Stanley, that was all he wanted now. The sooner he got to London and his new job, the better. He turned his mind to the letter. Taking a sheet of hotel notepaper he began to write.

> *My dear daughter,*
> *I am writing this in my hotel here in Athens. What am I doing in Athens, you might wonder! Well, two nights ago there was a problem with the ship and we were forced to disembark while they mended it. You can tell Mama that the shipping liner is paying to put us up for a few nights with all expenses paid. Isn't that good? This morning I saw the Parthenon and later it began to snow. Yes, Alice, I could hardly believe it, either. It is fantastic being away from Ceylon at last. You are a very lucky girl to be coming to England. How many other children your age can have such a chance to start again? You have your dada to thank for that.*

Stanley paused, frowning. He was almost certain Bee would be shown the letter. He could imagine what Bee would say. Only now he was a safe distance from his father-in-law did Stanley realise how much he disliked him. Low-class Singhalese, he thought, with some satisfaction. Well, he would never see him again, thank God.

> *I have just had my first bath, he continued. Because I was so cold after walking in the snow, when I got back to the hotel I filled the bath with hot water and lay in it. It was wonderful. And I thought to myself, this is only Greece. Think what England will be like! Even more civilised. A Swedish passenger on the boat thought all the problems in Ceylon stupid and, I must say, from this distance they are stupid. The people there are full of ignorance and primitive ideas.*

He stopped. No point in writing all this to the child. She wouldn't understand and Bee would see it as a direct dig at him. Well, so what, thought Stanley defiantly. Do I care?

> *I shall have to stop now as I intend to go out and find a stamp to post this letter.*

He had no intention of going out in the blizzard that seemed to be gathering outside, but he was getting bored with the letter.

Tell Mama not to worry; I shall write again when I reach England.
  With love,
  Your loving father

There was a knock on his door as he finished sealing up the letter. It was Marianna. She held out a bottle and two glasses.

'Chin-chin,' she said, laughing. 'Where were you?'

Stanley stared at her. She was wearing a blouse through which he could see her bra very clearly.

'Aren't you cold?' he asked.

'What?' she laughed. 'Cold? No, this isn't cold!'

'It's snowing outside,' Stanley said, blinking.

'Oh Stanley, you are funny! This little bit of snow, it's nothing. If you want to see snow, you must come to Stockholm. I will take you skiing.'

Stanley continued to look at her foolishly.

'Until that time, if you let me into your room I have brought some vodka for us to drink.'

'Oh, yes, yes,' Stanley said. 'Sorry, come in. Of course.'

And he opened the door wide, showing her the room with its cosy bedside light and the turned-down bedcover on which he had been sprawling.

Anxiety stretched like a cello string across the house the next morning. Alice woke and heard it play itself out in a long slow series of notes. Kamala woke dreading the sounds the day would bring. A labourer working in the coconut grove was sawing dead wood. Sita woke after only a few hours' sleep, full of energy. The house seemed to have sandwiched its tension between two thick slices of silence. It was a glittering morning, the sort that followed heavy rain. The sea made little grumbling sea noises and the breeze flicked smartly through the waves, leaving small white pieces of foam in its wake like rubbish thrown from a ship. Already the day had an inevitable feel to it, thought Kamala, watching Alice come out of her room. The child has changed, she thought. She's quieter, more obedient of late. The kitchen was scrubbed clean. The house smelled of antiseptic and steam.

'Two egg hoppers and a swim?' her grandfather said, intercepting Alice on her way to the kitchen, sweeping her away from the annexe like a leaf caught by a sudden gust of wind. Her aunt May had gone to school and her mother seemed to have disappeared too.

'Your mama is helping the doctors with the operation,' said Bee firmly.

Alice glanced curiously in the direction of the closed door. Only silence issued from behind it and her grandfather was impatient to be gone, so off they went down the hill to the bottom of Station Road, waving at the two men in the army truck, even though Alice disliked the look of them. Leaving the house with its quiet control and its morphine-numb concentration and its two doctors, doing what they had to do. On this dazzling, sun-kissed, ordinary day during the last of the south-west monsoons.

The beach was as smooth as a newly ironed sheet, for these days the fishermen no longer dragged their nets over this stretch of sand. The army collected the best of their catch from further up the bay, close to the lighthouse. Alice's footprints marked the ground like musical notation as they went towards Janake's house where his mother was waiting for them with hot coconut oil in a blackened *chatti-pot*. Janake, having been out earlier with the fishermen, was now starving.

'You want to play by the rocks?' he asked Alice, grinning. 'After we finish eating?'

They stood outside the small lean-to kitchen licking their greasy fingers. Alice nodded, her mouth full. The egg hoppers were the best she had ever tasted. Janake's mother smiled indulgently at them both and offered them another one.

'No, not by the rocks,' Bee warned. 'Not today. There might be currents left over from last night's storms.'

They ate their hoppers and went looking for treasures that might have been washed up by the storm. Bee sat under the shade of the coconut tree on a little mound of sea-grass and began to draw the rib of a boat that had appeared from the next bay. The sea had thrown up all sorts of things.

'I want all this wood,' Alice told Janake.

He watched curiously as she made a small pile of scraps of wood on the beach.

'What are you going to do with it?'

Alice frowned and Janake let out a loud guffaw.

'You look just like Mr Fonseka,' he told her.

The roar of the sea drowned their voices. The wood was old and wet. It had small marks, little flecks of red and turquoise paint embedded in it. She couldn't explain why this excited her, or why it should conjure up images of this place. She wanted to invent something to do with the things no one had a use for but still were beautiful. She wanted to save these things from extinction.

'I'm going to make a ... thing,' she said vaguely.

Ideas lurked at the back of her mind. Janake nodded. He didn't question her further.

'I'm going to make something too,' he said, going off to collect debris of his own.

He returned with more wood.

'Did you see Kunal this morning?' he asked abruptly.

Alice shook her hair out of her eyes. She had just found an enormous shell at the water's edge and was busy examining it. It wasn't a shell from around here.

'That was probably washed up from some other country because of the storm,' Janake said, peering at it.

'The doctors are taking Kunal's leg off today,' Alice told him.

Seagulls screamed. The sky seemed endlessly deep, teeming with light. They stood looking at the seashell together, solemnly.

'What will it be like, d'you think?' Alice asked, cautiously. 'Being without a leg, Janake?'

Janake didn't know. He stood experimentally on one leg and watched the sea pull the sand all around his foot. There were millions of tiny broken shells littering the beach.

'Do you think,' Alice hesitated, 'they have taken it off yet?'

They stared pensively at the waves. Bee raised his head, checking they were safe from the currents. Then he too stared at the sea before continuing to paint.

'He will adapt,' Janake said confidently, sounding like a grown-up. 'He'll be like the dog that comes near our house. When he first lost his leg under the train we all thought he would die, but after some time,' he shrugged, 'he could run as fast as the other dogs on just three legs. After a while, you know, nothing matters.'

Alice thought of the dog running on its three legs. Maybe it *could* run as fast as the other dogs. But did it *feel* the same as them?

Time passed; the afternoon wore on and the light changed again. Bee looked at his watch. A man walked by selling freshly cut king coconut and they bought some and drank the cloudy, refreshing liquid straight out of the coconut. Janake's mother had invited them for rice and curry to save their having to go back up the hill for lunch. Small paper-thin clouds passed swiftly by. Bee watched a man gutting fish beside a catamaran; it must be over, surely, by now, he thought. The man's knife glinted in the sun. There was blood on it. He was working quickly, throwing out the guts on the rocks and packing the fish into flat circular baskets. Afterwards he balanced the baskets on his shoulders and went off up the beach, heading for the town, his cries of, '*malu, malu*', getting fainter the higher up Mount Lavinia Hill he climbed.

'Look,' Janake told Alice, as they waited for their lunch under the shade of a coconut palm. 'See this bottle. It's come from a ship. From out there,' he pointed at the rim of the sea, which, while they had been talking, had become dark and thunderous.

'You can send me a message in a bottle from the ship,' he said. 'You can throw it into the sea. I'll stand here and wait for it to come.'

Alice laughed, delighted. She would do that, she promised.

'And when you get to England,' Janake told her solemnly, 'when you send me your address, I'll write to you. I'll always write. Until you come back. Okay?'

'Okay.'

Janake's mother brought out lunch. She had a plate of rice for Mr Fonseka too, but he shook his head and asked for a glass of *vatura*, water, instead.

'I'm not hungry,' he said, re-lighting his pipe. 'Feed the children.'

He went back to watching the sea. We swim in this sea of time like small plankton, he thought, only occasionally looking beyond the surface and catch a glimpse of how vast the ocean is. Overhead a flock of seagulls stabbed the air with their beaks and swooped down on to the rocks.

They stayed on the beach all day until the blistering heat began to retreat slightly. At four o'clock Bee looked at his watch and began packing up his paints. He folded the large black umbrella and put away his brushes. Then he carefully placed his watercolours between two boards.

'Let's go, Alice,' he said. 'I think it's going to rain.'

Alice gathered up her wood. The pile was so enormous that Janake started to laugh.

'It's bigger than you,' he said. 'Why don't you leave some of it here and I'll bring it up later?'

They waved good-bye to Janake and set off up the hill. As they walked, the rain that had threatened on and off all day began to fall in large dusty drops. The house was bathed in an orange glow. They saw the sea reflected in its long French windows and as they walked in through the gate they felt the difference in the air. The tension had drained away and a layer of peace had settled like fine sea sand. There was still two hours to go before curfew. In the kitchen the women were busy cleaning the table. Alice watched the hospital doctor go quickly towards the back door without looking at anyone. She caught a glimpse of the towel he was carrying. It looked red and white and crumpled, and the doctor was trying to shield it from view. He disappeared through the open door and Alice felt a sharp draught of fear rush towards her. She was too startled to speak. When the hospital doctor returned he went over to the sink and began washing his hands. Alice had a brief glimpse of red water swirling and draining away before her grandmother took her by the shoulders and led her gently away. Alice waited for them to mention Kunal's leg, but nothing was said. It was as though whatever they had been doing all day was an embarrassment to them.

'Come, Putha,' Kamala said, 'I've sewn the sleeves on your bridesmaid dress. Let's see how it fits.'

She sounded strained and tired. Once again the grown-ups avoided each other's eyes.

'Go wash your hands first Alice,' Sita called quietly after them.

Sita's hair was dishevelled. She looked completely exhausted. Only her voice, harsh for so long, had changed and was unusually gentle. They heard the gate click shut and each one of them tensed. But it was only May hurrying in. She stood in the doorway where Bee and the doctors were saying good-bye.

'Aunty May?' Alice asked.

But May did not answer. She looked as though she had been crying. She began talking to her father in an agitated manner, gesticulating wildly, ignoring the doctors.

'Wait a minute,' Kamala said, and she too went out to talk to them.

Curiously, Alice wandered out. The doctors shook hands with everyone. They too looked exhausted. The hospital doctor would not see them again but their own doctor would return in the morning, to check the patient.

'What's happening?' Alice asked, but nobody answered. It was left to Kamala to detach herself from the group and usher Alice back into her sewing room.

May had vanished.

'Come, I want to shorten your dress a little.'

Alice didn't want to stand still. There were mysterious things going on she wanted to investigate.

'Just a minute, darling. Be a good girl, please,' Kamala pleaded, her mouth full of pins.

And then, as Alice continued to crane her neck in the direction of May, she added:

'The army have taken a Tamil boy out of Aunty May's class. It's upset her a lot. As if we needed any more things to upset us.'

That night Alice heard the story from May herself. Two army men, she told Alice, had taken the Tamil boy. Her aunt, Alice saw, was still very upset. The local policeman had brought the soldiers to the school, she said. They simply took the boy from her class.

'*Anay*, Alice! No one did anything to help him.'

The school disgusted her, May said.

'All the pupils kept their eyes down, too scared to protest. Even the staff, although they had come out into the corridor because of the noise, stood there and did absolutely nothing! Can you believe it? Spineless bastards!'

Only May had protested. She had tried to stop the men from taking the boy. He was just a child, she had begged.

'I told them he had done nothing wrong. He was the cleverest boy in the school; he wasn't interested in causing any trouble. But you know what, the policeman gave me a look and told me I'd better watch out and not make a fuss. Ayio! I didn't care, Putha. I hate the bloody man.'

The police told May they wanted the boy's father for questioning and in his absence they were taking his son. May knew, once they had their hands on him, the boy would never be seen again, so she had tried to hold on to him, pleading with the soldiers, but they had pushed her roughly aside. The boy had gone and later the headmaster had called May into his office to warn her never to behave in this manner again or he would be forced to ask her to leave the school.

'I'm not without sympathy,' the head had said. 'But you must understand, ours is a tricky position. We don't want this school closed.'

May had begun to cry after that and the head had been nice to her, telling her to think about her wedding and not to dwell on what had happened. May had only cried all the more. Now, she told Alice, she hated the school.

'They are no different from the morons at your Colombo school,' she told Alice. 'I really believed there was a difference here in the south. But I was wrong.'

Alice's eyes were round as saucers. She had never seen her aunt like this.

'You know what, darling, I'm actually *glad* you're going to England. Glad you won't be subjected to any of the terrible things that are happening in our country. It will be so different where you are going. In England you will learn about justice and truth. When you grow up, you'll look back on all this and be disgusted.'

There was something Alice wanted to ask. It had been bothering her throughout this strange uneasy day.

'Is that why Janake doesn't go to school?'

May paused and shook her head.

'No,'she said abruptly. 'Since his father was killed, Janake's mother has no money. But I've been giving him private lessons, and one day I hope he will go to a university in India just so he can get out of this hell. Your grandfather has a plan to send him there, you know.'

Alice stared out of the window. Janake would not be waiting for her message in a bottle after all. Once again the feeling of being close to a precipice crept over her. What if everything vanished? What if all of this – her grandparents, her aunty May, the house itself – disappeared and, when the day came, when she had finally grown up and tried to come back, she could never find any of them again?

'You needn't worry,' Aunty May said, suddenly seeing the look on her face. 'We'll still be here. Waiting for you to return!'

Outside, the rain increased to a downpour. Lightning flashed across the sea, revealing the darkened horizon. May kissed Alice goodnight.

'Grandpa will come to give you a goodnight kiss when he's finished visiting Kunal,' she said.

Then she left, turning out the light. Lying beneath the mosquito net, turning towards the window, Alice saw a ship white as a swan against the night sky, carrying its cargo of human lives. From this distance it seemed to be sailing slowly over the edge of the world.

All that night, and the next and the one after that, Kunal lay delirious with fever and heavily sedated. Twice the generator broke down and the power was so low that the lights in his room cast dim shadows on the walls. They took it in turns to sit with him, Bee, Kamala, and Sita. Even the servant woman stayed up, boiling water constantly.

Only May, who had school in the morning, and Alice slept, although the latter felt her dreams disturbed by a steady stream of footsteps. At the end of the first week, when the doctor came through the grove he brought them the news they were waiting for. The army had gone. Removing the road-blocks, lifting the curfew, climbing into their trucks, they left without warning. The people in the little costal town watched surreptitiously from behind shutters. The army drove away in a thundering line, a convoy of green-and-brown camouflage, leaving heavy caterpillar tracks across the beach.

The town had been holding its breath and now it let it out. Outwardly nothing had changed; the bougainvillea still cascaded across the white-washed houses, the kade beside the Grand Hotel continued to play *byla* music and smell of Old Roses tobacco, while the catamarans put out to a sea full of fish. Only in May Fonseka's class there remained one empty seat. It would stay empty. None of the other children wanted to sit in it for fear of what might happen to them. May left them to their superstitions. *She* was one of the things that had changed. No one saw this change. It was too subtle and too deep inside her, but she was no longer the same young woman waiting to be married. The staff, glad she had calmed down, breathed a sigh of relief and began questioning her about the wedding. She answered smilingly, but inwardly it was a different matter. She no longer cared whether her pupils, all from rich neighbouring Singhalese families, passed their entrance examinations or not. Once, on her way home, she caught a glimpse of the Tamil boy's mother. The woman hesitated, not wanting to approach May, so that May, in her new mood of indifference, careless of any watching eyes, went up to her instead. The family, what was left of it, a family of women now, were packing up and leaving for Jaffna. Of the woman's son and husband, nothing had been heard. May listened, nodding, promising to try to get some information. The woman could barely speak for crying.

'I'll do what I can,' May told her.

She feared it was hopeless, but the words once released, seemed to bring some small comfort.

Another week passed. In the Sea House, too, all appeared normal. Alice had received a postcard and a letter from Stanley. She placed the card on her window ledge. Nothing in her life made sense any longer and the postcard added to this sense of unreality. She had not been allowed to see Kunal since his operation. The Sea House no longer smelled of antiseptic. The doctor, who visited daily, had wanted him to rest as much as he could. So most mornings her grandfather took Alice to the beach to play with Janake and by the time they returned Kunal was usually asleep. Since the alms-giving, Alice had seen nothing of Esther Harris. Once or twice on their way back from the beach she had caught a glimpse of her walking up the hill with the boy Anton, but apart from that she too seemed to have vanished. Then one afternoon Dias arrived to talk to Kamala and Sita.

'Hello, child,' she said absent-mindedly, squeezing Alice's cheeks. 'My goodness, you look well. Not going to school suits you, hey?'

Alice frowned. Who had told Esther's mother about her school?

'Why don't you come over sometime? Esther is back from visiting her aunty now that the curfew had been lifted. Come and see us tomorrow, ah? What d'you think, Kamala?'

Dias was preoccupied and disinclined to talk. Bored, Alice wandered off. She couldn't even be bothered to eavesdrop. She had been making a box with the old pieces of driftwood. It was a smallish box that could not be opened. Three nails kept it closed, but through a gap in the construction of it you could see a seashell inside. You could see it but not quite reach it. When she had first shown it to Bee he had been surprised. She wanted Janake to see it too. Picking up the box from where it stood beside the picture postcard from her father, she hurried out.

Stanley was disappointed. He was having such a wonderful time here in Athens with the beautiful Marianna that he did not want to leave in the morning. But they had lost three days already and the engine had been fixed. The ship was ready to set sail again.

'Good!' Marianna informed him. 'My fiancé will be waiting for me at Southampton. I shall have to tell him I have found someone else, now!'

'What?' Stanley asked, startled. 'Wait, wait a minute … I say, I'm a married man, you know. It isn't easy … what I mean is … look …'

He peered anxiously at Marianna, who was lying face down and naked on the bed. They had taken to coming back to the hotel after lunch with a bottle of vodka, courtesy of Marianna. Stanley had felt it was too cold to do much sightseeing.

'That's not what you said when you first got here,' Marianna had scoffed. 'Then it was all, "Oh, I must see the cradle of civilisation!"'

'Well, I've seen it now,' Stanley said. 'It's you I haven't seen enough of, yet.'

Marianna had been happy enough to oblige, taking her clothes off as easily as she cleaned her teeth. It made for a refreshing change. But he hadn't known of her desire to be rid of her fiancé. He looked sharply at her and she burst out laughing.

'Don't worry, Stanley, it's quite safe. I'm not going to leave Cedric. You can relax. This is what is called a holiday romance, didn't you know?'

Stanley swallowed. Soon it would be the end of April and they would be on their way to England.

In the days that followed the amputation Sita found herself praying. Kunal continued to be delirious. He had lost a lot of blood and the doctor still came twice a day to check on him. Sita had become an expert at changing his dressing, washing him and making sure he drank enough. Kamala and Bee continued to take turns sitting with him, but it was Sita who did the bulk of it, remaining beside his bed most nights. Kunal did not recognise any of them. Outside, the days had become hotter, the sky was a pitiless blue and along the coastline the currents changed. The fishermen on stilts moved further up the coast to where it was safer. The doctor tried not to show it but was worried. The first few days after such a serious operation were always tricky, but by now Kunal should have been improving.

'Try to get the temperature down,' he insisted. 'He must have plenty of fluids. The longer he has this temperature, the more debilitated he will become.'

Sita nodded. In spite of the anxiety, she felt wonderfully assured, utterly certain; Kunal would recover. The feeling of calm that had come over her before the operation remained and both Kamala and

Bee watched astonished as she organised the rota for the patient's care. Everything in the house revolved around it now. At night, while Kamala burnt incense at the house shrine, Sita sat beside Kunal in the darkness breathing in the musty scent that spread slowly across the garden and in through the half-closed shutters. 'Please get better,' she prayed silently, all thoughts of her own life wiped out for the moment. And then she would get up and adjust the bedclothes or wipe his face or hold the glass of cool water to his lips, restraining him when he thrashed his one good leg across the bed. Nothing Kamala could say would persuade Sita to move from her post beside Kunal's bed. She was determined to be present when he awoke.

Another week passed before Kunal realised that the month of April was almost over. Blown out like a candle. He had taken a turn for the better, but it was one more day before he remembered the operation. Waking, he felt the sunlight falling strongly across his bed. He stared, puzzled at the enormous expanse of sky before he suddenly noticed Sita standing beside the bed holding a cup of tea. She was smiling. Kunal began to sit up and as he tried to put his foot out of the bed and on to the ground in order to steady himself, he overbalanced. He would have fallen, had not Sita caught him swiftly with one hand. There was stunned silence and Kunal burst into tears. It was how he learnt the news of what had become of his leg. Sita's face moved into focus for a moment, a little blurred and passive, and in the part of his brain still functioning he registered once more how beautiful she was. He saw too that she was sorry for him in an uncomplicated way that had nothing to do with pity. He realised these two things in the same instance he understood that he would never again walk unaided by crutches. The thoughts moved simultaneously in Kunal's head, filling him with a mixture of black despair and confusion.

Later he learned other things. He learned that the curfew had lifted, so for the time being he was safe and that the shutters that had been closed when he arrived were open very slightly now, which was why he could see the sky. The doctor came to check him. Kunal asked him how long he had been lying here.

'Oh, not long,' the doctor said lightly. 'But we're going to move you somewhere closer to Colombo soon. It will be better there, and once you are strong enough we're arranging transport to Jaffna.'

Kunal gazed at the doctor, his eyes clear of fever, astonished all over again by the kindness of these Singhalese people. The heat had been rising steadily. In spite of the sea breeze everywhere was blisteringly hot. Kunal could feel it through the bars of the window. He had no idea how long he had lain here but as the days wore on and he grew more alert he became aware of the rhythm of the house. Sita was nearly always beside him and when she was not, either Kamala or Bee was present. They told him the current news. There was an election due soon. It would be best for Kunal to escape to Jaffna before it took place. Bee usually visited in the early morning with the doctor, before taking the child to the beach, and then again in the evening. Sometimes he came with the doctor, sometimes alone. Only Sita was there all the time. It was she who told him the things he was desperate to know so that bit by bit he was able to piece together the story of the last few weeks.

'It was a very long operation,' she said. 'I was worried. I didn't think they had given you enough morphine. What if you woke up? What if you started to feel the pain? I was frightened.'

She sounded as though she was talking about someone else.

'You were delirious for days. We took it in turns sitting up with you.'

He remembered shadows, someone wiping the sweat off his face, a fan blowing on him, water being held to his lips.

'Was it you?' he asked wonderingly.

'Most of the time,' she admitted.

These talks always took place during the evening. One evening she came in just as the sun was setting, and sat for a long time staring out of the window. The sky glowed with the light. Watching her face, he could see clearly the weariness that came from living in a place full of uncertainties. But, he thought, she's still young.

'We are living through a terrible history,' he said tentatively, picking up the threads of an earlier conversation. 'In the end, we're just part of that time. We don't matter in the way we think.'

He wondered if she knew what he meant, but instantly she nodded.

'So I have lost a leg. See how I say it as though it is a little matter!'

'You're adapting,' she agreed. 'That's good.'

'In the scale of what is happening, a leg isn't much to lose.'

'Or a child,' she asked quietly. 'Is that what you mean?'

He held out his hand. A moment later the sun had begun to set and was out of her eyes. Darkness would come swiftly after that.

'I mean, I have a hand that can hold yours. I am grateful to have that, in this time. We cannot expect more at this moment.'

If she wanted to, Sita could still make some sort of life for herself, he thought. But that perhaps was the problem; he could see she had stopped caring about her life.

'You are stronger than me,' she said quietly. 'Look what you have survived. And you are determined too, thank God!'

She was referring to his desperate fumbling attempts at getting out of bed, his balance, learning to walk again, differently.

Kunal nodded. On one of his visits, the doctor had pointed to a crutch leaning against the door. It seemed to Kunal the crutch had been there forever, since he had first moved into the room, long before any talk of the leg coming off. He saw his life like the drawing of a pyramid with everything being a training for this event.

'Don't give up,' he told Sita fiercely, surprising himself.

Bee had told him a little about her husband. It wasn't so much what Bee had said but how he had said it; dismissively, as though they, and Sita in particular, would carry on regardless of the husband. Don't go to England, was what Kunal wanted to say. The servant knocked and came in with a tray of food. Bee put his head around the door.

'Alice wants to show you something she made today,' he told them both. 'I'll bring her in later.'

Night fell while they sat talking and the stars had begun to come out. Through the open window they appeared very bright. It was as if some strange disturbance filled the sky.

In the end none of them wanted him to be moved, whatever the risk of his staying meant. May and her new husband would sleep in his sister's house after the wedding until Kunal left. May, more than anyone, had not wanted him to leave.

'He isn't a dog, to be kicked out,' she told her parents. 'He's so helpless. How can I be happy, having done a thing like that!'

So Kunal would stay. No matter what the omens were.

'There are no omens,' Bee said. 'Omens are all in the mind.'

And Kamala agreed without believing him.

No one commented on the change in Sita. No one knew what to say. The fact was Kunal was doing her some good.

'But, Amma, they're leaving at the end of July,' May said, voicing things better, perhaps, left unsaid.

'Let's get the wedding over, May,' her mother told her.

'But what about Stanley?' May asked.

Kamala did not respond, although later in bed it was another matter.

'Maybe Sita has a different sort of life ahead,' she said tentatively. 'A different karma than the one we imagined.'

Bee looked at her with faint surprise.

'Why are you looking at me like that?' she asked defensively. 'Can't I hope? Kunal may go to England one day. Who knows what might happen!'

'You aren't that traditional girl I married, after all,' Bee teased her, with a straight face. 'I'm not sure I approve.'

'How can I be traditional after thirty years of life with you!'

She was glad to make him laugh a little and she was happy too that, in spite of everything, the house was coming alive with the life of the wedding. They were happy, at last. For the moment. All of them, that is, except the servant woman who scrubbed and aired the house hoping to remove every invisible trace of the man with only one leg. The servant lit sandalwood joss-sticks and brought in vases of mimosa in the hope of banishing any evil that might be lurking. She sprinkled rose water on the threshold of the front door and she polished the mirrors and the floors so they shone and the Fonsekas slipped as they walked.

'Not quite so much polish, Nauru,' Kamala said, amused, knowing what was in the woman's mind.

Since the curfew had been lifted and the army dispersed, the drums could be heard clearly at night. Occasional bouts of fighting broke out in the nearby villages, but by and large the town retreated into itself and became what it had always been, a sleepy backwater of no importance.

May had decided to keep her job after she married. All that would change would be her name. She had been waiting impatiently for the month of June to arrive and now here it was drawing to a slow languid close. At last her wedding day approached. She had invited six of the senior girls from the convent school to chant the *kavi*, the traditional verse, at the ceremony. The girls were all from Singhalese families. On the day they would wear half-saris and carry their *kavi* books. But before any of this could happen, a few days earlier, the astrologer arrived with his list of auspicious times and then the house was blessed all over again by monks chanting *pirith*. It was only then, the servant told Kamala, satisfied at last, that she could relax.

Bee and Janake began fixing coloured lights in the trees and Alice poured coconut oil into small lamps and placed them all over the garden. It was just like Vesak.

'There are going to be fireworks,' Alice told Janake excitedly.

'Catherine wheels?' Janake asked, his eyes round with amazement. 'No? Like at the fair?'

Alice stared at him, surprised. She had forgotten all about the fair. 'I had my cards read,' she remembered.

'So did I, when I was at my aunt's house. What did yours say?'

She wasn't sure.

'Water, I think. She said there was a lot of water.'

Janake nodded.

'Mine was funny too. The lady card reader saw orange cloth and fire. And she saw water too.'

'Maybe she told everyone the same thing.'

'Did she say if you'd come back?'

Alice shook her head, doubtfully.

'She didn't even say I was going!'

They both laughed and Janake did a cartwheel.

'Good!' he said. 'Then maybe you won't!'

* * *

Sita saw with satisfaction that Kunal was on the mend. Every day he became a little stronger. Now she no longer needed to sit with him all night they both missed it, although neither confessed this to the other. Both looked forward to Sita's morning visit to his room with his breakfast of fresh fruit and string hoppers. Must be because I'm hungry, thought Kunal as he turned his face towards the door at the sound of her footsteps. Sita coming in felt her heart leap. As the wedding drew nearer, because of the constant stream of visitors to the house, it was impossible to allow Kunal out. So in order to keep him occupied Sita began to take down her old books from her father's room and read to him several times a day. Apart from reading to Alice in the old days before the baby, Sita had not read to anyone. Stanley had never been sick or interested in this way.

'You have a beautiful voice,' Kunal told her, staring at the ceiling when she finished reading *A Girl of the Limberlost.*

As a young girl it had been her favourite book. Sita smiled briefly.

'I'm going to read you some poetry next,' she told him, unaware that his eyes were on her.

'Why don't you start writing again?' he asked.

'Maybe,' Sita nodded.

She did not want to talk about the future. She did not want it to invade the calm certainty that had come to her, like a gift, since Kunal's arrival. So she read him poetry instead. And then she peeled a fresh mango for him, unaware that Kunal was unable to take his eyes off her hands and the juice running through her fingers.

Afterwards when they remembered May's wedding Kunal was the first image that came to all of them. He was the hidden memory, the prelude to the ceremony, hiding in the annexe, practising on his crutch. Tap, tap, tap on the unpolished floor. The day itself arrived swiftly. A morning of dazzle and light without a single cloud in the sky. It had not rained and scents from the jasmine and orange-blossom trees had intensified in the heat. Today was a Thursday, an auspicious day for a wedding. Everything that happened today would do so at moments ordained by the astrologer. It began with the servant sweeping up the fallen petals at a particular time. Watering the jasmine bushes that he had planted when each of his daughters had been born, even Bee did not complain. As usual he had awoken early. After he had finished the plants he went into his studio. He had done no serious work for weeks and his studio was strangely tidy. Kamala had given him strict instructions: no work today. Naturally, Bee ignored her. Lighting his pipe, he picked up one of his drawings abandoned before Kunal's operation. Kamala had told him there would be no smoking in the house today. She would have hidden his pipe had he not got to it first. Outside, the sea pleated itself into acquiescent folds. He heard footsteps and, turning, he smiled, thinking it was Alice. But it was Sita who joined him. A Sita he hardly recognised; happier than he had seen her for years. In a few weeks they would be gone. How had the time passed so quickly? he wondered apprehensively. The eldest following the youngest. Taking the child with her. God knows when he would see them again. No, not now, he told himself firmly, not today. Looking at his eldest daughter, in a rare, awkward gesture he put his arm around her. Then, feeling the bird-like sharpness of her bones, he kissed her forehead.

'Alice is sleeping late,' he said laconically. 'Must be tired, finally. Either that or she discovered the whisky bottle!'

'No, she's with Kunal,' Sita said, smiling suddenly.

Unexpectedly Bee's spirits lifted.

'Apparently there was something she needed to ask him urgently. There was no stopping her.'

Bee groaned. And then chuckled.

'She'll do him good,' he said.

They stood looking at the sea together. The day would be an ordeal in its own way for Sita. There was nothing either of them needed to say after that. In the final analysis, they would behave like the Buddhist people they were. His pain, her loss, all of it was in the gesture of his arm around her. She is like me, Bee thought, feeling a kind of peace settle over them both. Neither of us can speak easily. He saw that Sita had left years ago, long before Alice was born, probably long before she even set eyes on Stanley. She had needed to find her own way in life. It was what she needed to do on this journey to the strange place she was going to. He saw how it was, clearly.

'From out the fiery portal of the east,' he quoted lightly. 'You are going to the country that gave us Shakespeare, after all! Just think of that.'

'Thatha,' Sita said, so softly he bent his head to hear her, 'we may come back, you know. Alice and I.'

She struggled for a moment, then she turned, looking at him with Alice's large eyes. The very same eyes, thought Bee. And now pain clutched his heart.

'If it doesn't work out, I mean, if … if …'

'Wait and see,' he told her.

His arm still rested lightly on her.

'You know you can always return. When the time is right, if things work out differently.'

A small green bird hopped on to the bushes that screened the annexe from view. I am the man who travelled to far-flung places without moving an inch, thought Bee.

'I must go in to check on Kunal,' Sita said.

Bee nodded.

'Tell Alice she must come out now. It's the auspicious time to do so!'

They both laughed. It felt as though they had said their good-byes.

The *poruwa,* the canopy under which the bride and groom would stand, had been erected the evening before. May's schoolgirls had helped Alice and Esther decorate it with white flowers and gold ribbons. There were terracotta vases of temple flowers and sheaves of paddy placed beside the mini-stage while overhead the silk was shot through with silvery stars.

'They must stand facing the south,' the astrologer had said, consulting his chart.

The wedding ceremony was to be at three minutes past eleven, the time that was most auspicious for them both.

'And the bride,' the astrologer told them sternly, wagging his head from side to side, never having met a man as disobedient as Bee, 'must be dressed at three minutes to nine.'

Smells of *kiri-bath*, milk rice, that most auspicious of food, drifted through the house. Other scents and aromas crept in too, filling the air with celebration. The bridal flowers, a huge bouquet of lilies and stephanotis, was delivered and Janake, pedalling furiously all the way up the hill, brought the fresh fish. Cooking started as Janake stood at the back door looking for Alice, but there was no sign of her this morning.

'Come back later,' Kamala said. 'Alice is getting ready now. Come back just before eleven.'

In another part of the garden a marquee was being erected with much noise and laughter. The guests would dine here in its shade after the ceremony. A horn beeped; Kamala's younger brother Sarath and his wife and two children stepped out of a car and embraced everyone. They had driven from Colombo. As this was a Buddhist wedding it would be Sarath who would be giving his niece away in marriage. Several relatives arrived on the overnight train. This was the moment Sita had dreaded most of all, but now that it was here there was too much else to do to worry about the visitors.

They dressed, all together for the last time. Three generations of women under the same roof. May shivering with suppressed excitement and Alice agog in a white silk dress threaded with pink rosebuds. Kamala looked around for her elder daughter, but Sita had disappeared again.

'Mama's gone to see Kunal,' Alice told her.

'Oh no!'

Kamala looked alarmed. They had agreed that no one would go into the annexe for the few hours it took for the wedding to take place. She did not want to bring attention to it.

'Oh, Amma, don't worry,' May said. 'She'll be careful. Let her, she's happy. Leave her.'

'She likes Kunal,' Alice observed. 'She was holding his hand this morning. Aunty May, I can't do up my shoe properly.'

'Let me see,' May said, exchanging looks with Kamala over Alice's head. 'Oh yes, it needs another hole in the strap, that's all!'

* * *

Kunal was sitting on the end of the bed, wearing a pale blue sarong. In repose his face looked haggard. When he saw Sita, he broke into a smile. She closed the door. The room was full of the smell of the sea.

'Why aren't you resting?' she said, sitting next to him.

She said this almost every time she came in, for at the back of her mind was the worry that his temperature might return. She had been looking after him for so long now that it had become a habit. He had filled the space in her head that she thought would never be filled again. Certainty flooded over her at the sight of him. Her voice didn't sound quite right. It felt as if it no longer belonged to her. The warm line of her arm touched his briefly, a gentle frontier resting against him. Kunal looked at her, saying nothing, taking in her turquoise sari and the way it made her skin fairer and her eyes even darker. She had fixed her hair in a way that revealed her long slender neck. He stared at her for so long that in the end she averted her eyes, uncertain.

'What's wrong?' she asked.

'Alice will look like you one day,' he said. 'I hope I'll be there to see that day.'

She was so close he could feel the warmth of her breath. The smell of foliage and sun-drenched dew clinging to her.

'Have you been outside?'

She nodded, unable to speak. With a small sound of despair he leaned over and put both arms around her. He swayed slightly, almost losing his balance, feeling happiness bubble up.

'Don't,' he said.

'What?'

'Don't look at me like that,' he said, and then, because the ache within him had become unbearable, he kissed her.

Stanley was shocked. London was not as he had expected. After the excitement of Athens and the slight boredom of the voyage, he was unprepared for the seriousness of this new phase in his life. His brother Rajah met him off the boat train at Waterloo. Marianna had travelled up to London with him, but just as the train was slowing down, when he went to collect his luggage, she disappeared. He assumed she had gone to the toilet but when the train stopped she did not reappear. They had not exchanged addresses. His brother was waiting for him by the ticket office. Rajah, unfamiliar and pale from a lack of tropical sun, confused him with his fast talk and odd accent. Stanley could neither respond to nor assimilate anything being said. Everything passed him by in a blur. The traffic, the ride in the taxi.

'We can't do this too often, men,' Rajah told him. 'It's too damn expensive.'

Stanley sat shivering in his thin clothes.

'You cold?' Rajah asked.

'Yes,' Stanley said reluctantly.

He was aware that his brother was inclined to laugh, though what about, he had no idea. He felt like an amputee. And for the first time since he had left Colombo he wished Sita was with him.

Rajah had found him a house. At least, thought Stanley, he had done that.

'I promised Ma I'd pay the rent for the first month,' he told Stanley with a trace of resentment in his voice. 'But you'll have to start looking for work straight away, huh? Monday morning, okay?'

Give me a chance, thought Stanley. But he didn't say anything.

'Don't use too much paraffin,' Rajah continued. 'Only heat one room at a time. Everything here is costly.'

I thought this place was paradise, thought Stanley, remembering how Rajah had urged him to leave Colombo.

'You should get some proper clothes,' Rajah continued, eyeing Stanley's thin pullover with distaste. 'You can have some of mine to start with.'

The house was dirty and very dark. There was a damp unused smell and the long corridor that separated the sitting room from the hall was covered in maroon flock wallpaper.

'What's this stuff?' Stanley asked.

'Wallpaper, men!'

A wire curtain rail supported a sagging curtain. This, too, was filthy. What sort of place was this? wondered Stanley in dismay.

'It just needs a clean,' Rajah said, seeing the look on his face. 'The wife can clean it up in no time at all.'

He suppressed a laugh. The wife, thought Stanley, his dismay increasing. He was speechless with exhaustion, cold and unhappy. Why had Marianna disappeared?

'When's she coming?'

'What?'

'The wife. How long have you got before she comes?'

He was laughing openly now.

'Middle of August,' Stanley said shortly.

He had forgotten how Rajah always used to get on his nerves. Rajah rattled the loose change in his pocket. There was a pause.

'Right!' he said, taking charge, 'you've seen the place. Here's the key. There are a couple of clean sheets and some blankets on the bed. I've put some stuff in the fridge for the morning and there's paraffin in the heater. So you'll be all right for a bit. Now, I'm starving, so let's go to my place and I'll cook you some proper food. I know what that bloody ship's fare is like! Come on. Let's go!'

And he led the way outside.

But outside, things were no better. They took the underground, but the darkness and the noise frightened him.

'We're under the Thames,' Rajah said, adding to his confusion as they approached Charing Cross. 'This is the Northern Line, and I'm over here in Earl's Court. So we've got to change on to the Circle Line. See?'

Stanley didn't see. Rajah was racing ahead past crowds of people all with closed faces and intent silent expressions. His head spun. Where did Rajah get all his energy? At Earl's Court they left the tube and hurried across the road, pausing only at the traffic lights. Cars stopped obediently and without protest as soon as the lights turned red. No one beeped their horns, and it was pedestrians and not beggars who occupied the pavements. Stanley tried talking to Rajah but it was all he could do to keep up with him as they crossed and recrossed a confusion of roads, passing row after row of identical tall red-bricked houses with closed doors and windows. What sort of place was this?

'Here we are!' Rajah said.

He opened the door and they went in.

'Welcome to my humble abode!' he laughed, shepherding his brother into his flat.

In the colourless room, sitting at the table were three Jaffna Tamil men who looked up briefly and nodded at him. Outside the window the sky and the road were a dank, depressing grey.

'Alice!' Esther cried, coming in, impressed. 'You look really grown-up, today! I can't believe you are only nine!'

Alice, her eyes shining, was whirling around until Kamala scolded her, telling her the flowers were falling out of her hair.

'Come here, Putha,' Dias Harris cried. 'Stand still, there's a good girl, or I'll squeeze your cheeks!'

'Now, now, calm down everyone,' Kamala admonished. 'May, let me do your jacket up.'

'You look so beautiful, Aunty,' Esther said, staring at her.

'Ah! May! Of course she does. Even more than usual, I should say! You must be so proud of your girls, Kamala.'

'Where's Thatha?' May asked.

'He's getting dressed. I've finally got him away from his wretched studio. *Anay*, the man is driving me mad!'

'And Sita?' asked Dias.

'I'm here,' Sita said, appearing behind them.

There was a small silence.

'Why, Sita,' Dias Harris said faintly, 'I almost didn't recognise you.'

'Come,' Kamala told her carefully, 'your flower has got crushed. I'll turn it round.'

Sita smiled at her mother and, in the first spontaneous gesture in years, she turned to her sister and kissed her. Then she put her hand on Alice, restraining her.

'Let me comb your hair,' she said.

Just after eleven, the auspicious hour, Namil arrived and it began. Silver, gold and white. Love at the right time; love that was politically correct, thought Sita, but the thought held no bitterness. The bride and groom fed each other the sweetened *kiri-bath*, cut now into diamond shapes. Just like love-birds. At last May was emerging from her sister's disgrace, was the thought utmost in the minds of the guests. And Sita, they whispered to each other, she looked better than one could have hoped, standing quietly, holding the bride's flowers during the ceremony. A silver goblet was brought forward on a silver tray. May's little finger was tied to Namil's and water, blessed by the monks, was poured over them. The guests let out sighs of pleasure as rings were exchanged and the bridegroom placed a necklace around his new wife's neck. A white cloth was tied around them both as husband and wife were helped off the wedding dais by May's uncle Sarath. For a moment the sisters stood together. Well, thought Bee, glancing around the garden at some of the guests, there were still some prejudiced fools present today. He had tried to censor the invitations, but Kamala had overruled him, telling him to behave himself. It couldn't be helped, he thought grimly, but they could all go to hell if anything was said in his hearing about Sita. A sweet cloying smell of frangipani and jasmine drifted across the garden and behind, a backdrop of blue, was the sea, empty of ships.

After the registration of the marriage, Kamala lifted her daughter's veil and they cut the cake and lit an oil lamp so that any darkness they might have brought with them into this life was dispersed. Bee stood with the sunlight slanting on his face, watching them. Thirty years before it had been Kamala's face that had been unveiled in this way. Would she say it had gone well for them, if she were asked? Watching her, his face unusually soft, he saw she was smiling broadly. Lately she had not smiled much. He glanced at Sita, whose face today was glowing with something other than her sister's wedding. Here they were then, all together for the last time. Bee had no illusions but that it was the last time. Unless a miracle occurred. He wondered if he ought to slip out and check on Kunal. The hospital doctor was here today. Bee could see his dark curly hair, further back, watching the ceremony. He too was smiling. Turning his head, Bee caught Kamala's eye. She raised her eyebrows heavenwards. Don't go to check on him now, she seemed to be saying, you're needed *here*. Bee felt his face twitch. She had always been able to read his thoughts. He caught sight of Alice, her head cocked on one side, a broad grin directed at Janake. What were *they* plotting? He let out a sigh. Yes, he thought. Alice would travel the world, he was certain, doing what he could only dream of. And as he watched them all, Bee felt the day and the sunlight and the rustling, silky sea, become fixed into the last segment of his life. On this day when his youngest daughter was married. The kavi-chanters recited their last verse, the bride and groom walked together to greet the guests, laughing and chatting to them. Lunch was about to be served. Glasses of water were passed around and everyone drank to the health, wealth and prosperity of Namil and his new wife May.

Lunch was a grand affair. The guests washed their hands in small bowls of iced water. Then the servants brought around white towels. There were no knives and forks. This was a traditional meal; everyone ate with their fingers, as was the custom in these parts. Yellow rice and a dazzling array of curries. There was the fresh fish Janake had brought earlier that morning, *malu ambulthiyal*, tuna fish, flavoured with *goraka*, the skin of the mangosteen, there was every vegetable imaginable, the *mullungs*, and there were the *appa*, pancakes to be eaten with *bandake*, Maldive fish, *sambals*. Alice swallowed. Standing still for so long had left her starving. The afternoon meandered on. Janake, in unfamiliar clothes, neatly ironed, helped himself liberally to the string hoppers.

'Are you coming to the beach later?' he asked Alice.

Alice shook her head. She was too busy eating to talk.

'I've found you some more driftwood.'

'I won't be able to come until tomorrow. They won't be leaving until five today. You know, the auspicious time for their departure is late.'

Janake nodded. He helped himself to more of the excellent yellow rice and fish. Then he sneaked another *appa* as well, to be on the safe side. Alice eyed him. Would he really be able to eat all that?

'How's Kunal?' he whispered, his mouth full. 'Mr Fonseka said he's been trying to walk with the crutch. He's going to Jaffna the day after tomorrow, isn't he? Via Elephant Pass, I think. He's going to stay the night with someone he knows there.'

'Have you told my grandpa?'

'I think he knows already. Look, Mr Fonseka's talking to the doctor.'

Alice could see Bee was deep in conversation with the doctor. They had moved a little way out of the marquee into the boiling sun. Her mother and grandmother were standing together by the food.

'Amma, I want to take him some food,' Sita was murmuring to her mother.

'No,' Kamala said in a low voice. 'Nauru's taken him lunch. You stay here.'

'Oh God, look, Nanda is coming over here. I don't want to talk to her.'

'Oh, for goodness' sake, go in through the bedroom if you must. Don't go through the garden, you understand?'

But Sita had vanished.

'Hello, Nanda,' Kamala said, holding out a plate to her cousin and smiling. 'Here, have something to eat before it all vanishes!'

'Was that Sita I saw?'

'Yes, she's just torn her sari, she's gone to fix it,' lied Kamala, smiling sweetly.

By the time she had managed to get past everyone, shooing the children out of her parents' room, and found the key to unlock the connecting door, Sita was trembling. Kunal was eating, but he put his plate down as soon as he saw her and tried to stand up.

'Don't get up,' she said breathlessly. 'Is it true you're going the day after tomorrow? I just heard Janake and Alice talking about it.'

'I have to. There's a place, a safe house. I'll go there for a short time, then I'll go to Jaffna. I need to lie low for a bit.'

She was speechless.

'You will be going too,' he reminded her gently. 'Very soon.'

The words lay heavily between them. Sita could not think of a single thing to say. What was she doing? In his only letter home Stanley had said the thing he missed the most was the food. He hadn't said anything about missing her and Alice.

'We'll keep in touch,' Kunal said, looking at his hands, not knowing what else to say. 'I promise you.'

But you are married, he was thinking, and I am a cripple, wanted by the police. Even if I came to England, just supposing they took in cripples, what use would I be to you? Outside, a peacock screamed. A very bad omen, Kunal thought sadly, but he didn't say that either. Sita was crying softly. Only he had been able to reach her, she told him, her voice muffled, as she lay drowning. He was drowning too.

'Don't cry,' he said very softly.

'I'd better go.'

'Come back when they've all gone, please. Come back and just talk to me?'

She nodded, trying to stop her tears, trying to wipe her eyes. Through the opening in the window she could see the sea glittering as though it were filled with sapphires. In a week they would be on it. She could not bear it any more.

Outside on the verandah there were islands of light swimming through the trees as the sun dipped its late afternoon light. The auspicious time to leave was upon them. May, in her going-away sari of red and magenta, all ablaze like a sunset, stood poised for flight. Is this what happily ever after means? wondered Sita, her mouth like a twist of toffee paper. At this wedding there would be no crying ceremony, Bee had insisted. Not all old traditions were good and besides, there had been enough grief already, enough loss. So May went like a bright star, kneeling first at her father's feet, palms together, and then at her mother's. It was her thank you for her life. Namil smiled at his bride, impatient to leave, triumphant at his perseverance, pleased that it had been such a success, despite the past.

'Signed and sealed at last,' he teased her.

Stanley, thought Sita with her thin-twisted smile, never looked at me like that. Never. A harsh pronouncement, for a man too far away to defend himself.

Good-bye, good-bye they waved, watching them drive off into the sunset in the old Morris Minor to begin a new life together, for ever and ever. To drink flower-scented water at the groom's house before their marriage really began.

'God bless,' Kamala called out. She was crying, quietly. No, no, she reassured her husband, this wasn't to do with the crying ceremony. She was merely crying for the end of her daughter's beautiful day.

Esther giggled. There were young girl's thoughts filling her head.

'Never mind,' she told Alice, tossing her head. 'You're too young to understand. Wait till you are older.'

But Janake, who did not like Esther, scowled.

'She's just showing off,' he muttered. 'She can't make the kinds of things you make out of the driftwood. And anyway,' he added loyally, 'you're prettier than her!'

No one had said that to Alice before. She had given Janake the nailed-up box. It was an early leaving present. She gave it to him because she knew he would understand that it was not a box to open. It was a box of sealed-up memories. Hers. His.

Far out at sea, halfway towards the horizon, a boat bobbed about on the water, impassive against the sweep of sky and sea. The rain had held off all day, miraculously.

'Soon,' Bee said, lighting up his pipe, waving to the last of the guests as they drove off, 'it will rain again.'

7

THE WEDDING DAY, A DAY OF SKY-BLUE JAUNTINESS, had given way to a phosphorescent night. The moon was very full.

'This is a very good thing for the family, sir,' the astrologer said, pointing to it on his way out.

He placed his hands together and bowed, first to Bee, and then again to the rest of the Fonseka family. He had lied to them, for the sake of kindness. What was the use of upsetting them on such a day? It was not as if they could change their fate and get themselves a different karma, and in any case the day itself had gone well. The astrologer shrugged inwardly, thinking the bride was a good-looking woman and there was nothing more to be said on that score. The small child dancing underneath the murunga tree laughed and waved at him. If he remembered rightly, this was the child who was going to live in England. For a moment the astrologer hesitated. Perhaps he should offer to draw up her horoscope before she left? Perhaps this would be the one who escaped the fate of the others. He glanced at Bee. If the astrologer remembered rightly, Mr Fonseka was not given to horoscopes. What if the child's fate was the same as theirs? No, best to leave well alone, thought the astrologer, murmuring goodnight and slipping out without fuss through the gate. What will be will be, he thought, sighing.

'Let's play five stones,' Alice suggested.

'And then we can have a race on the bicycle,' Janake agreed.

'That's not fair,' Alice protested. 'You're much better at riding it than I am!'

Janake's mother, who had been helping the servant, came out. She was smiling.

'We have to go soon, Janake,' she warned.

'I'll take you back,' Bee told her. 'Don't worry.'

The servant came out with some iced coffee in tall frosted glasses.

'Does anyone want any more to eat?' Kamala wanted to know.

Her brother Sarath had gone, packing his family into the car and driving off. He had work in the morning. Kamala would not see him again for months.

'Your turn next, Sita, Putha,' he said, kissing his niece good-bye. 'If I can get time off work. I'll come to the harbour.'

Kamala winced. A thread of pain pulled sharply at her.

'Can I have some cake, Mama?' Alice asked.

She was dancing to Esther's rock-and-roll music.

'Haven't you had enough?' Sita asked dubiously, but surprisingly she was laughing. Alice thought her mother's tone was nice. Was her mother happy that Aunty May had left home? she wondered.

'No, of course not,' Esther told her, amused. 'She's got other reasons, child!'

'Why are you calling me "child"?' Alice demanded.

Janake, having given up riding Alice's bicycle while balancing a ball on his head, began eating again.

'You'll be sick,' Esther said disapprovingly.

She looked at her new wristwatch.

'How much did that cost?' Janake asked, stuffing another piece of cake into his mouth.

'How should I know,' Esther said, yawning. 'It was a present from Anton.'

'Esther, Putha, time we left,' Dias called.

Janake looked at her with interest.

'Is he your boyfriend?'

190

'Mind your own business,' Esther said crossly, and she went inside to collect her gramophone record.

Janake snorted.

'I don't believe anything she says,' he told Alice.

'Will you be on the beach tomorrow?' Alice asked. 'I want to ride my bike again.'

She wanted to surprise Janake by giving him her bicycle as a present when she left for England. By now it was time for Janake and his mother to leave too.

'Come, I'll walk you back,' Bee insisted, picking up his pipe.

'See you tomorrow,' Janake called out, and Alice nodded.

Sita was helping Kamala clear some of the dishes.

'I'm going to the annexe in a little while,' she murmured. 'I told him I would say good-night.'

Kamala pretended not to hear.

'Where's Alice got to?' she asked. 'Isn't it time she went to bed?'

But Alice had vanished, slipping through the gate, running after her grandfather, laughing as she followed Janake and his mother down the now empty Station Road. It was almost like the night of the fair, she thought.

In fact it was well past midnight before Sita was free. Kunal was waiting, his crutch resting against the wall, its outline thrown into shadow by the naked light bulb. Tomorrow night he would be gone. The doctor would arrive in his car to take him on the first leg of the journey to Elephant Pass. All afternoon he had practised walking with his crutch for hours on end, waiting for the wedding to be over and Sita to come back. Finally, exhausted, he had picked up the book she had left him and begun reading it. The moment the door opened he turned his head.

'Can you stay?' Kunal asked.

She nodded.

'Sorry I took so long.'

Kunal smiled.

'Yes, you were a long time,' he said softly, half teasingly. 'Many years late. But at least you're here at last. So I'm glad.'

He stretched his hand out. The light from the bulb cast a yellowish shadow, making his eyes very black. It crossed her mind that he had a fever again. A part of her hoped he did, so he might stay another day. He was looking gravely at her, saying nothing. She saw herself reflected in his eyes for a moment.

'I've been thinking,' he told her, 'you know, I no longer have any footsteps.' And he shook his head as if he was amused. 'A man without footsteps. Someone should write a *kavi* about it.'

'Don't,' she said, unable to bear it. 'Don't say things like that.'

Tomorrow he would be gone and already she understood that a part of her would follow him. How would she live? Like a ghost? Fear was a timeless thing. Kunal was pulling her gently towards him and in a dream-like state she felt his lips, full and soft and surprisingly cool. He had no fever; only his eyes burned. Somewhere on the roof a bird's feet scratched. The devil-bird, they both thought without saying a word. I am rudderless, she wanted to say. Without you I am cast adrift. Instead she asked:

'Shall l come back? From England. Shall I?'

He didn't know what to say.

'If you want me, I'll come back.'

Still he said nothing, looking at her, sitting with her back against the light. His entire life had retreated into shadow. It seemed a petty thing to say, but he said it anyway:

'I have only one leg.'

He meant it as a warning, but she shook her head, disregarding it.

'One leg, two legs, I don't care!'

She cried softly, leaning against his shoulder. He could feel her body shake along the length of him as he held her with his two good arms. At least I can hold her, he thought. Her hair was perfumed by a hidden flower. He would remember its scent forever now. Portions of her limbs seemed to become luminous in his mind as he touched her.

'I have no plan,' he smiled. 'If you do what you really should do, you will have what you want.'

He was quoting from something, she could not remember what. He has a beautiful smile, she thought. A sense of being alive, of being here and possessing all of it – this place, the hour, most of all him – overwhelmed her.

'Do you understand that, until I met you, I was just trying to survive?'

She nodded. She had slipped into the bed with him and he felt the heat of her very close and strong against his one good leg.

'Turn off the light.'

The noise of insects grew louder in the darkness. A bat fluttered against the bars of the window, confused, then vanished. The tropical night remained an ebb and flow of unfinished business.

'Can you imagine life with a Tamil cripple?'

'Why do you have to talk like this?'

He knew he was trying to hurt her, but he needed to make his warning strong. He wanted her to know the dangers. Only then could he be sure.

'Even if you lost the other leg it wouldn't make any difference. I will come back or you must come to England.'

He tried and failed to contemplate England. Living with her and his crutch. Daily life. For a moment he considered it.

'If you want it enough, it will happen,' she told him, reminding him of Alice. 'I will find out how to get you to England. Many Tamils go there. You can't stay in Jaffna forever.'

'And your husband?'

'He doesn't care.' Sita shook her head.

She was surprised to feel no bitterness. It had gone while she was preoccupied with other things.

'He hasn't cared for a long time. I did all the caring. I think …' She was more certain now: 'I wanted to be like Thatha. I wanted a cause. So I found Stanley.'

'Am I your cause now?' he teased.

In the darkness she shook her head vigorously. He could feel it moving from side to side, reminding him again of Alice. In spite of himself he smiled.

'No. *Stanley* was my cause, not you.'

She was crying again and he tightened his arms around her, kissing her hair.

'We are the same,' she told him. 'I can feel it. We are the same. It is unimportant that you are a Tamil. Whether or not you are a Singhalese is unimportant too.'

And then, her face buried against him, her voice muffled, she said. 'I don't want to go.'

She was pushing against the limits of his endurance.

'Shall I stay, then?' he asked, but now was not the time to tease her. His arms wound around her like some great enclosure, keeping out those many things she no longer wanted.

'You must go, for Alice,' Kunal said at last.

The sound of his words imprinted themselves on the night.

'Everything you've said makes me certain it's the only thing for her. She is young; you have to give her a chance of a better life. If I can, I will come to England. I promise. When I get to Jaffna, I know some people who have influence. I'll talk to them, see if it is possible. We can write. You must tell me what you decide about Stanley.'

'I will leave him,' Sita said. 'As soon as I can, I'll get a job. I can save money. Thatha would want it, I know. I can get a divorce. I don't think it will matter so much in England.'

She spoke eagerly. He remembered a time when he used to visit the Sea House, before she had married Stanley, when she had been like this, young, impulsive. Laughing, quoting Shakespeare, her long hair flowing as she darted through the trees. This is madness, he thought, mesmerised by what she offered him, unable to look away.

'Alice doesn't even care,' Sita said. 'All Alice cares about is Bee.'

'Alice cares about many things,' he admonished her, smiling. 'Don't underestimate Alice.'

'But what I mean is, she won't care about a divorce between her father and myself. She never saw much of him when he was here.'

Kunal was silent.

'Will you write?' Sita asked fearfully. 'Will you keep in touch?'

He ran his hand across the length of her body. Her sari had come undone and he undid the hooks on her jacket.

'Is the door closed?' he asked.

She nodded and he could feel, suddenly, that she was very tired, and his regard for this filled him with great tenderness.

'You're tired, no?'

He placed his hand on her breast and left it there, without moving, feeling her heart beating beneath it. She was silent and he felt her breathing beneath him.

'How do you know?' she asked, finally.

'The way you kissed me is tired.'

It was difficult to hold her and lie with only one leg for balance and he turned her slightly to face him. He began to kiss her breasts, first one and then the other, holding them gently. He feared these were their last moments together. Pulling her jacket gently away from her shoulders, he felt her move herself so that first one arm, and then the other, was free. He could feel all the upper part of her body, naked and silky smooth under his hand. She turned and half raised herself and she was almost on top of him, lying across his body so that he felt her against the stub of his severed leg. He felt the pain of its absence break from him in a small cry of agony. Instantly she moved away. Through the cracks in the window he could see the outline of her face and when he touched it he felt it was once again wet from her tears. The room seemed to wait, as though it was witnessing an unfinished act.

'This is not a good idea,' she said. 'You are still not recovered.'

'Will you do something for me?' he asked.

Outside in the garden there was no longer any light; the sea was simply a dark, silent swell. His tenderness as he touched her once more stretched into the darkness. Someone in some future time will think of us, he thought.

'I will do anything,' she said.

Bee smoked on the verandah alone. The light had faded hours ago in the abrupt way of these parts. Tonight there were no stars and into this darkness, sweeping an encircling arrow of yellow at regular intervals, came the beam of the lighthouse. A small breeze rustled the trees and Bee breathed deeply. The wedding had gone well. Even he could not complain. Given their precarious situation, there was nothing more he could have asked of the day. But still he could not sleep. Kamala slept, Alice slept and Sita, he knew, was with Kunal. Maybe that was why he was wide awake. What am I worrying about? he thought. She is not a child; she is not a stranger to heartache. The beam from the lighthouse could be seen swinging with brilliant regularity across the bay and in one of these spells of darkness left by it every twenty seconds or so he caught a glimpse of the water, deceptively calm and docile. Bee stared at the beam without seeing it. He hoped May would be happy in whatever way was possible. If there were any hope of contentment it would be May who would find it. Bee was not a man of words. He knew it to be a fault; didn't Kamala tell him, every day, he should talk more? Words were not his thing; explanations were best done with brushes. The colour of a place, the angle of the light, a tree, these spoke volumes. But words? No, he was useless with words. Bee sat very still on his planter's chair, without creaking, drinking in the silence. A shape moved and came towards him, slowly, tiredly.

'Come to bed,' Kamala said. 'What good will it do, waiting for her? She will be all right.'

He wished he had Kamala's optimism. But as he turned to do her bidding he caught the beam of light again, flashing against his eyes and cutting him like a sword.

The next morning, Kunal left. It was the hospital doctor who drove the car. They were all present. Even Esther's mother was there. Kamala had made a parcel of food for the journey. Bee would follow them in his own car as far as Colombo, then he and the hospital doctor would leave Kunal in the hands of the contact. After that he would rest for a while and then, if he was well enough, he would be taken by the back route to Elephant Pass and on, up to Jaffna. All in all, Kunal had been two months with the Fonsekas. Alice watched her mother walk with him out to the car. Kamala stood holding his arm with perfect ease, as if she had held his arm in this way for years and years. Kunal looked very frail; the skin on his face was the colour of the ash used by holy Hindu men and his clothes hung loosely on him. One trouser leg flapped uselessly in the slight breeze. Everyone avoided looking at it.

'Get his other bag, Alice,' Sita said. 'Quickly.'

She raised her hand to her throat and Alice saw she wore a necklace of milky moonstones. Alice was about to ask her where it had come from when Sita twisted her hand and suddenly the necklace snapped. It fell to the ground in a staccato of stones.

'Never mind, never mind,' Dias said quickly as they bent to retrieve it.

'I'll restring it,' Kamala added.

'Yes,' Sita agreed, faintly.

She was watching Kunal, who stood, helpless. A swell of regret seemed to pass through her and her voice sounded low and without colour. Looking at her mother, Alice saw she had become her old cross self.

At the last moment, just as Kunal was being helped into the waiting car, they heard the gate open. Alice saw her grandfather turn around sharply but it was Janake. He carried a small parcel done up in plantain leaves which he gave Kunal. Janake began speaking to Kunal in a low voice. He was talking in Tamil. Alice watched, astonished. She had not known Janake could speak Tamil. Seeing her staring at him, Janake grinned.

'You haven't been to the beach,' he said, switching to Singhalese.

'No, I know.'

Kunal smiled a sad half-smile.

'England will be better than you think,' he told Alice.

She did not want to talk of England. Really all she wanted was to go to the beach.

'When you stop worrying, you'll get to like it there,' Kunal was saying, but now he was looking at Sita, who had moved slightly apart and stood motionless beside the mango tree, her face pale against the lushness of the leaves. Again Alice had a sense of the tension flowing from her mother. Kunal held out his hand, hesitantly. For a split second Alice thought her mother was going to ignore him, but then she stepped forward and, putting both arms around his neck, she kissed him lightly on both cheeks. After which Kamala and Dias kissed him too and wished him a safe journey.

'Good-bye,' he said, and the word spoken in English had the strangest finality to it. They stood and watched in silence as the car turned around and headed in the direction of Colombo. And then, slowly, they went indoors. There were only three weeks left.

On the afternoon of the last day, while her mother shut herself in her room, Bee took Alice to buy some fish. The men selling the catch were on the beach, carrying their huge flat baskets on their heads, trailing seagulls.

'You'll be sailing close to the equator before turning towards colder waters,' Bee informed her. 'Tomorrow,' he added, pointing to the horizon, 'you will be out there. And I will stand here, at this time, and watch for you.'

'I shall wave,' Alice told him and he nodded.

They were both determined to hold on to any certainties they could find.

Once again Alice had a curious feeling of standing on the edge of that shelving beach, with the sea dropping steeply, fathomless and mysterious before her. If she moved she would fall into the void. The day and all its iridescent loveliness were as insubstantial as a dream. A train rushed across the bay, hugging the coastline. Through the heat haze the brilliant blue carriages and the swaying coconut palms took on an air of unreality, as though they did not exist. Panic struggled in her. It was very simple. She did not want to go to England. A cry, mute and unheard, rose in her heart. And then her grandfather's voice, already from some distance, came to her.

'So will I,' he said, quite seriously.

He was looking crossly at her.

'No more biting your nails, huh!'

'No,' she agreed, but he didn't seem to be listening.

Something was stopping her from breathing. Perhaps she was ill, she thought, and would not be able to go. Bee went on staring at her and then beyond towards the sea. Fishing boats filled their view. Was it her imagination or did the men on stilts stand nearer to the shore? The sea was like crushed sapphires.

'I'm coming back,' she said again, uneasiness curdling and clutching at her stomach, for he seemed suddenly, unalterably old. 'You'll see.'

She tugged his hand and he nodded. After that he took a long time choosing and buying her favourite red mullet for lunch, even though eating seemed an irrelevance.

'What a bit of luck,' he said. 'There must have been a good catch last night!'

She was puzzled. He talked as if the buying of the fish was of the utmost importance. They walked towards the hamlets in search of Janake, but he was still out with the fishermen.

'He is coming to see you in the evening,' Janake's mother told Alice, smiling. 'Don't worry, he hasn't forgotten you are going. He will come.'

It shocked her that life carried on, regardless of what was about to happen. Janake out in the boat, getting on with his life, just as he would tomorrow and the day after. But where would she be tomorrow? And one day, Bee was thinking, she will be a grown woman. I will not see that. This is the end of my sightline. The rest will be imagination.

Towards evening, when the house was a frenzy of last-minute packing, they went for a final walk on the beach. Sita had come out from her room and was collecting up the jars of pickles that Kamala was labelling. She looked pale and subdued. The servant wrapped each jar carefully in plastic sheeting and wedged them in the trunk. Then she slipped in a bag of *curra pincha*, curry leaves, and *umbalakada*, Maldive fish. There would be nowhere else in the world that Sita would find these ingredients, the servant knew.

'Be careful,' Kamala said. 'Make sure it's wrapped tightly.'

'Don't go too far, Father,' Sita called. 'It's getting late.'

'Just up to the hotel and back,' he promised.

'I've finished packing, Mama,' Alice told her.

'Good girl!'

Both were speaking carefully to each other as if aware that from now on they would be thrown together for a long time. The house was stifling. Alice tugged at Bee's hand. She wanted to get out.

They had walked the same stretch of beach hundreds of times, but tonight was different. Tonight they walked slowly and in silence. Darkness was descending, shadows lengthened imperceptibly and still there was no sign of Janake.

'He'll come,' Bee consoled her, puffing at his pipe. 'Maybe in the morning. He knows what time you're leaving.'

Pausing, they watched the late Colombo express rush past. Two kites floated lazily in the rosy sky and the sounds of *byla* music came towards them on the breeze.

'You're coming to the boat, aren't you?' Alice asked suddenly, but Bee shook his head, sucking on his pipe.

'No,' he said. 'No, not tomorrow. It's important for you to remember this place. If I say good-bye here, you will always remember it.'

And even though she was dismayed and tried to make him change his mind, he would not be budged. Some time later, when she sat on the verandah, and Bee had disappeared into his studio, Alice asked Kamala.

'Why aren't you both coming to the harbour?'

Kamala began combing Alice's hair. She combed it silently and for so long that Alice thought she would not answer her. Then at last she spoke.

'He can't bear it, darling,' she said. 'He can only just manage to get to the station. Don't make him.'

Kamala's hands moved with soft and wide sweeps against Alice's head, lingering against the dark hair, combing it into silk.

'But I'll be back,' Alice said angrily. 'Doesn't he know that?'

'Aha! Look what I have here,' Bee cried, returning with false joviality.

He had made a present for her. A painting of the house, and the beach, with the sea glimpsed in the distance. He had used only cerulean blue and an emerald green and most of the light was defined by the brilliance of the white paper so that it seemed as though the land and the water existed within a bowl of sunlight. On the back he had written, *For my beloved granddaughter Alice, from her grandfather with his blessing.*

'It's a watercolour,' he told her, tapping his pipe, watching her. 'You are going to the land of the most beautiful watercolours in the world. Did you know that?'

Alice did not know.

'Well, you are, so go and see them for me, when you've settled in London. Tell your mother to take you. Look at the Turners and the Boningtons and the Cotmans. I believe you'll be able to see Constable's skies, too. The English are the best at using watercolours. You will have to look very closely at them to understand how they use the light.'

No one spoke. Alice could not bear the look on her grandmother's face. Almost everything in this house will survive us, thought Kamala. We are already ghosts on this verandah. Each night, when my girls were small, I sat out here, but nothing could have made me imagine this night.

Outside, the darkness seemed full of ghosts. A bullock coughed nearby and the frogs that lived in the ditches began to croak quietly. Two lizards circled each other under the yellowing light. Tonight was full of insects, the servant complained, bringing in a mosquito coil.

'I wonder where Kunal is,' Kamala murmured.

'Oh, he'll be at the Pass by now,' Bee told her.

Sita moved her head slightly. No one could see her face in the darkness. She was thinking of Kunal's last night and how, when she had left his room, she had found her mother hovering outside, a worried look on her face, ready to hold her as she wept. At last, Kamala had told her, stroking her hair, she had found love. But that night now seemed like a million days ago.

'He must be nearing Jaffna,' Bee observed.

'I'll find a way,' Kunal had told Sita. 'I'll come to England somehow, you'll see.'

And she had whispered:

'Or I'll come back.'

'I have the strangest feeling about leaving this place,' she had admitted to Kunal. 'Not only am I going to miss you, but I'm going to miss the person I am now, at this time, too. None of us will ever be the same again.'

And now he was gone, carrying his loss like luggage, his crutch under one arm, leaving her to continue alone. The day was almost over; tomorrow would bring the thing she had waited so long for. She saw how her desire to be gone had set her apart from everyone around her. It had put her into the same category as a person with a limp or an extra thumb. Her aunts used to say it had made her different, had attracted the wrath of the gods. Whenever she had observed any injustice, each time another Tamil was discriminated against, she had thought, I will leave. I will go away to a better life. Stanley had been merely a step in that direction, and the lost baby had compounded the feeling, making her need to flee even more urgently. But she had reckoned without Kunal. Meeting him, seeing *his* pain, had made her waver, fatally.

'I am too burnt-out to stay and fight,' she had said.

'You don't know what courage you possess until you are called to show it,' he had replied. 'You are the bravest of women. Wherever you are, here or in the UK, it doesn't matter; you will remain brave. You represent all the women of this island to me.'

That was what he had said, lying there in the stifling heat, day after day with his phantom limb. But now the exodus, planned for so long, was almost upon them, and her mother with her mending, and her father in his planter's chair, sitting as they would tomorrow, was too much for her to bear. A cockroach buzzed past. The servant began sweeping the verandah and all around the simple sounds she had listened to all her life gathered together with great sweetness in Sita's head.

Alice sat quietly on the step.

'You'd better go to bed,' Sita murmured at last and her daughter, without protest, without fuss, stood up and kissed them all goodnight.

As she climbed into her small bed under the net, Alice heard the tell-tale whine of mosquitoes moving invisibly in the room. Far away in some other part of the bay she heard a heavy thud followed by the plaintive noise of a police siren. It went on and on, an endless hyphenated crying, and it kept her awake for a long time. Her grandparents and her mother were moving outside. Sometimes one of them spoke in a low voice so as not to disturb her, but she could not sleep. Great tropical stars shone over the sea and she wondered once more if tomorrow night she would be able to see the house and her bedroom from the ship. She had made a flag and stuck it on a branch of the paw-paw tree outside her window. She had done it for Janake, but Janake too seemed to have vanished into thin air. For a long time she lay in this way, looking at the stars, until finally she fell asleep and sometime between midnight and dawn she dreamt her grandfather pushed aside the mosquito net and kissed her good-bye. Sighing, she turned over.

Morning came; the morning of departure. Issued to them with ease, fresh as a newly laundered sheet, clean and ordinary. There was nothing in its arrival that suggested any significance, nothing to prepare them for such a momentous moment. Too late, the day had arrived without fanfare or thunderclap. England, that strange amorphous shadow, had become a reality at last. Sita stared blankly at the sky, joined now so seamlessly to the sea, wondering if it had always looked this way. The morning lay before her in exquisite beauty. Blue softened the water, reflecting the light as never before, piercing and very lovely. She gazed out through her window, a stranger already in her own home, dimly wondering how all the years of her life had led so inexorably to this moment. She was thinking about Kunal. She had not stopped thinking of him. She did not expect him to ring. Realistically, she could not expect to hear news until she reached England.

'I'll try to telephone, before you go,' he had said. 'Before you leave, I want to hear your voice one more time.'

'Don't promise,' she had told him quickly, 'in case you can't. I'll write. Every time the boat docks, they post the letters. It will take weeks to get to you, but I'll write.'

Kamala was calling. Breakfast was ready. It was no longer possible to bear the dazzling light coming in through the bedroom window. I am nearly on the other side of saying good-bye, thought Sita.

Alice avoided looking at the sea. Instinct made her turn away, strangely restless to be gone, to be done with the waiting. The servant opened the shutters; there was the smell of milk rice.

'Has Janake come yet?' Alice asked sleepily.

'Not yet, baby,' the servant smiled, coming in, pulling back the mosquito net around the cot that Alice had slept in since she had been born. Suddenly she felt stripped of identity. The wardrobe door was open and in its mirror she could see the stag's head with the bowler hat still on it. If she opened the door a little wider the sea swung into view, sun-lit and very clear all the way to the end of the horizon.

'A good day for sailing,' she told herself, just as she had heard the grown-ups say.

The wardrobe door moved and the sea and the sky and the large black spider on the edge of the ceiling tilted out of balance. Somewhere there was another house and another school with a new best friend. But she couldn't imagine it looking any different from this one. Her grandmother was waiting with a breakfast of the milk rice and half a paw-paw and some fleshy rambutan. An auspicious meal for a journey. Soon, Esther and Dias arrived noisily to say good-bye. They had presents.

'Here, I've bottled you some of your favourite *seeni sambal* to take on your journey,' Dias said, handing Alice a jar of her famous vegetable pickles.

'You won't get this in the UK, men. This is to my own devised recipe, child. Your mama will be glad of it, too, especially if any of you fellows get sea-sick!'

Alice had no idea why they should get sea-sick.

'I've got you something, too,' Esther was saying, and she handed Alice a record cover.

'It's my favourite Elvis cover, child.'

Esther, Alice noted, was still trying to be grown-up.

But she was being kind.

'I've got two, so you can have one. And if they sell records in England, you could buy one and put it in this cover.'

Nobody knew if they sold records in England, but Alice thanked Esther, anyway.

'Here, let me write on it,' Esther said, snatching it back.

And she wrote in small curvy letters: *Be good, sweet maid, love from Esther.*

'Wait, I'll write something too,' Esther's mother said.

And she wrote, *Refuse to promise anything you cannot do, from Aunty Dias.*

Alice took the record cover from her. Then, in the awkward silence that followed, she picked up the jar of pickle from the table. Esther and her mother watched her. The day shifted from one warm tone to another. Orange blossom and temple flowers drifted in from the garden as with a slight squeak the gate opened and Janake came rushing in. He had been cycling with only one hand, he told them, grinning.

'Look what I've found you!'

He gave Alice a small turquoise tin with a lid that wouldn't open. Esther giggled, covering her mouth.

'What on earth would she want with that on the ship!'

Janake scowled.

'You wouldn't understand.'

'Janake!' Alice cried, and she threw her arms around him and hugged him. 'I love it!'

Janake moved away uneasily, glancing at Esther, but Esther had gone to talk to the grown-ups.

'I can't stand her,' Janake whispered. 'I'm not going to talk to her when you've gone.'

'I'll write to you,' Alice whispered back, 'when I'm on board ship. And I'll send you things, too. Will you wave tonight?'

Janake nodded.

'We're all going to stand by the rocks and wave at six o'clock, so make sure you're looking!'

From inside the house there was a noise and the servant gave a cry. She had broken the clay pot with water in it and Kamala was scolding her.

'Oh my God!' Janake said. 'Let's go and see.'

Alice felt a small shiver run down her spine.

'Don't worry, child,' Aunty Dias was saying. 'It wasn't very full and the water fell near the door, so it doesn't matter.'

'Is May meeting you at the jetty?'

'How are the newly weds?'

Everyone was talking at the same time as if to cover up the awkwardness. A neighbour had placed a devil offering across the road. The woven basket looked fresh and tempting. It was filled with mangoes and ambarella fruit and spilt over with rice and freshly fried fish. Beside it was another basket of cut flowers.

'There are new people coming into this place,' Aunty Dias said in a loud complaining voice. 'Everything is changing. Yesterday there were two army trucks in Main Street. And they say the curfew will be back now because of the general elections. You know, Sita, it's a good thing you're leaving.'

'How are you feeling? About going, I mean?' Esther wanted to know. 'Are you feeling anything?'

'No,' Alice said.

'What a stupid question,' Janake scoffed.

He looked suddenly in a bad mood. But it was true, Alice couldn't feel anything. Janake turned to her.

'Thanks for the bike,' he said shyly. 'I'll look after it till you get back.'

Alice nodded. Her chest felt tight and she was finding it difficult to breathe.

'You weren't meant to find it till we left,' she said faintly.

'It's nine o'clock,' Bee called. 'I'll put the luggage in the car.'

'Thatha, I think I'll leave this other holdall. We've got too much stuff,' Sita told him.

'Is this war definitely coming?' Alice asked Janake.

'Maybe. But I'm coming to visit you in the UK anyway,' Janake told her. 'Just wait and see. I'll turn up one day!'

The bravado in his voice did not escape her and she wanted desperately to say something more to him. She wanted to ask him what this war would be like, whether he and her grandparents would be safe. She wanted to assure him that she did not want to leave, but she seemed to have lost her voice and in any case instinct told her it was too late for such sentiments. She looked at Janake as he stood squinting anxiously at her and saw with horror that she was going to miss him too.

The morning with its mists rolling in from the sea, its fishermen shouting, '*malu, malu,*' and the rush and panic of getting to the station, finding a seat and forcing the window open, was too absorbing to leave room for anything else.

They snatched at words.

'Have you packed your new Enid Blyton book?'

'Don't forget to look out to sea tonight and wave.'

'We'll write as soon as we're in London. In twenty-one days!'

'Look after yourselves,' the grandparents said, smiling funny lop-sided smiles. Standing close together, not like her grandparents at all but like an old married couple. Bee and Kamala left their hugs until the last possible moment.

'There's a new merry-go-round on the hill,' was all there was time for Alice to notice before, with a shrill whistle, the train began to move.

Suddenly, when it was too late, when their faces had begun to move away from her, she started to cry. And as the faces on the platform passed swiftly by, she saw, also, that all around and beneath her was the sea, huge and wide and filled with sunlight. In a few hours they would be on it.

There was nothing for it. Sink or swim, thought Sita grimly, her arms and legs aching as she climbed. They had said their good-byes to May and Namil and Uncle Sarath. Neither sister had cried. Something had stuck in both of them, stopping them from doing so. The noise and the stifling heat, Sita's tiredness and tension were inexorably caught up in a turmoil of confusion. She saw that May looked well. Her honeymoon was over, but there was still the excitement of the house being built and then there was the choosing of furniture to come.

'Now then, darling,' May told her niece, 'mind you look after Mama for me. She's all the sister I've got.'

And that too was it; once again the swiftness of departure was what they remembered. All around them people were crying. Sita watched impassively; she could not cry. Not even when they were on the launch, moving unsteadily across the bay, not even when May waved and called her name was she able to respond. The small motor boat took them out to the furthest tip of the sun-washed harbour, close to the breakwater. Then the boatman helped them, one by one, on to the narrow gangway. Children screamed as they stood up and the boat rocked madly. Before them, thin and insubstantial, was the rope ladder, each rung seeming higher than their legs could ever reach. Would it hold their weight? The sun beat relentlessly on Sita's back and her head throbbed as she followed Alice higher and higher up the gangway. Reaching, it seemed, for the sky.

'Hold tight, Alice,' she said faintly. 'Hold tight.'

Everything happened too quickly. I wasn't ready to leave; there were things I forgot to say. And now, she thought, it will last forever. They reached the top of the gangway. Below was a mass of swaying, saried women, their oiled heads bent in concentration, their voices a sad chant of farewell. In front of them were the neat dark ankles, the bright patterned silk of an unknown sari, fluttering like a useless flag in the breeze. And far beneath them was the sea, turquoise and restless. There was no going back.

Hands reached out to help them up the last steep step and she saw humanity hanging out of every porthole, from every deck. Ribbons floated down into the sea, someone was flying a kite. The strange unfamiliar smell of diesel mixed with the salty air made Sita nauseous. From somewhere inside the ship they heard the faint strains of the national anthem, its sad sweet melody, haunting and full of all that they loved, all they were leaving. The music, heard only at state funerals and other such occasions, drenched them in sorrow.

'Alice,' Sita cried in a panic, 'where are you?'

But Alice was beside her, her small face streaked with grime, her mouth firmly shut. In silence, somehow they managed to find their cabin. It was in the bowels of the ship.

'C Deck, next stop the engine room,' said the steward jokingly, pointing them towards the door.

Almost instantly they noticed the deep bass vibration, the vast hum of the engines. Staring at their small cabin in dismay they saw that this was all they were to have for the next twenty-one days. Two bunk beds, the sea, and each other. They made their way back up on deck again, negotiating the maze of stares, wrinkling their noses at the unfamiliar smells, staggering a little as the ship creaked gently. Pushing doors almost too heavy for them both, they went out into the fresh sea air to feel the warm breeze of their home and the painfully broken light. In the distance were the bare slabs of white-hot sand. Beyond was a coconut grove, sharply defined against the extraordinary sun. And it was then, suddenly, that Alice wanted passionately to get off the boat. She had had enough. Sita found a space to lean out over the edge, but the harbour and May and Namil were no longer distinguishable. In this way, slowly, with a creaking heaviness of metal and hearts, the *Fairsea* inched its way out of the harbour towards the open sea. Ahead was the pilot ship guiding them as far as the breakwater before it too turned back home. It was how Alice became aware, watching the island's sandy beaches recede, its dense coconut palms vanish, that the raised voices around her were broken by another, unfamiliar sound. The sound went on and on, rhythmically, unnoticed by everyone in the confusion of the moment, but as she listened Alice heard it clearly and was rendered speechless. For it was the soft swish of the waves as heard from a boat, pulling them away from the land where they had been born, washing over her mother weeping.

Night came. A night with no tomorrows, Bee thought, standing at the water's edge. Far away in the distance was a ship that moved flatly on the horizon like a child's drawing. Was it them? Was it their ship?

'Eat a little,' Kamala said. 'Try.'

His heart was hanging on its hinges. Broken. They dared not speak for fear of conjuring up the evil spirits of the day. Should they have gone to the harbour? Should they have stood and waved like May? I can bring nothing of this back, thought Bee. Every room seemed to describe an unfinished act. The presence that had filled the empty spaces of the house, *that* presence, had gone. May and Namil arrived, as planned, with tales of the last moments. As though it had been an execution, Bee thought.

'No, Father,' his daughter, the only one left to him now, said. 'It happened so quickly, they hardly had time to say good-bye and they were bundled on the launch. You would have upset yourself needlessly. As it was, no one cried.' Bee disagreed silently. It would have been better if they had cried. Better then than later, with no one to comfort them. May sighed. She could see her father was beating himself with a stick.

'How will Sita manage Alice?' Kamala worried. 'She has hardly recovered herself.'

'Stanley will be at the other end to meet her,' May soothed.

That's generous of him, Bee thought, bitterly. But he didn't say it. And the child, he had wanted to ask May. What about the child? Tell me? Did she grieve? But he couldn't ask that, either.

'She sent you this,' May said, knowing how it was for him.

And she gave him a drawing Alice had done in the train, going up to Colombo. It was a self-portrait.

'Wait, I'll put the date on it,' Bee muttered, going out to his studio.

They let him go, nodding at each other, saying nothing.

So now it was night. Bee's grief walked silently with him along the narrow spit of beach. He was too old for grand demonstrations or declarations. He knew when he loved and he knew about those things from which he would never recover. Here she had grown, a child with only small hints of what she could one day become. He would walk with that small child for what was left of his own life, here on this beach. Every night. Across the water a sickle moon trod a pathway of light and suddenly a sound carried across the breeze from the next bay. It was the long, lonely hoot of the night train as it rushed along the line. How often he had heard it. But tonight the sudden sound, this silhouette through the trees, was Bee's undoing. It was how Janake, wheeling the precious bicycle Alice had given him, hurrying to make a shortcut through the trees, found him, leaning against an empty catamaran.

'I knew what it would be like,' he told Janake, finally. 'Yet knowing doesn't make it any easier.'

Janake scuffed the sand with his bare foot. As it happened he had been on his way to see Mr Fonseka. The doctor, unable to leave his surgery for the moment, had given him a message to deliver. Janake had been about to blurt the message out, but Bee Fonseka was too upset. How can I tell him? Janake thought. I can't, not now. When Mr Fonseka had composed himself and Janake had promised to come for an English lesson later in the week, he said good-bye. Guiltily he rode off without saying a word.

'You tell him, Amma,' Janake begged his mother. 'How could I say Uncle Kunal had died in the car?'

On their very first night on the boat, the passengers were given strange things to eat. Italian food, long slimy strings of a substance Alice had never seen before. Sita did not want food, all she wanted was to stay in the cabin and write a letter to Kunal. She wanted it to be ready for when the purser made the collection.

'You go,' she told Alice. 'You know where the dining room is, go and eat with the other children.'

But the food was inedible. Like worms, Alice announced at the children's table, making everyone snigger, and the Swiss girl sitting next to her, vomit.

'Why can't we have some rice?' Alice demanded of the steward.

'There's no rice where you're going,' he sneered. 'Better get used to proper food, you little savage!'

The Swiss girl had to go to bed.

'See what you did,' the steward said crossly, clearing up the sick.

Several other children left the table. Alice didn't care. She wasn't hungry either. She took one of the strange-smelling orange fruit and went on deck to wave to her grandfather and Janake and Esther as she had promised.

Later, one of the staff knocked on the door of their cabin to complain to her mother, telling her Alice had been disruptive at supper. Sita regarded her daughter with a glazed look after the man had gone.

'This isn't like you Alice,' she said helplessly.

Sita looked hot and unhappy with the thought of the days and nights yet to be spent in the darkness of the cabin. When she had finished scolding her daughter in this half-hearted way, she placated her with a spoonful of the precious vegetable pickle from one of her grandmother's carefully packed jars.

'After tonight,' she told Alice, 'there are only twenty days left before we'll be on dry land again.'

The morning after his family had begun their voyage, Stanley awoke with a feeling of well-being. It was Monday, almost three months since his startling arrival in London and at last he had a proper job. He had been temping, washing dishes, addressing envelopes and generally odd-jobbing. Sunlight streamed in through the thin brown curtains of his bedroom, falling on the drab, peeling wallpaper, the yellow eiderdown, the oddly heavy furniture. For a moment he wondered where he was as he stared at the painting of a woodland scene on the wall. What leaves there were on the trees were brown. Autumn, thought Stanley, half in a dream, and he remembered Sita reciting a poem about autumn to him when he had first broached the subject of their migration to England. A picture of Sita swam before his eyes and he sat up with a start. It was seven o'clock and he was due to report at Rajah's office at eight thirty.

'Don't be late,' had been Rajah's words to him as they had parted.

Last night Stanley had again had dinner with his brother. Still disorientated, he had been determined to cook something for himself in his new home, but Rajah had been insistent.

'I'm going to take you to an Indian restaurant, men. It's very cheap and I want you to meet some of the people there.'

'Indian?' Stanley had asked, startled.

This was a new idea. Rajah had given him a peculiar look.

'We've all got brown skins so far as the English are concerned,' he explained patiently. 'Forget about the rules at home. They don't apply here.'

He had laughed at the look on Stanley's face.

'You've got a lot to learn, Putha!' he had cried. 'And you've got to learn fast, before that Singhalese wife of yours arrives.'

Rajah had been driving at the time, having picked Stanley up from the house at Cranmer Gardens. They were heading over the river.

'Why you wanted to saddle yourself with a bloody Singhalese woman was one thing. But to book her a passage to this place at the same time was sheer madness. What were you thinking?'

'Her father insisted on it,' Stanley said lamely. 'And I thought it might help.'

'Help? In what way, for God's sake? When has a Singhalese ever helped a Tamil!'

His brother turned towards him, roaring with laughter.

'Christ, Rajah, keep your eyes on the road!' Stanley cried nervously.

After their meal, Rajah had taken Stanley to a meeting at the house of a Tamil friend. Stanley had been surprised to see so many Tamils gathered together under one roof. Arguing about the state of Sri Lanka.

'There's a civil war about to break out, men,' a dark Jaffna man was saying belligerently. 'Just wait a while and you will see. The Singhalese shits have a lesson coming bloody soon!'

Stanley sat in a corner of the room, listening. A man handed him a can of beer. The man from Jaffna was shouting again. Stanley sighed. He knew the type. There were plenty of them in Colombo, stirring up trouble, aggravating an already delicate situation. Why was his brother mixing with such people when at home he wouldn't have dreamed of doing so?

'We need money for weapons and for training in the use of those weapons.'

'We have to help our people and stand by them,' another man said.

At the end of the meeting, a tray was passed around. Everyone placed their donations on it. Then a piece of paper was given to Stanley for his name and address. How much would he be able to donate each month?

'He's got no money,' Rajah said, waving the tray away. 'He's still temping. Wait until he gets the permanent job I'm organising for him!'

The woman in charge of the collection smiled at him before turning to Stanley. He saw a flash of gold in her teeth.

'Is it true your wife is Singhala?' she asked.

Stanley had been taken aback and had nodded uneasily. It was some weeks since he had last felt uncomfortable about having a Singhalese wife. He had thought all that was behind him.

'Never forget your brothers,' the woman said quietly.

'But is a civil war the answer?' Stanley had asked timidly, surprising himself.

The island and all its dysfunctional problems were less important, somehow. He looked around for Rajah, but his brother had moved off and was deep in conversation elsewhere. Stanley saw him take out his cheque book.

'Pay next time,' the woman with the gold teeth said.

She was smiling at him, but he sensed her watchfulness too.

'Would you like to come to my temple at the Oval next week? For prayers?'

'I'm a Catholic,' Stanley had said.

The woman had fixed him with her eyes for a moment longer. Then she smiled again.

'You might not always be a Catholic,' she said. 'And I can tell there is some sort of problem in your marriage. Your wife's holding you back.'

'How d'you know?' Stanley asked, mildly surprised.

'*Anay!* I can tell from your face. You're struggling a little, hah? Your wife isn't religious either. Come to the temple, just for once, before she arrives. It will do you good, you'll see, make you very prosperous.'

Stanley didn't know how to respond to this. The woman was not good-looking, she was too thickset for that, but her eyes were arresting. Half frightened, half mesmerised, he couldn't think of anything to say.

'Here,' she said, 'have this.'

She pushed a small packet into his hand.

'Put some of this on your tongue every evening. After you have taken your bath. Say a prayer to the Bhagavan. He'll hear you, I promise.'

Still Stanley didn't answer. The woman laughed.

'What's your name?'

'They call me Manika. Come to the temple, if you want. Next Thursday.'

And she went.

In the car going back, the small packet tucked inside his coat pocket, Stanley had been quiet. Rajah was talking enthusiastically about the evening.

'It's our duty to help other Tamils,' he said. 'These are our people.'

Stanley agreed, only half-listening. He was thinking of Sita. She would be arriving soon. The thought of her filled him with dismay. What, aside from survival, had kept them together? Somewhere between the mountains of Greece and the Mediterranean, the intensity had gone out of his life in Colombo. He had shed his anger like a skin.

'Have you thought of divorce?' Rajah asked slyly, taking him by surprise.

Stanley looked at him. What had he said?

'Come on, men, don't look so shocked. What's the matter with you? In this country anything is possible. I've been telling you for years.'

But later, back in his own flat, Stanley felt less certain. The packet, when he looked at it, turned out to be ash. Holy ash? wondered Stanley. Before he went to bed, he put some experimentally on his tongue and closed his eyes. There were unknown expenses ahead. The future was full of uncertainties. Perhaps the ash, holy or not, would bring him good luck. He had no idea what he wanted.

This morning, with the thin sunlight streaming in, he considered all of this. Swinging his feet on to the cold carpet, he got out of bed and hurried into the bathroom. He needed to get to Rajah's office. At last he had a proper job and could give up the temping. The sun through the window was not bright but it no longer felt as cold as when he had first arrived. He thought of the woman with the ash. She had probably been a servant in Colombo. In Ceylon, associating with such a woman would have been a huge social taboo. Here, such things were of no importance. This thought too was exciting. Staring at himself in the bathroom mirror, whistling, he considered his prospects. He had entirely forgotten his hurt over the Swedish girl.

Days passed. Travelling the ocean, chased by monsoons, sending messages to her grandfather in the bottles she threw overboard, Alice felt the time pass slowly.

I miss you … I want to come back … Please write to them and say you've changed your mind and I can live with you.

The seas had changed colour as they travelled, from an inky-blue ocean, deep and unfathomable, to the skittish, calm Mediterranean, but still Alice threw her bottles almost daily overboard.

'If the Purser sees you doing that,' one of the other children said, 'you'll be in trouble.'

Alice didn't care. She needed to talk to her grandfather. She had never been away from him for this long.

'He's coming to rescue me,' she said, sticking her chin out in the way that she knew he liked.

She wished she could hear his laugh.

'Don't be silly,' the girl told Alice disapprovingly. 'The bottles will never get back there!' Alice ignored her and redoubled her efforts.

Send a telegram, she instructed. *We'll be in Port Said soon, send a letter. Tell them to send me back on another ship.*

'You're mad,' the girl scoffed. 'Anyway, I don't care, I'm going home.'

And she skipped off to find someone else to play with.

My dearest Kunal, Sita wrote, sitting on her bunk.

All my other letters will be posted from Port Said. How many letters? I hear you ask. Maybe you will even laugh. (How I wish I could hear your laugh.) Well, I have to confess to having written seven! I have got to know you as I wrote. All the things I was unable to say that night I have said. Here in this little cabin, our home for almost twenty-one days, I feel as if I've summoned you up like a genie from a lamp. This is what happens to people who do not fit in. Ah, Kunal, if only you were really with me now, how different the seas would look. We would watch the flying fish together and the storms. The sunrises and the sunsets. We will be in Gibraltar soon. Alice wants to go ashore at the next port, but I can't bear to. All I want to do is to get to England, to get to the address where I'm hoping all your letters will be waiting for me.

With the first brushstroke of evening the moon slipped blood red over the sea. The last of the light seeped across the beach as though it were a line of watercolour. Everywhere was silent, for there would be no more trains tonight. The railway line gleamed like a silver fish. Coconut palms cast thin shadows across the rocks and the slight breeze smoothed the black silky water. It was as it had always been with the land and the sea and sky as one, joined invisibly. The sea pulsated like a heart. His heart. Cicadas vibrated in Bee's ears, lamenting his losses, while the moon-polished water brimmed over with unspoken memories. The land had lost something precious; the vast starlit sky had lost it too. And I am bereft, thought Bee. It was unrecoverable. He would never again have what other people took for granted. Continuity in old age, that was what he had lost. What became of a country that sent its people to the four corners of the world, indifferent to their fate, uncaring of the history they carried within them? Bee could not imagine. What would be left here in this paradise when all that was good and brave was slaughtered, and all those who cared were broken and dismissed? It was beyond his understanding. No longer able to rationalise this bereavement, he saw his eldest daughter and his only grandchild as distant, mythical creatures, standing on the prow of a ship, facing a new world not of their making, not of their people. Earth would be broken, he feared, lives too, in the making of their new home. His heart wept for them, it would go on weeping until his life was over. He could not see how, in what way, they could belong there. Someone, in some future time will tell of this. Not now, not in my lifetime, not perhaps for many years to come, he thought, but one day this uprooting will be counted. Threading his way back to the house, in the pale glow of the moonlight, he heard the familiar low dull thud, followed soon after by the scream of sirens.

Inferno

8

THE SEA AT DAWN WAS MOTIONLESS. Before them, rinsed by rain and approaching steadily, was the land. They stood on deck watching their ship slice through the muscle of water, bringing them inexorably toward their new life. In all, it had taken twenty-one days and seven thousand watery miles. The morning unfolded starkly, white as a shroud. What little could be seen through the fast-moving mist was bleak and devoid of trees. England huddled in darkness; ancient cliffs secretive and uninviting; settlers' land. Small pockets of fear exploded within them even as they watched. Everything they had seen – the Red Sea at dawn, memories of the Mediterranean – in one single blow was reduced to a crumpled blur in the face of this new reality. Alice, standing mesmerised beside the wrapped figure of Sita, heard her grandfather's voice very clearly in the cold morning air.

'This is your first home, Putha,' he had said, on that last day, 'you were born here.'

There had been a warning in his voice and she had ignored it. He had had the strangest look on his face.

'I promise you, it will be beautiful in England,' he had told her. 'In a different way. You'll have to search for it.'

In the twenty minutes or so in which they had been leaning against the rails, the sun had struggled to rise. Seagulls glided above them, their wings touched by an alien silvery-grey light. And again, unmistakably, close in her ear, Alice heard Bee.

If you are capable of seeing beauty in one place then you will see it in another. You must simply learn the way of seeing it. You must make it a habit, Alice. In order to survive; in order to become a painter.

I will be a painter, she thought, dully. She felt the long journey and the time spent surrounded by the sea had changed her. Water, pearly grey and smooth, spread out before them in delicate, enamelled hues. Alice was riveted. She had never seen an ocean of such colour before. She noticed that the land ahead of them was at perfect ease with the sea, and that even the green fields were touched with grey. Here is my new home, thought Sita as they approached, shivering in her thin clothes. She had dressed in her best sari, rising early, knowing that in a few hours they would be on dry land, but the sari, packed so carefully by her mother, worn only once, no longer looked right. Something about the greyness of the light and the murky green landscape con-trived to dull the yellow and pinks of the silk. Soon it would be September. Autumn was beginning to lay siege over England. Alice wore her blue embroidered frock, dark arms hugging the railings, face unsmiling and closed. This place, thought Sita, is where my only daughter will grow into a woman. She shivered, as other hidden thoughts pushed against her. The mist lifted a little and there before them was the harbour, drawing closer. Kunal, Sita pleaded silently, please come. I can bear it if you are here. Three weeks of yearning was on the move within her, nudged by the sight of this land. Imagining the pile of letters that would be waiting, in spite of all that still lay ahead, joy flooded her heart. The cliffs were coming up with an alarm-ing speed; their future approached. While they had been watching, the throbbing of the engines, their deep-throated companions for so long, changed their rhythm. There was no longer any doubt; they were slow-ing down.

'Look, Mama, I can see cars,' Alice said, her voice piercing the air like a thrown knife.

And what of me, thought Sita, looking up at the gulls. What will it be like for me? When I have lived in this place for years. She thought of the baby buried in what had become an impossible distance. Oh God, she thought, Kunal, save me!

The ship's horn reverberated across the water and a voice crackled indistinctly over the tannoy. They were coming into the docks. There were people standing silently on the quay, watching this ghost ship bringing its cargo of life to its shores. Somewhere in the crowd was Stanley. My husband, thought Sita, testing out the words; the man who I can no longer recall. By now the light, pearly white and slightly warm, was beginning to soften the land. A few yachts glided past, their sails as transparent as wings.

'There he is,' Alice said, 'I can see him!'

Her voice was flat against the throb of the engine, so different from the voice that had cried out at the sight of Mount Lavinia Station. But what have we done, coming here? thought Sita mutely. What have we done? The faint sunlight falling on her face gave no warmth, no comfort.

'We'd better get our bags,' was all she managed to say.

Turning her back on the view and taking her daughter's icy hand, she made her way slowly down to the cabin. The ship groaned as with heavy, scraping sounds its anchor was lowered. There followed a long, slow shudder. In less than twenty minutes they would feel dry land beneath their feet.

Stanley, waiting on the viewing balcony of the Passenger Ocean Terminus in his first proper suit, a rolled-up copy of *The Times* under his arm, saw them through the crowds and was catapulted into reality. Sita's face stained dark by a far-away sun, and the child, his child (had she always been this thin?), frightened him. He had not thought about Alice. His daughter was searching the crowd for his face and in her look he recognised the features of her stillborn sister. Unexpectedly, without any warning, kinship tugged at him and the day was knocked off balance.

Stanley had been dreading this moment. The sight of the huge ship, looming up so startlingly close, paralysed him with fear. Last night he had pleaded with Rajah to accompany him to the harbour.

'For God's sake, men, she's your sister-in-law. You've never even met her!'

But Rajah was not to be drawn. He would see Sita soon enough and in the end Stanley had caught the train alone. And here he was now, facing his past. The last few months had been like no other. Living as he had done, without responsibilities, feeling neither married nor really a bachelor, with the safety of one state and the freedom of the other, Stanley had enjoyed the best of both worlds. He had begun to notice with some amazement that there were women who were attracted to him. At County Hall, where he now worked as a clerk, he began an affair with a thin, mousy-haired colleague called Jacky. It enchanted him to find sex so readily available, so without consequences. Lying in Jacky's bed in her small flat in Streatham, watching her take her daily pill, he began to feel young in a way he had never felt before. He began to spend more time at her flat than his own house and somehow the decorating he had meant to do before Sita arrived never got done. June had disappeared in this way and was followed by a hot July. Stanley stared lazily at the sky as Concorde soared over South London on its daily flight.

'Where the hell have you been all weekend?' Rajah would ask him when he emerged bleary-eyed and late for work on Monday morning, and Stanley would smile dreamily and shake his head. In July, when London emptied of office workers on annual leave, Manika rang Stanley.

'Why you never come to my temple?' she asked him in a rasping voice.

The sound of her made Stanley uneasy. Time was running out. Once again the thought of Sita's imminent arrival made him break out in a cold sweat.

'Come for prayers,' Manika urged. 'Don't worry. I will help you.'

Quite how she would help him was a mystery, but curious about her prayer meeting, Stanley went.

Manika lived in a dingy flat on a council estate on Dorset Road, close to the Oval cricket ground. As he entered, he was struck by two things: the cooking smells that reminded him sharply of home, and the bright amaryllis flower that grew in a pot on the dining table. The house was packed with an odd assortment of Tamils. They sat cross-legged on the floor or perched on chairs waiting for Manika to finish spooning the hot food into brass bowls. Then, when she was ready, someone lit the joss-sticks and the chanting began. A dark Jaffna Tamil began to beat a drum and Manika carried the tray of food into her spare bedroom where the bright-brass shrine was set up, complete with chrysanthemums and coconut oil lamps. Stanley followed behind, but there was no room to move so he watched the proceedings from a corner of the doorway. First Manika bowed low, offering the food to Shiva. She asked the Bhagavan to bless their meal and answer their prayers.

'We are so far from our home,' she cried in Tamil. 'So lost, so needy of your protection. Help us, Bhagavan.'

The drumming reached a crescendo, the chanting got louder. Outside in the scuffed and drying grass of the council estate two children kicked a football. A police siren wailed in the distance. Manika produced some holy ash from behind the statue and touched each worshipper on the forehead with it. When she got to Stanley she paused for a moment, her breasts heaving. There was a faint odour of sweat and ghee surrounding her as she bent towards him and smeared his lips with the ash. Everyone was chanting and watching Stanley and he felt his face grow hot. For a moment longer he felt aroused by her as she swayed and moaned. But suddenly there was a knock on the front door. Because he was nearest, Stanley opened it.

'Will you stop that bloody noise,' the man outside shouted. 'I can't hear the telly any more. If you don't, I'll call the police …'

'No need, Mr Patrick, sir,' called Manika, smiling, closing the temple door and screening the view. 'We finish now. Please, no problem. I pray for your wife too, Mr Patrick!'

'I don't care what you do, just do it quietly,' the man muttered before shuffling away.

After she had shut the door, Manika took hold of Stanley's hand in her own hot one. Once again Stanley felt excitement grow in him. He caught a glimpse of the bedroom with an unmade bed and a bra hanging on a chair. Then Manika drew him into the sitting room, where the meal, blessed by her Bhagavan, was being served. The red amaryllis glowed brightly against the window. Manika began to eat using her fingers.

'You come back tomorrow,' she told Stanley, her mouth full of rice. 'I give you ash again. Make you very, very prosperous!'

It had been what he had done for the remaining four weeks, dividing his time between Jacky, who was beginning to bore him, and Manika, who held all the excitement of forbidden fruit. And then, without warning, the month was up and here he was at Southampton waiting for the passengers to disembark.

Much later, having travelled on the packed boat train to Waterloo, arriving by taxi at the house at Cranmer Gardens, Stanley fed them. He forgot for the moment about Jacky waiting in Balham and Manika at prayer in her council flat. He cooked hot rice and watched as they ate the *seeni sambals* they had brought. The smell of the sea was trapped in all their possessions: their clothes, the books he had requested, the food, packed too tightly in cheap plastic containers. And when Sita opened the heavy trunk, moments before she hid it, he saw the old shoebox with the dead child's clothes. So, he thought grimly, that has come too.

'Are there any letters?' Sita asked eagerly.

Stanley shook his head.

'No letters,' Sita said. 'You're sure?'

She stared at him, dismayed.

'It's Sunday,' Stanley reminded her. 'Don't worry, I'm sure they've written. Wait till tomorrow.'

On closer observation, Alice was even more of a stranger to him than before. She filled the house with her noise, rushing about, chattering, carrying the heat and the sense of his home strongly, like an aura. A patch of brightness seemed to be following her around the rooms of this new, dark home. Watching her, Stanley was confused. He had no idea the child could carry this much memory within her. He wondered if Sita was aware of it.

'It's not very nice,' Alice declared, having examined the rooms. 'Why is it so dark?'

'It's the way things are here,' he said, shrugging, not knowing what else to say. 'This isn't Mount Lavinia.'

'Why are there no letters?' Sita murmured.

She swallowed. Even if she panicked, what good would that do?

'Aren't they getting through?' she asked, unable to stop herself.

'There's the card I sent you,' Alice said suddenly, pointing to the postcard of the ship sitting on the mantelpiece.

Stanley drew the curtains shut and poured more paraffin into the heater.

'What's that for?' Alice asked him, her voice insistent.

'To keep us warm,' he said shortly, feeling hemmed in by their questions, by their crowding presence.

He wanted to be free to leave the house, go to the pub, visit the grey-eyed Jacky even.

'But there's no view,' Alice said, staring in dismay through the curtains at the darkened street outside.

People were walking through the fallen leaves; lamplight fell across the pavement, darkly cross-hatched by shadows. Just like some of her grandfather's etchings. She saw that it had begun to rain.

'Why is there no view?' she asked again, tonelessly.

Stanley sighed heavily.

'Because in this country,' he said slowly, carefully, 'only rich people can afford views.'

'Grandpa Bee said it would be beautiful here,' Alice said in a small voice.

The mention of Bee's name made her eyes prick. Uncertainly, she looked at her father, seeing him as if for the first time. There was nothing, she realised with dismay, either in his face or the scene outside the window, which she wanted.

'What does your grandfather know about London?' Stanley asked her, not unkindly. 'He's never been here. It'll be all right,' he added into the silence, trying to be encouraging. 'You'll get used to it.'

Alice said nothing.

'Let me show you how to fill the bath,' Stanley continued, aware of the bleakness of her stare.

Her face remained unchanged. What does a child of nearly ten think about? he wondered uneasily.

'We don't have showers here, only baths. You have to fill it with some water, hot and cold, and then you can put some bath salts in. Come, I'll show you how it's done.'

Once again he was met by a stony silence.

'Alice,' he said sharply, 'come, I'll show you, then tomorrow you can fill it yourself.'

Later, when the child was finally in bed, exhausted by the effort of getting her there, he tried talking to Sita. He realised that he had no means of communicating with her either. Their talk had stopped long ago. Watching her unpack her saris, he was puzzled. The silks he vaguely remembered as being saturated with colour now merely looked gaudy.

'Evenings come early,' Sita observed, making an effort.

He could see she was still worrying about the letters. Didn't she know that letter writing would become an apathetic activity with absence acting as an impermeable barrier?

'Yes,' he agreed.

She looked at him with her large trusting eyes, reminding him of how she used to look when they had first met. For a moment he was unnerved.

'Once the clocks go back it will be darker quicker but lighter earlier,' he warned her, knowledgably, sounding gentler than he had felt for many years.

Maybe it wouldn't be so bad, after all, he thought, as he lay listening to her breathing when she finally slept.

'My first night on dry land,' she had said and, hesitating a moment, awkwardly, he had kissed her, finally.

He had been surprised by her response and the way she had clung to him, weeping suddenly, asking him to hold her. Oh no! he had thought, trying not to panic. What does she want of me? Not more children? Had she forgotten the doctor had told them there would be no more? Stanley stared into the darkness. He would have to get rid of Jacky. That much was clear. But what shall I do then? he wondered unhappily. He thought of Manika. As always, at the thought of her, feelings of excitement rose in him. Manika was playing hard to get. Stanley moved restlessly under the blankets. Beside him, Sita slept like a stone, exhausted. I can't leave her, thought Stanley uneasily. It will kill her; she will never survive. Then what will happen? I'll get the blame. It was all very well for his brother to issue orders, but *he* didn't have to do the walking out, he didn't have to lie beside this needy, desperate woman. Sighing, Stanley turned over. He had work in the morning, the child needed to be registered in a school, there was a lot to do. Sita needed to find a job. First, I'll make her financially independent, he thought, shelving the problem for the moment, and falling, with no difficulty at all, into a dreamless sleep.

In her tiny attic room with its sloping ceiling and fading wallpaper, Alice lay staring into the darkness. Rain fell lightly against the window and once or twice she heard the screeching of tyres. The streetlight shone through the threadbare patches in the curtain so that when she moved Alice caught glimpses of condensation on the window ledge. The room was cold; she shivered and pulled the pink eiderdown up around her chin. She was far away from her parents; she had never been so far away from anyone. She had never been so far away from the sea, she thought. And then, swelling up within her, she felt the pain of her grandfather's absence.

'I want to go home,' she muttered, tears trickling slowly down her face. 'I want him.'

Later, when she could cry no more, when her throat was dry and she needed a drink but was too frightened to go in search of the kitchen, she sighed. She felt sleepy now. The sharpness of her longing had blunted slightly and her bed seemed warmer, so that turning over, facing the window, she slept. Towards dawn when the rain ceased and the streetlight was finally turned off, she dreamed she was running across the beach towards her grandparents' house.

Both Sita and Alice slept late into the next morning. The early autumn sun was high in the sky and Stanley had left for work several hours before. There were still no letters.

'I'm cold, Mama,' Alice said.

Sita looked at her daughter in despair. I have made a mistake, she thought, staring at the empty mat. Oh God! What shall I do?

'The paraffin heater has gone out,' she told Alice, pulling herself together. 'Come and help me light it, like Dada showed us. Then we'll eat the cornflakes he's left out for us. Come, Putha.'

Alice was shocked at the endearment. Her mother's voice too was softer than she had heard it for a very long time. Opening her mouth to ask a question, she decided against it and nodded. She sensed her mother missed Kunal.

There were no letters all that week or the next. Stanley felt he was being driven mad by Sita's pitiful questions. She was behaving like Alice, he thought, amazed, half inclined to laugh. What's the matter with her? Doesn't she know they've probably forgotten all about her by now? That out of sight usually means out of mind with those people! Stanley hadn't dared to visit Manika. He had already warned Jacky that their meetings were at an end. Jacky's unexpected tears had made him want to flee. He was beginning to feel hemmed in all over again, trapped wherever he went.

'Rajah,' he pleaded, 'you've got to help me.'

Rajah fixed him with a stare.

'I found you a house, I got you a job, what more do you want? Are you having an affair with Manika, by the way?'

'No!' bellowed Stanley. 'For God's sake, I can barely cope with a wife, let alone a bloody Tamil mistress!'

Rajah laughed.

'Ma always said you'd get yourself in a mess. Well, you'd better bring your Singhala wife to meet me, I suppose!'

Another week went by. Stanley took a day off work and went with Sita and Alice to the local school.

'I don't want to go there,' Alice said.

'You have no choice,' Stanley said. 'It's the law.'

He spoke more harshly than he had meant, but seeing the look on his daughter's face he paused and ruffled her hair.

'Don't worry, Putha. You'll enjoy it here. The schools are not like the ones in Colombo, thank God.'

Alice said nothing. This unexpected gentleness reminded her of Bee. She blinked. And the school, with its high grey walls and empty classrooms, reminded her of a prison. The headmistress talked to her parents, ignoring Alice.

'Will she be having school meals?' she asked. 'Or will she bring a packed lunch? Some children go home but we don't encourage it.'

'Mama …' Alice began, but Stanley was already nodding.

'She'll have the meals,' he said. 'My wife will soon be getting a job, so it will be more convenient.'

The headmistress looked doubtfully at Alice.

'Here's a list of what she'll need for her school uniform. She's quite small for her age. Try Morley's in Brixton. They might have her size.'

And that was that. She would start school in the first week in September. On the way back they took the bus into Brixton and Stanley bought everything on the list, grumbling at the cost. The clothes were too large for Alice.

'I'll take them up,' Sita said.

Her voice was strained, but she was nodding encouragingly at Alice.

'Good!' Stanley said, glad it was all settled. 'And tonight when we go to see Rajah you can ask him to find us a sewing machine.'

For a brief moment a feeling of solidarity encircled them. They caught the bus back. Sitting on the top deck, Alice stared at the park with the children's playground. Three boys raced around the roundabout and a small child swung standing up on a swing. A man walked his dog across the park and disappeared between the trees. Sita was looking at the row of shops as they passed. There was a launderette and next to it was a funeral parlour with memorial stones on display. Faint music from the bandstand drifted towards them through the open window. Someone rang the bell on the bus.

'Vassall Road,' shouted the conductor, and they got off.

Maybe the letter is waiting for me, now, thought Sita, as she watched the postman cycle past on his second delivery. The palms of her hands were suddenly clammy.

But there were still no letters, and that evening they went to Rajah's place. Sita, feeling as if she was suffocating, changed her sari. In her entire married life she had only met Stanley's mother half a dozen times. None of the visits had been successful. She did not want to meet Rajah.

'What's the point?' she asked, combing her hair and putting it up. 'I'm not in the mood for meeting him. We've been married for fourteen years and haven't met. I don't think it will make much difference, now.'

Stanley sat on the end of the bed watching her. He felt he was living in a nightmare.

Taking a deep breath, he tried to stop his temper from flaring up. Alice, coming into her parents' bedroom unannounced, saw a vein throb on his forehead.

'You can see a bit of London on the way,' Stanley told the child encouragingly, 'get used to going out. You'll be starting school in a few days' time, after all. So, best to get acclimatised.'

There was an uneasy pause. Two nights ago when he had kissed Alice in his usual perfunctory manner at bedtime, she'd noticed he smelled of perfume mixed with whisky. But when she had asked him what the perfume was he had flown into a rage.

'Let's go,' Stanley said now. 'Come on, I'm starving and Rajah will have cooked a damn good curry.'

Rajah lived with two girls. He was, Alice saw, an older version of Stanley. Both girls talked to her in a friendly way. They were Swiss Germans, working as au pairs in Golders Green.

'You look like your father,' one of them told Alice, admiringly.

'If you like, we can look after her one evening, so you two can go out,' the other one told Sita.

Sita smiled timidly, and shook her head. Her Kandyian sari appeared out of place and she had begun to talk in a kind of broken English as though she was unused to the language. Alice looked at her mother in surprise. She sensed her father was irritated too.

'Stanley told us about the baby who died,' one of the girls said casually. Alice saw her mother stiffen. She held her breath, hoping nothing more would be said. She suspected her parents would fight later. But the Swiss girl, oblivious to the hostilities, continued talking cheerfully. She bent towards Alice and Alice caught a whiff of the perfume her father had worn two nights before.

'Your daddy told me how he bribed the grave digger,' she said, *sotto voce*.

Alice watched her father help himself to another glass of whisky. Suddenly, without warning, she heard her grandfather's voice:

Listen, Putha, it will be fine in England too. You'll just have to be patient, that's all.

Confused, she turned to Sita.

'I want to go home,' she said uncertainly, but her mother wasn't listening.

Later, as she had expected, her parents fought. Her mother started shouting.

'How dare you talk about what happened,' she raged. 'How dare you talk to that tart about my private affairs?'

'The Queen of Hearts, she made some tarts,' Alice recited softly, looking at the lights of the passing cars on the ceiling of her room.

It was impossible to sleep. She could hear her father's voice, slurred with the whisky.

'What makes you think you have the monopoly of grief?'

'The Queen of Hearts,' said Alice, getting out of bed and going to the window.

Condensation lay across the glass. She wrote her name on it. Then she drew a face. Then she added a bubble coming out of the mouth. *Help*, she wrote. She wasn't sure who could help her mother. The front door closing marked her father's absence at breakfast the next day.

'Life has moved you to a different part of the ring, men,' Rajah said the next day at work. 'You can go on straining at the ropes, bouncing back, smashing each other senseless. Or you can recognise that a Singhalese will always *be* different, *think* differently even. And here's the problem in a nutshell. The bastards even do their grieving differently. If they could have their way, they would convince us that grief is something peculiar to them alone.'

He looked at Stanley's blank face.

'Think about it, Stan. How can you go on? We Tamils have been oppressed for far too long for these injustices not to matter.'

'But that's politics,' Stanley said uncertainly.

His brother, having got hold of the idea, would not let go of it.

'It's all politics, men, all of it! Love and death. And birth, too. The accidental nature, the pity of it. Mark my words, you will not be able to live with this woman forever. How soon you leave is up to you.'

'But there's the child.'

'The child is half-caste, men! For Christ's sake, you're such a damn fool. Why didn't you think of that in the beginning? Your trouble is you don't plan ahead. You'll have to ditch the child. Let her find her own way in the world.'

He paused, glancing sharply at Stanley.

'She'll probably do quite well in this country. Look at the untouchables who come from India. They all qualify as bloody doctors, men. So you see, you've done her a big favour!'

'Stop!' Stanley shouted.

His brother was going too far.

Another week went by and Alice started school. The weather had turned cooler and the sun that had been so bright had become watery and pale. The air became damp and here and there amongst the very last of the summer nasturtiums, wasps crawled drowsily, occasionally stinging a passer-by as they neared the end of their life. The weather was disappointing; there would be no Indian summer, after all. Sita took a silent Alice to school wearing her new uniform.

'You'll be fine,' she told her daughter hesitantly.

Preoccupied though she was by her own problems, Sita had registered Alice's reluctance. Once or twice as that first week progressed she tried and failed to find out what Alice thought of the school. Alice would not be drawn. Then on Friday she brought home a drawing she had done.

'Did you do that?' Stanley asked, noticing it.

He, too, was preoccupied.

'Yes,' Alice said, and she went upstairs to her room.

'Good,' Stanley said absent-mindedly. 'She's settling.'

Sita had begun to cook. She had discovered where the market was one morning and had begun to enjoy shopping for vegetables on her own. On the way she had found the main post office. She hesitated. Then she walked timidly up to the counter and asked how long it would take for a letter to reach London from abroad.

'The delay's at the other end, probably,' the man behind the counter had said. 'Could take several weeks.'

His words had a miraculous effort on Sita, who cheered up considerably after that. She would wait patiently for one more week. Kunal's letter *would* arrive, she was certain. The food that night was a feast of love in abeyance; she allowed herself to remember their last night together.

We'll get her a job next, thought Stanley, noticing. She needs her independence. Things will improve slowly. Probably it was all due to Manika's prayers. Stanley had not seen Manika for a fortnight but he spoke to her regularly from work. On Friday he would visit the temple and give thanks, he thought.

'I'm working late tomorrow night,' he told Sita casually.

The clock in Bee's studio had stopped the day they left. It was not an old clock but for some reason it had given up at sixteen minutes past nine. The news of Kunal's death had taken on the aspect of a nightmare that refused to end. No one had told Bee for days. They had let him deal with the loss of Sita and Alice first. Finally, late one night, when he was in his studio, the doctor risked a visit.

'Killed by a bomb,' he told Bee, drinking the whisky his friend poured out. 'Planted deliberately for him.'

'After all we did,' he kept repeating, again and again, 'after all we did to save him!' Bee clenched and unclenched his fists. The shock was physical. Kamala was shocked too, but Bee understood she was thinking of something else. Kamala was thinking of Sita.

'Who will tell her?' she cried later, when they were alone.

Alone after months with a house that had been bursting at the seams.

'I will tell her,' Bee said grimly. 'I will write to her once she is no longer on the ship. She can get the letter when she has begun to settle on dry land.'

He had been keeping track of the days. Even allowing for the delay in the post, he calculated she would get the letter by the second week of September.

'She fell in love with him,' Kamala said, weeping softly. 'She was hoping.'

Bee didn't say anything; he could not trust himself to speak. He was frightened of what he was capable of doing. What he would have liked to do was walk up the hill to the army headquarters and find the sergeant in charge. Swallowing hard, he began to compose the letter he would write. A letter that would be delivered to her by an unknown postman. A stranger in an alien land.

My dearest daughter,

By the time you get this you will have arrived in your new home with the little one. I expect you will be tired. I hope Stanley will have found you at the harbour without difficulty. I hope too the journey was bearable, that leaving your home was an easier thing than we all feared. I have some news for you. It is not good news, Sita. My poor, dear child, before I tell you I want you to promise me, even as you are reading what is in your hand, that you will write straight back. I want you to talk to me as you once did, pouring out your thoughts. Do you remember, Sita, what it was like, when you were a child? How, just like Alice, you would follow me around talking, telling me things, your worries, your anxieties. Sita, I do not want you to feel alone. I cannot alter the distance, nor can I change the course of your life, but as long as I am alive, you will never be alone. So promise me, when you have finished reading this letter, you will write to me? Please?

What I have to tell you is this. Your mother and I have only just had word sent to us. Sita, my news is about Kunal. There is no easy way to tell you. Kunal died on his way up to Elephant Pass …

As September drew to a close, Sita's optimism began to falter. She had waited patiently, had stopped talking about the absence of post, but now Stanley began to urge her to look in the newspaper for jobs. As her longing for word from home returned she was once more para-lysed with unhappiness. Since arriving in London she had written to her parents twice and still there was no letter. Walking back home, having dropped Alice off at school, she felt bitterness rise within her. They had been living here for a whole month. Had Kunal lied to her? she wondered. Had she misread him too? And why hadn't her father written? Or her mother, or even her sister?

'We'll write home tonight,' she had told Alice as she left her at the school gate, giving her something to look forward to. 'I'll buy some aerogrammes, huh?'

She felt a faint sense of optimism at the thought. Taking a short cut through Durant Gardens she noticed for the first time a small blue plaque on one of the houses. *Van Gogh lived here 1873–74*, she read. The house was tall and elegant. In the basement as she glanced in a woman was lifting a small child out of a high chair. The woman was smiling at the child. Sita walked on. Late summer roses tumbled over a high fence and the scent brushed delicately against her. She felt as though her heart would break.

When her mother did not come to collect her from school, Alice eventually decided to walk back home by herself. There had been some talk that, once Sita started a job, Alice would have to walk home alone, anyway. Perhaps, thought Alice vaguely, her mother had got a job and forgotten to tell her. There was no one to ask. After some time when the playground had almost emptied, the caretaker began to shut up the building and noticed her standing at the gate.

'Is your mum late?' he asked.

Alice nodded.

'Well, you'd better come into the office and we'll ring her.'

Alice shook her head. For some reason she felt ashamed to admit they had no telephone.

'I just live over there,' she said, pointing. 'I'll go back.'

'No main road to cross, eh?'

Again she shook her head and then she hurried out before he could ask her anything else. The road was empty. Everyone from her class had gone; not that she had any friends there, for although she had tried attaching herself to various groups of children, no one had taken the slightest notice of her. Puzzled, she had not known what to do. It was clear to her, from past experience, that the friendship groups in the class had already formed. Feeling instantly defeated, she withdrew. However she did not altogether dislike school. The art room was very bright and she enjoyed using the powder paints on the rough sugar paper, although here too she felt a difference. Most of the children used the paints straight out of the tub, while Alice liked mixing other colours from the ones she was given. At one point the art teacher had noticed and praised her. It had been a moment of brightness in an otherwise silent, grey day. But the art lessons were only once a week and the playtimes were three times a day. Today they had had PE, which she disliked most of all as it brought her into a more intimate contact with the other girls. The effort of pretending she did not mind being ignored was more exhausting than the lesson itself. But at last it had been over and the bell had rung, signalling the end of the day.

Crossing the road, Alice hesitated. Never having walked home alone she was not sure if this was the right way. All the houses looked the same. A ginger cat jumped up on a low wall and she went over to stroke it.

'Hello,' she said. 'Is your name Roger? I used to know a cat called Roger.'

The cat purred loudly and rubbed itself against her hand. I'd like a cat, thought Alice. Perhaps her parents would let her have one. The thought was a good one. She began to hurry along the road and the cat jumped down and followed her for a short distance before disappearing. But she was going the wrong way, she thought in dismay. She did not remember seeing a postbox here. Turning, she crossed the road and tried to make her way back to the school but the school seemed to have moved. Confused, she stood still. The cat, having lost interest, had disappeared. Her school bag felt heavy. She re-crossed the road and made her way frowning across another street. There was no sign of her own road. Two children playing hopscotch stopped and stared at her. Alice walked on, wanting to cry. She was breathing hard. Looking back she could see the children were still staring after her. Suddenly she began to run. A church clock struck the hour. There was definitely no church near their house and now she had reached a main road. There was no main road near them either. Uncertain, she hesitated, wondering what to do next. Try as she might, she could not remember the name of the road where she lived. Panic fluttered within her. Her shoulder was hurting with the weight of her bag. She had no idea how long she had been lost. What if she never found her home again? She did not want to walk back past the girls playing hopscotch. There was nothing for it; she would have to cross the main road.

'I'll find the traffic lights,' she said out loud.

She had no idea what she would do next. She was at the traffic lights when she saw Sita waving at her.

'Alice! Alice!'

'Mama,' Alice cried and, forgetting where she was, she stepped straight out into the road.

'Wait!' Sita shouted. 'Don't cross!'

But it was too late. Two cars flashed their headlights at her, swerving and beeping their horns. There was a screeching of brakes and a sharp glint of metal as Alice ran across the road towards her mother.

They were both crying. Sita clutched her daughter.

'You nearly got killed! Why didn't you wait?'

'I thought you'd got a job. I got lost coming home.'

'Oh, Alice!' wailed Sita. 'Alice, you're all I have.'

She went on crying for so long that Alice fell silent.

'Mama,' she said, bewildered. 'I didn't *get* killed.'

But Sita didn't seem to hear. She was crying in great gulps as she walked, her face averted. Alice swallowed.

'What's wrong?'

Sita shook her head, hurrying on.

'I'm sorry I was late,' she said finally. 'It will never happen again.'

And Alice, exhausted though she was, knew with absolute certainty that her mother was talking about something else. Later, after she had had a bath and while Sita was cooking, she saw a letter open on her parents' bed. Recognising the Ceylon stamp, she picked it up and saw too that it was written in her grandfather's hand.

The letter, which had taken Bee several hours to compose and had cost him many sleepless nights, had gone. Nervously, he waited for the reply. But silence had fallen. September drew to a close and the air cooled as the monsoons began again. In October, finally, a letter arrived, but it was from Alice. Very long and rambling, it described the house where they were living and her new school. There were several drawings and a list of all the books she was reading. The letter seemed muffled in some way.

We have a library in school, Alice wrote. *You can take out two books a week. There are books on all sorts of subjects. I have been looking at watercolour paintings. We will be going on a school trip to a place called the Tate Gallery. My teacher says I can see the Turner watercolours there.*

Bee read swiftly on but there was no mention of Sita until right at the end.

Mama says to send her love and she will write when she can. She has been a bit busy settling in, she said to say.

The letter was oddly dispassionate. Both Kamala and Bee read it several times, but neither could put their finger on what was missing. May, too, commented on Sita's silence.

'How can she be so busy she can't write!' she asked indignantly.

'Let's not judge her,' Kamala told her quickly. 'Who knows what trouble she's having with Stanley, or how the news of Kunal's death has really affected her.'

Kamala hesitated.

'Your sister's life has been terrible, May,' she said softly. 'Until Kunal came. He was her last chance, you know.'

No one knew what to say.

Bee wrote back immediately, both to Alice and to Sita, long, loving letters. Another month went by. May had now been married five months and was pregnant. On the day Bee heard the news of the coming of his next grandchild they received two letters from England. I cannot love again in this way, he thought heavily, opening Alice's first, with trembling hands. Sita's letter, when he came to it, was brief; its text documentarily plain.

I'm sorry I couldn't write earlier. I have been busy getting used to the house and the place where we live. Then we had to find a school for Alice. Anyway, she's now settled in. The money Stanley earns isn't enough and I shall get a job as soon as I can. When we do so I think we'll be able to afford a telephone. England is not as I expected. Things are much more expensive here. People work much harder than in Sri Lanka, but the results are to be seen everywhere. There is a pride in this country in a way we never had at home.

Bee was astounded. He read the letter in silence to its end. Then he handed it to Kamala without a word and went outside, taking Alice's letter with him. There was, Kamala saw to her own astonishment, not one single mention of Kunal.

'Perhaps she never got your letter,' May suggested later.

She had come over after school to see what her sister's reaction was.

'Perhaps she still doesn't know? Have you thought of that?'

No one knew what to make of it. Then Bee remembered.

'She *must* have got it, you know, because Alice said something about being sorry Kunal died.'

It was a pointless discussion. Thank God, thought Kamala, May's news will give us something different to think of. Her youngest daughter was looking radiant. In spite of all the uncertainties of their future, still *she* bloomed. Kamala could see that, until this moment, it had not occurred to May to consider the possibilities in her own life.

'I've decided to work right up until the birth,' May told them happily. 'And I'm going to have the baby at home, just like you, Amma.'

No one dared to disagree; no one mentioned what had happened with Sita. Calmly, such was her certainty, May told them that she would write to her sister with her own news.

I wanted you to hear from me, she wrote. *I know that in spite of everything that has happened you'll be glad for your sister.*

When she was alone, Sita re-read her sister's letter. The distance helped to ease reality. There was no Kunal. She found it hard to remember her past optimism; that naïve belief that she might have seen him again. Strangely, almost immediately after reading her father's letter, Kunal's face had begun to blur in her mind. She did not even have a photograph of him. Like her dead child, there was nothing left. It must have happened when they were on the ship, she thought listlessly. The anguish of her father's letter had been overlaid by the horror of what had very nearly happened to Alice. In spite of her utter desolation, it occurred to Sita that Alice understood what had happened. Later, when she had looked for the letter again in order to destroy it before Stanley came home, she realised that Alice had read it. But what did it matter? thought Sita. Alice, having eaten the hot rice that Sita handed her, had finished her homework and went up to her room to draw. She too was exhausted. Neither of them said another word, but that night, when Stanley had still not still returned home, before she went to sleep Sita had given Alice a kiss and the child had put her arms around her and hugged her. That had been all. By the time

Stanley returned smelling of whisky and cheap perfume, a thick sheet
of glass had fallen between Sita and her heart. It locked her out,
mercifully anaesthetising her with practised efficiency from the pain.
It had been a blessing. Stanley had noticed nothing; Sita was already
in bed feigning sleep.

It began to rain during the October half-term. Alice spent most
mornings in bed and then in the gloom of the afternoon she would
venture a few streets away to the children's library. It was warm in the
library and, as there were no children to stare at her, she would while
away a few pleasant hours reading the art books. The leaves had begun
to fall in earnest now and it became dark early. Returning home laden
with books she would sit in her room and draw the view outside her
window, staying there until her mother called her downstairs for
dinner. To her surprise, Alice had begun to love her bedroom. It was,
she discovered, the warmest part of the house and the only place that
really had the sun fall on it. The faded strawberry wallpaper and the
threadbare velvet curtains comforted her after the long silent days at
school. The room had the added advantage of being far enough from
her parents for them to hardly bother to come in, but not so far that
she missed any of their arguments. Lying in bed, listening to the
muffled sounds of her mother clearing up and her father's radio, she
felt safe at last to let her mind wander back over her life at school.
She had made no friends. Last week there had been a new arrival in the
class. The girl had recently moved up to London from a place called
Poole and the teacher had made her sit by Alice.

'I lived by the sea too,' Alice had volunteered. 'It was a very, very
blue ocean.'

But the girl had not been interested and a few days later had made
a friend of another child. Alice pretended she didn't care. Snatches of
the past drifted in and out of focus during the long and tedious days
that led up to half-term.

'Daydreaming, again, Alice,' the teacher had said, exasperated,
shaking her head.

'You're weird,' one of the boys told her, pulling faces at her.

Confused, Alice had become even more silent, longing for the moment when she'd be back at home, climbing the stairs to her room. And safety.

Towards the end of half-term Alice noticed something else. Her mother had begun taking out the baby clothes from the shoebox and ironing them. The clothes looked shabby and even the cotton lawn, once so fine, was unremarkable in the wintry light. Alice felt a tremor of shock go through her. She understood with a hopeless sinking of her heart that her mother would never be the same again. Her father, too, was changing. Alice registered that he no longer hid the fact of the strange perfume that surrounded him. And she saw too, without a single word being passed between them, that from now on *she* would be the one who would protect her mother. So when her mother started taking out the dead baby's things once more, Alice kept quiet, not drawing any attention to this change, knowing instinctively that Stanley would not like it. Sure enough, her father, who seldom missed anything, soon began to question her mother with increasing anger.

'Why don't you throw them away?' he asked her, lying in their double bed piled high with lemon-coloured blankets and eiderdowns, watching his wife fold the wretched things over and over again.

Alice stood outside the bedroom door, listening intently. It was important that she heard everything. She wanted to be ready to rush in and distract them the moment her parents started fighting. She felt the need to be fully alert, ready to avert a disaster. It was an exhausting business, but she had to do it; it was her job. Two and a half months had passed since their arrival and her parents were arguing more than ever.

'Say something, men,' Stanley was shouting. 'Don't just ignore me. You'll go off your head again if you don't talk. Remember how you were before I left?'

Alice pursed her lips, just as she knew her mother was doing at that moment.

'If you don't throw them out, Sita,' Stanley threatened, 'I will. It's for your own good,' he added, sounding uncertain, now. 'You've got to stop brooding in this way.'

Then Alice heard his voice soften as if he was talking to himself. And a moment later, as she strained her ears, there came the eternal sound of her mother's weeping.

'Your aunt May is going to have a baby,' Stanley told Alice a bit later on, over dinner.

Alice stared at her plate. Why on earth was her father talking about Aunty May's baby when he *knew* it upset her mother so much? She shivered.

'I don't feel well,' she said, not looking at him. 'Can I go to bed?'

They ate in silence for a moment longer. Sita, her face swollen with crying, appeared to make a huge effort.

'Yes,' she said absent-mindedly, 'you'd better go to bed in that case.'

Janake walked up the hill with some fish and a letter from his mother.

'Go and see how they are,' his mother had insisted. 'Mr Fonseka will be feeling terrible after the things that have happened. Go and see them, and give him this letter.'

Janake's mother could not bring herself to discuss the events of the last couple of months. The loss of his granddaughter had been bad enough for Mr Fonseka without the news about Kunal. A few days ago, the doctor had visited them. He had come walking on the beach, crossing the railway line at a point some distance away from the level crossing. There were police at the level crossing, the doctor had told them, so he had had to run across the line when the signal was green.

'Be very careful, sir,' Janake's mother had warned him. 'Sometimes the signal doesn't work. It's dangerous, you could get killed.'

The doctor had looked grimly at her. He had come to tell her something, he said.

'I can't visit Mr Fonseka for the moment,' he said. 'I think I'm being watched and I don't want to lead them to the Sea House.'

Janake's mother nodded. She understood.

'I need a message to be taken there. Can the boy do it?'

'Yes, sir.'

'No one will question him. Everyone knows he played with Mr Fonseka's granddaughter. It will be quite normal for him to visit because he misses her.'

'Yes, yes,' Janake's mother said. 'Don't worry. I can send them some fish.'

'Good!' the doctor said, looking relieved. 'Give him this telephone number. It's my brother's number at the hospital; he needn't be afraid to call it. We're going to have to find a different safe house for the next refugee. I don't want the authorities to get suspicious of Mr Fonseka.'

Janake's mother nodded once more. She would send Janake this afternoon, she promised.

So Janake went, taking the fish and the letter. The blistering afternoon light bathed the beach and the sea-heat burned the back of his neck as he walked. A few stray dogs trotted behind, smelling the fish he carried, but Janake turned several times and shouted threateningly, shaking his fists at them and in the end they gave up and wandered off. Since Alice had gone, the children no longer played beside the rocks. Most of them had been rounded up and sent to the local army camp where they would stay until they were trained. All except Janake. He had other plans. And this was one of the reasons he wanted an opportunity to talk to Mr Fonseka. He walked quickly across the burning sand, his feet bare, his head unshaded from the sun. Soon he passed the rocks where he had helped Alice carve her name. Glancing at it, he grinned. Yesterday he had examined it again and her name, carved with his own sharp penknife, was as clear as ever. He had told Alice she would return but since she had left he was less sure. She had vanished with such speed, and the enormity of her journey, never very comprehensible to him, had become unimaginably distant. Janake missed Alice. Right from the start, even when she had been a toddler, holding his hand, taking her first unsteady steps along the beach, he had known that she was different from the other children who played by the fishing boats. After she had gone, after the night when he had seen Mr Fonseka crying on the beach, Janake had moped for a while, staring at the ships eternally placed on the horizon. They all looked the same to him; remote as stars, impossible to imagine what life, if any, they might carry within them. It was exactly how he thought about England. With Alice gone, Janake had no desire to play with the other children; they seemed inferior by comparison. Occasionally he had glimpsed Esther walking up Station Road, but he still loathed Esther and so avoided her. There was a free school in the town now, but Janake refused to go to it. The town itself was full of edginess. Janake's mother didn't want her son to be idle. If the army saw him loafing around they would pick him up, so she sent him out once or twice with the fisherman. But whereas once this would have been enough for Janake, these days it no longer interested him. He talked constantly of Alice, imagining what it must be like for her in her new life.

'Alice will be at a proper school with proper lessons,' he told his mother enviously.

Weeks passed and Janake became quieter, less inclined to either go to school or out with the fishermen. The only pleasure he took was in reading his English books. In every other way he lacked motivation. It was then his mother had hit upon her idea, the one he wanted to talk about to Mr Fonseka. She had needed an excuse to send Janake to see him, and here it was.

Janake hurried across the beach with the sun on his back, walking close to the water's edge, absent-mindedly weaving in and out of the waves to cool his feet. The light beat relentlessly on his eyes, angular and sharp, making him squint. The Colombo express rocked past. The news from the capital was disturbing. All over the city riots were springing up like an epidemic, but after Kunal's death Janake's mother had stopped taking any interest in the news. When she first heard what had happened at Elephant Pass she had cried for days, refusing to speak to anyone. Janake too became silent with shock. Then after about two weeks his mother stopped crying and cleaned their hut, grimly turning her face away from what was going on in other parts of the country. She had recently got a job in the hotel kitchen. They would now have a little more money. And that was when she devised her plan.

'Go and talk to Mr Fonseka about it,' she said, parcelling up the fish and sending him out. 'Mr Fonseka will tell you if it is a good idea. Go now. And don't forget to give him the letter.'

So here was Janake with his parcel of fish.

'Be quick or the fish will go off,' his mother warned.

He counted the ships as he walked. Today there were four, all lined up close together, white as swans, their black, beak-like funnels poking into the sky. Having tried and failed to imagine Alice on one of them, he turned away from the sea and climbed the hill towards the Sea House.

The road was empty; this was the dead time of the day. The gate was unlatched. It was the first thing he noticed. The garden was silent save for the chirping of giant grasshoppers. An air of neglect hung everywhere; dead flowers dropped from the hibiscus bushes on to the cane chairs out on the verandah and a small metal tray with unwashed teacups stood on the table. The house too was quiet. Janake walked around the back, hoping to see the servant woman, but there was no one there. He paused, uncertain whether to go in or not. Clearly there was no one about. Then he noticed the studio across the garden was open and Mr Fonseka was working inside. Janake hesitated. He remembered Alice saying her grandfather never liked anyone except her going into his studio when he was busy. But Alice was no longer here. Aware of the fish wet against his arm and the unopened letter, Janake hesitated. As he stood wondering what he should do, Bee wiped his hands on a rag and came to the door. Janake saw him strike a match and light his pipe. And he saw with a sharp spurt of shock that the old headmaster looked terrible.

'Sir,' he said, before he could stop himself. 'Sir, are you ill?'

'Come in, come in,' Bee said impatiently, not hearing. 'Don't just stand there, boy. What d'you want? Is it the cook?'

Janake swallowed. Mr Fonseka didn't seem to recognise him.

'It's Janake, sir,' he said cautiously.

Mr Fonseka had a reputation of being fierce if annoyed.

'I know who you are,' Bee said, irritated. 'I'm not senile yet.'

He stepped back, letting Janake in.

'What's this?' he added, spotting the soggy parcel Janake was carrying.

'Fish, sir. From my mother. Caught this morning.'

'What am I supposed to do with it?' Bee asked, glaring at him. 'I'm here alone at the moment. Mrs Fonseka has gone to visit our daughter.'

Janake stood awkwardly, not knowing what to say.

'I'm sorry, sir, my mother insisted. And she gave me this letter to bring to you, from the doctor.'

'Why didn't you say?' Bee said, taking it hurriedly from him.

He seemed to relax a little.

'All right, go and leave the fish in the kitchen. And wash your hands before you come back.'

The walls of the studio were hung with etchings. Bee was staring at them when Janake returned. The letter was opened and on his table.

'They aren't quite right yet,' he said, seeing Janake looking at them, adding in a different voice, 'When did the doctor visit?'

'I don't know, sir, I wasn't there.'

'Well, if he comes again, which I doubt, tell him I'm going to Colombo soon and that I'll see what I can do to help. Okay? Will you remember that?'

Janake nodded. The prints on the wall were small, intense images in black and white. In one a girl stood staring at a severed sheep's head served up on a plate. Behind her a group of children jumped in and out of the sea, silhouetted against the sun. The girl had the unmistakable features of Alice. The whole feel of the image was one of suppressed violence. The black was very solid; the etching marks were furious.

'I wanted to ask your advice,' Janake said at last, hesitantly.

Bee appeared lost in thought.

'Sir?'

Bee turned.

'I was … my mother …' Janake swallowed. 'She wanted me to join the Buddhist monks, sir. I would be able to get an education and …' He stopped.

Bee was staring at him. For a moment he thought Mr Fonseka was going to shout at him.

'You see, sir,' Janake said quickly, 'it's the only way for someone like me to get any sort of education. I want to do something for this country. I don't want to be a fisherman. I would like to be able to help people like Kunal. I would like to do something for the good of this country. We are a Buddhist country, but we don't behave like Buddhists any more.'

He swallowed.

'I'm nearly thirteen, sir. I want to do something.'

There was a silence. A thread of a breeze tugged at one of the etchings and it fluttered to the ground.

'One day I know Alice will be able to; she will study in the UK and learn many, many things. But I do know about what it means to be a Buddhist and this is the way I think I can be of help.'

It was the longest speech he had uttered and Mr Fonseka was looking at him with an expression in his eyes that was hard to decipher. He still looked terrible, but he was no longer frowning. There was something helpless about the way he was looking at Janake.

'That's a very good idea, Janake,' he said faintly, at last.

At the beginning of December in this first year in their new home, Sita got herself a job doing alterations for a dry cleaner. She began mending zips, turning up trouser legs and changing the hemlines of skirts.

'Is this the best job you can find, men?' Stanley asked her, astonished.

But Sita didn't care. She wanted to work from home, in order to be there when Alice returned from school. Unlike her father, Alice loved hearing the comforting sound of the sewing machine. It reminded her of her time at the Sea House. She walked home alone now, no longer getting lost, never again making the mistake of crossing a main road before the lights changed to red. Time moved slowly. She had written two letters to her grandparents since their arrival. She hoped her grandfather would not mention Kunal again and in any case, after her last letter, Alice had become strangely reluctant to write another one. It was difficult to explain her life in England. Then, as Christmas approached, Esther wrote. Her letter came inserted into a greetings card. Alice opened it cautiously. Esther's handwriting, like her grandfather's, brought a sharp stab of longing.

Are you enjoying life in your foreign country? Esther asked.

And:

The fighting is very bad now. Mother does not let me go out at all, even with Anton. D'you remember Anton? He wants to marry me!!

Faintly, Alice heard the strains of fairground music.

Are your English friends better than the people here? Esther went on.

Discarded life leapt from the pages of the letter. Another sort of life. The fine curled script, the thin cheap paper, the thought of Esther sitting on the verandah step as she wrote, was too much to bear.

'Nice of Esther to write,' Sita remarked, her mouth full of pins as she made huge garish-patterned shift dresses for the West Indian women who now appeared regularly at the house, like crows around a rubbish tip.

Stanley read Esther's letter when Alice showed it to him but made no comment. Of late, her father spoke less and less.

Christmas was round the corner. Alice's school was busy with the nativity play and the carol concert and the Christmas party, but by a stroke of luck and by staying silent, she had managed to avoid being involved in any of them. The days had drawn in. On most days, by early afternoon, heavy low clouds descended, obscuring the light. Alice found this lack of daylight oppressive. It seemed to rain all the time in slow, never-ending motion. The plane trees were now bare and piles of unswept leaves rotted on the corners of pavements. Sometimes on her way back from school she had a fleeting picture of the sea in

Mount Lavinia, but mostly she just felt as though she had been living in darkness forever.

One evening Stanley came home with a surprise for them. It was a television set.

'Now you don't have to spend all your time in your room,' he told Alice with a thin smile.

He smelled of drink and later when she was in bed she heard her parents fighting yet again. Alice stared at the faint outline of flowers on her wall. The shouting increased its muffled anguish, going on for so much longer than usual that she wondered if she should go downstairs. She wanted to shout to them to stop; she wanted to tell her grandfather. *He* would have known what to do. Sometimes she wanted Bee so badly that the knot in her stomach grew into a physical pain and her head ached constantly. She waited, her body like a coiled spring, for the coconut shells to be thrown and her mother to rush out screaming, but nothing much else happened. Her parents just went on and on, their voices rising and falling to a mysterious rhythm of their own. Finally Alice must have fallen asleep. When she woke it was morning and the house was still.

She stared at the drawings pinned up on her wall. Most were of Sita and Stanley and the dead baby, but one or two were of Bee and herself. Her father would have flown into one of his rages had he seen them, but as neither of her parents ever thought to come into her room she felt safe from discovery. In the finely tuned sensibilities she was developing, she was beginning to be aware of certain changes in her father. One night she heard the sound of a car stopping and, looking from her window, had seen Stanley get out. The woman driving the car got out too and then she began to kiss him. Riveted, Alice had stared through a gap in her curtain. After a moment her father laughed, pushing the woman away; then he came in. Alice told no one, but the next day she had asked her mother to teach her to cook so that she might help her a little in the house. A few weeks after this incident Stanley asked her to hang his coat up in the hall. Without thinking, Alice slipped her hand into the pocket and took out a piece of paper. Later in her room she examined it. It was a receipt. One bottle of Blue Nun (What was that?

she wondered), two chapattis, rice and a chicken curry. She stuck the receipt into the back of her sketchbook. Then she drew another picture of her father and the woman who had kissed him. Listening to her parents row she began to compose a letter to her grandfather.

I don't want to live here, she imagined writing. *I want to come back to you.*

She would not write that, she knew. Tomorrow, she told herself as she drifted into sleep, I will write to him about the school play.

On New Year's Day with the arrival of evening Bee took his usual walk on the narrow spit of beach. Kamala watched from the window, thinking how like a great sea bird he looked. With his wings clipped.

'How beautiful my parents are,' May observed, smiling at Namil, waiting for her child to be born. 'Even when they are not together, they remain as one.'

All three of them remembered Sita, calmly contemplating their collective failure to save her from her fate. I have been useless as a parent, thought Bee. I could not stop her suffering. In spite of all his love for his daughter, Sita had snatched her life out of his safe-keeping.

'Where will it end?' he murmured, looking at the sea, but the sea gave him no answers.

My eldest child, Kamala was thinking sadly. She was the one bound up with my youth and my unsustainable hopes. I was very different with May, more realistic, stronger.

Very soon, thought May, entranced, as her child moved within her, I will feel what they feel about us!

They sat down to the evening meal together. It was delicious, in spite of the shortage of food and the fact that the cook had gone away to see her relatives further south. Two unset places nudged them silently. There is new life on its way, thought May, both guilty and happy. Fresh life was what was needed in this place. Sita had not written since May had told her about the baby.

'If I had had my way,' Bee remarked to Kamala later, when they were in bed, 'no more children would be born in this country. I would let this place rot and prune itself like a garden. And start again, many years from now.'

Today, as usual, he had been thinking of Alice. Through no fault of her own, the child would drift from him. He could no longer visualise the places she inhabited. Her only letter to date had made him aware that there were things she did not speak about. Was she aware of what she was doing? How could he ever hope to help her and understand her struggles? With what optimism had he expected to keep her close in all that lay ahead? And while I grow old with longing, thought Bee, she will be changing, becoming unrecognisable. One generation could no longer live beside another. That was a thing of the past. But I will never stop loving her, he thought. I will continue as always. The years ahead, lost even before they occurred, were suddenly unbearable. Ah! Alice, he thought.

In the darkness, Kamala searched for his hand. For over thirty years their hands had sustained each other at the start of sleep.

'Don't think such things,' she said, very quietly. 'Don't tempt fate.'

January on the island was the most beautiful of months. The heat lessened and the air thinned. It rained, but not in torrents, and the breeze from the sea cooled the coastline. That January the war began drumming again. After months of silence it marched in two/four time. Soon an orchestra would be playing; a two-conductor orchestra without direction. Playing to several different tunes. Ceylon was no more. In its place was a monster that destroyed anyone in its path. The country appeared to be fighting for its life, eradicating the foreign rule with a new, faceless, persona. Bombs went off like firecrackers, killing first one tribe and then another. Newspaper headlines screamed the statistics. Thirteen men in the Singhalese army were killed by the Tigers; fourteen Tamils killed by the army. The dead all looked alike, blackened, burnt, unrecognisable, strewn across the crossroads so their souls would not rest. A deep hatred lay like lacquer over the land, seeping into hitherto tranquil places.

'Fools!' cried Bee scornfully. 'The British *were* here. That's a fact. Can't they see they will *always* be present in our collective psyche, one way or another? They will be present in the language, our love of it, our use and mis-use of it. Our tastes, the feelings we have about parks and landscapes. These idiots call it Imperialism, but to me it's simply a collective memory. They'll never be able to destroy it.'

In just six months Bee had aged. He understood that this kind of growing old was different from the sense of ageing he had felt before. Now he felt physically old and helpless. Alice was getting on with life out of sight, her letters crossing with his, losing continuity with the distance. He hadn't expected any of this. And although he would continue to circumnavigate the world in his mind, in his heart, Bee knew he had given up. Kamala, watching over him, saw she could no longer help him. Their shared life was an illusion, she decided, for what use was any of it if you could not carry another's pain? But still, in spite of all this, Kamala was less desperate than Bee. Even the rumblings of war affected her less. There was another child on the way, a life to bring a glimmer of hope, at last. It would never replace Alice, but the child would bring its own gifts with it. This was how Kamala thought, whereas the little strip of time left to them both was all Bee saw. So Kamala went to the temple and prayed. She prayed that the wheel of suffering would be stilled and her husband might find peace, that he might see his daughter and granddaughter again. She was beginning to understand, with simple insight that the familiar Buddhist teachings she had always followed were there to make sense of their everyday lives. Of late, she saw clearly, they *lived* their karma. This grief, the struggle, what else was it, but karma?

Meanwhile the Tamils were fleeing for their lives. Slowly they were being pushed back into the north and the east of the island; the nationalist Singhalese concentrated on campaigning against them, while unnoticed by all of them a different violence, simmering quietly in the background until now, began to boil over. It was clear to those who cared: the point of no return was fast approaching.

One morning, soon after the New Year, Bee awoke and went out to his studio. Dawn had just broken. It had been his practice to wake at this hour whenever he could. The best light, he used to tell Alice, was the early light. He remembered how the child used to follow him out, her eyes full of sleep, refusing to go back to bed. She always wanted to help mix the colour. Both of them, young and old, needed so little sleep. Today the dawn was violet and pink over the sea. Two days ago he had begun some paintings based on the etching Janake had seen. They were part of a series he had called *Alice in Wonderland*. The dealer from Colombo had visited him to see the new work, wanting to know what he would sell. In one painting a small child stood in the doorway of a room watching a man having his leg sawn off. Behind her was the sea, tropical and very blue. The man from Colombo had raised his eyebrows when he saw it. The painting was beautifully executed, the sea shimmered and the whole canvas glowed under the slowly applied glazes. With no hesitation, the man from Colombo had bought the painting outright, even though it wasn't dry. He had paid Bee cash, telling him to finish the one of the fairground he was working on.

'I'll be back,' he told Bee, nodding, disappearing as swiftly as he had come.

'I wish you hadn't called it "*Alice* in Wonderland",' Kamala grumbled. 'Couldn't you use some other name?'

'Why not?' Bee asked. 'I've nothing to hide.'

'Thatha,' May said worriedly when she heard, 'I admire what you are doing, but is it wise? Given the type of people who are around these days?'

May had finished work for the moment. The baby was due in February and the new house that Namil had been building further up the coast near Galle was ready. They no longer went to Colombo. Colombo had become a dangerous place and as May's confinement drew closer, they had become more cautious. The curfew was in place again. Someone had attacked a train going up-country and two villages in Trincomelee had been razed to the ground.

'Don't talk to me about wisdom,' Bee said angrily. 'What can any of the local thugs do to me? I am a painter. A *Singhalese* painter. I can do what I like.'

When he had finished two more paintings, in spite of Kamala's protests, he decided to take them up to Colombo. Because of the shortage of petrol he would go by train.

'I won't be late,' he promised Kamala, seeing the look on her face. 'Just a quick trip and then I'll come back straight away.'

Kamala said no more. In the mood he was in she had no hope of stopping him, anyway, but she went to the temple after he left for the station. Bee was hoping to avoid the rush hour. It was the crowded trains that were dangerous, he told Kamala. The suicide bombers wanted maximum damage for their efforts.

The road was empty. The flower-laden bungalows that perched along the hillside were silent, their shutters closed. Bee could hear the soft sounds of water sprinklers behind closed gates. Pink and white oleander blossoms lined the walls. He passed Dias Harris's house. It too was shut, for Dias and Esther were now in Colombo. They still owned the house but visited only occasionally. It's a dead town, thought Bee, brushing past a branch of orange blossom that overhung the road from the Harrises' garden. Perfume filled the air. When Alice had been here it had been a fine garden. Now all of it was overgrown. Seagulls floated lazily across the sky, calling to each other, swooping down on the catamarans as they were dragged on to the beach below. Gihan the station master, watering his bitter gourd, raised his head when he saw Bee approaching.

'Ah! Bee,' he greeted him, smiling. 'An early bird. Come, come!' He shook his head from side to side, looking pleased. 'Haven't seen you for ages, men. There's half an hour before the train arrives. Come and take some tea with me.'

He could not refuse without seeming churlish, so Bee followed the man into his office where the peon was making tea. Gihan eyed Bee openly.

'Still missing the child, eh?'

He raised a hand before Bee could speak.

'No, no, don't say anything. I told you not to let them go, men.'

'What was the alternative?' Bee asked quietly. 'Watch my grand-daughter be beaten in school because she has a Tamil father?'

It was the only reference he made to Sita's marriage. If Gihan was surprised by Bee's bluntness, he did not show it. Instead he turned his oleaginous smile on his old friend and continued sipping his tea, considering his friend over the rim of his cup. Clearly, Bee had no idea that some months ago the rumours around him had started up again. One such rumour was that the Fonsekas were in the habit of hiding Tamil refugees trying to flee to the north. It was common knowledge that, in spite of the army's presence in the town, several Tamils had escaped being caught.

Bee was talking to the peon in Singhalese. His Singhalese was elegant and old-fashioned. The sort of correct, grammatical Singhalese that wasn't often heard any more in these parts. Gihan didn't know what to think. In his opinion, Bee was capable of almost anything. It had been what he had told the plain-clothes man from the army who had visited him.

'Yes, sir,' he had said, 'I *have* known him for a very long time. Yes, his daughter married a Tamil. No, no, they are in the UK now.'

The plain-clothes man had been very interested.

'So they send money to arm the Tigers, do they?'

Gihan had been dubious. He didn't think Bee and Kamala had that kind of money.

'But your friend, Mr Fonseka,' the man had insisted, 'would you say he was pro Tamil policies? A threat to the government, perhaps?'

It was all a game, Gihan thought, uneasily. Boys playing a match on the cricket field; nothing more than that. But he agreed to keep an eye on Mr Fonseka all the same. For his own sake.

'Have you heard from your daughter recently?' he asked, now.

He wondered if Bee had any idea that he was being followed. Bee smiled. A light hovered faintly across his face.

'Alice has started school. She's learning French, imagine that!'

His voice was full of wonder. French had not been a language that had occurred to him.

'And the school is taking the children to France for a daytrip.'

He shook his head, amazed.

'Well, England is a civilised country, why am I so surprised?'

Don't, thought Gihan. *Don't* say things like that.

'At least she's getting a fine education, men. Look at it that way.'

'Yes,' Bee said faintly.

He stood up and walked to the door, facing out to sea, his face remote and withdrawn. He must be coming up to sixty, thought Gihan, his unease growing. What harm can he really do? He was thinking about the comments of the army official.

'Men like him are what stop this country from progressing,' the man had said.

'Where are you going in Colombo?' Gihan asked.

'Just to see Suriesingher. Take him two new prints. Do you know what time the curfew is today?'

'Six o'clock from Maradana to here. Can I see?'

He pointed to the small portfolio Bee was carrying.

The etchings were called *Dangerous Games, 1* and *2*. And both figures bore a strong resemblance to Sita. In one of the images she appeared to be balancing the skull of a buffalo with one hand, while in the other hand she carried a bowl of curd. Gihan stared. Buffalo skulls were not something found in the south of the island. Buffalo skulls and curd were a speciality of Jaffna and symbolic to those parts. In the second image Sita juggled six bags of money while screaming in terror. In the background was the Sri Lankan flag, ripped and partially obscured. The station master was genuinely shocked. The likeness to the real Sita was staggering. It was as though Bee had taken a photograph, he thought, momentarily awed by his friend's talent. The train was approaching. Bee packed away his portfolio and tied the ribbon.

'Come and see us, men,' Gihan called, without conviction.

Both of them knew he would not.

'And don't forget the curfew. The four o'clock train will be crowded. Try to get an earlier one.'

Bee nodded. He stepped into the compartment and was lost in the grime and dust of the dirty windows. Gihan waited for a moment. He waved his hand and blew the whistle. With a heavy puff of smoke the train began to pull out. He went back in to his office and picked up the telephone. Then he dialled the number on the visiting card the man from the army had given him.

When he had found a seat facing the sea, Bee opened the filthy window, using his handkerchief to do so. The carriage was almost empty. Below him was the beach, fringed by cacti and coconut trees. Most of the fishing boats were still out with the night's catch and the sky was made transparent by a subdued sun, not quite up yet. Once again the air felt fresh with the strong smell of seaweed and ozone. A hiss and spit of waves flowed towards him, bringing with them a strong current of memory. The sense of bereavement cut deep into his flesh, its wound would never heal. Like a lost limb, he felt their absence constantly. Looking out of the window, he saw the view and the place, unmarked by his loss, unchanged by his pain, and he marvelled at the indifference of the land. The long, wide stretch of beach was completely empty. Only the waves moved, rising and falling regardless, while seagulls sailed against the rising sun. Closing his eyes, Bee began composing a letter to Alice. Across the aisle a man in a sarong picked his teeth systemically. When he had finished he stood up and spat out of the window. Then he began combing his hair with a thin broken comb. Bee opened his eyes and watched him for a moment. There was dandruff in the spaces between the greasy strands of hair. The man put the comb away and began wiping his nose. Humanity grooming itself, thought Bee, wanting to draw him but resisting the urge. The man shifted his feet. Underneath his sarong Bee caught a glimpse of army boots. The train rattled on, winding its way across the coast, rushing towards Colombo central station. Carrying Bee and his sorrow along with it.

9

SO THIS WAS SPRING, THOUGHT SITA. Soft and acquiescent, with its sudden squalls of rain, its nearly warm breezes. Birdsong pierced the air. Like love. And with their repeated call she realised she was not going back. They were here to stay. For Sita, April was indeed the cruellest month. Looking at the young green leaves sprouting everywhere, she remembered last year. In Colombo they would be celebrating Vesak. Alice was now ten years old. Silence issued from abroad. Sita had not answered her father's first letter in the manner in which she knew he had wanted, and she had not mentioned Kunal. It was impossible for her to think of his name, let alone write it down on paper. She had no idea if her father understood, and she no longer cared what he or anyone thought. Dangling by a thread, existing by invisible means, Sita ignored May's last letter, too. The longer she left it, the harder it became to express how she felt about her sister's pregnancy and the birth of her baby, a boy they had called Sarath. What did she feel about her nephew? She had no idea. Working at her new occupation, sewing, endlessly altering grey trousers, turning up hems (she had begun to get some white customers, much to Stanley's relief), Sita thought only of the next row of stitching. She seldom went out. Alice, returning after school, found her exactly as she had left her. Silent, her sewing machine whirring.

'Is there anything to eat?' Alice would ask, eyeing her mother, watchful.

And more often than not there was nothing. Eventually Sita would put her bright red Petticoat Lane-coat on and hurry around to the local shops, only to meet Alice on her way back from the same shop, eating chocolate.

Stanley worked late most days. He had begun to hate the house. All his plans to decorate it, to remove the dark wallpaper and paint the rooms white, had fizzled out through lack of interest. What can you do with a pokey house like this? he thought. The windows were too high to be cleaned properly, the carpets were so brown that they always looked dirty, and he had become disheartened by Sita's lack of interest. Even the garden, if it could be called that, with its filthy dustbin and broken outhouse, was a mess. Sita refused to do anything with it, complaining it was too cold to go out there, and he had no time for it. Days passed with Sita glued to her sewing machine, leaving the house only to shop for food.

'What's wrong with you?' Stanley asked, fuming at her stubbornness. 'Why don't you go out? Why are you behaving as if you are a coolie who can't speak the language?'

Sita shook her head.

'It's too cold,' was all she would say.

'For God's sake,' Stanley said, losing the temper that was always close to the surface. 'Have you *no* interest in the country you're living in?'

'Not much,' Sita said, refusing to be drawn.

'I can't cope, Rajah,' Stanley told his brother privately, holding his head in his hands. 'She's going round the bend, men.'

'Well, get her to see a doctor, then. Or leave. One or the other.'

Stanley did not know what he should do. Increasingly, the sense of alienation within his own house was becoming unbearable. Spring was beautiful but cold. In May, he would have been away from his homeland for a year, but the strange new and impenetrable atmosphere that surrounded him only drove him mad. When she wasn't sewing, Sita spent her time washing and ironing. What the hell was there to wash so much? thought Stanley. He was being driven insane by her. Then, when he thought he would explode with pent-up rage, one Sunday morning, without any warning, she went out. One of her customers had told her about the Sunday street markets and this had interested her. She bought an *A to Z* of London and, armed with an umbrella against the threatening rain, she went first to Petticoat Lane and then to Brick Lane. Stanley was speechless with astonishment. Elated, desperate to find some common ground, he decided they should all go as a family. The following Sunday they took the tube and walked in the rain amongst the noisy crowds shuffling between the stalls. But the markets with their endless rows of shoes, their cheese-cloth shirts, their stalls of love-beads bored Stanley. He would have liked to nip into the local pub for a pint of bitter, but Alice's presence made it impossible. A few more Sunday trips went by and Alice began to find them repetitive. She was no longer a rebellious child but even she had grown bored with the markets.

'Do I have to come, Mama?' she asked Sita.

'Isn't it better than staying at home?'

Alice shook her head. She did not want to hurt her mother, but she preferred staying in her room, drawing. Sita shrugged. It made no difference to her. She enjoyed wandering through the rubbish-strewn streets listening to the voices of the stallholders, smelling the frying onions and beef burgers, while picking up a bargain. No one knew her, no one even noticed her, but in a strange and uncomplicated way, in spite of the dull soot-ridden rain and the lack of sun, the place reminded her of home. She could not explain why this was so. London in itself had no significance for her except as a constant contrast to her home. She walked with her sights turned inward. Occasionally, as the months went by and a stallholder, recognising her, smiled a casual greeting she raised herself as though from a dream to acknowledge this strange place that she had landed in, under the railway bridge with its roosting pigeons. Soon it became accepted that she would be out every Sunday from seven in the morning until midday. Stanley and Alice stayed in bed. By the time they woke, Sita was back and with a rare show of energy was cooking lunch.

ROMA TEARNE

The house now began to fill up with random objects. This new
obsession had clearly replaced the one of waiting for the post, Stanley
decided, not knowing whether things had got better or worse. A set of
pillowcases with bright pink flowers and a pair of turquoise towels
made for the beach.

'What do we need with more towels?' Alice asked, staring at them,
puzzled. 'There isn't any beach.'

Sita unpacked some sheets.

'But they don't match the pillowcases,' Alice observed.

Sita ignored her. She bought framed maps of Britain, which she put
up around the house. She bought soap, boxes and boxes of the stuff.
Bargain plastic containers, small Chinese lanterns, ornaments. As the
weather began to improve and the Whitsun school break arrived, the
house continued to fill with all kinds of junk.

Stanley was struggling. He felt he was drowning under an excess of
rubbish. He could no longer have a proper conversation with his
brother about the sorry state of his marriage. The only person who
seemed to understand his dilemma was Manika.

'I can't just abandon Alice,' he told her. 'She is my daughter, when
everything is said and done.'

Manika raised an eyebrow. Then she put holy ash on his tongue and
pressed a peacock feather on his heart and slowly, in this way, summer
returned.

Alice noticed how the evenings stayed light for longer. Coming
home from school on these early summer days the earth had a smell
that she liked and would always remember. Although now there was
a small group of girls who tolerated her and allowed her to hang
around them at break times, she had made no real friends. No one
questioned her; no one took her into their confidence. When she heard
about the new school she was going to in September, she was driven
by a strong impulse to write to Bee.

I will be starting my new school, she wrote. *Mama thinks I will like it.*

She paused. The mention of her mother made her uneasy, so she
crossed out the sentence. She wondered what she might say instead.

I'm reading a book about a painter called Constable.

It was a lie. She was only looking at the pictures.

And I've been drawing a lot.

That at least was true. She wrote a few more sentences, but because she censored them so heavily, even she could see they were dull. Almost without thinking, she withheld all information of her parents' rows or her mother's remote air. She never mentioned her own loneliness or the fact that the house they lived in was constantly cold even on the warmest of days. Neither did she tell her grandfather that she was always hungry or that she quite often prepared her own food with whatever was left in the kitchen.

Sometimes Stanley took her to her uncle Rajah's, but her uncle, Alice sensed, did not like her much. Their own house, so empty when they had first arrived, was slowly taking on another, different kind of bleakness. In that first summer in London Sita discovered the vegetable and fruit markets of Balham. This was closer to home and full of the exotic produce she had given up hoping to find. Joyfully she began to buy boxes of over-ripe mangoes and ladies fingers that had to be thrown away before they could eat them.

'I can't eat this shit,' Stanley bellowed, pushing the crates of rotting fruit off the Formica table so they crashed to the ground. 'Why are you wasting money on this rubbish!'

Sita watched him silently, making him apoplectic with rage.

'Why don't you open the curtains, for God's sake!' he screamed at her.

'What for?' asked Sita calmly. 'There's nothing to look at outside.'

In answer Stanley stormed out of the house and headed for Dorset Road where a prayer meeting was under way in Manika's bright brass shrine. The lignums, the picture of the beloved Bhagavan, the smell of incense and cooked rice was a comforting compromise.

The following September Alice started at Stockwell Manor School. She was the youngest intake in the school. It was further away from the house but still within walking distance. She had felt lost in her primary school but this new one was so vast that she found disappearing in it was easier to do. By now the winter came as no surprise and another

Christmas came and went unremarked with a sprinkling of snow followed by a series of bitter grey days when the wind blew harshly as if from the Steppes. Sita bought Alice a pair of fleece-lined boots from Petticoat Lane market and a thick coat for herself. There was no card from Esther this year and no letter from Bee either. Looking at the unmovable blanket of clouds overhead, Sita felt her mind stretch into a perfect blankness.

This second winter seemed endless and spring, when it finally came, had no effect on Sita. The young green fritillaries, the pale glow of cherry blossom, the delicate tint of a sky becoming lighter, earlier, all these things were of no interest to her. She felt only the cold north wind, drying her skin and making her bones ache. It was the final straw for Stanley. After a particularly protracted row he told Sita he was leaving. Consumed with guilt, he glared at her.

'I can't waste any more time. I need to have a life.'

'And me?' Sita asked him, her mouth twisting. 'What about me?'

She knew the answer.

'I don't know,' Stanley cried in despair.

He was taken aback at how painful this was proving.

'Go back, perhaps.'

She saw his guilt before he did. He thought it wasn't his problem. In the face of Sita's blank, helpless face he just saw freedom, tantalisingly close, strained at the leash.

And so the door to their marriage clanged shut. Without fuss, without tears, with Alice watching, wordlessly.

'Don't!' Stanley cried, seeing his daughter's tearless reproach.

Oh God! he thought, she's becoming like her mother. Oh God! Two of them are too much for me.

'You can come and visit me, I promise,' he told Alice, slipping up, giving Sita another handle on his guilt.

Rubbing it in. Ending what should never have begun, after breakfast, with the taste of Ceylon tea still on their tongues. It was a bittersweet moment, much to Stanley's surprise, with his brother's don't-be-a-fool voice ringing in his ears and Manika's buck-toothed smile. That was how it was; both so easy and so hard to leave. On his way out he noticed he had taken Sita's smile with him. Her early-on-in-their-marriage laugh, her I-am-going-to-defy-convention determination. Unexpectedly, leaving behind his own convictions. Becoming even more disorientated than this migration had already made him.

So there it was. Done. Hope you are satisfied, he thought, looking at his brother with a new indifference. Giving money to the Tamil cause without passion, and finding himself saddled with a Sri Lankan servant woman. Ringing the changes while persuading himself of her worth. Had Sita discussed it with him she could have told him there were no winners in this game. But Sita was too busy with the voices living in her head to talk to anyone very much.

Alice could never quite remember the actual moment of her father's final departure. The emptiness of his presence was simply replaced by his absence. They had been rudderless for so long that a further drift was hardly noticeable. She saw that the most important thing for her mother was the fact that the shoebox could now come out of hiding, its contents displayed like market-stall wares on her unnecessarily large bed. Perhaps the most significant change was that at last Alice could daydream about her grandfather more than ever.

'Do you remember the eclipse?' she asked out loud. 'The way the darkness swallowed up the day and came rushing into the house?'

How wonderful it had been when the light had faded and the sun disappeared over the sea. She remembered the darkness muffling the bird sounds. A solitary crow perched on a gutter pipe in the gloom. Growing afraid, it had begun to moan like a lost soul, until at length, gathering what vestige of courage remained to it, it had flown away.

And then it passed, her grandfather's voice reminded her in the daydream. *And we had two dawns in one day. Don't forget, it passed as all of this will pass too.*

It was a conversation she was to re-run regularly.

10

THE MONTHS THAT FOLLOWED STANLEY'S DEPARTURE turned slowly. But at least they knew what to expect from the changing seasons now. On one occasion during the holidays Alice went to visit her father at Rajah's flat. The two Swiss German girls were long gone and Rajah seemed mellow. There were a few presents for Alice, a meal of rice and curry and later, as she was leaving, some money.

'I don't want you to do without,' her father said, giving her an unexpected hug.

Rajah winked at her.

'You'll have to stop being so shy, Alice,' he said, not unkindly.

Alice was relieved to return home for unexpectedly she found she enjoyed living alone with her mother. The atmosphere in the house was peaceful now. Stanley still paid the rent but Sita had taken on all their daily expenses. She doubled and trebled her workload. There was a great deal of sewing available for a good seamstress and plenty of men who needed their trouser legs shortened. At least, thought Sita, bitterness never far away, they all had two legs. Months passed in this way. The long summer holidays came and went with stretches of idleness when Alice lay on her bed staring into space or simply drawing. Sita bought back poster paints from one of her foraging trips to the market so Alice began to paint small still-life studies interspersed with startling blue images of the sea.

In September Alice went reluctantly back to the brutish building and harsh environment of her school. She was a second-year pupil now, slightly below average in her work, conscientious if somewhat uninspired. She had still made no real friends to speak of. The following spring, when Stanley had been gone for a whole year, Alice discovered hawthorn buds, shrivelled by a late, destructive, frost. She hadn't noticed the hedges before. She began to walk home through the park and she saw that the sky was exactly like a painting in the National Gallery. Forever after she would think of spring having Constable skies.

Sita was working hard and with more energy than she had ever had, but she had also begun to forget things; little things, things that were not really of great significance. Turning off the lights, finding her glasses; Alice frequently found the kettle had boiled dry.

'Oh, never mind,' Sita would say carelessly when Alice showed her another burnt-out pan. 'I'm too busy to think of everything.'

So Alice got into the habit of checking that everything was switched off before she went to bed. Their life was not exciting, but in a way they both were content. Every evening, after she packed away her sewing Sita would at the kitchen table writing out her accounts into a small notebook, adding and subtracting the details of her finances. Alice could see that this moment at the end of the day, with the house so tranquil and the sewing machine stilled, was the best moment of all for her mother. Because of this she loved it too. Something about its peacefulness always stirred the distant memory of nights at the Sea House. There was no sea, no express train rushing past; but the sound of cars starting and stopping, of dustbin lids rattling and Cockney voices calling to each other made her feel safe.

'We'll be fine as long as we're careful,' Sita informed her. 'Your father's money covers the big items. I can make up the rest.'

It was her only reference to Stanley.

Alice had no reason to address her father's departure at all until the October of her third year at the school. It happened by chance during an art lesson. The teacher was taking the register when someone pushed her and she slipped off her stool, knocking over a tray of green paint. The class rocked with laughter. The teacher looked up and glared at Alice, causing more guffaws.

'Pack it in,' he said wearily. 'Alice could you clear it up, *now!*'

Alice stared hard at him, stung. Silently she went to the sink.

'Cheer up,' the teacher said flippantly, noticing the look. 'It's not that bad.'

A bit later on she became aware he was watching her mix some colours. When the lesson was finished and the children were rushing out he called her over.

'You okay?' he asked.

She nodded without speaking. The teacher hesitated fractionally, considering her.

'Why didn't your parents come to the parents evening last week?' he asked, not unkindly.

Alice stared at her feet.

'My mum doesn't like going out on her own, Mr Eliot,' she mumbled.

The bell had just gone announcing the lunch break. The art teacher stubbed out his cigarette. He waved the smoke away and pulled a face.

'Don't tell anyone,' he said, pushing the contents of the ashtray into the bin. 'I must be an addict!'

Alice looked at him so expressionlessly that he sighed and perched himself on the edge of the table. He picked up the construction she had just finished painting.

'I like it,' he told her, glancing slyly at her.

She didn't know what to say. The thing he was holding was shaped like a cupboard. When opened, a boat emerged. He looked enquiringly at her.

'I found the wood in the skip outside school,' she volunteered finally.

'I know that skip,' Mr Eliot said.

And he grinned suddenly.

'I've watched you foraging in it!'

Startled, she fell silent again. Unlike the other children in her class, Alice had made several pieces of work. All of them were constructions; all had the same peculiar originality. They were dotted around the room.

She had painted her cupboard white. David Eliot felt around the sides of it, checking the glued edges. Frowning, he closed the doors again. It was not his usual policy to comment on work in progress, but this was work of a more sophisticated nature than he was used to seeing in this rough-at-the-edges inner-city school. Here, in this concrete wasteland, as Mr Eliot often complained, talent was thin on the ground.

'What are you going to do now you've painted it?' he asked, noncommittal.

'I want to make it look old,' Alice said.

She spoke reluctantly. He waited.

'I'm going to rub cardamom powder along the edges and then paint it with glue and water.'

David Eliot raised an eyebrow.

'*Cardamom* powder, Alice? Where on earth will you get cardamom powder from?'

'My mum's got loads of it in her spice drawer,' she said. 'We brought it with us from Ceylon, but we never use it.'

She hesitated again, uncertain. The art teacher was turning over the construction in his hands and frowning slightly. He has nice hands, Alice thought suddenly. The sun appeared from behind a cloud highlighting the grubbiness of the long windows and the dust on the still-life table. The art room felt warm and safe.

'Of course!' the teacher said absent-mindedly. His words dropped into the empty classroom. 'Couldn't your dad have come to the parents evening instead?'

Alice shook her head. She shook it so hard that her hair went over her eyes.

'My dad's left, sir. He left last year.'

It was her first acknowledgement of the fact.

'Oh, okay,' the teacher was saying, easily. 'Well, finish the piece and let me look at it when it's done.'

He smiled down at her again, catching her unawares so that without thinking she smiled back. There was the smallest of pauses. Then

Mr Eliot stood up and nodded before sneaking off to his makeshift office for another fag.

Some weeks later, during one of the double art lessons, David Eliot handed Alice a book to look at.

'Heard of her?' he asked.

Alice shook her head. The book was full of the strangest pictures.

'They're sculptures,' the teacher said, watching her turn the pages.

Several other children came over curiously to look at the book. Towards the end of the lesson Mr Eliot wandered casually back around the room looking at the work. When he came to Alice's table he stopped. Her cupboard-boat construction was finished. She had rubbed cardamom powder mixed with dirt all over it and had scratched and gouged holes in the wood. She had papered the inside of the doors with an old Singhalese newspaper.

'Where did you find this?' David Eliot asked.

His voice was neutral.

'We lined the trunk we brought to England with it,' Alice told him, aware the class was watching her, too.

She felt her face grow hot with a mixture of emotions, but all Mr Eliot said was, 'I hope you're planning to do GCE Art.'

'Yes,' she said, adding, 'I used to make things like this when I lived in Ceylon.'

She stopped abruptly. For one sharp moment her grandfather's studio flashed before her eyes and she smelled linseed oil. A shadow fell across the whitened beach. Then it was gone and Mr Eliot was speaking to someone else in the class.

After the lesson ended Alice took the book back. She could see Mr Eliot in his office, tapping a cigarette on its packet before putting it between his lips. Alice noticed his fingers were nicotine-stained. She frowned. His fingers reminded her of someone else's, but she couldn't think whose. Once again an image flashed past her.

It was of her grandfather tapping his pipe.

'Yes, what d'you want?' asked one of the other staff, sharply, seeing her hovering. 'Always knock before you come in here, please.'

'Sorry, Miss Kimberley.'

An inexplicable stab of anger, not evident for years, rose within Alice. It took her by surprise so that her face glowed. She had never liked Miss Kimberley.

'What is it, Alice?' asked Mr Eliot, coming out. 'Oh, the book. Would you like to borrow it until next week?'

She nodded and scuttled off before he could change his mind. But not before she heard the art teacher say to Miss Kimberley, 'Stop being a dragon to her, Sarah. She's scared.'

The idea that they thought she was scared mortified Alice. Embarrassment flushed over her. She felt humiliated. Momentarily she saw herself as the teachers did. Was that what they thought of her? The rage made her want to cry. Vowing to stand up for herself against Miss Kimberley, she hurried home with her book.

That night in her bedroom Alice read the book from cover to cover. There were facsimiles of some of the artist's diaries. The dedication in particular caught her eye and she read it with some difficulty.

May this book of your childhood become a guide in your later life: in it you'll realise how you grew up, you'll find names and dates, you would otherwise forget; events that might drown in the stream of experience, but are important for you. None of this may get lost, my beloved child. Because there is nothing that sustains us more in the hardship of our lives than a review of our childhood.

Alice read very slowly, twice, not fully understanding everything. Then she paused for a moment before copying it down in the front of her sketchbook. She could not understand why her chest tightened at the sight of the words.

As the school year moved slowly on, Alice found she spent more and more time in the art block. With David Eliot's encouragement, she began to work on her constructions and paintings in the much-hated lunch break. At home, life had settled into a rhythm. It was the happiest it had been for years. Conversation between Alice and her mother was desultory. Relieved to be let off the communication hook, they both sank gratefully into what passed for a companionable silence. The summer of 1976 turned out to be blistering hot. It was their third summer in England with hardly a cloud in the sky and day after day of sunshine and dust. London was emptied of its residents, beating a steady path to the sea. Sita, busy with her orders from the dry cleaners and her private clients, barely noticed the heat. In her mind the sound of her sewing machine had completely replaced the sound of the Indian Ocean. For both mother and daughter, keeping their heads above water took most of their effort, and when they saw an advertisement in a shop window for a holiday let beside the sea, they simultaneously looked away. They had no need to consult each other; the sea was part of an intractable past. In the first week of the summer holidays Sita took a week off work, telling the dry cleaners that she needed to spend some time with Alice. In fact she had decided to dig the garden up. She planted three rose bushes of such garish colours that the old woman next door objected.

'I don't want yellow roses growing up against my fence,' the woman said. 'Can't you see mine is a blue-and-white cottage garden?'

Sita apologised and uprooted them. She didn't mind. It had been a half-hearted attempt at gardening. She disliked going outside. In the autumn of that same year, with some of the money she had saved, she concreted over the garden, leaving only a small square patch of grass that was soon overgrown with dandelions.

The new school year began and with it came another letter from home. When she opened it, a photograph of May's young son fell out.

'Can I see,' Alice asked.

I haven't heard from you for such a long time that I sometimes wonder if my letters ever get through, Bee had written. *It would not surprise me in the least if certain parties censor them. But never mind. I will continue to write all the same and hope something eventually gets through. Here is your little nephew, Sita, and your first cousin, Alice. I do hope you get a chance to write to May and Namil, Sita. I know they would love to hear from you. Life here has hardly changed since you left. The way we miss you has not altered with time either! Your grandmother has a touch of arthritis; I continue to smoke, much to her annoyance, and every evening I walk along the beach and think of you all.*

Sita read the letter and passed it on to Alice. She made no response and once again silence fell.

At Christmas, two more photographs arrived. This time they were of May, with the sheen of motherhood on her, holding Sarath's hand. Alice ignored the pictures, only to pick them up when her mother was not around and stare at the blurred black-and-white images, searching for signs of anything she might recognise. There was one picture of her grandfather carrying the child.

You must be very busy, her grandfather had written. *But when you have a moment, do write.*

Sita, coming in from the shops, found Alice staring greedily at the photograph.

'I thought you couldn't be bothered with any of that,' she said sharply.

Alice handed them to her guiltily.

'I'm not,' she said. 'I was just curious.'

They said no more on the subject, but that night Alice wrote a brief letter to her grandparents.

At the beginning of term, she wrote, *I went with the upper school to an exhibition. They were big sculptures made with all sorts of things. My art teacher said it is important to try to use different sorts of material. He wants me to choose Art as one of my GCE options.*

She paused, wanting to say more about the art trip and the exhibition at the huge gallery beside the river. She wanted to say that the day had been the best in her life since leaving Ceylon. She wanted to tell her grandfather how the exhibition had enthralled her. That the delicate latex sculptures, the small vigorous paintings and detailed pencil drawings had reminded her of Bee's studio and the work he did in it. But when she came to actually write this down she found her enthusiasm dried up even as she wrote. It seemed her happy memory of that day was locked away, refusing to be voiced. All she was aware of was the desperate need not to mention her parents. In the end, unable to think of anything more she signed off lamely sending them her love. It was some time before she wrote again.

Over Christmas, Stanley surfaced once more.

'Here,' he said brusquely, handing Sita an envelope. 'Get yourself a telephone.'

Sita wouldn't touch the money. What did they need a phone for?

'Alice can ring me,' he told her. 'Can't you, Alice?'

Alice shrugged; she had no idea why she would need to ring Stanley. Her father smelled strongly of a new, slightly sicklier perfume.

'What's that smell?' she asked.

'Incense,' Stanley said, shortly.

'Taken up religion, then?' Sita asked.

Stanley ignored her. He doesn't care, thought Alice, amazed. However much he hurts her he doesn't care.

'You've grown,' Stanley was saying with mild surprise, staring at her.

He lit a cigarette. Out of the corner of his eye he could see that the house was in a terrible state.

'Why don't you get rid of these paraffin heaters and get some electric ones?' he asked irritably.

Sita didn't bother to answer him. She lit the gas and put the kettle on the ring. Alice took out a butter cake that Stanley recognised as the sort Sita used to make.

'Would you like some cake, Dada?' she asked, the old name slipping out.

She raised her eyes and it was then that Stanley saw, with a small jolt of shock, that his daughter's face had changed subtly. A faint but unmistakable air of youthfulness, not noticeable before, was evident. He smiled at her and Sita, handing him a cup of tea, saw that the old Stanley had transferred his affections seamlessly to their daughter.

'Didn't you get a Christmas tree?' he asked, sensing Sita's hostility.

'A Christmas tree?' she laughed. 'We're Buddhists, have you forgotten? Have you forgotten everything about us?'

'Well, this is a Christian country,' Stanley mumbled. 'Your friends must all celebrate Christmas, Alice. Don't they?'

'What friends?' Sita asked him. 'Your daughter doesn't have friends; not that you'd care.'

Alice glanced from her mother to her father. Sita's voice was rising; it meant that she would soon start screaming.

Okay, okay, sorry, men,' Stanley said. He set his hardly drunk tea down on the kitchen table. Then he picked up his hat.

'Look,' he said, 'there's the money. Get a telephone put in, will you? Then I can call Alice; see how she's doing. All right, Alice? Maybe you'd like to come over to my place in Ealing sometime too? See where I live.'

He smiled awkwardly, his eyes pleading with her. Alice, watching them both, was torn.

'She's my daughter, after all,' he added defiantly.

'Of course!' Sita said bitterly. 'And your daughter must meet that woman. See who her father left her mother for. Is that it? Is that what you want? Is that why you've come here?'

But Stanley, taking fright, was gone, banging the door shut, fleeing from the accusations of his almost divorced first wife.

In March a letter arrived in time for Alice's birthday. It was from Bee and had been written before Christmas but had taken three months to arrive. Once again their letters had crossed. Bee's letter had been censored so that what Alice was left with was disjointed and difficult to understand.

We think of you all the time, Bee had written. *The beach is just as it always was. The rocks are still there, of course, and the stretch of sand where the driftwood always appeared. D'you remember, Alice?*

But Bee's letter, like her own, had become wooden; Alice could no longer hear the sound of her grandfather's voice.

Esther and Dias are moving to Kultura after the Singhalese New Year. They will still keep their house here. Something happened to prompt them to leave.

A sentence had been crossed out in red pen.

Dias hopes to get her married off sometime this year. And Janake, do you remember him? He is studying to become a Buddhist monk. Soon he will be moving to Colombo. So the old crowd is moving on.

And then, faintly, at the end he had written:

Love to all of you, to your dada, your mother and yourself, Alice, from your loving grandmother and grandfather.

'Doesn't he know Dada has left?' Alice asked.

Sita looked at her daughter. Since Stanley's last visit she, too, had become conscious of changes in Alice. Dimly she felt the presence of an inner life, hitherto invisible. It shone faintly in the child's face, casting a new and tender light not apparent before. Sita registered this change with furtive wonder. There was no one she could share these thoughts with, but a frail, tender motherliness, never until now given an airing, began to work in her. Several times she almost sent a school photograph of her daughter back home so they too might see this change. But each time, at the point of doing so, some timidity always stopped her. Perhaps it was the traces of the absent Stanley that remained in Alice's face and the shame of his leaving that got in the way. No one in Mount Lavinia had eloped, let alone got divorced.

'They wouldn't understand,' she said with finality, and the subject was never referred to again.

* * *

They did not see the years go by after that. Living took up too much of their energy. Another spring, thought Sita, drearily, uncaring. By now it was 1979 and Kunal was merely a dull pulse in her memory. The letters from both sides of the ocean were brief epigraphs of news items. Soon the decade was over, swallowed up by an indifferent world. For Sita, life had begun to feel like a walk across a mental desert. She travelled slowly, with a mind-map that coursed its way along the dried riverbeds of her old life. She would walk this route, she suspected, forever, singing her voiceless, wordless song. She would walk like a bird that had lost its wings. Mute. With her head held steady and her eyes firmly on the arid path. Occasionally something would catch her attention briefly, making her aware of a milky-soft May morning or the cornflower blue eyes of a passing stranger. Then, for a moment, she would find herself in an unexpected oasis. But mostly there was nothing. It was no longer possible for her to move out of her desert territory. She continued to take in alterations from the dry cleaners and had begun to work for a tailor's shop as well. There was always plenty to do. So that, turning her back on the past, she was content to drift far out into the Atlantic greyness. For *this* was her life now; England in its peculiar way was the only home she needed.

After the Christmas holidays that year Alice found to her surprise that she had won a prize. Mr Eliot had entered one of her constructions for a competition and she had won.

'Did you have a good Christmas?' he asked, after he had told her the news.

Alice felt her mouth become stiff with the effort of not smiling.

'My mother's a Buddhist,' she volunteered. 'We don't really celebrate Christmas.'

'Well, anyway, you can inform your mother what a talented daughter she has!' Mr Eliot said. 'There's a photographer coming to take a picture of your sculpture. Have you got a name for it yet?'

Alice looked at the teacher. Overwhelmed, she wanted to run and hide.

'It's called *Catamaran House*, sir,' she said solemnly.

'Goodness me!' the teacher said in a friendly way. 'Pretty *and* talented! Look pleased then!'

She blushed.

January was bitterly cold and in February it snowed heavily. Sita brought two more paraffin heaters. Small birds rested on the fence in their neglected back garden. Alice drew them from her bedroom window. She was a permanent presence in the art room now. A week later, Stanley read about her prize in the London evening paper.

Alice Fonseka, who won the first prize in the junior section of the Discerning Eye (Sculpture Section), is not quite sixteen years old, yet her winning piece shows great maturity. Although the Ceylonese girl has been living in Britain for four years, her memories of her homeland are still vivid. 'The catamarans on the beach were very old,' she says. Wrinkled and scratched, the wood shows glimpses of painting and re-painting over many years. 'There are lots of stories in the wood,' Alice adds. 'From years and years ago.'

Some of these stories are in Alice's prize-winning piece. When asked why she had put the boat inside the cupboard she explains that the cupboard is a kind of house that keeps secrets. Her teacher, David Eliot, feels that Alice is a student worth watching. 'I think she has a natural affinity with materials,' he says.

Alice Fonseka attends Stockwell Manor School.

There was a photograph of Alice standing next to her *Catamaran House*.

'Well, well, well,' Stanley's voice came loudly over the newly installed telephone.

He sounded pleased.

'You're a bit of a dark horse! Looks like you're going to take after that grandfather of yours, after all! That should please your mother.'

At school, winning the prize and the newspaper article made a difference, too.

'Her grandfather is an artist, sir,' one of the children told David Eliot when he pinned the article on the noticeboard. 'Alice said he's quite famous in Ceylon.'

The art teacher nodded. He wasn't surprised.

'When did she say that?'

'Dunno, sir. Last year sometime. She brought a letter from him into Geography. With a stamp of their Prime Minister on it.'

Mr Eliot raised his eyebrows. The next time he saw Alice he questioned her.

'Grandpa Bee,' Alice said eagerly, caught unawares by the question.

She stopped what she was doing for a moment. Memories flashed past and the teacher looked sharply at her. Her hair, grown longer in the past few months, was tied up, exposing a slender neck. It made her look older than fifteen and her eyes, when she glanced at him, were almond-shaped and clear.

'He had a wonderful studio,' she said hesitantly. 'I used to make things while he made his prints.'

'A printmaker!' said Mr Eliot with interest. 'He's a printmaker? What's his name?'

'Benjamin Fonseka. You wouldn't know him, sir. He painted in watercolour too.'

Her grandfather's voice was suddenly close by in her ear. *You are going to the land of watercolours.*

'Good!' Mr Eliot said, nodding his head. 'I want to see you paint as well, you know. Not just make objects. D'you understand? When you start on your examination year, I want you to try your hand at watercolours.'

And he went back into his office for another fag, unaware that Alice's eyes followed him across the room.

11

By the time Sarath was six the war was a worn-out habit on the island. Slowly, the old ways sank under the strain of the conflict as though they were a broken boat shipwrecked on the reef. The Fonsekas had stayed on the boat while others had gone. Sita, having made a raft of her own, was sailing to oblivion. May, examining the crop of grey hair on her head, was saddened to discover how much time had passed.

Two shots from a Kalashnikov and another youth was felled to the ground.

'Be careful, Sarath,' May called out in warning several times a day.

Her beliefs and her sense of justice had altered since Sarath's birth. She continued to teach at the local school at the top of the hill where, ostensibly, nothing had changed. The view from her classroom window had not altered. It was still a sun-drenched, dazzling sea she gazed at. But the Tamil boy who had been dragged from his seat had been dead for many years and her own son had replaced him in May's heart. Nothing else, she now knew, mattered.

'Don't be long,' she called out. 'I want you to come straight home from school.'

And Sarath replied for the hundredth time:

'No, Amma, I won't.'

Sarath knew, even before he could walk, that he had certain responsibilities. Certain sections of the family guilt were stamped on his name. At his birth, for instance, his mother had lost her sister's affection. Sarath knew that. His aunt Sita had not been able to contemplate his birth because it raised the spectre of her dead child. Even though the chances of any of them ever seeing his aunt again were more or less nil, still Sarath felt the family guilt heavy as a gold chain around his neck.

Then there was his cousin, Alice. She might as well have been lost at sea, for all the contact they had with her. Sarath's mother had told him that Alice's leaving had broken Grandpa Bee's heart. Once Grandpa Bee used to paint beautiful seascapes in iridescent peacock colours. But now he just made etchings of disembodied faces that had brought him an official warning. Watching his grandfather, Sarath was aware that he wanted to do something for his country to stop the senseless war. With this in mind, on his seventh birthday, Sarath declared he was going to become a doctor. His parents listened with admiration. Their son reminded them a little of Alice, before she had gone away and lost her anchor.

Bee was watching too. He was watching with caution, keeping his opinions and his memories in a rusty old chocolate tin with the Queen's crest and the name Ceylon stamped on it. Long ago Bee had decided it would not do to get too involved. Thereby lay heartache. Alice had left behind a hole in his view of the sky through which she had sailed into eternity. Her mother had followed without once looking back. They had made a winter landscape of Bee's life, here, in the sun. So it would not do, he told himself, to get too attached to the boy. In order to guard himself, Bee took the following precautions: he never walked on the beach with Sarath; he never invited him in to watch him mix his colours; he never told him stories. There was no need for Sarath to stay the night with his grandparents as he lived so close to them anyway. Battling silently with himself, Bee argued that Sarath did not need him in the way Alice had, for both Sarath's parents plainly adored him. Kamala, understanding perfectly well what Bee was up to, observed all this without saying a single word on the subject. She never commented when he rang May every day to check the boy had got home safely from school.

Newcomers had moved into the town from the city, from the east, from the west and from the more remote parts of the island. The army had established permanent headquarters and there were always patrol cars racing along the beach at nights, playing shine-the-searchlight and round-up-the-terrorists. A rash of corpses appeared all along this part of the coast. Hell with a face on it; lips that would never kiss again, hair with no hands to comb it. In the years since Sita had left, Bee had lost count of the number of Tamils he had hidden, saved, dispatched to Jaffna. Except for Kunal, all had reached their destination safely. The fugitives came at night, silently through the coconut grove, never when the moon was high, in a steady stream of desperation. Mostly they were servants, sometimes as young as fifteen. Always they came via the doctor. The road across Elephant Pass had become impassable. And now, another, fresher activity was running silently across the island; one that no one wanted to talk about. It had not reached the south as yet, but in the eastern province it was big news. Here large white vans had begun to patrol the villages; late at night, under cover of darkness as though they were fishermen fishing with lamps, men in plain clothes rounded up their catch. Door to door they went, house to house, penetrating the night with the beam of their torches. Pouncing when they were least expected. Creating a new terror that would last for many years to come. One day someone would speak of this abuse of human life, but for now they were simply ghost-people disappearing softly through the rustling trees, voiceless and despairing. Those Tamils lucky enough to have relatives abroad tried sticking it out in hiding while they waited for a ticket. They went to England, to Canada, to Australia. Anywhere, really, such was the desperation for peace. But peace was in hiding, too. Bee, walking defiantly across the beach to visit Janake's mother, sensed it as he stumbled, horrified over the whitened remains of unidentified bones. Saying nothing to Kamala, he put new bars on the doors.

'Thatha,' May said worriedly, when one more Tamil had been dispatched safely to a ship, 'Thatha, please, you've done enough. I want you to stop. These etchings are madness, hiding these people is so risky. I think the neighbours are watching you.'

For months now, the post had been intermittent. The astrologer who had cast May's horoscope before her marriage came to visit Bee. He looked grave.

'Maybe you should leave this town,' he told him tentatively. 'There are people here who don't like you.'

He did not speak of the dark star that lay across Bee's horoscope, crossing the planet Saturn with the number nine. The astrologer remembered all this from the time of May's wedding. Nine was important, he told Bee, counting the steps that led down from the verandah to the gate. Nine lizards darted across the wall, and nine moths circled the shade of the single light bulb in the sitting room. May rang her parents daily. Had they had any news from Sita? She had seen the postman walking up the hill, perhaps with a letter for them. But no, there was no news from Sita.

Then one morning at eleven o'clock all the radio stations were interrupted by a news flash. A senior government official had been assassinated and the Tamil Tigers were claiming responsibility. Shockwaves reverberated around the capital as the government was thrown into chaos. All morning the radio broadcast the news, interspersed with the sonorous chanting of monks, their voices calmly rising and falling, for death, being part of life, did not perturb them. Several hours later, before the country could draw its breath, the Tigers bombed the holiest of Buddhist sites. A truck loaded with explosives rushing towards the sacred temple of the tooth was all it took to destroy three thousand years of peace. Those who watched in horror saw that at last the eye of the storm had appeared.

Bee listened to the news while he worked on his etching plate. The afternoon sun was low in the sky. In a little while it would be dark and the mosquitoes would descend with the curfew. He watched the etching acid frothing in its tray. After a few seconds the timer buzzed and he lifted the metal plate out and washed it in clean water. Then he began to ink the plate up. He had received a message from his friend the doctor. There was a Tamil man in the wrong place at the wrong time, on the run. Bee looked at his day's work. The etching was drying between blotters. On the white paper was an image of a naked body lying face-up across a trestle table. Four faces emerged from out of the black mezzotint, staring down at the begging figure. Bee stared at the image intently. He took his pencil out and signed the print. Then he wrote in his neat faint handwriting: *The Banquet.*

'I'm going up to the Mount Lavinia Hotel,' he told Kamala. 'I'm meeting the art dealer there.'

Kamala watched him go. She knew he was lying but she understood; if she wanted Bee to find a little feeling in his numbed emotions it was through this small seepage of defiance that he would do so. So with an eye blinded with love she left him alone.

At the hotel Bee ordered a glass of beer and went to a table outside. He waited. There was no sign of the doctor. The light from the sea pierced its way through his thoughts. A small spindly bird hopped on the sand. His heart ached. This war has cursed us, he thought. Staring at the kingfisher-blue sky he thought of Sarath and saw how great his fear had been, how frightened he was of loving again. But Sarath would be fine. Thank God! With his Singhalese father, his Singhalese name, he would be safe.

After finishing his beer, Bee looked around casually. Then he stood up and left. The barman watched him leave. He wiped down the counter. Under his waiter's uniform he wore army boots.

Because for once there was no curfew, they all ate together that night: Bee and Kamala, May and Sarath. Even Namil, having finished work early, joined them. Nobody spoke much and the fish was exceptionally delicious. If I had not lost Alice, thought Bee, when the plates were cleared and he sat smoking on the verandah, I would say it hasn't been so bad. But I would like to see her one more time, he thought. Afterwards, as they sat on the verandah under a sky punctured by stars, listening to the sweet, soft sound of the Indian Ocean, Bee brought out a pack of cards. No one, not even Sarath, said anything as he began to deal them out. In the light of the lamp that the servant had lit Kamala glanced at her husband's face. It was unutterably sad.

* * *

The dawn came up like the opening bars of a symphony. It brought the sea into view once more, cleaned smooth by night's hand. Gradually as the sky whitened it became possible to see the waves rising slowly above the horizon, high and incandescent in the softest of blues, impossible to replicate in paint. They moved one against another, spreading lacy fronds across the sands. And here and there glimpses of wet sand glinted like precious gems. An unseen hand had swept the beach. Slowly the dark line of the horizon began to glow, first with a faint rose, followed by streaks of yellow. And all the while the dark expanse of water turned a glorious, shimmering silver. Some other person will paint this stretch of sea after I am gone, thought Bee, rising to gaze at it. Unusually, he felt refreshed. The arrival of the light could still make him impatient to begin working. Perhaps, he thought, I should go back to painting what I see. Last night's unexpected tranquillity had left him hopeful. His sleep had been peaceful, uninterrupted by sounds of devil dancing or drums or the thud of an exploding bomb. For once, nothing had disturbed him until the arrival of this slow-spreading, astonishing, dawn. Beside him, Kamala stirred but did not wake. Turning over she snored gently. Quietly, Bee went outside.

In England the dawn was at least five hours away, he thought, examining his plants, still damp with dew. Last night Sarath had won the card game, laughing gleefully; watching him, Bee had felt a confusion of old emotions from long ago. Unlocking his studio he went in and began examining his etching plates, clean now of all ink, criss-crossed with finely bitten lines, like the palm of his own hand. Staring at them, suddenly he wanted simply to paint again. Taking out a sheet of watercolour paper, he stretched it across a board. Outside an army of enormous red ants marched across the gravel in wavy lines. Bee dipped his brush in a jar of clear water. The ants, moving as one, headed towards the threshold of his studio. Sunlight fell through the open door and on to their transparent, swollen bodies, making them look as though they carried sacs of blood on their backs. With one swift stroke Bee drew his brush across the board, marking the horizon across it forever. Aquamarine pigment bled across the paper.

He dipped his brush into the water again, completely absorbed in the movement of colour and water. A scene was growing under his hand, seeping out on to the white, rough paper, saturated, fluid and staining. He was so absorbed that he did not hear Kamala's voice calling out to him, over and over again, from the verandah. He did not notice the columns of ants flattened juicily by a pair of thick-soled boots. Only when the machete above his head came down in the first crack on his skull did he feel anything. Only then as, again and again it smashed against him, did he move, as with a whisper of breath, and the infinite grace of a marionette, he sank to the floor. Beside him the thin line of ants were no more. And in this moment Bee Fonseka was spared the knowledge that Kamala, seeing what was happening, running out towards him, had been gunned down, her cry and her life snapped off.

Silence. There was only silence. The sun rose fully. It was another cloudless, blank-blue day on this lovely island. First one bird, then another sang their indifferent melodies. Light fell on the leaves in the garden, casting shadows on the gravel where once Alice had stood, where neither Bee nor Kamala would ever walk again. Tenderly the shadows lengthened; it would be many hours before anyone called at the house. More hours still before May and Namil and Sarath would be brought the news by shocked neighbours. It would be a whole day before such news could travel across the oceans to England, and it would take even longer for Sita and Alice to comprehend what had happened. For distance would both protect and abandon them in equal parts, so that their wound would congeal instead of healing. But all this was some hours away. For now, those who would mourn still slept the sleep of innocence, protected for a little while longer. As the blood seeped into the land, and the sea rolled gently in a dazzling bowl of sunlight, all remained still.

It would be many weeks before the letter itself finally reached them. First there was the incoherent conversation with Namil. Still half-asleep, they struggled, grappling with the unfamiliar voice and the events that were unfolding elsewhere. They tried to picture the scene. Dawn on the coast? The sea? They had not heard its ebb and flow and hiss for years. They thought the sea had been erased from their consciousness. So her sister's voice, choking and crying, rising and falling across the ocean like an old familiar refrain, invading this drab, dark hall in which Sita stood holding the telephone with both her hands, seemed unreal. Afterwards, Sita had *known* she had sounded unfeeling.

'What time did it happen?' she had asked, woodenly.

And when the answer came back to her, broken up by the line and served up with her own echo, she had insisted:

'What were they doing, up so early?'

Namil spoke then, telling her unfamiliar things that made her want to scream, enough, enough, but instead she asked:

'When is the funeral?'

Later, when she began to register the shock, long before there were any tears, she imagined May saying, 'Have they forgotten how it is here already?' She imagined May judging her.

Like her mother, Alice had not reacted much. The sound of her voice echoing back across the telephone line had distracted her too. The hour and the rude awakening had made her clumsy and slow-witted. The line crackled. It was hard to imagine her grandfather's face, here in the cold, windowless hallway. The magnolia paint, Alice noticed irrelevantly, listening to her uncle's voice, was peeling in patches. Pink wallpaper showed through like raw flesh. Alice reached out and began to scratch at it a little more, delighted that it came off so easily in her hand. Her mother was speaking on the telephone again; the call would be costing someone a lot of money. This is my home, thought Alice, making a hole in the plaster as though the house was a living, breathing thing, so that her mother, still talking, still holding the phone with both hands, turned to her with a bewildered, half-wild look. Then, when the phone call was finally over (how many different ways was it possible to lament the dead), they wandered aimlessly around the house. Sita, walking into her bedroom, staring at the double bed she had leapt out of moments before, noticing the condensation on the windows, the cold linoleum floor, warm only near the two-bar gas fire, felt her thoughts stumble clumsily about. What sort of reality had she just heard?

'I'll put the kettle on,' Alice said.

Silent, slender Alice, with her mane of dark hair and her face pinched with shock, brewing tea as though it were tears. When had Alice the child become so inscrutable? Sita asked herself, bewildered. They drank tea with the electric light switched on and the paraffin heater spluttering fumes. They talked in shocked, low voices, not knowing how to communicate with each other. It had been so long since they had had anything to say.

'What shall we do?' Alice asked. 'Should we try to ring them back?'

It was a pound a minute. They could not afford it. Had May wondered why they had never rung before? Had they thought that Sita had plenty of money? Old anxieties surfaced. But in any case, thought Sita as the news renewed itself with another shockwave, her parents were no longer there to judge her. Relief-tinged bereavement.

'No. They're not in a state to talk. I'm going to write.'

'I thought you said that letters were being opened?'

It was true; those letters that did get through were still being opened. But what harm could words of condolence do? Sita looked at her daughter in the harsh electric light. Sixteen-year-old Alice, nearly seventeen. Here, in this single moment she had shed her childhood, freed herself like a butterfly; become someone else. The eager child was no more. She is almost a woman, thought Sita, surprised, seeing her daughter outlined against the wintry light. Beautiful and remote. Like her father, thought Sita, and unlike mine, she thought again, feeling a small prick of tears; a sensation of a dam that was blocked. Had it happened after Kunal? thought Sita.

'I'll send flowers,' Alice said, and for a moment her voice trembled before steadying itself. 'Don't worry, you don't have to go out. On my way to school I'll send flowers.'

She was thinking she would send white roses. An image of her grandparents burned briefly before her, but she concentrated hard to blank it out. Sita was remembering her sister's voice, swollen with tears, rising and falling, speaking in Singhalese; the only language possible for their grief. In the background, Sita was certain she heard the sea.

'Did you hear the sea?' she asked, frowning. 'In the background, I mean?'

'No, I don't think so. Why?'

'Nothing. It's just ... I don't know. It was hard to picture them, the place ...' her voice trailed off.

Alice nodded. They were both thinking the same thing. Outside, the light had become stronger. Surprisingly, this November day would be sunny. Icy, but with a blue sky. The tea in the pot was cold too and the paraffin heater, having spluttered a few times, went out. They would, thought Alice dully, have to buy an electric fire soon. Stirring herself with difficulty, she went to have a wash. She was due in school in two hours.

Alice went to the art block as soon as she could. Mr Eliot was washing paintbrushes, a cigarette dangling from his lips as usual. Every now and then he coughed and ash dropped into the sink. Outside in the bright winter sunshine a fight was in progress and once or twice he banged on the window.

'Oy,' he shouted, 'pack it in.'

No one took any notice. Opening the door, Alice rushed in.

'How many times have I told you kids not to use that door,' the teacher cried angrily.

'Sir,' Alice said, and then she stopped.

'Oh it's you, Alice.'

'They killed him ...' she cried before she could stop herself, and then with no warning she burst into tears.

Sitting in David Eliot's office she told him the story, slowly, bit by disjointed bit.

'He was my grandfather, sir,' she said. 'He loved me.'

Outside, snow had begun to fall heavily, transforming the playground, muffling the sound of traffic, as Alice haltingly described her last glimpse of her grandparents.

'The sun shone all the way to the harbour,' she said, and now she was crying in earnest.

Having started she found herself unable to stop.

'He wouldn't come to the jetty and when I asked my grandmother, she said he couldn't bear to.'

The teacher nodded, saying nothing, waiting.

'I was angry with him, sir, for not coming. I didn't understand. And then, later, I was angry he didn't send for me.'

The lunch break was nearly over. Children lined up, jostling against each other, laughing, while Alice talked to David Eliot about her home, her voice rising in a passionate flood of tears.

'He was the only one who ever loved me, sir,' she cried piteously.

Still the art teacher said nothing.

'And I never wrote, not often. I couldn't.'

Mr Eliot turned to her with a look of grave pity in his eyes.

'Alice,' he said at last, when there seemed no letting up of her tears, 'you are very young.'

Bemused, she looked at him with eyes magnified by tears and something of his confused thoughts communicated themselves to her.

'Alice,' he sighed, unable to find the words he wanted.

Then he put his hand on her thin shoulder and shook her very slightly.

'Alice … do you think you should go home?'

She didn't seem to hear; she was too busy shredding a paper hanky.

'Shall I send a note to your form teacher?' he asked finally. She shook her head violently. The thought of her mother was more than she could bear. David Eliot pressed his lips together. He could hear the whistle being blown.

'Listen,' he said, 'Miss Kimberley will be here in a minute …' He cleared his throat, gazing at her hopelessly. 'I've got to teach now. And you better go and wash your face in the girls' toilet. Come back after school, okay?'

Alice nodded, wiping eyes that continued to weep.

'Come back and tell me about your grandfather, okay?' David Eliot said. 'You are going to be a really good artist one day, you'll see.

I promise you. I've only had one other pupil like you before. And he wasn't half as good as you're going to be. You listening to me?'

His smile was wry. The look on his face was unreadable.

'I've been teaching a very long time, Alice, I've seen many, many students …'

Still she made no move to leave. The door opened and a boy put his head around the door.

'Sir, can we come in?'

'Get out, Joe,' the teacher bellowed. 'And remember to knock and WAIT!'

Alice stood up.

'Okay?' Mr Eliot asked, turning to Alice with a completely different voice. 'You'll come back after school?'

'Yes,' she said faintly, tremulously, catching at his heart.

'And remember what I said. One day you *will* be a really good artist! Hold on to that, will you?'

She nodded wanly and left.

'And one day,' murmured David Eliot softly, 'you will be beautiful too.'

She waited impatiently for the end of the day, wanting simply to see him again. But when she walked into the art room after the last bell it was Miss Kimberley who was there.

'Yes, what is it? It's Alice, isn't it?'

Alice nodded.

'It's okay, Kim,' David Eliot said easily, coming in. 'She's seeing me. Come on into my office, Alice.'

Aware of hostility Alice hesitated.

'What's the matter?' David Eliot asked, seeing her wariness, adding, before she could say anything, 'Oh, just ignore her! I'm going to have a cup of tea. Want one?'

Alice smiled and he considered her.

'Good,' he said. 'Nice to see you smile.'

At that her eyes filled with tears again.

'Listen to me, Alice. How long have I known you now? Since first year?'

She nodded.

'Well then. You come in here most days and work on your constructions, and right from the beginning I saw there was something, very ... I dunno,' he shrugged. 'Poetic, I suppose,' he said, hesitantly. 'That's it. You don't often see that in the daily shit that's given to you here, believe me!'

A faint smile crossed her face; a small dimple appeared in her cheek.

'So, listen to me,' the teacher continued, in a voice that made her want to cry once more. 'I know there's all sorts of things in your life feeding into your work.'

She looked at the ground, motionless, long eyelashes sweeping downwards. She could hardly bear the tone of his voice. She had not heard such tenderness for a long time.

'And that's great, you know. That's the stuff that will make the work terrific,' he was saying. 'The best thing about teaching is when, once in a while, you find an interesting student. So talk to me about your grandfather.'

Later, after he had shooed her out into the cold slushy playground, she watched him walk towards his car wondering where he was going, seeing the man who was her teacher in a different light. The sky was a hard fluorescent expanse, empty of any cloud. Her mother would be wondering where she was. It was so cold that there would be snow again, quite soon. Uncertain, exhausted with weeping on and off all day, she headed for home, her mind filled with lightness at the memory of the art teacher's voice.

By the time she was able to even contemplate writing the letter, the double cremation was over, the alms had been distributed, and the Sea House had been closed and boarded up. Time had arrived to lie heavily like an animal on May's hands. It was the school holidays and she did not even have her work to distract her. Putting aside old grievances, she wrote to her sister and her niece. When Sita opened the envelope, miraculously untampered, two photographs would fall out. Black-and-white images from a happier past. The photographs were blurred, but even so, thought May, her eyes swimming with tears, it was possible to distinguish Bee, standing under the murunga tree with the six-year-old Alice. Their father in his striped sarong, puffing his pipe, and Alice in the yellow cotton dress with the two ducks embroidered by Kamala. A wash of innocent memories spread before her.

By the time you get this all that remains of our parents will be ashes, May wrote. *I am in no mood for writing, but I must set down the events as they occur in case I forget. It will not be possible for you to imagine unless I do this. In any event, it will be almost impossible for you to believe what is going on here. They killed them both. You know how long Thatha had been under threat. So when it finally happened, why was I so shocked? And why did they pick this moment? Perhaps it was the etching he sold to the Tamil journalist. Did you know that his pictures were used in the* Asian Herald *published in Chennai? Namil and I had not been aware of this. How foolish he was. How brave. And then Amma. What had she ever done in her life that warranted this? Namil thinks she might have been killed after him, because she would have been a witness. Would we too have been mown down if we had been in the house?*

Let me tell you how it was. Dias found them. Can you imagine? Dias had come home, after being away in Colombo for so long, to clear her home. She and Esther are going to Canada. I don't know if they keep in touch with you, if you know what their story is. Did you know that someone in the army raped Esther? She might have AIDS; they are waiting for the test results. Dais's relatives have got them a visa for Canada and they are going in a month. They were both present at the funeral. The turn-out was huge. Father might have had enemies, but he also had many, many friends. Even the local policeman was present. He was so shocked, poor man; he was in tears. And the station master – do you remember him? – he came too. And then, at the last minute, of course, the army came; they told us it was to make sure there was no trouble for us. Can you believe it! Of course they have denied that they had anything to do with the murders. And of course they will get away with it. The news will be whitewashed, or the Tamils blamed, or, what is more likely, it will simply be forgotten.

You may be wondering how I can write in such an unemotional way. Why am I not more hysterical? The truth is, I am numb. In the past two weeks I have cried myself to a place from which I shall never again return. You might say I have lost all my illusions. Sita, you are my only sister. In the past we have not always seen eye to eye. I have grown used to saying nothing, but I think you knew I disapproved of many of the things you did. But I must tell you that the best thing you ever did was to leave this terrible place with Alice. When you left, I resented you going so much. I used to think, why is she leaving this sinking ship, why is she abandoning us to Hell? Don't we matter? I used to feel that Father preferred you to me. And then I would complain to Amma. Did you know that? When you married Stanley, father was devastated. And again, after Alice left, he changed completely. The grief was too much for him, and I resented that too. What about Sarath? I wanted to ask. Don't you love him? Is Alice all that matters? Even if she no longer bothers to write home? There, I have said it, I have removed the poison that has lain in my heart for so long. I am trying to be as honest as I can with you.

Sis, Sita, I want to start again. We have grown apart. Alice too has become lost to us. It is too late for father and Amma, but let it not be too late for us. This is the real reason for my writing now. When I heard your voice on the telephone, when we rang you with the news, I longed to see you again. I longed for Sarath to know you. Alice is his only cousin; they should know each other. Please write back; please tell me what you are thinking. There is too much hatred living in this place already, the world has gone mad. Let's not add to it.

It was Sarath who spoke at his grandparents' funeral. You should have heard him. I thought my heart would burst. He spoke of them both, saying how much he loved them and how they had wanted the war to stop. Oh, I can't remember what he said. He's only a little boy, Sita. But already I see Father in him. Father, and a bit of you, too! He keeps telling us that he wants to become a doctor, did you know? All that has happened has affected him and, small as he is, he wants to do something about it. I only hope to God his own karma is good. Namil says it is his generation that will change things. Sita, I must stop writing now. I am very tired and Sarath will be home from school soon. I have had this term off from my teaching because I just can't concentrate for very long. Please write back, don't let's lose touch again. I want to know everything. Tell me how you are coping without Stanley. I'm sorry I didn't say anything when you told me on the phone. I was in such shock over the news of what had happened here. But oh, Sis! Why didn't you tell us before? Did you think we would judge you? Tell me about Alice. Tell me what she's like, how she has changed, what her interests are. I hope your lives are going better than ours. One last thing, do you remember a boy called Janake? Alice would remember him, I'm sure, they used to play together on the beach. Well he is a young Buddhist priest now and he conducted the ceremony. He is a very gentle, peaceful person, all that a Buddhist monk should be. He was asking about you all and how Alice was doing. Ask Alice if she remembers him.

Our love to you both,
Your loving sister,
May

When she had finished reading the letter, Sita folded it back along the creases it had come with. She tucked the photographs inside the envelope and resealed it. Then she put it on the mantelpiece for Alice to see when she came home that night. And taking up her scissors she began her work. She had three pairs of trousers to alter before five o'clock. May's reply would have to wait.

Purgatorio

12

WITH THE BEGINNING OF THE RAINS, the steamy, oppressive heat and the spiders that curled in fistfuls of rigor mortis below the ceilings, an immense inertia took hold of the Sea House. Nothing could shift the humidity, the acidic smell of sea heat, which crept in through the boarded-up windows and the cracks in the doors. Their lives stilled like a painting. In this neglect, everyday objects, no longer in daily use, edged towards their own extinction. A table worn by years of constant use, useless now. A chair, its cane disgorged in upward movement like tufts of sea grass on the beach, empty of any human shape. There was no one to say who might have occupied it once, no one to blow away the fine sea dust that had crept in with the storms. Sunlight slithered in whatever slit it could find. But it was the moon, heavily pregnant with religious fullness, that lit the house where they had once all lived together. Shining on the leaves of the paw-paw tree that drifted in through the front door. Revealing the painting that had buckled with the damp. When the full moon shone a whole terrible history seeped out of fabric and wood, exposing un-erasable marks and stains on objects that had finished one life of plenitude and were moving into another of decay.

After a year had passed May returned, following the ghostly path trodden by her parents. She wandered the house and took away their wedding photograph in shocked silence. The photograph, fixed in innocent smiles, gave nothing away. It haunted May. How could she have known what effect this image would have on her one day? Her parents, not yet her parents when it was taken. A butterfly, sulphur yellow and enormous, drifted in through the window and settled briefly on her hair. Fearing madness, she fled. The landscape had an air of menace. I'll come back another day, she told herself, rage and grief overwhelming her yet again. But then she fled. When she was stronger, when many more months had passed, she crept slowly back to collect a few more things. A tea service, an embroidered jacket. Her books from the days of the Girls' High School. A rice-paper edition of the complete works of Shakespeare, the prize her father had won forty years before. A copy of the Bible. What made them own a Bible? Karma lay scattered everywhere, issuing its warning. It appalled May afresh. The violence of their death was stronger than the smell of the sea. It was stronger than the sunlight that dried the house up, turning it into a shrivelled skeleton. It was too much for May, who vowed never to return. She forgot the pair of shoes belonging to her mother tucked under the bed. She forgot her father's pipe, still with the toothmarks from when he chewed it. These things were left. Someone else in the future would have to rescue them.

Namil came and dismantled the studio. He sold the etching press and took whatever had not been already been destroyed by marauding thugs. He took what paints remained, encrusted and useless. He took a pot of brushes bearing traces of colour. There were no etching plates. Unknown hands had destroyed them. Then, tucked away behind a shelf, Namil found something else. It was a small painting made a short time before Alice had left.

'We should send it,' Namil suggested tentatively, wiping the dust off its surface. 'One day it might mean something to her.'

The painting was of the sea, viewed from what had been Alice's bedroom window. Time had not changed the view. However many years passed, it would not alter the blueness of the ocean, and Namil hoped the painting would move his niece.

'It is not her fault,' he consoled May, referring to the continued silence from overseas. 'Be patient.'

But even though they waited hopefully, nothing happened. The old doctor who had lived behind the coconut grove had gone. On the night of the Sea House murders, a van had come for him. His manservant told May how the men had bundled the doctor into the van. As it drove off, the manservant heard the doctor cry out with pain. He was not seen again. A new doctor, a younger Singhalese man, had replaced him. Time passed. Like the sea and the sky and the shoreline, the days and months blended together. The mango tree in the front garden bore fruit. Small boys from the fishermen's huts, seeing the house was empty, stole the fruit. Small girls, finding the dried mango stones, played hopscotch with them. No one cut back the undergrowth and the orange-blossom tree soon overshadowed the verandah, choking it of light. Nature entered the house, bleaching it, camouflaging it, making it its own. In Colombo and in other parts of the country the war continued regardless, appearing in small deadly pockets, creating craters of despair. The airport was destroyed. Suicide was the new destroyer, dropping its human remains as bombs everywhere. The cries of death were no longer distinguishable from the cries of birth. And while the world turned a blind eye and paradise blinded itself, the rich continued to travel home each night in armour-plated cars.

Alice saw him crossing the road before he even noticed her. He had a bottle of milk in one hand and a cigarette in the other. She knew he was hurrying to get back before she arrived at his flat. A bright August sun shone through the plane trees as she walked past the park and towards the block of Victorian flats where he lived. She was carrying a small portfolio.

'Alice,' he called, seeing her suddenly, waving the milk bottle. 'I'm here!'

She turned and stopped, waiting for him solemnly. Ever since the dreadful day of her grandparents' murder David Eliot had become her friend. He had seen her through two exams and a successful place on the foundation course at Camberwell. In the following July, after she finally left school, he'd invited her for the first time to his flat. She had been back several times since then, treasuring each visit. His flat, like his art department, was chaotic. She had never seen anything like it, except perhaps her grandfather's studio. There were posters on the walls, shelves rising to the ceiling, filled with books, photographs, plants and of course ashtrays full to the brim. She had discovered that, in the privacy of his house, David Eliot smoked a pipe. And although the smell of the tobacco he used was different, still the sound of him puffing on it filled her with contentment.

'Coffee?' he asked, closing the door.

She spread out the contents of her portfolio on his kitchen table. Sketchbooks, drawings, some paintings.

'What's this about?' he asked.

'I'm clearing up,' she said, smiling, unaware how changed he found her since the first time he had noticed her. 'And I found this –'

She held out a small oil painting of sea and sky, not her usual style.

'It's for you,' she said. 'I found it last night. I think I did it after my grandfather died.'

He was looking at the painting and did not look up. When he did his eyes were unreadable.

'I'll buy it from you.'

'No! No!' she said in horror. 'It's a present!'

He frowned and moved away from her. For a moment she wondered if she had offended him. He did not look pleased. She thought he was the most wonderful person in the world.

'But if you don't like it ...' she trailed off.

'I shall sell it when you are famous,' he said only half joking. 'Thank you.' He had told her many times that she was his best pupil. He would never have another like her again. All the others paled into insignificance, he often said. The difference is you actually have something to say, he had told her. She knew he was sorry to lose her but she was determined; she would always know him.

'I wish you were teaching the foundation course,' she said tentatively, sitting back on her heels, looking at the drawings in her portfolio.

There was a stale smell of cooking, and the rubbish he had once again forgotten to put out was everywhere, but she hardly noticed.

'More coffee?' he asked, his face helpless.

Misunderstanding, she looked at him anxiously.

'Can I still come and see you when I start the course?'

For all that she was constantly visiting him, there wasn't much they discussed that was personal. He did not encourage it and she did not want to be a nuisance. Which made the little she had told him about her life all the more precious. She fixed her eyes, beautiful and compelling, worriedly on him.

'Well, it'll cost you!' he said, lighting another cigarette.

'You smoke too much,' she told him bossily, adding, 'I can't manage the foundation if I don't keep seeing you!'

She almost bit her tongue, but he was still smiling, if a little ironically.

'Oh, I don't think so. You're your own person now, you'll see.'

Again the flippant tone she did not fully understand. August stretched luxuriously ahead.

'My mother works through the summer,' she told him. 'We need the money, sir.'

'Oh, for goodness' sake, call me David,' he replied impatiently.

Her father, she confessed, sent most of his money to the Tamil cause in Jaffna and there wasn't much left over for them. Besides, her father had another life now with a new woman. David Eliot listened without commenting. She had no idea if he secretly disapproved of her family. Once, during this long, wonderful August, he had taken her to a West End gallery to see the work of an artist he admired. She had stood for a long time staring dreamily at a painting called *Say Good-bye to the Shores of Africa*. On another occasion he took her to the Hayward Gallery and talked to her about a sculptress who was very old. Whenever he talked to her about art he was deadly serious. She loved listening to him talk in this way. Always he brought the subject around to her own work. Then, a few days before the bank holiday as a belated eighteenth birthday present he took her to a small restaurant he frequented in Goodge Street and gave her a first sip of wine, laughing when she wrinkled up her nose at the taste. He ordered lasagne and listened to the story of the first time she tasted pasta on board the ship that had brought her to England, and how she had for years hated the smell of tomato sauce because it reminded her of leaving her home. He had listened intently to her story. He always gave her his full attention when she spoke. Then he had asked her, hesitatingly, if she would ever want to go back.

'There's no point,' she told him. 'I have all of it in my head.'

'You should do more paintings from your head,' he said now, looking at the oil she had given him.

He began to cough suddenly and she stood up.

'Shall I get you some water?'

He didn't answer. When the coughing stopped he reached for his cigarettes again. Then he waved his hand towards the door.

'Time you went,' he said, with a small grimace.

Unknown to anyone, Janake had taken to visiting the Sea House. Memories propelled him towards it, pity kept him silent. Every time he returned from Colombo, on his way back from the station he would stop off to visit his elderly mother. He loved to listen to the sounds in the house, the murmuring and whispering that went on in it; like a shell echoing the waves. There was no one but Janake to listen to these unresolved voices. Alice, they called, Alice! Ordinarily the house would have been sold, ordinarily another family would have moved in. But these were not ordinary times and May and Namil were too crushed, too frightened, too traumatised to bother with the house. So it remained, sighing and whispering its tale of neglect. The death stains had all gone, washed away by wind and rain, veiled in dust, suppressed by time. The house stood eyeless and terrible. And the mango tree fruited and the coconuts fell to the ground and the frangipani blossomed under the blistering tropical sky. It was how this time passed, with slow indifference, with Janake as its only witness.

At eight Sarath already acted much older than his age. He still wanted to attend medical school. His parents said nothing. After what had happened, all that interested them was Sarath's safety. They had not heard from Sita for a long time; years. After May's last letter there had been silence for several months and when finally the longed-for reply came, it was cold and unsatisfactory, a mere formality that had hurt May more than she could say.

'She has become a white woman,' May told Namil, after reading it. 'She doesn't want to know about us, now.'

Namil had been more optimistic.

'Be patient,' he said. 'Your sister has had a hell of a life.'

May had cried herself to sleep for many nights after that. Who would have thought the Fonseka family would end up this way?

Some months later, after one of his visits to the Sea House, Janake called round to see May. Janake was twenty two, but still small for his age. Sarath was nearly as tall as him.

'How are things going for you, Janake?' Namil asked gently.

'All right, Uncle,' Janake said with a shake of his head.

Always after his secret visits to the Sea House, Janake was full of sadness. Full of memories of Alice. They had never written to each other as they had promised. By the time Janake had been able to write in English, the moment for writing had passed.

'There's a slight chance,' he said, and then he stopped.

He was thinking of the box Alice had given him on her last day. A box that would never open, she had laughed. And when he had asked her why this was she had told him she didn't want the memories to be lost. Janake hesitated. He had always been aware that a rift existed between the remaining Fonsekas.

'What sort of chance?' Sarath was asking.

'Well, it might not happen,' Janake said a little reluctantly, 'but next year I might go to the UK.'

'What!' May cried. 'Oh, Janake, really? When next year?'

She looked shocked.

'I don't know, Aunty. It's just talk at the moment. I have to finish my exams first.'

He wondered if they knew of his secret visits to the Sea House and if he could talk freely about Alice without angering them. He understood the hurt caused by Sita's neglect. But did they blame Alice, too?

'If I go, I shall want to see Alice,' he said, thinking how much he would love that.

'Bring some photos, if you do,' Sarath said excitedly. 'And ask them why they don't write. I'm going to England one day, too,' he said confidently. 'Not yet,' he added, catching sight of his mother's face. 'Not till I'm a doctor!'

Later that night when Janake had left and Sarath had finished his homework and gone to bed, May cleared up the remains of the evening meal. It was a Friday night. Janake's news had conjured up ghosts. The past contained relatives she no longer recognised. Sita was not the sister she had known. What was lost, she told Namil with finality, would never be recovered. In the year since the murders she had found it impossible to shake off her depression. While her sister had vanished to a better life, bitterness continued to cling to May, no matter how hard she tried to remove it. Soon, she told Namil, they should visit the Sea House and tidy it up for the last time. The idea filled her with dread.

'Perhaps we should sell the land,' she said.

'Go to sleep,' Namil told her. 'Stop thinking about the house. There's time enough to sell it, when Sarath needs the money for university. You never know how things will work themselves out. Our karma can't be bad forever.'

Outside in the moonless night, further up the bay, the Sea House stood silently, facing the ocean, in the way it had for a century. It watched the bay with its windowless eyes as though it were a living, breathing person. Filled with memories, waiting for a better future. And some memories were good and some were not, for the wheel of fortune was not easily stopped and the Sea House would have to take its chance just like the rest.

13

'How's your mother?' Stanley asked.

Alice nodded and helped herself to some mushroom curry. 'Okay.'

'Is she still working for that bloody dry cleaners?'

'Mmm.'

'And?'

Stanley frowned, exasperated. Alice continued eating and would not look at him. He poured himself another glass of beer and stared at this girl, his daughter. She had grown; not much in size, it was true, but nevertheless she had blossomed. Each time she visited the change surprised him. Even Rajah had noticed.

'A proper Tamil beauty!' Rajah had said admiringly, suddenly inclined to friendliness in the face of such a startling transformation. 'The ugly duckling has become a swan! Any boyfriends, yet?'

Alice had not responded and Stanley had been annoyed at his brother's tactlessness.

He was discovering within himself a belated and fierce protectiveness towards this unresponsive child. Surprised by it, of late he had begun to make overtures of affection towards her. Now that Alice had started at art school he tried to see her as much as he could, insisting she visited every Saturday. She came, without complaint, was always ravenous and mostly silent. He had no idea what went on in her head.

'Doesn't your mother feed you?' he asked, irritated, watching her help herself to some dhal.

'I do most of the cooking.'

'Why? What's the matter with her? She can't have that much work.'

'I can cook very well.'

'I'm sure you can, but I give her money to buy food for *you*.'

'She does … I do the shopping sometimes too. She doesn't like going out, much.'

'Why not?' demanded Stanley.

'Dad,' Alice said, and then she stopped.

The look on her father's face made her suddenly no longer hungry. She pushed back her plate. He still hates her, she thought. After all she's been through, he still can't say something nice about her. Alice sat very still until the feeling of pity for her mother died down.

'She's tired, Dada.'

How could she tell her father what her mother was really like? How to describe the fragile ghost that inhabited Sita's body for so long? Had her father forgotten the woman who had walked up the hill so long ago without her baby in her arms? Anger overwhelmed Alice. Anger, and a sort of despair at her father for his constant criticism. Anger at herself too, for not understanding her mother sooner.

'She's cold all the time, Dada,' she said instead, trying again.

Sita had never stopped complaining of the cold. She had never been able to adapt, never been able to wear Western clothes. Instead, she wore cardigans over her saris, thick socks on her feet and a headscarf tied on her head. For this reason as much as any other she had begun to hate going out. On those few occasions she was forced to do so, she took with her an old canvas tool bag which she used as a handbag. In it were her pins, her tape measure, her scissors. In spite of herself, Alice smiled. Nothing she said could persuade her mother to stop using the tool bag in this way. Quietly, with her head bent, wearing her heavy winter coat even in summer, Sita would venture timidly out. From a distance Alice always thought she looked like a broken doll. How could she make her father understand all this?

'What d'you mean, she's cold?' Stanley demanded irritably. 'Don't you have electric heaters now? I told you to get rid of those paraffin heaters ages ago. They're useless.'

'We have.'

Stanley's own, never-ending feelings of guilt made him angry at any mention of Sita. What about me? he wanted to ask Alice. Don't you feel sorry for me, too? But he said nothing, frightened of alienating the girl further. Life had not worked according to plan. Manika had left him. Once a servant woman always a servant woman, he supposed. He didn't miss her. The indoor shrines, the incense, the saffron washed offering were a bit much, here, amidst the London grime. His brother had disapproved.

'Filthy sex,' Rajah had called the infatuation, and Alice had kept away too. Surprisingly it was the child's absence that had bothered Stanley most of all. Anyway, it was over; Stanley lived alone now, with the occasional visitor that no one knew about. Now all his energy was taken up by the Tamil cause, back home. Not many people knew about that either.

'Neville's coming over this afternoon,' he told Alice. 'Do you remember Neville?'

Alice shook her head.

'No, I suppose you were too small. He was a friend of mine in Colombo. He was the person who got our tickets to come to England. We owe him a lot.'

'Can I have a glass of orange?' Alice asked.

'You must have been at the Sea House whenever he visited us.'

An image of the blue-painted gate and the dappled sunlight on the ground flashed by. She saw a piece of sea glass on the dusty shelf in her bedroom. The servant was polishing the floor with white coconut scrapings. She used to slide on the floor behind the servant. Laughing.

'Anyway, he's come to England. He does a lot of very good work for the Tigers. We all must help. These are our people. Your people, too, don't forget.'

In her mind's eye a lizard darted across the path and up on to the jak-fruit tree. In the light its skin was wrinkled like an old dinosaur. Old, like the land. Lime flowers dropped on the ground.

'You're Tamil too, Alice. You mustn't forget the suffering of your people,' Stanley urged, finishing his beer.

Only half, she thought, helping herself to orange juice. It was getting late, she told her father, she had to get back. There was a piece of work she had to finish for tomorrow.

'I saw someone called Neville,' she told her mother, when she returned. 'He knows you.'

But her mother didn't remember Neville either and Alice refrained from telling her that she had been made uncomfortable at the way Neville stared at her. She was in her first term at art school, living at home, partly for financial reasons but also because she did not like the idea of her mother being alone. It was something they never discussed. The slow changes on Sita's once lovely face, wrought by time and middle age, were painful for her daughter to bear. Aware also that, although she said nothing, Sita was secretly pleased to have her still living at home, Alice began to take over the day-to-day problems that arose in the house, the shopping and, increasingly, the cooking. Sita, claiming to be busy, continued her alterations, but Alice knew her mother had come to rely on her. It suited them both, this negotiating of the same space without friction. Outwardly, it was easy to pretend nothing had changed.

'I'm going to see Mr Eliot tomorrow,' she told her mother. 'I want to show him my new work.'

'Can you change my library books?' Sita asked before going back to the programme she was watching on television.

The next morning Alice caught a bus and went over to David Eliot's flat. She hadn't seen him for some weeks because of her workload. It was still David Eliot who Alice showed her work to first; it was *his* judgement she valued the most. Today she carried with her two parts of a new construction she was making, some photographs and a few drawings. As she let herself into the main entrance of his block of flats she caught sight of Sarah Kimberley walking down the stairs. Alice hesitated. She had a feeling that Miss Kimberley still disliked her.

'You going up there, again?' the woman asked.

Alice nodded.

'He knows I'm coming. I haven't seen him for two weeks.'

Somehow Sarah Kimberley made her feel guilty.

'Well, you *do* know he's not well?'

Alarmed, Alice shook her head.

'He should be resting.'

'He said it was okay to come over.'

Sarah narrowed her eyes slightly. She hesitated for a moment. 'Look, could I have a word with you?' she asked, lowering her voice, and before Alice could reply she found herself on the way back down the stairs. 'Let's go outside, shall we?'

Outside, the older woman whisked Alice to a café and bought them both a cup of tea.

'There's something you should know,' she said, not unkindly. 'You're obviously not aware, but David and I plan to get married.'

Alice stared at her.

'You had no idea, did you? He said nothing?'

Still Alice remained silent. Sarah laughed. The laugh sounded like a series of gunshots.

'He's hopeless,' she said lightly.

She paused for a fraction of a second. Then she sighed heavily.

'Now listen, Alice. This may sound harsh, but you are just *one* of the many ex-pupils that Mr Eliot has ringing him up, pestering him and ...' her voice tailed off and she gave another laugh.

This time the laugh was more embarrassed than angry. Alice continued to stare at the woman.

'And while I don't *mind* you visiting him now and again, I would appreciate it if you didn't come over quite so often.'

She smiled, showing a fleck of lipstick on one of her teeth. Alice was mortified. Something heavy lodged in her throat.

'Yes,' she said faintly, feeling her eyes prick with tears.

She looked away and then she stood up quickly. All she wanted to do was flee from this woman as fast as she could, get out of the café, bolt home.

'I hope I haven't upset you,' Sarah was saying.

Alice shook her head. Her hair had fallen over her eyes.

'Was there something in particular you wanted to ask him, just now?'

'No, I ... tell him I hope he gets better, and perhaps I'll come over at the end of term.'

'Of course,' murmured Sarah Kimberley, looking at her hands.

She did not go back to see David Eliot that term. And she hardly did any work either. Art school was proving problematic without him to talk to. Her intense sense of privacy meant she hated the communal nature of the studios. Not surprisingly, the students living in rented accommodation around London had bonded together early on, enjoying a social life while Alice simply went home at the end of each day. For the first time she began to wish she had made more of an effort to make friends, but it was too late. She saw she had alienated herself. At the end of the spring term, during the vacation, she helped Sita take in extra sewing. She was still only nineteen. Making an effort, she went to a few exhibitions and even on one occasion to the theatre. She did all this alone, never venturing near David Eliot's flat. The vacation drew to a close. Sita was getting more and more absent-minded. She left the iron on and burnt a dress, she forgot to switch the television off, she lost her purse in the street.

'Mama, what's wrong with you?' Alice asked her, exasperated. 'You're working too hard. I think you should take a holiday.'

But they both knew Sita would never do that. By 1984 Sri Lanka, as it was now called, was in the throes of a long and senseless war, the brutality of which was hardly noticed in the West. Other wars, more important ones, in larger, richer countries, hit the headlines. Occasionally, if something was mentioned on the Six O'clock News, Sita turned the television off. If she closed her eyes she knew she could blot the country out. In June the weather became suddenly lovely and the students in Alice's year decamped to the park in Camberwell. It was a time of parties and end-of-year shows, of champagne and ebullience. Soon they began to help clean the studios of all the winter rubbish in preparation for the degree show. A skip appeared and began filling up. Bit by bit, paintings that had never been seen before began appearing and were hung on the newly painted studio walls. The students from Alice's year helped the third-year finalists as labels were printed, floors scrubbed and invitations sent out. Summer light flooded the spaces and the smell of turps and oil was now mixed with bleach. Alice did whatever was asked of her willingly enough, but she disappeared as soon as any social gathering was planned. Then, just before the end of term, she decided to attempt one last visit to her old teacher's flat. Sarah Kimberley's warning off had brought out in Alice one of her uncharacteristic flashes of anger that, try as she might, she could not control. She was amazed by the strength of it, for the truth was she desperately wanted to see David Eliot once more. But when she got there the flat was closed up and a neighbour told her he had been taken ill.

'He left in a hurry,' the neighbour informed her. 'His cough got worse. The fags were the problem.'

'Where is he?' Alice asked with sudden, utter, desolation.

'Dunno, me ducks. First he went off in an ambulance. Then he came back, then his missus came for him – carrying a suitcase, she was. Dunno. I think he don't work no more, anyway.'

Seeing Alice's face, the neighbour paused before shutting her door.

'You one of his kids?'

Alice nodded.

'Why don't you drop him a note, darlin'? Someone comes to collect 'em every so often. Try it.'

That evening, angry and hurt, telling her mother she was going to the cinema, she went out alone into the summer rain. The chestnut trees in the park gleamed in the twilight and all around was the earthy scent of dry grass, watered at last. London washed away its dust as the roads steamed. Alice stood at the bus stop waiting for a number 3 bus. The church clock struck six. There was one other person waiting for a bus. Standing, hunched and with her hands in her pocket, she thought dully, I've never been able to make friends. Ever since Jennifer discarded me there's been no one else. What a fool I was to think David was my friend. Her eyes filled with tears. It would be difficult to visit him ever again without feeling bad. Suddenly, without warning, she thought of Janake. It had been so long since she had thought of him that she failed to notice the empty bus that sailed past.

'Did you see that?' the man beside her said crossly. 'I've been standing here for twenty minutes and the first one that comes along doesn't stop!'

Alice pulled a face. It had begun to rain harder.

'Oh no!' she said, looking at her watch. 'I'm going to be too late, now!'

The man, he was quite young, about her age, shook his head irritably.

'It's a disgrace,' he said. 'I was going to the pictures. Hardly worth bothering.'

'Me too,' said Alice, without thinking.

They stood for a moment longer. The rain increased. Alice raised her hand to her eyes and wiped them. The man glanced at her.

'Oh Christ!' he said irritably. 'Call this a service? We're both going to be soaked. Look,' he glanced at her, 'want to go for a drink in the Russell?'

Alice was taken aback. In the early evening light the man looked very pale, his long floppy reddish hair fell over his forehead. She hesitated, but the rain was falling faster.

'Okay,' she nodded, making up her mind.

Which was how she came to meet Timothy West.

In Sri Lanka, a series of suicide bombers were creating a spectacle of horror. People who should have been in control had lost it. The Tigers, having begun a series of backlash retaliations, were finding that what had started in desperation was becoming a necessity for them. India watched and waited. India had its own vast problems. It had no desire to be netted by this tiny castaway island. Janake walked home from the railway station. The sun beat down on his head and his orange robe cast shadows as he moved. The road was hot and old tar had melted in some places. Janake put up his umbrella and crossed the railway line, heading towards the hamlet by the coconut trees. Scraps of washing hung out to dry. The sea shimmered. Janake had not been back for some weeks. The sea breeze felt cool and wonderful after the heat of Colombo. When he had finished his studies, he wanted to return to this part of the world. His heart belonged to the south. He wanted to do what he could here, teach at the local school perhaps. He closed his umbrella; there was no need for it in this breeze. Shading his eyes, he stared at the horizon where a white ship appeared pasted to the sky. He was nearly twenty-four now Some would call him handsome. Children's voices came towards him faintly on the wind; a coconut scraper sounded flatly; two men walked past and bowed to him, hands together. Janake bowed back. He felt relaxed. Tension drained out of him as he stared at the sea. How he loved it here, he thought, breathing deeply. He could never leave it. Unexpectedly and with no warning, he thought of little Alice Fonseka. She had loved the sea, just as he did. Later, after he had seen his mother, after his furtive trip to sit on the verandah of the Sea House, he would walk up the hill to visit May and Namil. He had brought a small present for Sarath.

By the time Alice sent her letter to David Eliot's address, Timothy West had put down firm roots in her life. She wrote to the teacher with a certain air of triumph, telling him her news. She had left art school, she wrote. And, she added, with unusual confidence, she was getting married. There was a small gleam in her eyes as she posted the letter. Her father had told her she was a fool to leave art school, but she had ignored him.

'At least get your degree,' he said, making no attempt to hide his disappointment. 'I say, when you won that competition I had such high hopes for you,' he added, forgetting the absent years. Alice shook her head, surprisingly stubborn. Tim West had wanted to marry her and she was very happy to accept. David Eliot wrote back eventually, giving her some of his news. His letter was guarded, as though, thought Alice, the effort of writing to her was too much.

But we'd love to see you again, he wrote.

Stung by the use of the word 'we', misunderstanding him, Alice did not follow it up.

In September of that year England basked in a heatwave of spectacular proportions and things moved with surprising speed. Both Sita and Stanley were mildly surprised by the news. Stanley had secretly hoped Alice would find a nice Tamil boy, further the cause; bring more Tamils into the world to fight the bastards.

'Sacrifice a few more lives, you mean?' Sita asked, when he confessed his hopes.

Stanley glared at his former wife. There was nothing vague about *her*, he decided. When she wanted to, she had no trouble in sharpening her tongue. But his daughter was a different matter.

'What on earth do you see in him?' Stanley asked, bemused.

Unbeknown to him, Timothy West's mother was asking the same question. Sita didn't question Alice quite so openly, but when Alice introduced Tim to her the mutual apathy was so great as to be almost comical.

'I know why you're marrying him,' Sita said shrewdly.

But then she sighed and, with one of her rare gestures of affection she placed her hand on her child's head in benediction. For a moment, Sita's face looked startlingly like Bee's.

'Still,' she continued, 'maybe you'll have less trouble this way.'

She did not explain further. Alice was puzzled by her mother's choice of words. She was doing a painting of the sea at the time and the water looked the colour of moonstones. It was a sign, she decided; she was doing the right thing. Cautiously she allowed herself to feel alive. Tim had more to him than met the eye. There were many good points to him, she told herself. She liked the way he had no time for disorder in his life, or superstition or other useless sentiments. And he hated obtuseness (his words, not hers). She did not feel what she had felt for David Eliot, of course. She did not love him as she had loved her grandparents, or Jennifer, or Janake. But she was not marrying any of them, she told herself. It was better this way, she decided, reassured. This way it was more real, more down to earth, more lasting. Feeling magnanimous, eventually she sent David Eliot and Sarah Kimberley a wedding invitation. David replied with a postcard almost instantly, accepting. He was too preoccupied with his illness to write more.

Alice, thinking he was being sarcastic, put the matter out of her mind. Then, after years of silence, Alice decided to write to her aunt May. It was a tentative letter, brief and to the point, informing May of her imminent marriage. Sita, rousing herself, wrote too. Now at least she had something to write about. Neither wondered what effect their letters might have on the recipients.

Time has flown, wrote Sita, feeling some satisfaction, *like a flock of birds. We thought it never would, and now it has, thank God! The past has almost gone.*

Far away in the little costal town fringed by coconut trees where light spilled wastefully everywhere, May opened both her letters.

'What does it say, Amma?' demanded Sarath excitedly, wanting the stamps for his collection.

Even though she was unable to read between the lines, May could see the curious mixture of defensiveness and desperation present in the letters. Emotions moved within her.

'Poor thing,' the soft-hearted Namil said. 'It can't have been easy with such parents. *Anay,* send her a sari!'

May tried to imagine her elder sister.

'Maybe when Alice has a child, things will heal within Sita,' Namil suggested.

'A white boy,' May said, wonderingly. 'What will the children be? Will they be English?'

'What does it matter? They don't have wars about caste over there. The English have better things to think about.'

May tried and failed to imagine what England was like. None of them had seen even a photograph of Alice for years.

'People are the same all over,' Namil told her.

But surely karma applied to everyone in the world, thought May, puzzled. It was hard to be sure of anything any more.

'Send the child a sari,' Namil said again. 'The girl has lost out on most things.'

In spite of all that had happened, May still only ever wanted to heal the rift between them all, so with this in mind she sent Alice a wedding sari of crimson rose. It was perfumed with rose petals and had been the one she wore at her own marriage.

It was a marriage of all kinds of dependence, that much was clear. A needy, hasty, possibly desperate September marriage. Sita tried to imagine them in old age.

'Well, it's up to them,' Stanley shrugged.

He still found Sita impossible.

'What's wrong with your mother?' he asked Alice irritably.

Alice would not be drawn. Her mother was a little forgetful, that was all. Sita, displaying a new slyness, watched as Alice became annoyed with Stanley. Whatever this marriage was doing for her daughter, it was making her wake up.

'My sleeping beauty,' she murmured; but no one heard.

In the last days of Alice's presence in the house, Sita began to give her some of the tenderness reserved for the dead baby. She bought her daughter a wedding sari and even though Alice had never worn a sari in her life, she agreed, touched by the gesture, to wear it. Next, Sita, taking out an old, forgotten emotion, sewed a bridal jacket for her daughter, picking the pearl buttons with care, sewing them on by hand, slowly and painstakingly in the fading evening light. Mother-love, she supposed it was.

Something dropped off the ledge in Alice's heart and, eleven years after she had last seen him, she began to dream of her grandfather, Bee. She smelled the soft perfume of her grandmother's Yardley apple-blossom powder, and then, a month before her wedding day, she heard Bee's voice once again. Close in her ear:

This bridegroom of yours, her grandfather asked in the dream. *Is his hair really red?*

He sounded exactly as he used to. In her dream, Alice giggled. When she woke the next morning she could still hear his voice, very clearly. All that day and for most of the next, the voice stayed with her, and a few nights later she dreamed of him again. This time he was smiling, his eyes crinkling in the sun, and she could smell, very distinctly, pipe-smoke. In fact, when she woke up the following morning, her whole room smelled of tobacco.

'Can you smell anything?' she asked her mother, who had risen early and was doing her whirling dervish act with her sewing machine.

'Only the paraffin heater,' Sita replied. 'I'll probably die of paraffin poisoning,' she said in conclusion. 'Years of breathing in these fumes will kill me off.'

Alice laughed; her mother was being silly. They no longer had paraffin heaters.

'I dreamt of Grandpa last night,' she admitted cautiously.

She had not mentioned her grandfather since his death. Now that his voice was filling her head, refusing to go away, she looked for and found the painting her uncle Namil had sent her. Propping it up on her table in her bedroom, she drank in the view.

Later, on her weekly trip to the temple, May saw Janake.

'Alice is getting married soon,' she told him.

Janake glanced at her. May looked as though she had spent the night weeping. If he was shocked, Janake hid it. In all his childhood memories May had been the more beautiful of the two Fonseka sisters. Whereas once she had been the family joker, now she was simply depressed. He had heard rumours that she was no longer liked at the school where she taught. There seemed nothing specific, but things had changed, life had moved on. Her parents' death had taken its toll; her sister's absence didn't help. Janake understood all this. But why had Alice forgotten them? Since he had become a monk, meditation and prayer had taught Janake to observe many things. He often thought about Alice and how he had helped her carve her name on the rocks. She had not known it, but afterwards he had carved his own name underneath hers, in the hope that some of her good fortune would rub off on him. There had been a time when he had envied her good fortune. But not now, thought Janake, shaking his head. Not now. It was impossible to imagine Alice being married.

'I am happy for her,' he said, at last.

In a year or so, if the war lessened and the new government was able to reach a peace agreement with the Tamils as they hoped, Janake would go to England. To study at the Buddhist Centre, in Chiswick, London.

I shall definitely see her then, he decided. I'll be able to meet her husband too! he thought. But all he said to May was:

'Do you know what time the ceremony is? I would like to pray for her.'

Timothy West, accidental bridegroom-to-be, the man who hailed a wife instead of a bus, was shocked to see his bride walk into the registry office looking like a 'proper Asian', as he privately told his mother afterwards. David Eliot thought Alice breathtaking. He almost missed the ceremony, slipping in at the last moment looking very frail and disconnected. His hair had all fallen out, there was hardly anything of him, but he had been unable to stay away. He didn't wish to be seen; all he had wanted was a glimpse of Alice, beautiful in white.

The wedding reception of Mr and Mrs West took place at an old coaching inn called the Three Horseshoes, in a room that seemed too large for the small group of people who attended it.

'It's not a very auspicious hour,' Sita told one of the guests, who didn't know what she was talking about.

She had not wanted to have her daughter's wedding on a Saturday.

'Better if it had been on a Thursday,' agreed Stanley.

He was with a new woman and was wearing a cheap, badly altered suit. Sita pursed her lips. All she wanted to do was laugh at the sight of her old love.

'Hello, Sita, this is Sarah.'

Stanley walked with a slight swagger and refused to be embarrassed. Life was life, people moved on. He would have liked to move on much more, he thought, eyeing one of the waitresses, but this new woman had him by the throat. He sighed, reminding himself that he was here to dispatch his duty as the father of the bride and give her hand away. The elder Mrs West smiled wanly, trying not to cry, She knew if she wasn't careful she would lose her son in foreign waters. Alice's reticence frightened her. She had thought Asians talked a lot, but she saw uneasily that this was not necessarily the case. There were all sorts of Asians.

'Very exotic!' mumbled the elder Mr West, trying to inject some humour into the proceedings.

The bridegroom, hearing his father's jokes, frowned. But then they cut the modest little cake and it was the moment for cheap fizz and paper roses.

'She shouldn't be carrying lilies,' Sita told Stanley's new woman. 'Not right for her stars.'

'Her sister would have been eleven!' Stanley said, forgetting himself. The two women, both past and present, glared at him. Luckily, they were distracted, for the groom began to make his speech, about his new life and the home he hoped to make, and the children he hoped to have. The groom was still speaking. Some of the guests shuffled, laughing uneasily. Sita watched in a dream. Her mind had blanked out temporarily. It was late summer here in England but in Colombo it would be the hot season now. Sita could not remember if she had written to her sister about the wedding. Frowning, Sita tried to remember the name of her daughter's husband. Perhaps Alice was right and she *was* becoming forgetful.

'Hello,' said David Eliot, coming up to her. 'I used to be her art teacher.'

'Can you remember the name of her husband?' Sita asked.

'Haven't a clue. Is she happy?'

'I've no idea,' said Sita, suddenly gloomy. 'Alice has always been a mystery to me.'

'A bit of a dark horse!' laughed Stanley, coming up to them. 'Always was. Cared for no one except her grandfather, no, Sita?'

'Shut up,' said Sita coldly. 'You've no business being here. You were my mistake.'

'Well, let's hope he's not her mistake,' Stanley said, moving his head in the direction of the groom. 'Like mother, like daughter!'

And he moved off. After that exchange, David knew he could not leave without kissing the bride.

'Be happy,' he murmured, as she turned towards him with her sudden smile.

Was she happy? Her eyes were shining. Life had begun for her, he saw. In the emotion of the moment she put her arms around him and kissed him on the cheek.

'Thank you,' she said.

'For what?'

'For simply everything.'

And then she was gone.

In their new home in Brixton, after a honeymoon of a week of cloudy weather in the Lake District, a sudden memory of the Sea House broke over Alice like a squall of monsoon rain. It caught her unawares and took her breath away, floating in the September sky like a kite released from its string. Because of this when they returned she gave their new home in Brixton a name. She called it Brixton Beach.

'What?' asked Tim, confused.

He watched her fixing up the sign she had painted. She seemed uncharacteristically determined. He remembered his mother's warning.

'Are you mad?' he asked. 'What will the neighbours think?'

Far away, beside another, bluer sea, the Sea House creaked slowly in the slight breeze. A plank of wood that had swung loosely by the kitchen entrance gave way and crashed to the ground. Two nails rolled under the paw-paw tree and the haunting view came in through the hole. The sea sent out a sigh, as though it was a mayday signal across the bay. Sita, sitting at her kitchen table drinking tea, dropped her cup noisily. Lately she kept dropping all sorts of things: needles, scissors, pieces of cloth. She cleared up the mess made by the broken cup. Then, with a small sound of relief, now she was completely alone, she went into her bedroom to fetch the dresses of her stillborn child. Recently she had bought a large doll from the market. The clothes, made eleven years ago, were small enough to fit the doll. Taking it out of its hiding place, she began to wash it. After that she dried and dusted it with talcum powder. And began to dress the doll in her dead child's clothes.

14

ALICE LOVED BRIXTON BEACH. Even at the very beginning she knew the house was not the problem. Once she had named it she set about painting the rooms. She painted the bedroom first; a deep aquamarine turquoise. But Tim hated it. It was an unhappy moment and brought on their first argument. Something had to, she supposed, surprising herself with a sharp flash of defiance. She apologised quickly, but the room was already painted. Then, after their disagreement had been brushed aside, she lime-washed the kitchen a delicate duck-egg blue. Feeling the urge to go back to her painting again she decided one of the rooms would be her studio. Tim agreed; he didn't want her mess all over the house. So she turned the third bedroom into her studio.

'Although,' Tim said, frowning, 'where will the visitors sleep?'

But there were no visitors, Tim's parents, and Sita too, preferred to be visited in their own homes.

That was that. The routine of married life commenced. They both wanted it to work. In that at least there was no doubt. Around this time Sita began forgetting to telephone them.

'Why don't you ring us, Mama?' Alice asked when she went round with the shopping.

'I don't know,' her mother admitted. 'I think I must have lost the phone number.'

'Oh, for goodness' sake! Let me write it down, again.'

On the third occasion, Tim looked at Alice archly. He understood what the problem was.

'It's obvious,' he said, not unkindly. 'Can't you see?'

'What d'you mean?' Alice asked him, a flash of anger crossing her face. 'There's nothing wrong with her!'

Tim grimaced.

'I know she's a bit young,' he said. 'But it has been known to happen. Take her to the doctor.'

Alice ignored him. Her mother was just fine and she herself was working well. She had stopped making the constructed pieces she had made at art school and was beginning to paint again. As she stood sorting out her colours, she thought suddenly about David Eliot. She had been angry with him because of Sarah Kimberley but, she thought a little wistfully, she would have loved to have a conversation with him about her work now.

'I might build a conservatory,' Tim said, 'when we've saved up a bit. It will be cheaper if I do it myself.'

Alice had no interest in the subject.

They had been married for only three months when a package came through the post with her name on it. Luckily she was alone when it arrived. The parcel contained all the artwork Alice had given David Eliot. Included was the painting she had done when her grandfather had died. A hastily scribbled note was attached with the date of David Eliot's funeral, which had now passed. His death had come as a shock because she had assumed his treatment was working. The uncharacteristic anger, seen only twice before, welled up in her so powerfully that she crumpled the note up and threw it violently into the bin, along with everything else. Then she burst into tears. Afterwards she rescued the painting, simply because it was of the sea. When she propped it up in her new studio, her anger died down almost instantly. Soon after, she began having conversations with her grandfather. These increased when, a few weeks later, she discovered she was pregnant. The shock seemed to energise the voices inside her head. They swam like great shoals of fish around her. The past, returning out of banishment, was paying her a long overdue visit.

'Nonsense,' Tim told her, not really listening to what she was telling him.

His new job and his new status as a father-to-be were preoccupying him. He was pleased, though his mother, when she heard the news, was less certain.

'Alice,' Tim said, 'it's no good, all this living in the past.'

He paused for a moment, searching around for the right thing to say. He didn't wish to be too harsh, but sometimes he felt she should stop indulging in all this sentiment.

'The past is best forgotten,' he told her firmly. 'You can't live with a foot in two places. It's too disturbing.'

Alice saw he had a point. But, as if they sensed her desire to do away with them, the voices became more insistent.

Sita received the news of the pregnancy several times over. As always, she kept forgetting about it.

'I've told you,' Alice said after the fourth time. 'I told you yesterday too.'

Sita shook her head and swore blind that this was not the case.

'Oh God!' Alice cried, despairingly.

'I told you,' Tim replied. 'I think you should get some tests done. I think you should find out, once and for all.'

But Alice couldn't bear to.

'Is she doing this to punish me?' she asked him now.

Tim shook his head. He had a clearer view of things. It was what Alice liked in him, although he did express himself clumsily.

'She's going batty, of course,' he observed. 'Haven't you noticed how she forgets *everything* you tell her? Alzheimer's, I'd say.'

He was not speaking unkindly and was unprepared for another of her flashes of rage. But there it was, the word was out. Alzheimer's!

'Stress can trigger it,' Tim said knowledgably. 'And she's certainly had plenty of that!'

Alice had a sudden memory of her mother walking in through the gate at the Sea House. The image was shockingly clear. Bee stood behind her mother in dappled sunshine, his face grim. The baby began it, Bee said. And later, Kunal had finished it. Alice swallowed.

Perhaps losing her memory was no bad thing to happen to her mother, she thought, given that she had no happy memories. Looking back over all the years of her mother's forgetfulness, Alice wondered if Sita had in some way willed this to happen.

By and large, Sita ignored the pregnancy. She was still busy dealing with the facts, as she remembered them, of her own failed one. One afternoon when she visited her, Alice was startled to see a row of dolls lined up on the sofa. The clothes looked familiar and seemed at odds with the straight blonde hair and pink skin of the dolls. Seeing her daughter's face, Sita began to put them away.

'I wasn't expecting you for another hour,' she complained, without looking at Alice.

'Where are they from?' Alice asked, confused, but Sita turned her back on her and began packing them away under her bed.

Alice stared at the familiar yellow and tan eiderdown and the piles of folded clothes that she associated with her mother's bedroom. Something caught her eye as Sita hastily arranged the bedcovers.

'How many of them have you got, Mama?'

Sita did not answer.

'Mama,' Alice cried, alarmed, 'you've got loads more under the bed!'

Sita refused to be drawn. Pursing her lips, she marched crossly into the kitchen. All the way back to Brixton Beach, sitting on the bus, Alice puzzled over her mother's collection of dolls. She could not put her finger on what was wrong.

'I never knew she had them,' she told Tim urgently, later that night.

'Well, maybe you didn't,' Tim said reasonably. 'There's nothing wrong with that.'

But Alice knew; something was not quite right.

'I think she's dressing them in the dead baby's clothes,' she said quietly.

'Oh Gawd! You really should take her to the doctor, you know.'

His obvious irritation reduced her to silence. It was only on a subsequent visit that Alice discovered that it was the boxes and not the dolls that were the problem. When next she visited Sita she took a furtive look under the bed. Each box had been lined with white silk. The dolls were lying face up in them. And when Alice put the lids back on, she saw the boxes were coffin-shaped. Trembling, she had no idea what she should do. Her mother had constructed these coffin boxes, carefully, using cardboard and glue. It would have taken hours of work. When had Sita done this? Had she been making coffins while Alice was still living at home? Had she been making them *before* Stanley walked out? Why had no one noticed? While she was crouched down beside the bed, Sita walked in.

'Satisfied?' she asked coldly. 'What are you going to do now? Take them away from me? Tell your husband, Ted?'

'Tim,' Alice said automatically.

'Tim, Ted, what's the difference?' Sita asked nastily, but she too was trembling. 'Are you going to take them away from me? Answer me!'

'Mama,' Alice said. 'We should talk …'

But what was there to talk about after all this time? Who was to be blamed, who called to account and made to pay for what had been done to her mother? Me, thought Alice, with sudden, clear, insight. I will. And as she grasped the thought, the child inside her sighed and turned over in its sleep. She waited.

'No, Mama,' she said finally, softly, shaking her head. 'No one will *ever* take them away from you.'

She did not tell Tim. She did not feel it was a betrayal; there were simply some things that she thought were best kept from him. So she remained silent. But she had reckoned without Tim himself.

'You shouldn't upset yourself,' he told her reprovingly after one of her visits home. 'Think of the baby. And,' he paused, an idea turning slowly in his mind, 'it might be better if you didn't see her on your own, any more.'

'She's my mother!' Alice cried and, once again, rage swelled unexpectedly.

And died down again. Tim shrugged and the baby kicked Alice sharply.

The next time she saw her mother she noticed the coffins had disappeared from under her bed.

'Where are the dolls?' she asked casually.

'Why?' Sita demanded suspiciously.

She had made a cake and iced it with pink royal icing.

'Are you hoping for a girl?'

'No, no, not particularly. We don't mind what we have,' Alice said. 'I think Tim would like a girl, but I don't care, really.'

'No!' Sita said, grimly. 'Your husband isn't getting his hands on your sister's clothes. And if you must know, I've buried them in the garden,' she added.

Alice was frightened. Her mother was getting worse. She decided Tim was right after all and they would have to see the doctor.

'Well, if she does get worse, she'll have to go into a home,' Tim said when he heard. 'There's no two ways about it. You aren't going to be able to cope.'

Alice ignored him. Lately Tim had begun to make her feel hopeless. Was this how her mother had felt for years and years? The shine that had surrounded her marriage had become less bright. She had not bargained for that.

'It's an old grief,' the doctor told her, after he had spent time talking to Sita. 'I would have expected it to pour out at some time or other. It's just happening now.'

The doctor made it sound logical and Alice was slightly reassured. She did not tell Tim everything the doctor said. Nor did she speak of the unexpected intrusion of her grandfather's voice in her dreams. And then, when she had almost come to believe she would remain in this state of swollen, ungainly limbo forever, on a night of velvet stars, without any warning her waters broke and the baby, a boy, was born.

Nothing had prepared her for it.

'I wish my grandfather could see him,' she told Tim.

They had called the baby Ravi. Tim had been inclined to argue, but Alice had suddenly become fierce. She wanted the child to be called Ravi, she told him, in a manner that brooked no argument. Tim had no idea she could be so stubborn.

'Hormones,' his mother said, pessimistically. 'It's a pity, but I'd give in on this one. He can change it when he's older. No doubt he'll want to!'

Alice's mother looked confused when she heard the name.

'I remember that name,' she mumbled. 'Was it your father's?'

Tim guffawed.

'No, Mama, his name is Stanley,' Alice told her patiently. 'Can't you remember how you loved the name Ravi?'

There was no point in bringing up the past, but she wished with passionate longing that her grandfather was alive.

'Just so I could hear his opinion,' she told Tim, unable to drop the subject. 'I would have loved to know what he would think of his great-grandson! Although,' she added, laughing, 'I could just imagine it.'

Her face was startlingly animated. Tim stared at her. She looked flushed and desirable, reminding him why he had wanted her in the first place.

'So could I,' he said. 'Didn't he hate the English?'

'Oh no, I don't think so. It was just that ...' she paused, struggling. 'In any case, Ravi is half English, so how could he hate the English?'

But Tim was suspicious.

'From everything you've told me, he might have caused trouble. Best the way things are.'

Hearing this, she wished she had kept her mouth shut. She had thought Tim would love everyone she loved.

'He was very funny,' she said faintly, unable to let go of the subject, yet having no means of expressing what she felt.

The child in her arms woke and cried. It was at that moment, as she rocked him back to sleep, that Alice began to realise how much she longed for the sea again. All her homesickness, dealt with so efficiently for so many years, had, with the momentous event of motherhood, returned to torment her. She felt an urgent desire to replicate those things that once had been hers for the sake of the sleeping infant; her son, Ravi. Sensing the impossibility of making amends, she was glad that at least she had won the right to name him. Ravi, the name of her mother's forgotten dream-child.

Thinking this contentment would last, she watched as spring turned slowly into summer and the child grew. Sighing with a happiness of sorts, she believed life had at last moved full circle. Her dreams for Ravi began to grow. At last she had someone to dream for.

So, our Alice has a son, huh? she imagined her grandfather telling her grandmother. *What d'you say to that?*

And she imagined him nodding, for of course he would have been delighted by the news.

'One day I will take you home,' Alice told her sleeping child. 'One day I will take you back to where I belong and you will see a sea so blue that it will appear joined to the sky, seamlessly. I will show you the rock where I carved my name,' she planned. *Alice Fonseka, Age 10, Colombo, Sri Lanka, The World, The Universe.*

The child opened his dark eyes and in the moment before he cried, she saw herself reflected in them. Motherhood fluttered within her. By the time Tim returned from work, she had lost another day in dreams.

His wife's island within its reef of bright waters was out of sight, and life teemed noisily in his own house but Tim was uneasy. His innate sense of order was being eroded. Ravi was what mattered, he insisted, needing to be sure that Alice's past was erased. Tim knew he would have to be the one to banish it. The two lives could never be compatible. The sea and all it stood for would simply have to go.

'I don't mind,' he said, reasonably. 'I don't have a problem with Asians, obviously, and I like the curries. But,' he added, warming to the subject, 'at the end of the day ...'

Her heart sank. She was becoming a little too used to the idea of what happened at the end of Tim's day.

'At the end of the day, I don't think of you as *Asian*, not really. You're British, you're one of us. You've lived here so long you wouldn't know what to do even if you were forced to go back. In fact,' he continued, glad she was not arguing with him for once, 'I guarantee you'd be scared if you were suddenly told to go back to that bloody place!'

The thought amused him and Alice saw with relief that it was possible to hide all she felt and join in with his laughter. But later on, when he thought she was asleep in front of the television, she heard him telling his mother unhappily that he had married her without understanding this whole Asian thing.

'They're a bunch of weirdoes,' he had said. 'Not Alice, but I mean generally speaking. They've got a lot of mumbo-jumbo attached to them!'

He was silent.

'It's not Alice's fault,' he mumbled, finally. 'I blame her parents.'

Tim sounded confused. He had married Alice in good faith, he told his mother.

'It could be a touch of post-natal depression,' the doctor said, when Alice visited him. 'I wouldn't worry too much about your dreams. How's your mother?'

Tim cooked their meals. Alice, up all night with the screaming Ravi, was exhausted. He cooked two sorts of meals. One where he emptied piles of spices into the chicken curry, and a second meal with mashed potatoes and cheddar cheese, for himself. They coped somehow and every morning, with more than a little relief, Tim escaped to work. The Health Visitor soon got the picture.

'It's your grandpa, luv, isn't it?' she asked, gently helping Alice clamp the baby's pink mouth on the nipple.

Breast is best, she told the girl, thinking what a pity it was that these girls looked so lovely just when they felt so exhausted. Nature is full of wastage, the Health Visitor thought privately. And she didn't like the husband either. The baby waved his tiny hand, suckling greedily.

'Did you do these?' the Health Visitor asked, picking up Alice's sketchbook.

The book was filled with drawings of her grandfather.

Don't take any notice, Bee's voice so close in her ear made Alice jump. *Get on with bringing up the child, my great-grandson. I don't know where you found the fool you're married to, but you are a mother now, so enjoy it. And don't forget to plant those seeds. You've been a long time in growing them. I gave them to you when you were nine and you are twenty-one now. How long do they have to wait?*

She heard the plaintive circular cry of a bird and for a split second could not imagine where she was, or even where reality began and ended. Her grandfather's voice was very clear. It came from beyond the reef, floating somewhere on the horizon. There was a ship sitting on the horizon too. I wish you were here, she thought.

I'm already with you, her grandfather replied. *And for God's sake, feed the child. I can't stand the screaming.*

Out of the blue she got a letter. It had come via her mother's address; Alice picked it up on one of her weekly visits. Sita welcomed her vaguely. She had given up her work some time ago, finding it too confusing to remember the names of her clients or the instruction for alterations. After a few disasters she was forced to stop, and now she lived on a disability pension. She showed only a marginal interest in the baby. When he cried she covered her ears with her hands, shouting to Alice that she couldn't stand the sound, and she refused to hold him. After a while she tolerated his presence although she still would not touch him. But it was Tim whom Sita had begun to really loathe, confusing him with Stanley. Eventually, much to Tim's relief, Alice began visiting Sita on her own, taking the baby with her. She went several times a week, doing the shopping, clearing up the kitchen, checking her mother was eating properly.

'She'll have to go into a home soon,' Tim kept warning. 'It's a matter of time, that's all.'

Alice continued to ignore his warnings. She was becoming adept at ignoring the things she didn't want to face. The thought of her mother in a home was more than she could bear. On the morning she received the letter, Sita seemed more distracted than usual.

'Have you brought me some fish?' she asked.

'No, should I have? Have you had breakfast?'

'I'm very busy,' Sita said coldly. 'Can't you see how busy I am? I don't want any of the neighbours nosing around here.'

'Mama,' Alice said, and then she stopped.

The dolls were back out of their coffins.

'Why have you got them out again, Mama?'

Ravi began to cry in his pram in the hall.

'Don't let any of those doctors near him,' Sita said, disappearing into the kitchen.

In the hall was a pile of unopened letters that Alice picked up, with Ravi in her arms. A Sri Lankan stamp caught her eye, but she didn't recognise the handwriting. It was not her aunt's. The letter was addressed to her. There had been no response to her announcement about Ravi's birth several months ago and she had assumed the post was not getting through again. But the letter, when she opened it, was not from May. It was from Janake.

'Who?' asked Sita frowning.

She had cooked Alice some hot boiled rice and was slicing a very ripe mango into it. Alice was feeding Ravi and reading her letter. Sita sliced some green chillies into the rice and served her daughter.

'Who?' she asked again.

Alice ate a spoonful of rice absent-mindedly.

'He's coming to England,' she said. 'Don't you remember Janake? I used to play with him by the rocks.'

She paused, her eyes sparkling. The beach came back to her fresh as a new day, served up with the fragrance of the hot rice her mother had cooked and the drawing sensation of Ravi's small mouth as he fed on her.

'He's coming to Chiswick, to the Buddhist temple. I'd forgotten he was a Buddhist priest,' she said, amazed.

And she saw again, with extraordinary clarity and a long, lost ache, the rocks, dark and cool against the sun as she carved her name on them. Her grandfather sat under the shade of the coconut palm, his back resting neatly against the broken catamaran, watching them splash in the shallows, listening to their laughter, knowing he was soon to lose her, unable to follow where she was going. How had the memory been lost?

'I've begun to remember all sorts of things,' she told Tim that evening when Ravi was asleep and they were eating their supper in front of the television. Tim grunted, his eyes fixed on the news. He reached for his can of beer. Since Ravi was born, there seemed less conversation between them.

'I thought we would go home on Saturday. The little 'un has grown so much since they have seen him last, I don't want them to miss out on anything.'

Home, the word struck her with new resonance. The letter from Janake was in her studio; somehow it wasn't the moment to mention it.

Nor did she, a month later, mention her meeting at a small café near the Buddhist temple in Chiswick. Janake stood at the entrance to Ravenscourt Park tube station. She knew it was him, even from behind; she recognised the back of his head. She had not known what to expect. Would he be in saffron robes like the Hari Krishna tribes who wandered the streets of London with their tambourines? Would people stare at them? At the last moment she hadn't wanted to go. But Ravi was in his pram asleep and the day was one of late winter sunshine, casting shadows on the pavement. Fake spring, thought Alice, knowing by now how the weather could take a turn for the worse when it was least expected. It was too late to change her mind. Janake saw her as she crossed the road. He stood uncertainly, recognition instant. He's grown up, she thought, confused by the current of emotion that flooded over her.

'Alice?' he asked as she hurried towards him, tangling up in his mind with the flower stall selling tulips beside the tube station.

'Alice? Is it really you?'

He was wearing a thin coat and dark trousers. She saw he was wearing closed-toed shoes. No, she decided later, it wasn't what she had expected.

'Janake! Oh my God!' she laughed, delighted, feeling the warmth of this February sun as though it was suddenly tropical. 'I would have recognised you anywhere!'

'How long has it been?'

'How are you?'

They spoke together. And then laughed together. She's beautiful, he thought, astonished. Why does he look so sad? she wondered.

The moment froze even as the traffic moved. Like parts of a silent film, thought Janake. Red buses, dark blue cars. Everything must look so dark to him, she thought, seeing the street with his eyes. But he was looking at the tulips, wishing he had some money to buy her some, thinking how bright they looked. Just like her.

'So?' he said instead, peering at the contents of the pram where a tightly bundled Ravi slept.

Alice was lost for words, wreathed in smiles. They were *both* lost for words.

'There is a café nearby,' he said when he had hugged her, taking her arm.

It amused her that he showed such confidence here in London after such a short time. There was so much to talk about and she wanted to make a start before Ravi woke. The last time they had seen each other had been with the sea as a backdrop.

'So long ago,' she sighed as she stirred her tea. 'How long are you here for?'

'One month,' he said helplessly.

He should not have come, he realised. It had been a foolish desire to see her again. It astonished him, the look of her, the instant effortless connection, the way the day had begun to clutch at his heart. He swallowed. There were things he had to say.

'I know we've lost touch,' she was saying. 'Ever since …' she stopped, not wanting to mention her grandparents.

Janake nodded. He could not stop looking at her. It was as though he had been denying an undetected thirst for a long time.

'You know my aunt never even replied when I wrote and told her Ravi was born,' Alice complained, before she could stop herself. 'She has forgotten us.'

Janake glanced at her. Again he swallowed.

'No,' he said.

He could not bear this. Alice did not seem to hear him.

'Sometimes I think I just dreamed my childhood,' she said, shaking her head so that her hair loosened itself from the pleat at the back of her head.

Laughing she brushed it away from her face. Time is like the sea against the rocks, thought Janake. Changing everything, very slowly, as if by magic. We were both such children.

'It hasn't been all that easy for us here,' she said, thinking of her absent father and her mother, absent in a different way.

She wanted to tell Janake about her mother's dolls. She wanted to tell someone who would not judge her for it. Someone who would still love Sita even though her mind was going. She wanted, she realised, her own people.

I must have always felt it, Janake thought. I must have always thought of her in this way, without knowing it. He felt he was in danger of losing his grasp on everything he had built up; his life, without her. I shouldn't have come, he thought again. Danger lurked within his heart.

'I know the war was terrible,' Alice said. 'But –'

'There is something I must tell you,' Janake said quickly, interrupting her.

The palms of his hands were clammy.

'Alice … your cousin Sarath has disappeared,' he said. 'One night there was a dawn raid on the town and a white van appeared driving up the coast. The van went on a house-to-house search. Everyone was asleep, but one by one the street was woken. The men knocked at your aunt's house. When your uncle tried to put the light on, they hit him until he was unconscious. Your aunt was screaming and the noise woke Sarath. He switched on his torch and as he came out they grabbed hold of his arm and tried to drag him away. Your aunt was crying and holding on to him, but they pulled him away even as she sobbed. She begged them in Singhalese, as she had begged over a Tamil boy in her school, many years ago. You won't remember, you were small. But it was no use. They hit her and punched Sarath across the face. Then they dragged him out into the van and drove away. The whole thing must have taken about five minutes. That was all. Your uncle Namil was lying in a pool of blood.'

Janake stopped and took a deep breath. Alice sat motionless, her face frozen.

'That was ten months ago. Just before Ravi was born. Your uncle was in a coma for several weeks. The local doctor would not touch him. A neighbour took him to the hospital in Hikkaduwa. Eventually he regained consciousness, but then he had a stroke and now he is an invalid. May has to do everything for him; she bathes him, feeds him – everything. He cannot speak. But sometimes he starts crying, and that is the worst thing for her. Because, however hard she has tried to find him, there has been no news about Sarath. He has simply vanished,' Janake said, lowering his voice, looking into Alice's dark and luminous eyes.

Alice saw Janake once more before he returned to the university in Peradeniya. The temple in Chiswick allowed him no more time for anything else. His face had looked pinched with the cold, and the sense of the sea that he had brought back to her so vividly had faded. Already he looked as though he was preparing for flight.

'How do you stand this cold?' he asked, kissing her on both cheeks. 'It reaches my bones!'

She smiled and he thought that was what had been wrong with this visit. The childhood picture he had carried of her over the years had been of her smiling. But now she no longer smiled.

'And your husband?' he asked gently. 'Tell me about him.'

'Tim?' she said. 'He loves me. And he loves Ravi.'

The child looked a miniature version of her, wriggling and wanting to be on the move.

'You should bring him back,' he said. A feeling of helplessness engulfed him. What could he offer her? 'When the war is over, I mean.'

He couldn't bear her suppressed unhappiness, nor she his. Was she aware how lonely she was? he wondered. He has the look of someone who is barely alive, she was thinking, shocked by the reality of it. She wanted to ask him why Sri Lanka cared so little for its own people. He listened to the traffic rushing past and watched the rain dripping slowly along the window of the café where they were sitting as she spoke softly, for the first time, he suspected, of what had become of her life since she had left the island. Loneliness consumed her. He felt it had probably done so since the moment she left. Listening to her talk, dimly he saw the effort it cost her. No one had thought of what the experience would do to her. They had been children, caught up in hatred not of their making, he thought sadly. Accepting whatever life threw at them.

'There was this teacher,' she was saying. 'He was called David Eliot. He was the only one who understood.'

Janake could not bear it. Alice hugged the child, holding him like a shield.

'But you know, he was just a teacher,' she told him lightly. 'I wasn't the only pupil with problems. I think I leaned too heavily on him. I think he got fed up with me.'

She laughed without joy, and he saw that this too had hurt her. They talked about Sita.

'She's losing her mind, Janake. She sits in the house all day. Luckily, the rent is fixed and the landlord can't throw her out. She would never live with us, even if Tim felt she could. They don't like each other much, you see. It's a little difficult.'

He saw that the situation was an impossible one.

'Can I visit her before I go?'

'Of course. But I warn you, she won't remember you.'

Of her father she said nothing. They had gone in the rain to Cranmer Gardens to see Sita. It was only then that Janake realised the extent of what they had been through. Sita, unrecognisable, staring at him blankly, was uneasy with his presence in her house. So they had left. It was late afternoon by now. Tim would be returning from work in a few hours and Alice needed to get home to tidy the house and cook a meal. She was beginning to get restless.

'I have to go and pack,' Janake said.

He felt the afternoon break up before his eyes. His plane was leaving at midnight.

'Will you come back?' she asked.

He thought she was going to cry. For a moment she had a look on her face that held traces from her lost childhood. He saw that he was taking her home away from her, all over again. But he could not give her false promises. He could not tell her that the war would end soon, that her aunt would reply to her letters, that her cousin would be found. Or that he and she would ever be free to explore other avenues. While they were looking elsewhere, their lives had taken different paths. It had been ordained in this way. They were passing like ships in the night. That was all. Sitting on the bus that was taking him away from her forever, waving, smiling his promises to write, he thought they had loved one another in a different life. Perhaps they would meet again in some other time.

Spring when it came was bitter that year. The daffodils were scentless and the wind was relentless. Everyone said it was the worst spring in decades. Tim repainted the front door and Ravi, crawling now, put his hand on it before it was dry.

'Alice, where are you?' Tim said crossly. 'Take him away – can't you see I'm doing something?'

But Ravi had triumphed. The ultramarine imprint of his hand remained forever on the door of Brixton Beach.

Sometimes, in the months that followed, Alice began to imagine she had dreamed Janake's visit. She had not expected to feel as she had done when he kissed her good-bye. Confused she had run back home with Ravi and put the moment out of her mind. But the image of Janake's face as the bus took him away kept replaying itself. He is like my brother, she told herself, but the thought did not satisfy her. It seemed as though they had shared a whole life together instead of the few years it had been in reality. Feeling unhappy and worried at her disloyalty to Tim, she decided to bury herself in looking after Ravi, but all she did was spend hours staring at the sandpit outside the newly built patio. The sandpit was small and made of a surreal blue plastic. There was a spade and a cheerful red bucket beside it. Ravi had been sitting in it earlier that day. He was a year old now and on warm days she sat with him outside and let him play in the sand. He loved throwing the sand outside the square box. In fact, he preferred it to anything else.

'Try to stop him doing that,' Tim told her almost every day. 'Otherwise, we'll have bloody sand all over the place. Look, it's in the flowerpots.'

Alice could hear Tim's unhappiness in his voice. She knew that he too was beginning to feel things were not right. Something seemed to have stuck in the throat of their marriage, making it impossible for them both to breathe. But he's a good man, Alice scolded herself. He's not like Dada.

'That was the wind,' Alice said, referring to the sand.

She had not worried about things like that, she told Tim, when she was a child.

'Well, this isn't *your* childhood,' he told her, crossly.

She saw how right he was. But what else had she to go on?

'If it's a beach you want, then how about we go to Cornwall?' he said after some time, not wishing to prolong what he thought of as her sulkiness, wanting to compromise. 'I went there when I was about five.'

Organising a home-help for Sita, they went to Cornwall.

'July!' Tim declared, glad it was all settled. 'I'm owed time off then.'

Cornwall was a long way from Brixton. The car was burdened with beach paraphernalia, windbreak, inflatable rubber dinghy, bucket and spade.

'Okay, little 'un,' said Tim with a touch of excitement in his voice. 'We're all going on a summer holiday!'

And so, with the thrill of her growing son refusing to be denied, Alice spent every summer on the beach. The slightest hint of sun turned Ravi brown as a berry.

'Looks like a proper little Asian!' said Tim, not unkindly.

She saw that at least she had picked a man who loved his child. The thought comforted her in the long, featureless days sitting on the sands watching Tim sunbathe and Ravi make sandcastles.

'I might do some drawing again,' she said out loud.

Tim nodded, pleased.

Good girl, her grandfather's voice said, alarmingly close and approving. *Took you long enough.*

Alice jumped. To begin with, she drew everything she saw on the beach. But sometimes other things, things not there at all, appeared in her drawing. She had no idea how the Colombo express strayed on to the page, or how the wardrobe in her grandparents' old garden wandered into their rented cottage, which in turn had a distinctly odd interior.

'Weird!' Tim laughed, when he saw. 'What sort of chair is that?'

'A planter's chair,' she told him.

Tim groaned.

'You'll damage the boy, at this rate,' was all he said.

For five years they returned like the tide, nearly always picking the weeks that rained, missing the summer sun, effortlessly getting it wrong. The cottage waited for them with its rented furniture, faceless and noncommittal. Tim clearly enjoyed every moment of it; Ravi delighted in the beach, running towards it as soon as they began their descent from the car park. Alice followed, shivering.

For five years. Then, one dark January, when a cold watery moon was high in a frosty sky, with the unexpectedness of a fairytale gone wrong, Tim left. There was no warning. The moon filled the small leafless garden, light outlining the motionless, empty swing. Apart from the few stray hairs on the bar of soap in the bathroom, embedded like ticks, advertising his vacancy, there was nothing left. Had she not been involved she would have raised an eyebrow, such was the efficiency of his departure. He had discovered something that corresponded more easily to his idea of love, he told her. Someone *normal*, he added. Someone who had grown up with the cold, so that sleeping with the windows open in winter was not difficult.

'I've had enough!' he said, sweeping away the years they had spent together in a gesture of farewell.

She could see he had.

'Some marriages,' he cried, looking suddenly as though he might weep, 'are not meant to last forever.'

He was more upset than one would expect from somebody who had freedom in his sight. For the first time, Alice felt pity for him touch her. It was not his fault.

'I am tired of hearing about all your dead relatives, the endless war in your savage country, your talk of politics, your spicy food, your foreign ways.'

His words lay between them. Everything had become irreversible, she saw. He had been stretched too far and for too long. But so have I, she thought in silent despair.

'I have found someone more balanced,' he confessed.

And now he began to sound angry.

'Someone who actually loves being part of *this* country. Someone grateful. D'you know what that is like?'

'Who?' asked Alice, before she could stop herself.

'She's Jewish,' Tim said. 'Her mother was in a concentration camp.'

Alice was paralysed. Tim loaded his bags into his car and returned to the house, carefully wiping his feet on the mat for the last time. He wanted to say good-bye to his son. He had a pile of photographs in his hand.

'Look,' she heard him say to the six-year-old Ravi, 'this is the house where I am going to live. Here is the sitting room, here is the kitchen, and look, here is the garden. I'm going to put in a climbing frame and a swing for you. And your bedroom will be here. It's all ready and Ruth can't wait to meet you. Okay? So think about what you would like to do next weekend?'

He left soon after that, taking with him all her own anger. Ravi was sitting in his room, building the Starship *Enterprise* out of Lego bricks. The photographs of Tim's new home lay scattered on the floor beside him. Turning one of them over, Alice began to draw.

'This is the coast where I grew up,' she said, hesitantly. 'Here is the headland with the lighthouse that still flashes. Night after night, it flashes, right across the bay.'

She knew she must keep talking, that it didn't matter what she said so long as she didn't stop. She ran her hand across the boy's smooth, thin arm. She had read somewhere that the touch of a mother's hand on her newborn was different from her touch later on as the child grew. Instinct, she thought, stroking her son's bent head. Why then, since she possessed so much instinct, had she gone astray?

Now when she wanted most to hear her grandfather's voice it seemed to have deserted her. From this distance his promises seemed hollow. She thought of an old jumper, knitted by her father's office girl, that she had discovered in the back of her mother's wardrobe, shrunk and unwearable. Her mother's life had collapsed too, falling away without fanfare, insignificantly. This is how we have ended, thought Alice, stroking the bent head of her silent, beautiful son, wondering what long, sad shadows were already casting themselves on *his* life. Love was not enough. How will we manage? she worried, feeling the weight of all the years ahead. She saw that she had even less certainty in giving this child those things he would need in order to find his footing in this country. I am only half his story, she thought, too late and with terrible sharp understanding of the foreshortening of her own life. She had travelled the ocean and tried to understand this alien place, but she was *still* struggling, she thought in pain, astonished by the years of effort. And she thought again of all the messages she had thrown overboard, day after day.

I want to come back. Write saying you've changed your mind. Say I can live with you instead. Tell them to put me on another ship. Send me home.

The sea had changed its colour the further she had travelled from her grandfather.

Sitting on the floor beside Ravi with her drawing and Tim's photographs, she remembered again, as though it was yesterday, the faint smell of diesel oil and ozone.

'One day, when you are older,' she said, hugging her son's unresponsive body, 'you might like to visit the place where I came from. And see the Sea House.'

They did not go back to the sea in Cornwall ever again. Other events of more significance occurred. Sita moved into Brixton Beach. Her landlord was harassing her and, besides, Alice told her firmly, it was time for her to be closer to her grandson. Sita brought her dolls with her; she would not be parted from them, but she learned to keep them in her room. She was disintegrating fast.

'I'm potty,' she told Ravi. 'Your grandma has no memory left. It's worn out. From over-use!'

Ravi laughed, delighted. He loved his grandmother.

'I don't have any memory either,' he said. 'Let's just have *now*, Grandma.'

As he grew from six to seven and then towards eight, Sita sometimes mistook Ravi for someone else. Each time it was a different person. They grew used to it and hardly noticed her ramblings now.

'Take no notice of my grandma,' Ravi would tell his school friends when they called round for him. 'She's batty!'

But he always gave her a hug before he went out to play, Alice noticed.

In Sri Lanka things were in a mess. Janake's letters, which for a while had been frequent, now stopped altogether. Alice's own letters had trailed away, receiving no encouragement and although she had written repeatedly to her aunt, there had never been a reply. Tim came every fortnight to take Ravi for a sleepover at his new house. He nodded to Alice but avoided looking at her. With the money he was forced to pay her for maintenance and the money she made from her paintings, she was able to survive. Her paintings were always of seascapes, but she had begun to make small sculptures again using odd bits of wood and found objects that caught her eye. They reminded her of the box she had once made with the driftwood Janake had found buried in the sand. Sita watched her daughter. It was difficult to know if she knew who Alice was, but her eyes followed her around her studio without comment. The rest of the time she would fall asleep in front of the television. One night, having dozed beside Ravi as he watched his favourite programme, she decided to go to bed early.

'I'm tired,' she told Alice peevishly. 'I don't want anything to eat.'

'But I'm just serving the rice, Amma,' Alice protested.

'No, no, Bee, I don't want anything to eat. Good-night.'

And she disappeared into her room.

'She called you "Bee",' Ravi said, not taking his eyes off the television.

'Yes, I know. She hasn't done that before.'

Alice found her later when she went in to check on her before going to bed. Sita's eyes were closed. She was cold. Colder than she had been since the day, twenty years before, when she had left the tropics.

Bel Canto

15

ONE EVENING TOWARDS THE END OF May 2004, at the moment between twilight and darkness, a man approaching late middle-age stood gazing out of the window of a first-floor flat in Kennington Park Road. The man was Dr Simon Swann, senior vascular consultant at St Thomas's Hospital. Almost forty-five years old, he was the holder of what could be called a liberal, carefully compartmentalised life. In his quiet, focused way he had achieved most of those things a man of his age could want, with his teenage daughter Cressida and his wife Tessa of twenty years. It was a considerable achievement, given that this was post 9/11 with its rolling rogue wave of terror. It seemed only yesterday that Simon and Tessa had marched up to London, carrying one of Cressida's WAR IS NOT THE ANSWER placards. It had been a rare moment of unity between the Swanns, who had seen eye to eye with a feeling akin to passion for the whole of that hot summer's day. It hadn't worked, of course. Neither the eye-to-eye business as a family nor, as it turned out, the nation's desire to stop the war. Given the undermining clashes they suffered as a family, how could he be surprised by the subsequent decision of the government to invade Iraq? Simon merely lost a little more hope. For a while he saw the years ahead rattle like dead leaves. But then time had gently blunted his dismay, turned it into the more acceptable philosophical approach, shifted his melancholy a little. So that now, a year later, the whole sorry mess was something one read about in the newspapers and occasionally shook one's head over. For after all, what could anyone do? Realistically speaking, life had to go on. So in order to ensure this dreary fact, Simon continued to do the bit he had always done, and was good at: saving what life was put in his hands without discriminating between race or class or creed. Patients, those in the know, always asked for him.

The Swanns still had two houses. One an angular and efficient flat in town, close to the hospital where Simon worked, and another, softer, more faded house in the country, where the china was Eric Ravilious and there were Nicholsons on the walls and some wonderful Bloomsburyish and delightfully English curtains. Outside this house there were sheep, the cliffs and the sea. The beautiful Sussex coastline. Now, as he stood in the London flat listening to his favourite opera broadcast live over the radio, Simon Swann felt the approaching summer flex its green fingers, reaching upwards towards him through the open window. It was still light outside, the pure full light before twilight. He could see the park reflected in the windows. The air was pleasantly warm and the sky was stained pink with the remains of an unusually beautiful day. Tomorrow will be fine, he thought, watching the evening star rise above him. Below him, the traffic was flowing easily at last in the busy London street. The rush hour was almost over as the music he listened to began reaching its climax. As he listened, in a silent space inside him, muffled by his external life, he felt another self, marking time. Overhead the twinkling lights of a plane coming into land at Heathrow was followed almost immediately by two more planes hovering into view. The voices on the radio rose and fell, supported by a sweep of violins as he stared with blank eyes at the activities outside. However many times he listened to this final act of *Tosca* it never failed to move and remind him of another time, a lifetime ago now, when he had first heard it. So many years later it still sounded fabulous.

A tissue of memories floated along with the final moments of the opera, carrying him with it. He had been a young man then, sitting in the darkness of the Royal Opera House. The world had become a different place since that evening, changed beyond recognition – 9/11 had altered everything. The country he lived in was no longer what it once was. Terror had returned to Britain and it was here to stay, leaving the inhabitants of this small island xenophobic and fearful. Once we had an Empire, he often thought, wryly; now we just have the suspicions left by the Empire! Simon hardly ever played this recording, knowing he would remain possessed by low-level depression for hours afterwards. It was a foolish thing, this conjuring up of a fragmentary time from his youth for which there was no room in his life now. He had been at medical school, going to the opera as often as he could afford to, hiding from everyone else the passion that had no place in his mundane, hard-working, existence. The girl had been sitting in front of him, close enough for him to see her profile, close enough for him to see she was alone. When the lights went on at the end he saw she was wearing a red dress. Her hair was very long and black. Something made her turn her head and their eyes met. He was close enough to see the dark downward sweep of her lashes and the perfection of her teeth as she smiled before he stood up to let someone pass. When he looked back at her seat, she was gone. On an impulse, brought on no doubt by the music, he left the auditorium but could not find her anywhere outside. She was lost amongst the crowds. He had bought a book of cheap tickets for the season but, by the time he saw her again, he had given up looking for her. It was a different opera this time: Mozart. As soon as the first act ended he saw her stand up and, making up his mind he hurried out, determined to accost her. But once again she disappeared. It was the same in the next interval. Then at last when the performance ended he followed her out of the building until, as they were both hurrying towards the tube station, he managed to talk to her. It was nothing really, he would tell himself later, nothing worth making a fuss about. They had gone into a pub for a drink, she had looked anxiously at her watch, not wanting to miss the last train, and they had talked. She was training to be a schoolteacher, she sang a little, there was no one special in her life at the moment, she told him. They had talked without stopping for over two hours. She missed the last train and he had found her a black cab. She gave him her phone number, scribbling it on a scrap of paper (why had he not given her his?) and he had promised to call her the next day. But carelessly, as he made his way home he had lost it. Perhaps it had fallen out of his pocket when he took his ticket out. Simon had gone back to Covent Garden, even though it meant he missed his last train and had to walk back to his lodgings. But although he had scoured the pavement he never found that piece of paper.

In the days that followed, he had looked everywhere in the street, going back again and again to the opera, queuing outside for returns. Paying far more than he could afford. Then, when he still did not see her, he had taken to waiting for the crowds to come out at the end of some of the performances, but to no avail. Cursing himself for his stupidity, he was unable to stay away from Covent Garden. Finding the girl had become a kind of obsession and for a time it was impossible to concentrate on anything else. His work began to suffer. A few months on, he met Tessa at a party. She had been surrounded by a group of people, mostly men. One man in particular appeared utterly infatuated with her, causing Tessa much amusement. Simon had noticed her derisive laughter and had been appalled. Unwisely, when she had come over to speak to him, he told her so. They had had a terrific row that had somehow ended with her going back to his place. She was not his type, their interests were very different, but a few weeks later he caught chickenpox and Tessa arrived to nurse him. One thing led to another. Too late, he saw what he had done. Fleetingly he thought of the dark-haired girl at the opera. But Tessa with her blonde hair and icy blue eyes had become his reality. Soon all their friends began to see them as a couple. Their mutual, hidden loneliness formed a cocoon around them both. It had been enough. He proposed marriage and she accepted without hesitation. Twenty years later here they were, with the life they had built together. Solid as a monument.

The music was over. Sensing someone had come into the room behind him from a waft of perfume, Simon turned. He picked up the invitation on the mantelpiece.

Drinks at six, he read. *Followed by dinner. And please bring Tessa if she's free! I haven't seen you two together for ages.*

So that was what he was doing. And they were late because of the music. It was his fault, he knew. Even before Tessa pointed it out to him.

'I'm on call,' he warned her as they left. 'I might have to leave early. You'll have to get a cab.'

She nodded slightly.

'You never know, it might be interesting,' he said, knowing Tessa did not want to go but wanting to break the slightly frosty silence.

He knew she was annoyed and trying not to be. She hated it when he listened to opera, particularly this one, aware it did strange things to him. The opera was one of many bones of contention between them, he thought heavily, manoeuvring his way through the traffic. Another was that he played his music too loud. She didn't understand you needed to hear everything as though it were a live performance. She just thought he was going deaf. The evening light was beautiful. The mild depression had settled over him, just as he had known it would. The music threaded through his thoughts, regardless, conducting a conversation of its own. He had never told Tessa about his foolish non-encounter at Covent Garden.

'Meeting his new woman, I mean,' he continued regardless, glancing at her sideways.

'Nothing could be worse than his last,' Tessa said shortly. 'She was truly dreadful.'

And she shuddered delicately, making him smile inwardly, in spite of the fact he'd rather liked the last one. He stopped the car and they got out in silence.

'Well, here we are, Ralph!' he said too heartily as the host opened the door.

And then they went in.

'Just orange juice for me,' he said. 'I'm on call tonight.'

He watched as a beautiful nineteenth-century glass was filled with wine for Tessa. Tessa was looking around discreetly for the new woman.

'I'm Simon Swann,' he said to the man standing near him.

He turned to introduce Tessa but she had been whisked away by Ralph. There were hungry, admiring lions waiting, he guessed, pleased for her.

'On the wagon, then?' asked the man next to him.

'Pardon?'

'Not drinking?'

'Oh, I see. No, no, I'm on call at the hospital tonight, that's all.'

'Really? Can't have an inebriated doctor, I suppose!'

'No, exactly.'

'What d'you do? Stitch up drunks?'

'Bit of everything really. Emergency surgery, on nights like these,' he said, sipping his orange juice and surveying the room.

There were a lot of people tonight, mostly here out of nosiness, he suspected. It would certainly not be for the food, Tessa had remarked earlier, for the host was well known for his uncertain culinary talent. The man next to him was looking a bit green. Liverish, thought Simon, out of habit.

'So they know, when they see you, what's coming, eh?'

Simon smiled gently, not minding, knowing how people were about the subject: squeamish, not wanting to see what might be around the corner of their own lives. So he smiled.

'They're not usually conscious,' he said mildly.

Excusing himself, he went in search of Tessa. Snatches of music filled his head like ghosts. He could see her talking to the host's new woman with a look of intense curiosity. He hoped she was not disappointed.

The empty glasses were cleared away by the new woman in a proprietorial way. They went into dinner, and Ralph, himself a medic, served up the veal.

'*Vitello Brasato all' Uve!*' he announced, holding it high above the table, raising their hopes and expectations, toying with their appetite only to dash it hopelessly, so that several guests would stop at the fish-and-chip shop on the way home, and snuffle down a double cone of chips, all salt and grease and warmth straight from the fryer, before they would at last feel sated. But that was later. For the moment he simply brought in this dish, conjuring up in their minds the beautiful early summer full of expectancy and colour and surprise, the grapes plump and softened in the wine, the warm tartness of the fruit against the sweetness of the veal making a fine marriage. The guests waited with the fine claret in its cut-glass glinting ruby-red, and the candles in the polished holders glowed in the lit room, a token reference to bygone ages. The host placed his dish, rather as a conjurer would, on the mat on the high-gloss mahogany table to the soft sounds of appreciation around him. The women all wore black.

Tessa Swann glanced at her plate, her eyes glinting sharply. She's in good form, thought Ralph, with the sharp eye of the psychiatrist. It did not stop him noting shrewdly that she had begun to wear the shadow of disappointment sometimes seen on the faces of once attractive women. She was not ageing well, he mused, chewing on his veal, frowning slightly with the effort. It wasn't obvious to the casual observer yet, but Ralph wondered how conscious she was of the fact. Tessa Swann had always relied on her good looks, he decided, warming to his ruminations. But they had let her down now! Ralph imagined her forging ahead each morning with her brushes and her cover-up creams, unable to believe in her body's betrayal. She had such an air of holding on. With a small frisson of excitement he began to think of her naked and in bed with him. Tessa smiled, aware of some approval on his part. Satisfied that his new woman wasn't up to much, she relaxed. Triumph made her sharply defined, like a newly sand-blasted statue. The host grinned. He felt a stirring in his elderly groin, a rising of what might pass for sap. He breathed in spring, when for him it was really autumn. It was a pity, but the new acquisition would have to go, thought Tessa, leaving the field clear for their continued, gentle flirtation conducted over many years and wholly undetected by Simon himself.

At the other end of the table Simon Swann was only half listening to a convoluted story told by the new woman. He had forgotten her name and was waiting for a pause in which to ask her it again. She was a long woman, he saw, with a torso that took up most of her frame, giving the appearance of a body stocking accidentally stretched in the wash. And, he observed mildly, she had a hypnotic manner. She was American and every subject that she raised – motherhood and adoption (she had tried neither, she told him), psychoanalysis and the nature of the soul or literacy in Bradford – *every* subject discussed was washed with the all-consuming twanginess of her voice. How did she do it? marvelled Simon. She had a lot to say, mesmerising them all, so that even the veal became unimportant in the face of so much energy. When she began to talk about the war in Iraq, Simon felt his eyelids become heavier. He stifled a yawn; he had been working late just recently. The American's voice seemed to be running down, like vinyl being played at the wrong speed. Or perhaps she had simply lost interest in him, for she was now addressing her remarks to the man on her right. The veal was inedible, a discovery that spread slowly around the oval table, but even this did not bother Simon too much as with professional instinct and courteous manners he pushed the congealed cream, like regurgitated sick, around his plate. And then, just at that moment, the woman to the left of him spoke.

'I'm so sorry,' he said, startled out of his dream. 'I didn't quite catch that.'

He had not seen her sitting there beside him, she was so small and the American woman had absorbed too much of the atmosphere, he realised, belatedly. The woman beside him sighed. She flashed him a look from huge dark eyes and for an instant Simon could not conceal his astonishment.

'I was talking to myself,' she said, slightly defiantly. 'I was wondering how much more of this I would have to endure.'

Taken aback he laughed out loud. An alarming amount of defiance here, was his first amused thought.

'I was thinking the same thing,' he said before he could stop himself.

Across the table Tessa's crystal earrings glinted dangerously. The light seemed to have a surge of sudden power, falling on the sparking table with new force.

'I'm so sorry,' he said, wishing the woman would look at him again. 'How rude of me. I should have introduced myself. I'm Simon Swann.'

'I'm Alice,' the woman said unsmilingly.

He had to bend to hear her and then he caught a glimpse of her eyes once again. That was what he saw first, those eyes.

'Are you a psychiatrist too?' he asked.

She smiled unexpectedly. Her eyes went on smiling far longer than they needed to, he noticed. There was something very arresting about her appearance, which was dark. Exotic, he supposed, was the word.

'Oh God, no!' she was saying. 'I'm not quite sure why I'm here. Antonia invited me. She thought it would be good publicity.'

'Antonia?'

'The woman you were talking to,' she said, nodding in the direction of the American, who had moved on and was now deep in conversation with the man across the table.

'She's a friend of yours?'

'God no! She just exhibits my work. I believe she thought it would be good for my next exhibition. Actually, I think she wanted me as moral support. Not that she needs any.'

Simon looked confused.

'She's just met Ralph,' Alice said patiently. 'Our host. And she told me this would be a dinner for medics and she wouldn't know anyone. So,' she shrugged, 'I said I'd come. I must say, he can't cook, can he?'

Simon gave a shout of laugher, hastily stifled, and the woman stared at him.

'I'm sorry,' she said, not sounding sorry at all. 'But he can't, can he?'

Again he noticed her eyes. They were truly enormous, he thought, mesmerised. And a little at odds with her manner, which had a curious flatness to it. He hesitated, wanting to ask her where she was from, but afraid of giving offence.

'What sort of work do you do?' he asked instead.

'Me? I make sculptures.'

'*Really.*'

She glanced at him sharply. Evidently he passed the test because she seemed to relax a little.

'What sort of sculptures?' he asked once more, encouragingly.

'About my life.'

He registered the deadpan inflection in her voice again and was silent, not knowing what to say.

'What I mean is, they're not pretty nudes,' Alice said, with the faintest trace of amusement in her voice.

She took a small sip of wine and pulled a face, keeping her eyes lowered. He had the distinct feeling she didn't want to have anything more to do with him, maybe even regretted talking to him. In fact, he had a strong sense that she had withdrawn from the table altogether. Her face in profile was arresting. Also her voice had no trace of an accent, he thought, puzzling over this. Obviously she was from some Asian country but he could not decide where it might be. It was not, he felt sure, India. And although he would have liked to ask several questions, the woman's shuttered face seemed to forbid it. Her dark lashes covered her eyes, turning them into elongated buds. He stole another look at her.

'Ah! I see you've met Alice,' Ralph cried, appearing from behind and removing their plates. He replaced them with small pudding bowls. 'Alice is an artist, you know.'

'So I hear,' Simon nodded.

'Has she told you, she's got an important exhibition coming up soon? I've told Antonia she must send us an invitation. You mustn't forget,' he added loudly, smiling broadly at Alice. Tessa was staring steadily at Simon across the table.

'Yes,' Alice said softly. 'I do understand. I speak English!'

Only Simon heard her. Touchy, he thought, noticing Ralph had had a bit too much to drink. Antonia must have had the same thought, for suddenly she was beside him, holding a dish.

'Now, who's for summer pudding?'

'Not for me, thank you,' Alice said.

Simon had the feeling that she was fuming quietly. He opened his mouth to say something and, just at that moment, just as he felt he had discovered someone interesting in the evening, his bleeper went off.

'Damn,' he said gently. 'I'm on call tonight.'

'Oh dear! Now you won't be able to sample my excellent pudding,' Ralph said plaintively.

'Lucky you!' murmured Alice.

Tessa, watching across the table, made a small moue of irritation and the man next to her laughed sympathetically. Twice in two days.

What's the point? Tessa was thinking privately. After all, he hardly ever saves them.

'Should I drive you?' she asked, her concern suddenly and sharply proprietary.

'Oh, goodness, no,' murmured Simon. 'I'll drive myself, no need to worry. I'm afraid there must be a rush on if they're calling me.'

He took out his pager.

'Bad luck,' Ralph commiserated.

'For whom?' asked one of the guests nervously.

Simon Swann pushed back his chair regretfully.

'If I could just use your phone, Ralph. Very nice to have met you, Alice. Sorry I couldn't stay. You must send us an invitation to your exhibition. When is it?'

She was looking at him as if she didn't believe he was interested. Again he noticed how small she was. Her eyes reflected the candlelight unnervingly. Fleetingly she reminded him of someone he had met many years before.

'In about a month,' she said.

He searched in his pocket and found a piece of paper and scribbled his address down.

And then he was making for the door, checking he had his house keys, telling Tessa not to wait up for him. With a quick peck on her cheek, he was gone.

Far away in another time zone, dawn was breaking. It had been breaking for years on an unrecoverable past. The Sea House sighed and sank a little more into disrepair. Over the years it had slowly given up, loosening its hold on its past life, gently absorbing all that the elements threw at it. Accepting defeat. Only memory remained, possessing each of its rooms; folded inward with dust, undisturbed by human presence. There was no one to pick them up and shake them open. May had not been back. She had not found it possible to walk the path beside the coast, bending low under the bougainvillea branches grown heavy and unruly with neglect. The path held too much for her to bear. It was filled with the footsteps of her journeys to school; it had been the way she had walked as a young bride and then with her beloved son. She had thought his absence had defeated her completely, but then she had received a bundle of clothes. Only then did she understand the true depths of loss.

Through all of this, the Sea House soldiered on regardless, wreathed in neglect and unshed tears. The monsoons swept through it, making the rooms their own, and when they passed, the garden claimed the house again. Birds settled all over it while the paw-paw tree thrust its branches in through the open window. Chairs and tables, beds and hammocks, everything that once held life crumbled while the Sea House buckled under its fate. Janake visited it after Namil's funeral. When the bundle of clothes had arrived, Namil, like the house, had given up. May had thought he had not understood, but it seemed he had. He died in his sleep a day later. A blessing, Janake said, when he came to comfort May. At her request, he went back to the Sea House in search of a letter Namil had written when he had first met May. But the letter was not to be found, even though Janake looked everywhere. Instead he found other things that had been overlooked. A pair of child's shoes belonging to Alice, a lump of glass that he had given her, some driftwood they had found together on the beach, and then, to his delight, a photograph of her standing beside the rocks with him. Janake stared at it for a long time. His heart contracted. Buddhism was about letting go, he knew, but he longed for the simplicity of his past. He took the photograph, adding it to his small collection of possessions. He would keep it, he thought, in case the time should ever come when he might give it to Alice or her son.

Eleven years had passed since Alice's uncle Namil died. Peace of a sort had come to her island home. Sri Lanka had become a place that many people knew about. Thanks to cheap air travel, it had become a honeymoon destination, but for Alice the place held nothing but painful memories. Her aunt had disappeared, like all the people in her life, unintentionally, inevitably. Ravi at almost eighteen was a handsome boy with a shock of curly black hair. Although he did not know it, he had grown into the image of his great-grandfather, Bee. Every time he smiled, Alice's heart missed a beat. They still lived in the house in Brixton. She had converted one of the rooms downstairs into a proper studio and here she had begun to make the large sculptures that were becoming increasingly well known. Yet she was not happy. As he grew, Ravi began to change. The slow breaking away process, the growing distance between mother and son that was so necessary for the boy's entry into adulthood, had come as a shock to Alice. She felt each step away from her as a terrible wrench. There had been so many separations in her life. She saw her son's apparent indifference as one more. Ravi had always visited his father regularly, his parents' divorce having made little difference to his relationship with Tim. The plan of Tim's new home as he had drawn it on the day long ago had changed and changed again. Tim was no longer with the woman for whom he had left Alice. Other loves had come and gone with only his affection for his son remaining intact. Now, as he grew independent, Ravi began to take himself to his father's house on the other side of Brixton more frequently. He went after school, without bothering to inform his mother, letting himself in before Tim returned from work, and the first Alice knew of it was when she rang Tim's house. Often Ravi ended up staying the night. Shocked to discover feelings of jealousy within herself, struggling to acknowledge them, silent with hurt Alice watched as Ravi drifted away from her. Adolescence had brought the end of his love for her, she believed. All that she had tried to hold on to, she told herself, had vanished into nothing, and only her work remained. This was beginning to be noticed, first locally and then in a slow, haphazard fashion, further afield.

One day a woman from a newspaper came to interview her. She was about to have an exhibition in a gallery on the Railton Road. The journalist had come wanting to see her studio. She smiled with pleasure when Alice opened the door.

'I love the name of your house,' she said. 'Where's the beach!'

Alice had looked at the woman, unsmiling.

'It's in my head,' she said.

After she had made a pot of tea in her blue kitchen with its brightly painted shelves, its cheerful pottery and geranium plants that dotted the room, she suggested they look at the work.

'Who's the boy?' the journalist asked, peering at the photographs pinned up everywhere.

'My son,' Alice had answered shortly, and then they went into her studio.

Later, when she read what had been written about her studio, she was surprised.

Her studio gives the appearance of emptiness, apart from the solitary armoire and table. At first glance nothing is out of ordinary, yet the effect of stepping into a room lit from above by two spotlights gives an uneasy edge that is bewildering. There is something a little shocking about walking between table and armoire, their very ordinariness, the break from the daily business of living that invites one to view the experience of the 'disappeared' in a new and shocking light. This, the Sri Lanka-based artist tells me, a little hesitantly, is what she wants, this bridging of the spaces between one person's experience and another's.

Alice read the article over and over again, feeling an inordinate sense of pleasure. Put like this, those things she had wordlessly tried to do from a young age began to be clearer to her. Reading the article she felt close to tears. Someone, a person who had no connection with her, had understood. After so long this seemed a miracle. She toyed with the idea of contacting the journalist but was ashamed at her desperation. Instead she began to work with renewed determination, trying to forget Ravi's indifference towards her.

Soon after the piece in the newspaper, she was offered two prestigious exhibitions. She began to have recurrent dreams that she was back at Mount Lavinia. Always she would enter the house in these dreams, crossing the threshold of the boarded-up rooms where many years of darkness pressed against her. Butterflies fluttered before her eyes, thin and transparent as rice paper intermingling with the sea, a distant, repeated, inescapable sound. And always now, her grandfather's voice:

The jak-fruit have all burst.

362

He would shake his head.

I told your grandmother to get the boy to cut them down before they rotted. But she forgot.

In her dream, Alice saw her small self, spindly brown legs hurrying along beside his. Her grandfather was rubbing gingili oil on his legs. The black *pottu* in the middle of her forehead, put there by her mother to ward off the evil eye, had the effect of making her look fierce. Perhaps that was the effect it was meant to have.

I don't know why your mother insists on such rubbish, her grandfather laughed, watching her scratch it off.

Something happened to her when she got married. You mustn't get like her, Alice. You mustn't become frightened by life.

She never wanted to wake up from those dreams. But when she tried to tell Ravi, she only irritated him.

'You're insane,' he groaned. 'You and your bloody memories are nothing to do with me! I belong here.'

At other times he would shout:

'The people in that place make me sick. Your country is nothing to do with me. Don't you understand? I'm English!'

And he was. He looked like her, but his personality, all his gestures, even his laugh, was his father's. She could not hold him responsible for her folly. He stopped eating rice and curry and asked for Shepherd's Pie instead. He told her she did not make apple crumble like his grandmother. He began walking around the house with his headphones on in case she tried to talk to him, and then finally, one late spring afternoon halfway through his A levels, he told Alice he wanted to live with his father.

'Until I go to university,' he said.

Alice was speechless, what had she done?

'Nothing,' Ravi said, avoiding her eye. 'I just need to think of the best option for me, don't I. Dad can help me with my Maths homework, that's all.'

'And make you apple crumble, I suppose,' she said, before she could stop herself. She heard her mother's bitterness in her own voice. Ravi stared at her.

'I'm nothing like you,' he said quietly and with the certainty of youth. 'I don't think like you, I'm not interested in the things you are. It's best we do our own thing.'

He sounded like his father. Alice felt winded. The tall, leggy youth towering over her looked blankly back.

'But I am your mother,' was all she could whisper.

'So? I never said you weren't! You're just too emotional for me.'

It was the most she got out of him. Nothing would change his mind. He had hit upon the best course of action and would now stick to it. She had always known he possessed this cold determination. She could not beg, and as she watched him load his things into his father's car it was Tim, surprisingly, who came to her with an air of faint embarrassment.

'It's just a phase he's going through,' he mumbled, without looking at her. 'I expect he'll be back in the holidays.'

Tim's voice was softer than usual. She saw traces of something in his eyes. Some feeling that clearly disturbed him.

'It's his age,' he added, and the unexpected kindness pressed on her wound the harder. 'He does love you.'

The sudden generosity on Tim's part caught her unawares. I have nothing left, she thought through a waterfall of grief as she watched the car drive off.

Nonsense, her grandfather said, unexpectedly. *You have your work, that's what you must get on with. What d'you think I did when you went?*

The room was empty. Outside in the deep soft dusk of early evening, light poured over the garden she had tended for so long. The sandpit, the swing, the childhood toys had all gone. The apple tree had matured and grown. In a few weeks a flush of roses would cascade across the weather-beaten fence. She could hardly breathe. Somewhere far above her in the limitless sky an aeroplane moved slowly, its sounds faint against a coloratura of birdsong.

See, her grandfather said. *Look what a beautiful evening it is. Don't cry, my darling. The boy will be back; even his idiot father can see that! Come now, dry your eyes. I'm here.*

She had laughed, for her grandfather had not changed a bit. And then she had done what he said, burying herself in her work, welcoming Ravi when he came home, hiding the pieces of her broken heart, disguising her pain, pretending it didn't matter. A year later, having done brilliantly in his exams, Ravi was offered a place at Oxford to read Mathematics.

All the mathematicians come from the south of India, Bee told her. He sounded slightly disapproving. *The boy will grow up soon enough, you'll see,* he said.

A few weeks after he went up to Oxford, kissing his mother briefly on the cheek for the first time in years, Alice got a phone call from an American curator. The woman's name was Antonia Stott and she ran a gallery in the East End of London, close to Hackney. She wanted to show some of Alice's work. It was the breakthrough she had waited for.

Well done, her grandfather said. *That's the best news you've had in a long time. Now, work! This woman will lead you to other things.*

What those things were, Alice was not to find out for some months.

By the time the invitation arrived he had forgotten all about her.

'It's from that woman you met. At Ralph's place,' Tessa said, handing it to him.

'Who?'

It was a Saturday afternoon. This time he wasn't on call.

'You were chatting her up. She was Indian, I guess.'

'Oh … *her.* I was not! And I don't think she was Indian, but she was interesting.'

'So I noticed,' Tessa said.

Simon glanced at her. Something was irritating Tessa.

'Could you clear up your mess on the dining-room table, Simon?' she asked. 'The idea is you use your study to work in. Not the whole house.'

There, he thought triumphantly, having found the obstruction. That was the problem! He picked up an apple from the fruit bowl and bit into it.

'Oh, for God's sake, Simon, stop *eating*! You're always eating whenever I look at you. We're going out to dinner soon.'

'It's only an apple,' he said mildly. 'And we're not going out for ages yet.'

But Tessa had gone, crossly clattering her way into the kitchen. He could hear her on the telephone. He glanced at the invitation. It was printed on glossy white card. *Alice Fonseka,* it said. *In Search of Lost Time. Private view: Thursday 14 June, 6 p.m. to 8 p.m.* And underneath was the address of the gallery. Not too far, he thought, turning the invitation over. He would be back in the flat in London next week. On the other side of the card was an image of a glass-fronted cupboard. The glass was covered in white plaster. Embedded in it were glimpses of clothing: men's shirts of different patterns. He could see cuffs, frayed at the edges, parts of collars pressed against the glass, partially covered in the plaster, looking as though they were struggling to get out. Interested, he turned the card over again and stared at the title. What did it mean, *Searching For Lost Time*? he wondered. And then, without warning, he remembered Alice's extraordinary eyes. Had he taken her number? He couldn't remember.

'Simon,' Tessa said, coming in again. 'As you don't seem to have anything to do, could you put the rubbish out, please? I'm fed up with doing everything. You're never here. I might as well be living alone.'

She was getting in a froth, he thought tiredly.

'Well, I'm on call-out all weekend,' he said, making it sound as though he were giving her a present, making her crosser.

'What difference does that make?' she asked. 'You're absent whether you're here or not.'

He didn't say anything, speculating on the nature of absence. He knew she was watching him as he tried to toss the core of the apple into the pedal bin and missed. Everything he did, thought Simon, picking it up again, irritated her. He lifted the black bin liner out of its carcass.

'Shall we go to it?' he said, his mouth still full of apple, pointing to the invitation.

'Simon!' shouted Tessa. 'Mind the rubbish, for God's sake. Look, you're spilling *everything* on the floor. Oh, give it to me, I might as well do it myself!' she cried, snatching it out of his hand and going outside.

In the end he went on his own. Probably Tessa didn't want to come up to London so soon, or maybe it had been something to do with Cressida that stopped her. Whatever the reason, he was alone when he next saw Alice. The gallery was filled with people he did not recognise. Simon had not been to a smart exhibition in London for ages. Usually the only art he saw was when he went with Tessa to some dreary local show of paintings to buy another charmless landscape. This exhibition, he saw immediately, was different. For a start, the first two rooms were strictly minimal. On the floor in front of him were three piles of shirts, neatly folded and stacked into high columns. Behind them on the wall hung an exquisite seascape, shimmering with light. Simon stared at it. A woman in a low-cut black dress and red high heels clipped over to him, her hips as flexible as a scorpion's tail, a flute of champagne in her hand. A group of people stood in a corner of the room staring down at something he couldn't see. They were making a lot of noise. After a while he tore himself away from the painting and walked around the stack of shirts. Then he wandered into the next room. Alice was nowhere in sight.

There were two more rooms, each with a couple of free-standing sculptures. One was the wardrobe that had appeared on the front of the invitation. It was filled with shirts pushed up against the glass. What was it about shirts? he puzzled, staring at it. In the last room there was a painting on the wall. And again it was a small luminescent seascape. The sculpture here was the strangest of them all. He wondered how he could describe it later on to Tessa. A cross between a table and a cupboard, perhaps? It occurred to him, all these things were hybrids of some sort. That's it, he thought, pleased with himself. Another piece of unusable furniture with bits of other furniture grafted on to it, like limbs, taking on a strange alien life of its own, filled the room with its oppressive personality. He moved closer and peered at it. The object had been limed and rubbed over with plaster. Now it was partially white with traces of paint from some other life showing through here and there. Simon stared at it. Lost in thought, he sipped his champagne, puzzled over it. He saw the whole surface was scratched and covered in fine hair. For some reason he felt certain the hair was human. A sense of menace struck him forcefully. He went closer and examined the table. Again he had the vague sense of knowing what he was looking at but still he couldn't put his finger on what it might be. Was it an operating table, he wondered? No that wasn't quite right, he frowned. Under the pool of gallery lights it no longer was a table. The sense of a sinister presence deepened in his mind. Had he been asked he would have said the room made him think of a torture cell. He was trying to work it out when he heard a small sound. Glancing up, he saw Alice Fonseka watching him with an unreadable expression in her eyes. He stared at her for a moment crushed by the complexity of his own thoughts. Again, he experienced the feeling he'd had the first time he met her: she reminded him of someone.

'Oh it's you,' she said, unsmiling, in that disconcertingly flat voice that he had forgotten, 'I didn't think you would come.'

'I almost forgot,' he admitted, smiling boyishly, taking her aback, so that she wondered how old he was.

Later, after the private view was over they had a drink together before she went home. She had wanted to duck out of the party Antonia had laid on, she told him, because she wanted an early night. She was talking on the radio in the morning. At the last moment she agreed to Simon's invitation to go around the corner with him to a small bar for a quick drink. All she wanted was a cup of tea, she said.

'Tell me about your work,' he asked, really wanting to ask her if she would have dinner with him, but knowing instinctively this could prove tricky. He didn't want to frighten her off, he was thinking. The light from the window was unnaturally bright as though a storm was brewing. All around them were the silvery shadows of the summer evening. The unusual heat was making him drowsy and he felt the whole of the day come to a halt as she spoke. She seemed unaware of the sorrow in her voice.

'I loved the paintings,' he said carefully. 'But the other things disturbed me.'

Instinct told him honesty was best. She was looking him full in the face.

'I'm just a medic,' he said self-deprecatingly.

She smiled then and the unexpected force of it threw him.

'You were right to be disturbed,' she told him. 'They disturbed me too. What happened.'

'Where are you from?' he asked before he could stop himself.

In the slight pause that followed he felt a faint fragrance drift towards him. He wanted to touch her hair. Outside a police car screamed and faded as it passed. Dust motes filled the air. Time stood still.

'I'm from Sri Lanka,' she said, and he realised she had understood his nervousness and was enjoying it. He laughed, delighted. A last ray of late sun caught the edge of her hair and the urge to touch her grew stronger within him.

'Do you go back often?'

She shook her head and he saw again how dark her eyes were.

'I haven't been back for thirty-two years,' she admitted. 'I've been carrying that stretch of beach around with me for a long time.'

She had a way of speaking very quietly so he found he had to lean forward to catch her words. Again he could smell the unidentifiable fragrance.

'But how old are you?' he asked, puzzled.

With a flick of her hand she pushed her hair back, watching him with dark brown eyes that held him with something between gravity and the gentlest of irony.

'I've just turned forty-one,' she told him, pulling a face, and now she was laughing at him openly. He felt a stab of excitement leap up in his heart. She seemed, even as he looked at her, suddenly identifiable with all the rising summer, exquisite and still young, desirable as sunlight and exotic. What was there to do? What should they talk about? Words clothed his turmoil. Frightened, he suggested instead he drove her home after a snack. Again Alice smiled. Light danced in her eyes. A dimple appeared on her cheek, and vanished. He longed to see it again. She looked him unexpectedly full in the eye, and shook her head. Tea, she just wanted another cup of tea. Maybe next time.

So there was to be a next time. Who would have thought this simple certainty could bring such joy?

Simon was talking; telling her about Tessa. With a compulsion only barely understood, he knew he wanted to explain Tessa, to sweep all obstacles aside so nothing and no one should stand between them from this first moment. The impulsiveness of his youth, denied for so long, returned with a rush of intoxicating certainty. If he could have explained this he would have said simply that he had no time to waste.

'We've been married for twenty years,' he told her.

In the diaphanous sky, still light, for it was not quite midsummer, small birds darted about. There was nothing more to discover, he told her, candidly. Not even anger. Just nothing. They had read each other completely. Some books you read only once. Alice was looking at him unflinchingly. She nodded and he watched her hands as she folded the bill into a small boat. Then she uncreased the paper and smoothed it flat. She told him about Tim, and less easily, about Ravi.

'He comes home very occasionally,' she said. 'We are very different. That will always be a problem.'

She hesitated.

'He wants to simplify his life. My presence in it makes it messy.'

She laughed nervously. Again he looked at her hands, the long slender fingers of a sculptress. She was thinking she had never had this kind of conversation with anyone before.

'The young need to have a fixed position,' she said, her eyes searching for some invisible horizon.

'They go on about the world being a global village,' Simon said. 'I thought a fixed position was the last thing they wanted.'

Certainly it was what his daughter always told him.

'Cressida tells me she could live anywhere in the world and feel comfortable because of this.'

Alice shook her head, smiling.

'Ah, but your daughter looks like you and your wife, I imagine. It's different for my son. He feels as if he is neither one thing nor another. Really,' again she hesitated, 'it would have been better if he looked more like his father. People would see him simply as an English boy.'

'You mean his looks cannot hide his connections?'

'Yes.' Again she nodded, her eyes steady on him.

'But it's such a rich connection,' he said, wanting to say it was exotic, but not daring to.

She grimaced.

'Theories are fine if you have a secure life already. My son has had to carve out an identity for himself. Ordinarily, divorce muddles things. In Ravi's case the choices are harder.'

Simon was amazed. Vast oceans stood between them both and his mind was in turmoil. He talked of Cressida and the strange cyber world she lived in. Perhaps it was reality.

'My son has no use for my memories,' Alice was saying. 'They aren't his memories, so,' she shrugged, 'why should he care?'

He could see she was hurt.

'The thing Ravi needs most of all is to belong somewhere, totally. He needs to be grounded in an identity before he can feel at ease.'

'But you'll see,' Simon said lightly, wanting to offer some comfort, 'he will find out one day that belonging is not about appearance.'

A little later on when he saw she was getting restless he drove her home.

'I shouldn't ask,' he said, when he stopped the car.

He smiled. He could barely see her face. It had become dark without them noticing.

'But can I phone you?'

'You needn't ask,' she said, and he sensed with enormous relief she was smiling too.

Briefly, he placed his hand over hers. Then she was out of the car and gone with hardly a breath's disturbance to the air.

When he got back to his flat, the answer phone was flashing. Tessa had left a message about a quote from the builders.

'I don't know where the devil you are, Simon,' she said in her economic and clipped way, 'at some opera, no doubt. But *can* you ring him in the morning? I think we're being overcharged. And can you let me know *when* you're coming home. I wanted to invite the Richards to supper.'

A shock like cold electricity darted up Simon's arm and into his heart so that he pressed the delete button abruptly and began searching through his collection of CDs. He knew exactly what he wanted to listen to and here he was free to turn the volume up. He went to the window, through which the lights of London were strung like jewels across the night sky. All summer spun in his head. The music swept over him in a wave of pure joy, swamping him in an ache of wanting to see the woman he had just left. The longing surged over him, quivering through his body. A complex web of happiness had been thrown over the familiar view, turning it into something rare and utterly beautiful. He could not think. Thinking was too much tonight. All he wanted was to have this feeling go on exactly like this, with the music and the night full of stars and tomorrow somewhere nearby. He doubted he would sleep.

Across the river in Brixton Beach, sleep evaded Alice, too. Not since David Eliot had first befriended her had she had an evening remotely like this. Her skin felt stretched and tired as if she had been swimming for a long time. For some reason the feeling made her think of Janake. She allowed herself to bring out the memory of the last time she had seen him. Outside, the traffic rushed past. Night noises of police cars and ambulances flashed by and disappeared. The moon was full in the sky, shining through the curtains of Brixton Beach. Simon Swann, she thought, saying his name aloud. She was stunned. Then in order to calm herself, she tried out the sobering thought of his marriage.

That was broken already, her grandfather's voice said, close by. *You're living in a different era, both of you, to the one you were born into. Don't you know? A person has many lives.*

I don't want to do anything to his wife, she thought. I don't want to be the one to break anything. This is crazy, I don't even know this man, she said out loud. Her grandfather's voice seemed to have deserted her. What should she do? Sleep was impossible.

The next morning, having left it as late as possible, Simon rang her.

'Do you like opera? Would you like to go to *Tosca*?'

'The opera?'

He might as well be suggesting they went to the moon.

'I don't know any opera,' Alice confessed.

Her life had no history of opera, she told him, a little defensively. Had he forgotten she had different cultural references from his? Not British taste. She felt as though her grandfather was floating about near her, listening. Simon Swann glimpsed another, darker, more interesting layer that he would want to unwrap later. He tried to think of the Asians he worked with. He was a politically correct man, but he wondered if he had been thinking in clichés. He could not remember a time when he had ever given the matter much thought. How many had he worked with in his career at the hospital? Twenty, thirty?

'Well then,' he told her, easily, 'you have a treat in store! I've got two tickets for a performance next month. Friday the twenty-fifth.'

It was clear to him they would have to make another meeting. And another. And instinctively he knew these meetings alone would not be enough. Alice was thinking the same thing too, but Simon had no way of knowing this. She smiled into the phone. There were things she should have been asking him, but he beat her to it.

'Tessa's gone back to Mortimer. She hates London. And the opera.'

'Who's Mortimer?'

Her voice was so close to his ear. He badly wanted to see her.

'It's the name of the house in Sussex. It's been in my family for years. I think it was my mother who named it,' he said. 'She always felt the house was a person, you see.'

'How funny,' she said, faintly. 'That was how I felt too!'

And she gave him her address.

He was with her sooner than she expected, leaning against the door frame when she opened it, smiling at her, familiar already. How could this be?

'Did you sleep well?' he asked, and then he laughed.

The interior of the house had a tropical feel to it. There were cracks all over the yellow walls. All the way here his mind had been going over some lines from a poem he had once read:

> You are many years late,
> How happy am I to see you.

She was laughing too.

'You should take my pulse!' she said.

'I have to be at work by two,' he told her, regretfully. 'I've got a rotten rota for the next ten days but then I'm free again on Friday the twenty-fifth.'

They both sighed, paused startled, and then laughed. Oh God! thought Simon.

He had the feeling that a part of him had severed itself of its own violation and would now forever belong to her. He thought this sort of thing happened only to young men.

'I'm sorry,' he said softly. 'I'm a medic, you see.'

She saw. She was already getting used to the idea, she wanted to tell him. I will ring you every day he wanted to say, and think of you all the time. Neither said a word.

Alice took him through into the kitchen, which was surprisingly large. The cupboards were made of driftwood, bleached and blanched with sun and salt-water.

'I used to beach-comb in Cornwall,' she told him, seeing him look at them. Through the doorway he caught glimpses of other rooms, a length of ultramarine silk draped over furniture; sea glass of a piercing blue reflecting the light. He felt disorientated. The London traffic, still only a pace away outside, did not penetrate or remove the feeling that, somewhere, nearby there was bound to be the sea.

'I love the name!' he said. 'I mean, Brixton Beach.'

Alice handed him a mug of milky tea. The day was like a seashell. You looked inside it and it was impossible to see beyond the middle. And the end of course was in complete shadow. You put it to your ear and all you heard were the half-understood sounds of the sea: waves, voices, the wind. The walls of the kitchen were hung with a series of small paintings. All of them were very beautiful. All were of the sea.

'But the sea is everywhere!' he said with amazement.

'I grew up by it,' said Alice. 'It's inside me, I suppose, wherever I go. The horizons, the greys,' she waved her hands in the air. 'People think the tropics have to be all colour, jungle green and hot reds. But it's not necessarily so.'

They stood side by side, gazing at the paintings.

'I used to walk on the beach at dawn and the sky was often a soft grey and pearly white. And sometimes, far out on the horizon, was a touch of a very pale yellow. My grandfather would point it out to me.'

Tell him I'm dead, her grandfather said succinctly, interrupting her with a faint chuckle in his voice. *He's no fool; other people's memories won't frighten him.*

Startled, Alice smelt a whiff of pipe tobacco.

'Where do you make your work?' Simon asked, curiously. 'Do you have a studio in the house?'

Alice nodded. 'Would you like to see it?'

The room startled him further. Unfinished work was strewn every-where. The high ceiling light he had noticed in the gallery was here too, giving the room the same feeling of menace, completely at odds with the rest of the house. Simon felt as though he had stepped into another world; one he could only guess at.

'It's very powerful,' he said, uncertainly. 'What's this work about?'

Good! her grandfather's voice intervened. *Tell him, then!* So halt-ingly, she spoke of her mother's ordeal, the cousin she had never met, and finally, of Bee. They were the things that history remained silent about, she told him.

'He was the only person I've ever loved with all my heart,' she said simply. 'Apart from Ravi, of course.'

In the English summer daylight her words were more startling.

'My friend Janake said the floor was marked by their shoes. No one saw the footprints until afterwards, and by then it was all that was left,' she said. 'I remember being struck by his words, most of all by the thought of the struggle. It was somehow so utterly shocking that I could visualise it.'

She fell silent at the memory.

'These scratches?' Simon asked, pointing to the marks on a door resting against the studio wall.

'Yes.'

Simon too was shocked. He was used to death sanitised and made reasonable. He was used to kindness being drawn like a sheet across suffering, not this. Tessa, and his life in Sussex, seemed very far away.

It was this, this righting of a terrible injustice, that had informed her work, Alice continued, quietly. Made her turn from the fluid seascapes to sculptures.

'All my life is built on memories,' she said over lunch.

Her eyes glowed with dark intensity. Sunlight poured into her colourful kitchen, slanting across her face. She's beautiful, he thought, mesmerised.

'To be an immigrant is to be sandwiched between two worlds,' she told Simon Swann, without a trace of self-pity.

The flatness that he had heard when he had first talked to her had gone from her voice.

'The effort it takes to be a person who does not belong is unimaginable, you know. I am one of those people, living that life.'

But inside, she told Simon Swann; she was still Alice Fonseka who had once belonged.

They talked all that long hot afternoon with the hours flying around them like late summer gulls. Simon wanted to sort everything out in his mind, wanted her to understand that he was going to change the world she had inhabited.

'I'm too old to waste any more time,' he said firmly.

'How old?' she asked boldly, laughing.

'Forty-five!' he said, pulling a face.

She continued to laugh.

'You look younger.'

It was true. Sunlight on his greying hair gave him the look of a much younger man. He felt himself sink down into the dark place of awful loneliness she had been describing. He wanted to erase it. He wanted to do many things; to touch her, for a start, to trace an unwavering line from eye to eye and down across her mouth. Wanting to touch her shouted in his head above every other thought, but he ignored it. Smiling, she wanted it too, although what she wanted was slower, harder to put into words. Neither of them requested anything of the other. Both were filled with old-fashioned courtesy. Both waited for the other, averting their eyes, suddenly, conveniently, blind. Alice felt her heart was bursting.

Good, good, her grandfather said, sucking on his pipe. But on this occasion, Alice did not hear. There was an orchestra playing in her head. She was not altogether certain what it might be playing. Simon too was listening on invisible headphones. He was listening to Mozart.

'The twenty-fifth,' he said, in a voice he hardly recognised as his own. 'I'll pick you up at six and we'll go to the opera. I know you'll love it!'

16

ALL THAT WEEK AND THE NEXT two after that Simon Swann felt as though he was a wind-up bird functioning perfectly well on mechanical energy, but absent in spirit. His staff asked him questions and he looked blankly at them. The patients greeted him in their usual subdued way with the mixture of fear and awe the occasion demanded. Tessa rang him once to inform him the builders had arrived and were at work. They were trampling all over her plants and she was convinced they were stealing the best roses.

'I think it's the younger one who's the culprit,' Tessa said. 'I'm certain he's taking them home to his wife,' she said crossly. 'I need to catch him at it,' she added.

'It's just a few flowers,' Simon said mildly. 'Does it matter?'

'It's dishonest,' snapped Tessa. 'Why doesn't he buy his own, like the rest of us?'

Cressida wanted to speak to him and Tessa passed the phone to her.

'There's something wrong with my car, Daddy,' Cressida complained. 'The gears are sticking again.'

Simon placated her and promised to look at them when he got back.

'Can't you drive Mummy's car till I'm next home?' he asked when she continued to grumble.

'That's not the point!' Cressida said, impatiently. 'Tom hates her car!'

'Well, tell Tom to get a car of his own, or else fix yours.'

'Why? When will you be back?'

'I don't know yet. I'm going to the opera on the twenty-fifth. Put Mummy back on, I want to talk to her.'

Cressida groaned.

'The opera!' she cried, handing the phone back to her mother.

'I take it from that you won't be here when the Richards come?' Tessa asked waspishly.

Simon sighed.

'You knew about the tickets ages ago! I'm sorry.'

'You're sorry! What good is that?'

It was the usual rejoinder.

'Look,' he said, reasonably, 'put them off till the following week.'

'No, Simon, I will *not*. If you're going to the opera on Friday, why can't you come home on Saturday? Cress needs her car fixed.'

There was a short pause.

'I'm not coming home just to fix Cress's car,' he said, suddenly riled.

He could hear his daughter shouting in the background.

'I think you're being exceptionally mean to both of us,' Tessa was saying.

That was how it had always been, he thought: Tessa and Cressida against him.

'In any case, I'm working on Saturday.'

The lie, taking him aback, slipped out with startling ease. The silence on the other end of the phone grew.

'Put the Richards off until the following week or have them without me.'

'Well, of course you never liked them,' Tessa said.

There, it was out. All the knives, he thought, wincing, slightly. Soon they would be sharpening them. When would they start drawing blood? Taking a deep breath, he wondered what he could do to resolve it. Feelings he had not thought he possessed were clamouring inside him, crying to be let out. He didn't want a scene but it was heading towards him like a tidal wave. He had never quarrelled with his life until now. Wait! he told himself. Wait! Maybe he was mistaken. But it was no mistake.

He opened his computer. His e-mails remained unanswered from days before. Invitations to dinner, to play squash, his friend Ralph offering him two tickets to a concert, another invitation to give a paper at a conference. A colleague, writing to him from the States. A long letter from the editor of *The Lancet* with queries about the article he had submitted some months ago on pain relief. They were going to publish it. Next Simon listened indifferently to his telephone messages.

The days crawled slowly on. He hurried back to the flat in the early hours of each morning impatiently, wanting only to ignore the telephone, his mobile, his e-mails, everything. Wanting only to listen to his music and wait. Friday the twenty-fifth seemed a lifetime away. He rang Alice twice in that time. The first time was a few days after he had seen her last when, unable to bear it any longer and with a feeling of slight sickness, he dialled the number. What if she had changed her mind and couldn't face the opera? After all, hadn't she warned him that opera was outside her experience? What if she couldn't stand the thought of an evening with a married man? The world was full of unattached men, he thought, his head swimming. Like a schoolboy, he plucked up courage and rang her. He let the phone ring and ring but there was no answer. Feeling let down, he went into the kitchen and cooked himself a boiled egg, opened the tin of anchovies he found in the cupboard and ate supper. Then he drank some whisky and listened to a recording of *Tristan and Isolde.* The old magic flooded over him so that for a while he was distracted. At ten o'clock, feeling unaccountably restless and depressed, he decided to go to bed but as he was cleaning his teeth the phone rang. Her voice sent him into paralysis.

'I was in my studio,' she said, sounding very young. 'I didn't hear the phone.'

'You're still working, then?'

'I can't sleep.'

There was a pause, as though she felt she had said too much. Unvoiced questions gathered in his head. But luckily she couldn't see. Neither of them knew what came next. He wanted to say, he couldn't sleep either, that all he had done was think about her, that if he had half a chance he would jump in a taxi and come over. But he said none of these things. Instead he told her about the music he had been listening to. It seemed safe to admit he was looking forward to Friday, so he said that too. He heard her laugh slightly, as though she was reading his mind.

'I was on the radio again, yesterday,' she said, 'promoting the exhibition.'

'Oh God, I completely forgot! How did this one go?'

'Well!' she said. 'I was nervous thinking you might be listening. I hate the sound of my voice. But it was okay. I'm glad you forgot!'

Again she laughed. So my opinion matters, he wanted to shout triumphantly. Instead he too laughed, delighted. They talked for a moment longer. He told her about Cressida's car and her reluctance to drive her boyfriend around in her mother's car. He tried to make the story funny, determined to mention their names, not wanting her to think he was evading the situation they were walking into. But the story came out all wrong. He heard the slight hesitation in her voice and then he asked her about Ravi.

'Have you heard from him?' he asked quickly.

'No. I don't expect to for a bit. He rang me last week. There's another two weeks of term left. I expect he's busy.'

Simon cursed his clumsiness. Was she comparing their different lives?

'You could visit him,' he said, trying to console her. 'I could drive you up to Oxford and go off somewhere while you visited him?'

There was a startled silence.

'That's kind of you,' she said formally. 'Maybe one day.'

Suddenly he felt worse than if she hadn't rung him back. Had he said too much too quickly? What was she thinking? He told her a bit about his work but at the same time he was thinking anxiously about what was going through her mind. There was another awkward pause.

381

In the end, Alice was the one who finished the conversation, saying she ought to go to bed as she had an early start in the morning.

'What are you doing tomorrow?' he asked, uneasy, now.

'I've got to take another piece of work up to the gallery and Antonia has someone from the press coming to meet me.'

'You'll be famous!' he said admiringly, and she laughed.

He was certain he was boring her.

'Sleep well,' he said.

'Thank you. You too.'

Putting the phone down he remembered the first time he had met her and how she had withdrawn from him. He felt she had done it again. Now he wouldn't sleep, he knew. Calm down, he told himself, this is getting out of hand. It's too quick. But he knew he wouldn't sleep. Going back into the living room he turned on the light in search of his recording of *Tosca*.

In Brixton Beach Alice washed her hands, scrubbing the plaster out of her fingernails. She didn't know what had made her ring him. Staring at her hands under the running water she thought, Why on earth should this thing work out? Why had she told him so much about herself? She shook her head. *Child,* her grandfather's voice came to her clear and real, *he is a very fine man.* It was possible, she thought. Best not to hope. Will he ring, again, she wondered? *Of course,* her grandfather said, mystified at her doubts. *I told you, this man is not like the other. And besides, the time is right.*

Neither slept well. On Wednesday Alice thought, Only two more days to go. She found it difficult to concentrate on her work and decided instead to go into Brixton. It was hot. Jumping on a bus she made her way to the top deck and sat looking down at the street. The branches of the plane trees brushed past. The bus was empty and Alice sat quietly lost in thought. Every part of the Brixton Road, she realised, was filled with memories of Ravi. But I feel so old, she thought. She smiled ironically, aware that it had been a long time since thoughts about her age and appearance mattered. They passed the park where she had taught Ravi to ride his bicycle, running behind him, holding on to the back as he pedalled. Round and round she had run, laughing, her hair obscuring her view, while Ravi shouted at her not to let go. And the passers-by had stopped to smile at the girl, so young and small, with the dark flowing hair, teaching her son to ride. Simon Swann would never know that girl. She had vanished. The bus stopped beside another bus and she did something she hadn't done for a long while. Years. She considered the face reflected in the window, scrutinising the ravages of time.

There's nothing there to worry about, her grandfather's voice intercepted. *You're still beautiful, child.* His voice came to her with the slap of waves carrying her youth with it.

But what shall I do? she asked him, wordlessly.

Nothing, Putha. Just be yourself.

The long hot afternoon seemed deliciously filled with a sense of Simon Swann. Whichever way she turned, she felt his presence, rich with possibilities. Reaching Coldharbour Lane she stepped off the bus and headed for a record shop. Walking amongst the rows of CDs she found the section marked 'opera' and began to look through it, but she couldn't remember the name of the opera they were going to. Frowning with concentration, she picked up one boxed case after another, not knowing what to do. A piece of music was playing. The voice was very deep and rich and melodious. Mesmerised, Alice listened. The singing was in Italian, she knew that much. On the counter was a notice that said what the music was: *La Traviata.* She was certain that wasn't the name Simon had said. The music held her for a moment longer before it came to an end. Alice hesitated, wondering whether to buy it. At the last minute, superstition made her decide not to, but she wrote the name down. If he ever rang her again she would ask him about it. *If he rings?* chuckled her grandfather.

But he didn't ring that day, or the following day either. Alice worked in her studio, chiding herself for her foolishness. Later in the afternoon the phone did ring and it was Ravi. Such was her focus on Simon that for a moment she was taken aback.

'Can you look for something in the loft?' Ravi asked, without preamble. 'There's a box with my school maths books in it. Can you post it?'

Yes, darling,' she said. 'When are you coming home?'

'I don't know yet,' he mumbled. 'I'm in a hurry, I can't stop to talk now. I'll let you know.'

And then he was gone, leaving her wondering again how they had become strangers. Alice went back to sanding the piece of wood she was working on. Then she began to lime it with a rag. A small coil of barbed wire lay on the floor. There were drawings strewn around, pinned on the walls. The work was looking good, but her hard-won equilibrium had been disturbed and she had to force herself to go on working. At six o'clock, just as she was finishing for the day, the phone rang again. It was a woman she knew only slightly, a local artist she had occasionally shown her work with. Alice waited politely for the conversation to finish. Her head was beginning to ache with the fumes from the solvents she had been using and also from hunger.

'What about coming over tomorrow?' the woman persisted.

Alice murmured her thanks and declined.

'I'm so sorry, I'm busy,' she said, wanting to get off the phone.

She felt dizzy and wanted to cry. After an eternity, the woman rang off. Alice went outside and cut some roses. It was as she was putting them into water that the telephone rang once more.

'What are you doing?' Simon asked, his voice very clear and close to her ear.

For a moment Alice could not speak. A constriction in her chest, a barely acknowledged longing burst inside her and she smelled the fragrance of old French roses, all in a bunch, in her arms.

'Cutting roses,' she said, and she described the pale creaminess of the flowers. She was breathless. Simon hesitated and then he laughed.

'I'm still at work,' he said. 'I'm afraid I will be here for some time, or I would suggest inviting myself over to Brixton Beach!' he said.

She heard faint music.

'I was worried that you might have misunderstood something I said the other night,' he told her.

She could hear his uncertainty and felt relief flooding over her. With new confidence she told him about her trip to the music shop and her curiosity to hear what an opera was like. Simon was delighted.

'Do you want to know the story before you go?' he asked, and proceeded to tell her the doomed story of the painter Cavaradossi and his dark-eyed Tosca.

'I once heard Maria Callas sing Tosca,' his voice went on. 'You know, I queued all night for a ticket and my God it was worth it! She was superb, brought the house down.'

Alice listened, not understanding but mesmerised regardless. Her life balanced on a knife-edge. A distant memory was disturbed as she listened to Simon Swann talk and she saw her younger self, listening to her grandfather telling her about his work.

'Just you wait,' Simon was saying in the same passionate way. 'In less than three days you've a treat in store. I'll pick you up at about six.'

She did something she hadn't done since her wedding day. She wore a sari that was the colour of the roses she had placed in her glass bowl. She felt as though it had been years since she had seen him last. He was late, perhaps he wasn't coming after all? At ten past six, feeling sick, she stared at herself in the mirror. What was wrong with her? Disliking the way she looked, she put her hair up in a French pleat. Simon Swann, arriving in evening dress, found himself gazing into a pair of dark eyes that had on them the late summer bloom of a grape. He had imagined this moment for so long that the reality of her took him by surprise again.

'What?' she asked, feeling shy, but he could only shake his head and smile at her. There were no words to explain the emptiness of his past. He smelled of shaving foam from another era, she thought. She left him prowling around the kitchen while she got her shawl.

'I've cooked something,' she called, 'if you want to come back here to eat?'

'Oh, that might be good,' he said. 'Let's see how we feel.'

He stared at the photographs curling at the edges, tucked into picture frames. The younger Alice, holding a small child on her hip. Ravi, he thought and then he saw other photographs on her dresser. Ravi blowing out seven candles on a cake, Ravi playing the piano, looking about eleven or twelve. The teenaged Ravi, thinned out, taller, with his mother's face lurking in his.

Simon had bought tickets in the Dress Circle. Twenty years had passed since his encounter as a student. On an impulse he told Alice the story.

'I've never told anyone,' he said. 'But you know, for years, every time I went to the opera I looked around hoping to find her.'

'Tonight might be your lucky night!' Alice teased and Simon, looking at her solemnly, replied:

'Tonight *is* my lucky night!'

She had been prepared for the story of *Tosca* but not the drama of the whole production. A vast theatre, lavish costumes and an orchestra, not to mention the singing itself. At some point before the first interval she found he was holding her hand.

'Are you enjoying it?' he asked when the lights came on and the applause had died down.

He felt a wave of disturbing tenderness at the sight of her. They drank champagne sitting in a corner of the crush bar. He told her something about the singers; those who were on top form tonight and the ones who were a little disappointing. She caught a glimpse of a world she had not known existed.

'I have never been to the opera with someone who's interested in going. Tessa would come when we were first married as a sort of duty.' He paused, gazing at his empty glass. 'That's no use.'

Embarrassed, she didn't know what to say. He glanced at her sharply.

'Look, Alice …' he hesitated. 'I was worried the other day when I rang you, in case you were annoyed I mentioned Tessa. But … I wanted to start with as clean a slate as I could. I wanted to mention her, so you didn't think … I was doing anything you won't fully understand.'

She was watching him gravely.

'It's too early for me to say anything …' he began again when she interrupted.

'There isn't anything to talk about yet,' she said, placing her hand on his arm.

He noted she used the word 'yet' and was thrilled.

'I'm still thinking about all this,' she said gesturing at the glittering chandelier and the plush crimson seats. 'Tell me about the next act.'

So he told her about the aria, *Vissi d'arte, Vissi d'amore,* I lived for art, I lived for love, and how when Callas sang it in the early sixties, there wasn't a dry eye in the auditorium.

As the lights went down for the second act he took her hand as though he had been doing this all their lives, and then it began again. Afterwards, as the curtain swept down and they sat for a moment in silence surrounded by the roar of applause, Simon looked at her. In the darkness he saw her face glistening with tears and the slow breaking of her smile seemed to wake him from his life's dream, so that he cleared the distance between them and kissed her. And, as he held her hand, listening to the sound of the applause, there woke in him such a flood of feelings that he felt the whole enchanted evening spin together. And he understood at last how far he had needed to travel before he could recognise with certainty that he wanted her.

They drove back to Brixton Beach quietly; an air of contentment had spread itself over them. Neither wanted to dine out.

'I'll make a salad,' she said, and went into the garden to pick some herbs, a lettuce and a few radishes.

From the house the light fell softly on her, deepening the darkness of her hair.

'I didn't know you gardened,' he said, and stopped as she burst out laughing, making him smile too, for there was so much he didn't know about her. The sky had no colour left in it except for the unearthly blue of the stars. Again he was certain that some part of himself had detached itself and now belonged to her. How ridiculous, he thought, again with happiness spinning around him like a carousel in a fairground. Taking her hand, he kissed it, fingertip by fingertip.

Excavating scents. Parsley, she has been tearing some from her herb patch; garlic, she crushed some earlier; hot rice, she has been sticking her fingers in it, he told her, like a fortune-teller, reading the traces of the journey of her hand. Then he enveloped her in his arms. He was hungry, but not for food.

'All the stars are out,' he said with amazement. 'Every single one of them.'

Her hair too was full of the scents of the garden, he told her, marvelling how everything had changed so swiftly since the morning. Stunned, he thought: So this is what has happened to me! Miraculously, he was falling in love at last, and for the first time. And all the stars were out. She kissed him back, shaking a little with laughter and again he felt the slow beautiful unfolding of emotions suppressed for so many weeks. They stood with the light from the house streaming over them. Whatever he had been searching for all his life was here on the moonlit beach of Brixton. But then she silenced his thoughts with an upward gesture of her arms, and with great sweetness he turned and took her in.

Later, he would think it was as though he had never seen a woman before, for the sight of her nakedness overwhelmed him. The night gathered in the hollow of her neck, the arch of her back, the soft rise of her body as he tried in vain to hold on to the moment. He began to kiss her again, stumbling across places he had not known of moments before. Here was a faint scar left from a childhood fall, the sweep of skin, silkily soft, from ear to shoulder, the place where once her child had been nurtured. The night filled his ears with whispers. She unbuttoned his shirt, placing her cool hands on his pale skin. Searching for him, guiding him, taking him towards all the lonely, uninhabited parts in her world. He was crushed, made speechless by the simplicity of her generosity as he realised that no one had been this way for many years. A chill passed over him even as he felt the completeness of the moment. No one had showered him with such gifts; no one had slowed the night in such a way, with tongue and lips, and trails of phosphorescent love. Never for him before. A feast of love was beginning, as both fell silent now. All his life had been but an overture to this. He rocked inside her tenderly, as though he was the sea breaking against her; wave upon wave, each one more dazzling than the last. Astonished, he saw he was crowning his life as in the intermittent light provided by passing cars he caught glimpses of her face. Through the woman she had become he was able at last to comprehend the girl she had once been. Later, much later, she began to speak, telling him *he* was the one to set her free. It was then that the last remnants of modesty broke free in her. So that kissing him back, encouraged by his tender consideration, she danced for him. All night long, like rain on a tropical roof, she danced for him. It was what she had been made for, he saw with astonishment. And when he could think again, when their closeness was the closeness of people who had travelled for a lifetime, they slept. Encircled in one another's arms. Two sides of the sun. Dark and light. United as one.

Morning saw them sleeping, stretched out across the bed like starfish in some far-flung paradise. The light woke him first; stirring, but never letting go of his hold on her, he traced the line across her body straight to her heart. She slept without moving, tidily and without fuss. Impatiently, remembering all she had given him, he wanted only to begin again. There would be many things to be explained to others, he knew. Tessa, Cressida, Ravi ... So many people. Already they floated past him, indifferent as fish from some other sea. They would deal with all of it, together. With her beside him, he could do anything. He would be guided by her, he thought. For the rest of his life, this would be how it was. Overwhelmed, he kissed the smooth brown shoulder, running his hands over the soft mounds of her breasts, towards her haunches and beyond. Waking her, so she came to life with a soft exhausted sound, like a person saved from drowning. Smiling, for the familiarity of the night had left its indelible mark, she raised her arms, wanting him again.

Finally they showered and Simon watched her comb her hair before putting it up with pins; girlishly slender and beautiful against the bluish morning light from the window. Unable to watch, he took her in his arms and kissed her. Laughing, Alice pushed him away. How ridiculous she felt, she told him, for a woman of her age.

'Let me make breakfast for you,' he said. 'I make a wonderful breakfast!'

And even this remark made her giggle like a young girl. He had insisted that she stay out of the kitchen while he crashed around in the unfamiliar space, so Alice went into her studio instead to stare at a painting she had started a few days ago.

'I want to take you back,' she said, eating the toast he had made. 'To my stretch of beach.'

He nodded. Saying it out loud made her realise how much she wanted this. Simon was following a thought of his own.

'I must talk to Tessa,' he said. 'Alice?' He took both her hands in his. 'I'm working tomorrow, but after that I'm going back to Sussex to talk to her.'

Alice was still, watching him, silently. The world stopped spinning and came to rest gently. She stopped eating and was no longer smiling.

'Don't look at me like that. I have to do it, face to face. I owe it to her – you do see, don't you?' he pleaded.

She nodded. The enormity of what had happened was beginning to hit her. She looked pale. What if it didn't work?

'It will,' he said quietly. Certain. 'You think it too. It wasn't of our choosing.'

'In Sri Lanka they would call it re-birth,' she said.

It was his turn to stare at her. Could it be that the morning light made her more beautiful than she had looked last night? He thought of all the love that evaded the great central chamber of his life. Until now.

'Let's not go out,' he said, looking at her seriously, feeling his heart melt. 'Let's just go to bed.'

When he had gone, her grandfather's voice came to her: *He will love you forever, you know, Alice. Be comforted by this. I always said, One day my Alice will find someone to heal her broken roots. That is why I have stayed close to you. To keep you from falling.* She thought his voice sounded weary and seemed to come from a long way off, lulled by the slow undulation of the sea, rich with the smell of ozone, deep as the deepest blue. *Brixton has its own beach now,* Bee said, breaking the silence. He sounded very sad.

17

SILENCE. THE BEGINNING OF AN ORDINARY summer's day. In the dark-before-the-dawn hour the streets are awash with night waves from an imaginary beach. A spray of tail-lights from a passing plane pulsates as it waits, poised to land. Behind is another plane. And another. A thousand people riding the air waves, as day breaks over London. Men and women returning home, tourists with dog-eared guidebooks crushed beside them. There are bleary-eyed children looking down on the Millennium Dome, the empty London Eye, the Thames. The flight attendants yawn over London and the business-man runs a large hand over his dishevelled hair. Pretty girls looking pretty even at this hour, the lovers peering out of the window, arms entwined. The pilot speaks. 'This is London. The Queen is in Windsor,' he says. 'See, her flag is flying.' Dawn-white and embalmed on a crack of sky, the day creeps up. The houses below sleep with eyes tightly shut, bat-blind and silent, too. The beach in Brixton is swept clean by invisible tides; the smell of seaweed, never far from the imag-ination, lingers. Invisible driftwood gathers like ghosts in pockets of this beach, but no one sees it. In Southey Road, between the junction of Brixton Road and Vassall Road, near the school where Ravi went long ago, sparrows gather like crumbs on chimney tops. Biscuit-brown flecks, rising and falling all together in a wave. While beside the children's park, empty swings remain motionless. Light creeps inside the old Victorian chapel, alabaster smooth against the tombs.

The inhabitants of Southey Road stir slightly, their eyelids moving rapidly as they watch the enactment of an undisclosed dream. Even the sound of the dawn chorus cannot penetrate their consciousness; cannot wake them. Maria di Stefano, sleeping above the Italian deli, smiles as she straightens a picture on the tea-rose wall of her Sicilian dream-home. She watches as her husband Giuseppe prises open a fig as though he is searching for a secret love-trinket. Giuseppe dreams on undisturbed. Outside their house an enormous tom cat investigates a dustbin overflowing with yesterday's rubbish. Standing on his hind legs, he sends the bin lid clattering to the ground. At that the baker opens his back door and shoos the cat away, frowning. Then the baker takes a batch of bread out of his oven. And yawns. He is the last independent baker in the whole of Brixton. More than that, he is the last Cockney baker, born half a century before within the sound of Bow Bells. He knows he is living on borrowed time. There are probably only ten thousand loaves of bread left for him to bake before the council will buy him out of his livelihood, selling the site of his bakery at a good price for the building of a mosque. The baker will be angry when this happens. He will begin blaming the people who worship in the mosque for everything that has gone wrong in his life. Lucky for him, he does not have an exact day for this event.

At Patel & Son, the greengrocer is up. His harried, hardly-washed face grimaces as he opens his storeroom door for the delivery of greengages. They lie half-ripened, between green and amber and remind him of the colours of India. His father and his grandfather have been opening this same door for longer than he has been alive. So this dawn is no different from any before. The Halal butcher sleeps, his mouth shaped like a meat cleaver, dreaming of the Lebanon. The woman he once loved ended her life as a suicide bomber in Tel Aviv. When he heard the news, the butcher slaughtered another lamb and refused to comment. His sister rang him, but even the sound of her voice could not bring a tear to his eye. Something was locked inside the deep-freeze of his mind. He hung the carcass in the correct way, watching its blood run cold. He was a butcher, after all. What could anyone expect?

In Cranham Park Road, SW9, in the top flat, Kavi Mustafa is praying. Dawn is a time for cleansing his soul in the warm summer air. Kavi is praying for peace. Not in the Middle East, that is something he has given up hoping for; no, he prays for peace in his neighbourhood. He is a citizen of this community, with a wife, two children and a sub-post office. Last week someone threw a brick through its window. It is the third brick this year. When he has finished his prayer, he will go to work, check his premises and do his accounts.

Two houses down a young man of Middle Eastern appearance stands in a doorway. Since he left his home, he has become a shadowy figure. As he stands watching the first plane over London, he notices a flock of sparrows rise from the trees. After his travels to foreign parts he has been living alone, moving from house to house, learning to sleep anywhere with the minimum of fuss. Last night he moved again. This time it is to a place south of the river. None of his family knows where he really is or what he is doing. His mother and sisters think he is elsewhere, studying. They have accepted that he has little time to phone them because he is so busy. The road sweeper walks past slowly and glances indifferently at him.

Inside Brixton Beach, behind its ultramarine-blue door and within its cobalt walls, Alice Fonseka lies asleep. She sleeps with her arms thrown back as though she has been swimming for hours and is now treading water. In her dreams she is watching the fishermen gutting fish into shallow woven baskets. They will balance these like scales on their shoulders when they knock on the doors of the squeamish Singhalese housewives, their cry of *Malu, Malu* resounding across the beach. And because she is so small in her dreams, perhaps no more than three years old, the fishermen appear very tall to Alice. Her bare feet burrow in the sand. Someone takes her hand and leads her away into the stone-dark coolness of the house, which after the blaze of heat, feels like water being thrown on her face. And she wakes.

Further away in a leaf-green cul-de-sac, nowhere near Alice and her dreams, an alarm goes off. It is an old-fashioned alarm, not electronic.

It wakes Simon, sleeping on the edge of his big smooth double bed. The night has turned restlessly towards the daylight. In his dreams Simon has been shaking an almond tree full of blossoms. His arms are aching with the effort. A beautiful woman wearing a yellow dress with a pattern of birds watches him as the blossoms turn to stones, clattering to the ground. Simon notices that the stones are really hailstones from a freak storm, crow-black and falling out of a blue sky. The alarm has woken him. In the still velvet darkness an owl hoots and for a moment he faces his fears squarely, lying all alone between clean white sheets. His feet, placed next to one another like kippers in a box, are cold and he wonders why he is so sad. But all in a rush he remembers he will never be alone again. Memory floods over him. This will be the pattern of all his waking days for the rest of his life. Last night he was late coming back but even so he had phoned Alice, unable to wait another moment. He has had a difficult two days with Tessa. He doesn't want to think of the last two days now. Today he will see Alice again. Impatiently he throws the bedcovers off and gets out of bed. At four, when he finishes work he will meet her. He has a very light shift for the rest of the week and together they will go back to her place in Brixton Beach. Tomorrow night they are going to another opera, but he wants to be with Alice *now*, he thinks, smiling to himself. Facing Tessa was more unpleasant than he had expected. She will not let go of what she is used to that easily.

'She knows, now,' he had told Alice, late at night.

His voice had been sad, for he is aware this is the price he has to pay. For breaking the rules. Alice cannot think what to say that will comfort him.

'If it helps, stay away from me for a while,' she said.

But that wasn't what he wanted to hear.

'I want to see you,' he had said into the phone. 'Tessa and I are nothing to do with how I feel about you.'

In the bathroom, in the shower, Simon thinks about the last two days. Everything has been compartmentalised so carefully and now it is thrown up in the air. Happiness never comes without its own price; he smiles. That is one of Alice's sayings, not his. He does not agree.

The thought of Alice makes him want her as he stands naked under the hot shower. In ten hours he will be with her. He will never leave her after this. In the shower he is transformed by the thought of her. A younger man once more. The dark rift of night has vanished and sunlight floods the bathroom; early morning and optimistic. The alarm clock has started bleating again and Simon hurriedly dries himself.

Alice wakes. The summer light enters the room with short stabbing marks across the floor. Her first thoughts are of Simon. It is the seventh of July. How her life has changed. Like a flick of a switch, everything is different. If only her grandfather were here to see it. She remembers the Sea House. It has belonged to her for years. One day it will be Ravi's. Smiling, Alice picks up memories as though they are discarded clothes. Long ago her aunt May had rung her to tell her the house had been left to her, but Alice had not cared at the time. What use was the Sea House in her life? she had thought. But last night on the phone Simon had expressed a desire to visit it with her.

'It will have rotted with neglect,' she had warned him.

'Then we'll clean it up,' he had told her, with a new youthful energy. 'Start again. You can show me the rock where you carved your name!'

Maybe that was why she dreamed of Janake last night, she thinks, smiling, eating toast and drinking tea in her sea-blue kitchen.

'Tomorrow is the last morning you will wake up alone,' Simon has promised.

Sunlight is pouring into Brixton Beach through a hole in the sky. Never has the morning felt so transparently beautiful. Alice wriggles her bare toes, remembering how she used to burrow them in the hot sand. Her earlier life is scorched forever in her mind. She, too, counts the hours until they are to meet.

It is not yet seven o'clock but Friday traffic delays Simon as he crosses and re-crosses the one-way system on his way to work. On the river it is high tide. At the Elephant and Castle the traffic comes to a standstill and he waits impatiently, unable to see the obstruction. Opera pours out of his car's CD player. The last act of *Tristan*. Simon notices as they crawl past that the police have cordoned off a part of the road. Something serious must have taken place. Large police dogs pace the roads on thick chains, sniffing a mysterious trail of their own. A car, completely burnt out, lies on its roof in a pool of wetness; a few people stand silently on the pavement. That is all. In spite of this, even though he is still upset over Tessa, the day and all its summery light catches him in a web of happy anticipation. This summer will stay in his mind as the summer when he cherished the last drop of his youth. A taxi driver with his window down is shouting and Simon leans out to hear him but the man's words plunge into a confusion of other words, other noise. Simon drums his fingers on the door of his car. Whatever has happened has been cleared up, the remains somewhere else, possibly in St Thomas's Hospital. He will no doubt hear more when he finally gets into work. For terror lives in London now. Such are people's expectations that no one is surprised. Yet for a fraction of a second, no more, he is unexpectedly fearful. He has always understood the fragility of life in practical terms, how to save it and when he cannot. He has lived his life with focused logic. Now he glimpses another side of this. Everything hinges on chance, he thinks. It frightens him for perhaps the first time in his life. Yet what has changed? Only him. The small ambitions of his youth, the desires, all his past aspirations are as nothing in the face of what he has acquired now. The traffic is flowing at last as he crosses Lambeth Road and heads towards Westminster Bridge. Impatiently, for he has lost nearly half an hour, he stops at another set of traffic lights. The last bars of *Tristan* draw to a close. He feels his heart rise. A huge advertisement features a picture of the Red Cross in some foreign war zone. The words ANYTHING CAN HAPPEN AT ANY TIME are emblazoned across it in large letters. The slogan sticks in Simon's head as he turns into the hospital car park.

Alice leaves the house and turns right into Brixton Road. A notice outside the White Hart pub announces it is closed for restoration work. The notice makes it sound as though the White Hart were a listed building. A toothless drunk gives the door a sharp kick before cursing and walking away. A not-in-service bus sails past. Alice decides to walk to the tube station, through the market and Brixton's darkest heart. She is on her way to the gallery where her work is showing. Someone has bought her wardrobe sculpture for their museum collection and Antonia wants her to meet the buyer. For the first time she will get a large sum of money for one of her pieces. Years of worry about money are coming to an end. Alice has left early; her appointment is at nine and she doesn't want to be caught up in the rush hour. She thinks she has plenty of time so she walks slowly. In her heart, unresolved emotions swell as sunlight falls slantingly across her path. Is it her imagination or is there a touch of autumn in the air? She walks past stallholders selling fruit and vegetables. Everywhere she looks there are yellow and indigo shapes piled high. African women in colourful batik headdresses sell guavas and dark African plums. She feels a strong urge to paint. There are images inside her, dark tropical things that flit across her mind. Perhaps painting is a happier occupation, she muses. Cautiously she wonders if this dream of going back to the Sea House and the beach might happen after all. Perhaps the troubles will finally end. She would like to see the place again, she thinks, with a thrill of happiness. The narrow spit of sand she played on, the view from the top of Mount Lavinia Hill, her beloved home. Now that they have started, memories are flooding out of her like love. Far away in the distance she hears the sounds of the carousel. The music, undisturbed in her head for decades, returns to astonish her, and her eyes fill with tears of happiness. She would like to introduce her aunt and Janake to Simon. Could this dream ever become a reality? She walks past the butchers with its sawdust spilling out on to the pavement. She has been walking this route for so many years that she hardly notices it any more. The large Muslim community, settled like a flock of birds on this part of Brixton, means nothing to her. They are merely another group of displaced people taking their chances like the rest, trying to make some sort of life. Alice is thirty years ahead in the struggle; she has done her time. Unfamiliar feelings tug at her heart as she walks. Her feet have wings. As she passes under the railway bridge she hears a run of piano notes and looks up towards an open window in a shabby house. Love comes from the most unlikely places, she thinks, smiling to herself. She can't stop smiling today. The day reminds her of her ninth birthday and the train that took her to her grandfather's house.

The young man washes in the public lavatory. He cleans himself fastidiously, for that is part of the process he is embarking on. He has no watch, he sold that long ago to help fund the cause, but instinct tells him he is late for his appointment. He has folded his bedding into his rucksack and now he slings it over his shoulder and hurries towards Stockwell station, the bitter taste of hunger growing in his mouth.

Brixton station is crowded. Alice passes through the barriers with her Oyster card and watches as two men scream at each other, only to be removed forcibly by an armed policeman. There are delays on the Northern Line. Glancing at her watch, Alice goes on to the north-bound platform of the Victoria Line. The wind from the tunnel blows against her soft yellow dress, making her feel like a young girl, uncomplicated and free. In nine hours she will be meeting Simon. They have been apart for thirty-six hours, she thinks, shyly, doing her sums, imagining his face.

Having finished his early-morning rounds on the wards, Simon goes into his secretary's office.

'You've had several calls, sir.'

'Who?' he asks.

'Just your daughter. And Mrs Swann. No message. Just to tell you they called.'

Tessa. What now? He is feeling jumpy again. How foolish of him not to see that Tessa will not let go without a fight. Things could get ugly between them.

'Anyone else?'

'No, sir. Don't forget you've got a meeting at ten, on level seven.'

'No, no. I'm going to make some phone calls, so I don't want to be disturbed for about half an hour.'

He hesitates.

'Unless it's someone called Alice Fonseka.'

Mentioning her name leaves him breathless. He feels himself blush, but the secretary has her head bent and merely nods.

'Oh, and I'm expecting some tickets from the Barbican. You don't know if they've arrived by any chance?'

'Yesterday's post is on your desk, sir. If they're not there and don't arrive in the second post, I'll give them a ring.'

'Okay, thanks,' he says and goes into his room, closing the door softly.

He is suddenly exhausted. I'm not used to this sort of thing, he thinks. He badly wants to speak to Alice. The scene with Tessa has disturbed him more than he realises. He sits uncertain for a moment and then he tries to ring her mobile, but it is switched off. She told him she would be leaving very early as she didn't want to be late. Most probably she's in the tube. Closing his eyes, he tries to rid himself of his tension and think only of her. Then he takes out the memories of all the nights he has spent with her so far. Piece by piece, he examines them, arranging them in a line before him. They are the beginning of a collection. A bare arm, a small dark breast with an even darker areola. A fragrant coil of hair faintly stroked with grey. Dark trusting eyes. Just now, in the ward, he talked to an Asian patient, a woman about Alice's age. He asked her where she came from, and even though it was nowhere near Alice's home, even though the woman was nothing like Alice, he had been interested. It had been all he could do not to mention Alice. In the end he had told the woman that he knew someone from Sri Lanka. Would he be a better doctor from now on?

'Oh, Sri Lanka!' the woman had said. 'They fight a lot there.'

Don't you know, he had wanted to say, how it is there? But he had a whole ward waiting and he doubted his ability to recount the things Alice had told him. We need to talk, so much more, he thought, happiness bubbling up. So that one day, many years from now, I will at last be able to understand more fully what it has been like for her. Glancing at his watch, Simon sees it is nearly eight o' clock.

* * *

The man with the rucksack has had his meeting.

'Your family will be proud of you,' they told him, praising him for his courage.

At this the man had hesitated for a fraction of a second. He did not want to think of his family.

'We need to take control, you understand? Before they control us!'

The man gives a nod as he gathers up his rucksack. Now he is on his way at last, heading for the tube station to catch the Northern Line.

At Oxford Circus Alice changes from the Victoria Line on to the Bakerloo. It's almost ten to eight and the journey has taken her longer than she has expected. With a bit of luck she will get there on time, although the underground is still beset by delays. She had hoped to talk to Simon before she goes to the gallery, but now there won't be time. She debates whether to take a taxi once she gets to Edgware Road but decides it would be quicker to walk.

At Baker Street they stop. This train terminates here, the public address informs them, ignoring their collective cries of annoyance. Everyone piles out, grumbling. She is going to be late, after all. Unless another train comes along immediately. She wishes she hadn't dawdled earlier on.

'One's just coming now,' she is told when she questions the guard.

From Baker Street it's only two stops. Once she's out she'll ring the gallery. Then, to her infinite relief, with a muffled roar and a warm sooty breeze, the next train appears at the tip of the tunnel. She won't be able to call Simon now, he will be on his rounds.

There is a hold-up at Waterloo and the man with the rucksack finds he has to wait five long minutes. When the train finally arrives he can barely squeeze into it and stands squashed against the door. People pushing against his rucksack make him angry. Seeing they are all older than him, all well-dressed office workers, he pushes them back savagely. Rage rises in him once again, almost making him pass out. This country, he thinks, is full of fucking idiots, ruining everything.

At Baker Street, Alice runs along the platform as the train pulls in, looking for a carriage with standing room. A security warning of extra vigilance is being played over the public address. No one has time to listen. Alice resists looking at her watch. She should have remembered there were always delays on the Bakerloo Line. This is the most important appointment of her career to date. Madness lurks on the platform as the train pulls up and the doors open.

'Mind the gap,' intones the electronic voice.

The crowd surges forward. Alice stands watching. There is still a bit of room in the carriage, but before she can squeeze herself into it the doors begin to shut. The board says there will be another train along in a minute. She has no choice but to hang on and wait, hoping one more minute won't make too much of a difference. Too impatient to sit down, she paces the platform. It's just a quarter to eight. She's cutting it fine, but she will do it. Just.

Simon sends a few e-mails. Then, before he goes into his meeting, he tries ringing Brixton Beach. He isn't surprised that Alice does not answer as he knows she is on her way to meet Antonia.

Alice steps into the carriage. The notice is correct; the train has only been a minute in coming. The carriage isn't full, but she doesn't bother to sit down. Two stops, that's all, she thinks with relief. No point in sitting down. She stands facing the door and watches the tunnel whizz past. Dark shadows and orange tungsten light, giving tunnel vision. Someone, a youth about the same age as Ravi, dark beautiful hair falling over his eyes, sits with headphones emitting a loud and rhythmic hiss. He is licking his lips nervously. He closes his eyes once or twice, muttering to himself, moving his head, she supposes, in time to the music. Marylebone. Some people get out, others come in. One stop to go. Two Australian girls with long fair hair sit at the furthest end of the carriage opposite a man with a laptop on his knees, a suitcase beside him. Another man, dressed for the city, sits staring into space. The Australians are laughing out loud. Suddenly Alice has a sharp clear picture of Simon's hands, long and thin and very tender as he held her. She sees herself for a single moment as she will be tonight; naked and in his arms. Young again.

The train begins to move slowly forward and the pale youth with the headphones moves towards the door. As she watches him idly, waiting for the train to come into Edgware Road station, Alice thinks again of Ravi. Without warning there is a blinding yellow flash. It reminds her of crocuses in spring or the insides of a mango. The colour seems somehow all wrong. The carriage stretches as though made of India rubber, first one way and then another. The yellow flash seems to go on and on for a long time, but there is no sound, only a stench of something sharp and bitter and impossible to understand. She opens her mouth to cry out and the smell fills her lungs, choking her so that she can hardly breathe. Hot liquid pours over her and she sees herself, falling like a star, as though slain by a streak of tropical light, forever leaving an imprint on the world. Her body curves in a graceful, impossible arc. Just like a child's drawing of a shooting star. And then, she has no idea how much later, she is outside. There is an odd eerie silence. Soft black dust motes fill the rosy sky in a long ellipse of shapes. Dust falling from the air, she thinks in amazement. After the pause there are other noises which she struggles to identify; the screeches and the screams and other, more elusive sounds interweaving with the distant sounds of traffic. Closing her eyes against the cacophony, she wonders who on earth is doing all the screaming?

'Don't move her, call an ambulance!'

'Clear the path,' a new voice says loudly. 'Move, move! And don't touch her.'

'Oh God, what could have done this?'

'Can you hear me?' a male voice asks.

He sounds agitated, and he's shouting. I'm not deaf, she thinks. Of course I can hear you. I just can't move.

'The ambulance should be here any minute.'

'Hold on, luv, hold on.'

'We're just going to cover you up.'

Like a mistake, she thinks. Or an embarrassment. A coat is draped across her shoulders and her legs. The coat is soft and smells of pipe tobacco. Voices come to her from a long way away. Whose are they? Muffled and secretive, like the sea when she was a child. Bone white and scorching in the piercing tropical light. Lace-edged with foam, and utterly beautiful.

'Hold on, luv,' the man's voice repeats. It sounds profoundly shocked. And close to breaking.

She has been holding on, for years and years. Holding on like grim death. Pointlessly, mercilessly crushing out her memories, hoping they would finally die down. But always they had seeped cunningly out, hovering like the insects that sat motionless on the broken ceiling fan in her grandfather's house.

You have to do your time, darling, her grandfather's voice comes back to her. *And one day I hope you'll come back.*

The ride in the ambulance is curiously soothing.

'Nearly there,' says the paramedic comfortingly, quietly checking her pulse.

He is reeling off a checklist, making it sound like a litany. Heartbeat, breathing, blood pressure, temperature …

'Can you hear me, luv?' the woman with the oxygen mask asks as it comes down on her. 'What's your name?'

She struggles and someone strokes her head again. Hush! Hush!

'There, there. Just hang on, hang on, we're nearly at the hospital.'

She is reminded of her bunk bed in the cabin. On C Deck. The *Fairsea*, the boat was called. The inky blue sea, just like the bottle of Quink in her grandfather's house. It brings tears to her eyes. But the sea had been a different blue when she was on dry land. Her grandfather's face is suddenly a blur. The ambulance is slowing down and a frenzy of activity begins. Simon, she thinks, feeling the tears begin to fall. I want to go home, I want you to see the Sea House. And she struggles to keep the beach in her sightline. But they are pulling her about, sticking things into her so she opens her mouth to shout at them. Go away, she wants to say. For God's sake, can't you see I've had enough? The voices drift towards her and recede again. The voices are fast and reassuring, so why is she not reassured? Her legs feel suddenly heavy. Haemorrhage, they keep saying. White light invades her lids.

Something is put over her. Are they going to bury me alive, she wonders? Simon, she thinks, with sudden urgency. Simon! He is her last chance. She has known this since the first encounter, but never with such force as now. He and Bee, she thinks at last, astonished, they are both part of the same thing.

'I'm coming back,' she tells them. 'Tell Ravi.'

'Good girl,' says a voice and she feels something sharp in her arm. 'Good girl,' says the voice again.

Opening her eyes she feels the sea breeze again, slight and youthful against her face. The voice sounds warm and familiar, falling on her ears like a benediction. It is filled with the memory of cheap tobacco and the noise inside the conch shell they used to keep for a doorstop. It is all she has ever loved.

'Good girl!'

Startled, she thinks she can smell the green scent of oranges, wet with the rain, and she feels her skin, tired and stretched as though she has been swimming in the sea. It is the very last thing she remembers.

He hears nothing. The room where the meeting is taking place exists like an inner chamber to a pharaoh's tomb, without outside light. A fish tank full of small tropical fish swim under the fluorescent bulbs, forever confined to plastic coral fronds. Someone in management had thought it good feng shui. Day or night, it makes no difference to the fish. The meeting continues regardless of the outside world. Simon feels his eyelids grow heavy. Lately all he ever seems to do is go to management policy meetings. They have now been sitting here for over an hour. What a waste of time, he thinks impatiently. He glances at his watch and catches Ralph's eye. Ralph gives him a considered look. Roughly translated, Simon takes the look to mean 'Why are you so tired?' He raises an eyebrow. The door opens and coffee is brought in real jugs with real cups and saucers. There are biscuits.

'Okay, everyone, let's take a short break before we deal with the last matter on the agenda.'

The coffee is hot and unusually good. Ralph approaches, cup in hand.

'Management does all right with their refreshments, I see.'

'It's where the money is.'

'Yes, well …' Ralph hesitates. 'So what have you been up to?' he asks, cocking an eyebrow at Simon.

'Nothing much, a bit tired, that's all. Why?'

'Rumours are rife! Had Tessa on the phone.'

'Ah!'

'Oh, for heaven's sake, Simon, isn't it a bit quick? Aren't you being a little rash?'

'I don't think so.'

'All my fault, it seems,' murmurs Ralph, with self-mockery. 'Better give up having dinner parties.'

'Thank God you had that one!'

'D'you want my advice …?'

'No thanks.'

Ralph grins and looks at his old friend. He opens his mouth with a rejoinder. But he never makes it. Three bleepers go off and the door opens simultaneously. The staff nurse from A&E comes in.

'There's been an incident on the underground,' she tells them. 'Reports are just coming in. An explosion – deliberate, they think. Nobody knows yet how many injured. We need the standby team, now. A&E to report to casualty, please.'

The meeting breaks up as everyone reaches for their phones.

'Oh, now what!' curses Ralph, looking pale. 'Now what has some God-awful fundamentalist nutter done?'

But Simon does not hear him. He has turned, as though struck with a sixth sense, towards the nurse.

'Where?' he asks, not recognising his own voice. 'Tell me? Which line, where was it?'

The nurse looks startled.

'I think it's the Bakerloo, sir, but we haven't had confirmation.'

A dark ugly flare shoots up through the bubbling water of the fish tank. It is the last thing he sees in the room as he makes for the door.

* * *

Grass and trees. The day's warmth still lingering in the shocked London air. It stunned him that desolation could be so peaceful. The heart of darkness is here in this incinerator of mangled metal and bodies. All that happened in a split-second will last forever. The willows by the river weep as he stands bareheaded and bowed by incomparable grief. A breeze comes up from nowhere; it carries his memories, for that is all they are now. He imagines her as she had been, answering the door to him, only yesterday; when he was young. Terror has come to Britain, he thinks, his mind bludgeoned and weeping. For at the end of this ordinary summer's day, he sees with finality that terror is all around. Everywhere love is, there is its possibility, and love has made him understand this.

The garden at Regent's Park is closing. All over, under a sky pricking softly with the subdued stars of this summer night, there is a drowsy ripeness in the air. In the dying light an overflowing of warmth, thick and heavy and inaccessible, engulfs him. The park-keeper mumbles and nods, his face shocked, shutting away the flowers for the night. Doing what he has always done, but differently, now. The park-keeper is changed forever too. Simon passes a border of red peonies as he leaves. Did she like red peonies? He never asked her.

Alice! his mind cries. All she had wanted was to be loved. She had wanted someone, one person in this country that had become her home, to acknowledge what she had tried to do. In spite of everything she had been forced to leave behind, she succeeded in transferring her allegiance. Yes, he thinks, she had wanted to be loved for this achievement. And he, Simon Swann, had loved her. But it had only begun, he cries; he has only just begun to love her. Too many years late in finding her, still, find her he did. And in this moment of being locked out of the garden, staring at the peonies through the railings, knowing what this must have meant to her, he is so glad that it has been *him* and no one else. Even though they have passed like ships in dark waters, and he is left alone; a foreigner in his own land, still he is glad. Oh, but that he might tell her this! Looking up at the sky, at the lights of a passing aeroplane leaving the city, he sees this night, the first without her, will pass, leaving him behind. And seeing this he understands with terrible, sweet certainty the thing that he must do. Turning his back on the garden, leaving the bunches of flowers piling softly against the pavement, the flickering candles, the messages of condolence, he heads towards Lambeth Bridge and hurries south. Towards the river, and a remarkable beach, transported by her many years before, moved inch by painful inch, reconstructed. For it is clear that he, Simon Swann, needs this beach; it is clearly and irreversibly part of his internal landscape now. Nothing and no one will erase it. And so he heads towards it, and the small house perched nearby. Where a young man called Ravi, with his mother's dark, unforgettable eyes, sits in stunned silence. Waiting for him to arrive.

ACKNOWLEDGEMENTS

As always to my agent Felicity Bryan for her belief in me and for finding me Clare Smith, my wonderful editor at HarperCollins, who continues to allow me the space to develop as a writer.

Essie Cousins for her tremendous support and encouragement.

Also at Harper Press, Taressa Brennan for making life so much easier and Anne and Sophie not least of all for their excellent maths.

Michele Topham and all at the Felicity Bryan Agency.

Charles, Nicky and Henry Chubb, old friends who gave me a brief insight into the workings of the emergency services.

Thank you.

'It's like a book, I think, this bloomin' world.'

RUDYARD KIPLING

BEHIND THE SCENES

'HISTORY IN STORIES'

'If history were taught in the form of stories, it would never be forgotten.' So wrote Rudyard Kipling, perfectly capturing the importance of the writer's craft. And yet the precise nature of the creative process is a mysterious one. What is it that inspires authors to put pen to paper: curiosity, sympathy, passion, obsession? In her own words, Roma Tearne reveals what inspired her to write *Brixton Beach* ...

Two years ago, while researching new work, I visited my old home in London. I had not been back there since my parents died but I wanted to write about a woman who searches for her lost past.

The house in which we had lived since leaving Sri Lanka is in Brixton. Always a little shabby it now seemed woefully rundown. In the boarded-up back garden a jasmine creeper my father once nurtured was still thrusting itself up, and a hydrangea bush, planted by him stood forlornly, its flower heads merely a frost-blackened memorial to happier times. The house looked closed and dark, its windows covered in grime, for life had fled and was replaced by neglect. I peered in at the room where my mother had died. There was nothing in it, not a bed, not a carpet, nothing. Unable to bear the sight, I fled, pursued by memories.

Back at home I began thinking of all the houses I had lived in as a child. They were places existing only in my mind and they formed a map of nowhere. Images from a lost time began to come back to me, superimposing themselves on the landscape of my current life. I remembered a sepia photograph of Mt Lavinia beach that used to hang in the sitting room. It was a view that had been part of my mental map for longer than I could remember. There used to be giant cacti growing on the sand dunes. Now, staring out at my own well-cared-for garden, and the cacti I grew in large pots, I understood the ways in which loss is carried into exile and the manner in which landscape can be altered by the longings of the immigrant who lives in it. How often does one see, on entering a foreign house in some corner of Britain, a place where two worlds meet and a sense of place overlaps?

I began to write the book that would eventually be called *Brixton Beach*. In its pages my female character shifts the memories from her childhood, inch by painful inch, until at last they bloom again in her new, alien, home.

ROMA TEARNE

'WHAT, WHY, WHEN, HOW, WHERE, WHO'

······································

'I keep six honest serving-men
(They taught me all I knew);
Their names are What and Why and When
And How and Where and Who.'

RUDYARD KIPLING

From Socrates to the salons of pre-Revolutionary France, the great minds of every age have debated the merits of literary offerings alongside questions of politics, social order and morality. Whether you love a book or loathe it, one of the pleasures of reading is the discussion books regularly inspire. Below are a few suggestions for topics of discussion about *Brixton Beach* ...

Brixton Beach opens dramatically with the horrors of the 2005 London bombings. Did you find this an effective beginning to the novel? How and why?

Alice is the daughter of a Singhalese mother and a Tamil father. How does this affect the way that she, and her family, are treated by others? In what ways does her parenthood influence the direction her life takes?

In chapter three, Grandpa Bee tells Alice, 'This is your first home, you were born here. That's a powerful thing, don't ever forget it. But it may not be your last ...' By the end of the novel which, would you argue, is Alice's true home? Sri Lanka or England? Or both?

How significant is the character of Kunal? What are your thoughts on his relationship with Sita?

Homeland, identity and relationships are all central themes of *Brixton Beach*. In what ways are these tested when the Fonsekas move to England? How are they developed throughout the book? And which, would you argue, is the most relevant to the novel?

What did you know about the Sri Lankan civil war before reading *Brixton Beach*? How has this book shaped your understanding of the conflict and Sri Lanka itself?

In chapter six, May says to Alice, 'I am actually *glad* you're going to England. Glad you won't be subjected to any of the terrible things happening in our country ... In England you will learn justice and truth.' How accurate do you think this statement is?

How do the Fonsekas adjust to life in England? Do their experiences in their new environment differ, and if so, why?

Kamala, Sita and Alice – three generations of Sri Lankan women. In what ways are their lives similar? In what ways are they different? What do you think *Brixton Beach* reveals about the role of women in Sri Lanka?

In what ways does Roma Tearne highlight the differences in landscape between Sri Lanka and England? Do you think the fact that she is a visual artist, as well as an author, has an impact on the way she writes?

Brixton Beach is the name Alice gives to her new home in London. What do you think this symbolises, and do you think it is a powerful title?

'IT'S CLEVER BUT IS IT ART?'

'But the Devil whoops, as he whooped of old: "It's clever, but is it Art?"'

RUDYARD KIPLING

Praise for *Mosquito*

Shortlisted for the Costa First Novel Award

'*Mosquito* plays with sensuous mixes of human bestiality and natural beauty ... It is in this continuing agency of remembered love – presented as the colours, sounds and smells of art, in dialogue with beauty and horror – that the uplifting politics of this fine novel lies.'   *Independent*

'Heart-rending ... Readers of this powerful novel cannot fail to be moved ... but they will also realise that, as well as being a rebuke to indifference, the book is also about hope and survival.'

CHRISTOPHER ONDAATJE, *Spectator*

'*Mosquito* lyrically captures a country drenched in both incomparable beauty and the stink of hatred.'   *Guardian*

'Lovely, vividly described.'   *The Times*

'Tearne brings her skills as a painter to her writing, creating some extraordinarily lovely portraits of Sri Lankan land and seascapes, a stunning backdrop to the changing horrors of the country's 20-year civil war. Anyone who has visited, or has a passing interest in Sri Lanka, should read this beautiful novel.'   *Sunday Telegraph*

Praise for *Bone China*

'Tearne's second novel also deftly reveals the corrosive effects of civil strife on private lives and the receptiveness of art, though in the more conventional, if highly readable, form of a family saga over four generations that turns midway into a migrants' tale. Probing loss and memory amid violence and displacement, her novels have affinities with Romesh Gunesekera's groundbreaking fiction.' *Guardian*

'Told with intelligence and grace, *Bone China* is a compassionate tale of an anguished spirit with an irrepressible quest for assimilation.'

Sunday Telegraph

'One of those rich, nourishing family sagas that seizes the imagination. The setting [is] beautifully evoked. The characters are wonderfully vivid … Tearne carries her story triumphantly into the present.' *The Times*

'This beautifully written account of a family in freefall addresses the experiences of victims of war and immigration, while acknowledging the love that exists within the family.' *Waterstones Books Quarterly*

'THE MOST POWERFUL DRUG'

'Words are, of course, the most powerful drug used by mankind.'

RUDYARD KIPLING

If you enjoyed *Brixton Beach*, you might be interested in these other titles from Harper Press …

The Lace Reader by BRUNONIA BARRY

The Whitney women of Salem, Massachusetts are renowned for reading the future in the patterns of lace. But the future doesn't always bring good news – as Towner Whitney knows all too well. When she was just fifteen her gift sent her whole world crashing to pieces. She predicted – and then witnessed – something so horrific that she vowed never to read lace again, and fled her home and family for good. Salem is a place of ghosts for Towner, and she swore she would never return. Yet family is a powerful tie and fifteen years later, Towner finds herself back in Salem. Her beloved great-aunt Eva has suddenly disappeared – and when you've lived a life like Eva's, that could mean real trouble. But Salem is wreathed in sickly shadows and whispered half-memories. It's fast becoming clear that the ghosts of Towner's fractured past have not been brought fully into the light. And with them comes the threat of terrifying new disaster.   *April 2009*

The Book of Fires by JANE BORODALE

Brought up in rural Sussex, seventeen-year-old Agnes Trussel is carrying an unwanted child. Taking advantage of the death of her elderly neighbour, Agnes steals her savings and runs away to London. On her way she encounters the intriguing Lettice Talbot who promises to help. But Agnes soon becomes lost in the city, losing contact with Lettice. She ends up at the household of John Blacklock, laconic firework-maker, becoming his first female assistant. The months pass and it becomes increasingly difficult for Agnes to conceal her secret. She meets Cornelius Soul, seller of gunpowder, and hatches a plan which could save her from ruin. Yet why does John Blacklock so vehemently disapprove of Mr Soul? And what exactly is he keeping from her? Could the housekeeper, Mrs Blight, with her thirst for accounts of hangings, suspect her crime or condition? *June 2009*

The Buried Circle by JENNI MILLS

Weaving fact with fiction, Jenni Mills's second novel is set in the village of Avebury, one of the most mysterious places in the English countryside. Surrounded by ancient standing stones, crop circles and burial mounds, this is a place where all is not as it seems. In 1938, the archaeologist Alexander Keiller – a millionaire playboy with a passion for witchcraft and ritual magic – plans to reconstruct Avebury's five-thousand-year-old stone circle. Frannie Robinson and her boyfriend Davey are among those who fall under his dangerous spell, and are nearly destroyed. Seventy years later, Frannie's granddaughter India sets out on her own quest to discover the truth. But digging up the past unearths the unexpected, and may prove lethal … *July 2009*

Swap by DANIEL CLAY

Angela Kenny wants more from her life. Sure, she's got a loving husband and a sweet teenage son, but she can't help feeling that there should be more. She's tired of going to work and filling in spreadsheets, fed up with cooking the same frozen pizzas every evening, and bored of waking up every morning to do it all over again. Lucas – her husband's best friend – seems to share her dissatisfaction, and over slow summer evenings in their small, settled suburb, their friendship slowly develops into a dangerous affair. When John sees his wife in his best friend's arms, his anguish will have devastating consequences for all of them. *January 2010*

Visit www.harpercollins.co.uk for more information.

CEYLON
POSTAGE
& REVENUE
WAR STAMP
2c
CEYLON
POSTAGE
& REVENUE
9c
COCONUT PALMS
FOR
SPACE MA
COLOMB